The doorway opened on an eerie, misty realm lit
with effulgent light
pale-greenish glow
enough to dim the
illumine the fog be
gusting from the fal
eerily above a balustraded stone terrace, and a
broad stair that led down and away out of sight.

The wisps of fog curled and drifted almost like
living things, swirling at the limit of the watchers'
vision. Then, to their amazement, moving figures
did start to take shape in the pale nebulosity—a
crowd of lurching, distorted shapes sweeping up
the stairway and casting long green shadows ahead
of themselves in the mist. They made a sound, too,
as they came—a growing, full-throated roar. In an
instant the raiders were matching it with their own
cries of terror and alarm.

For across the stone terrace and through the
doorway swarmed bellowing demons, crocodile-
headed monsters who rushed up out of the glowing
pit with eons-old hatred flaring in their eyes, as if
summoned by the sound of the falling doors. They
charged among the raiders, snarling with misshapen
mouths and flailing with strange, antique-looking
swords and clubs . . .

CONAN
THE
RAIDER

Look for all these Conan books

CONAN
THE RAIDER
BY
LEONARD CARPENTER

TOR

A TOM DOHERTY ASSOCIATES BOOK

CONAN THE RAIDER

Copyright © 1986 by Conan Properties, Inc.

First printing: October 1986
First mass market printing: September 1987

A TOR Book

Published by Tom Doherty Associates, Inc.
49 West 24 Street
New York, N.Y. 10010

Cover art by Boris Vallejo

ISBN: 0-812-54262-2
CAN. ED.: 0-812-54263-0

Printed in the United States of America

0   9   8   7   6   5   4   3   2   1

To
James Battersby

Contents

Chapter 1

The Poison Sea

Blue sky burned overhead like a torch. Beneath it lay the desert of eastern Shem: a vast, unpeopled expanse strewn with dry mountains and sand wastes like the dust and bones of giants. But here the land lay flat, baked white and hard as the floor of a kiln. And over it, like an insect creeping across the bricks of a blazing hearth, came a lone horse and rider.

The white mare moved forward at a trot, lathered and slack-muzzled from the heat. The horseman sat motionless, muffled in the folds of a long caftan, a garment made woolly and thick to keep the desert sun from parching the last drop of water out of the wearer's skin and roasting the brains in his skull like a pan of sweetbreads.

The folds and bulges of the dusty cloth showed the rider to be a large man, though he was swathed completely except for his eyes. These flashed blue from the slit of his cowl, scanning the desolation ahead with the alertness of a stalker. Once, too, he twisted in his saddle to search the rearward horizon with the wariness of a fugitive.

At this shifting of weight the horse's pace faltered, and the horseman cursed. "Crom! Steady, there! I don't want to end up afoot in this devil-haunted waste!" Stroking the animal's neck with a massive, sunbrowned hand, he spoke more soothingly in her ear. "All is well, girl—just keep up the pace!

Our pursuers have given us up for dead, if they have any sense. Now catch Juvius's overburdened nag for me, and we will regain the gem.''

For a moment the living image of the golden ring with its great blue sapphire, the Star of Khorala, seemed to burn in the air before him. He blinked the vision away impatiently, knowing it for the treacherous specter of delirium that it was. Instead he tried to focus his gaze on the heat-dancing horizon.

"Just tell me where, by Set's toils, that scoundrel Juvius is leading us!''

In his inmost heart Conan of Cimmeria knew the answer, and he was not pleased. Long had it been, two days and more, since the faint hoof-tracks he followed parted from the litter of bones marking the caravan road. Now the mountains that shimmered on the horizon, pale in the heat-haze, might be days away, or weeks, but they were not within the range of a lone and ill-provisioned rider. There were no landmarks nor vantage points to spy out the terrain ahead. Not even a scrap of shade on which to rest one's scorched, weary eyes. Conan knew that Juvius could be leading him only . . . to death.

No great surprise, he reflected. Back in the desert outpost of Uwadra, the rascal had been sly and unctuous in his approach to the Cimmerian. Juvius had quickly plied him to drunkenness with the heady melon wine of the region. He had been deft at robbing him of the Star and planting value-less pilfered goods in its place, and devilish clever in leaving him to the mercies of the local Wazir's garrison, to be throttled at dawn for a petty thievery he would never have stooped to commit.

But in all Juvius's accomplished knavery—considerable for a mere border-town thief—there had been no hint of courage nor of fighting prowess. The man was a street-crawler, out of place in the hostile desert. When he spied Conan on a stolen horse, freshly escaped from the garrison and coming after him with murder in his eye, he had pan-icked. Thinking of nothing but escape, the fool had galloped off into trackless country.

And Conan, raging after his gem, with the Wazir's angry guards close on his heels, had not hesitated to follow. Now the thief was lost, straying deeper into this roasting hell hour by hour, as the meanderings of his trail clearly showed.

"Well, if the desert doesn't finish him, I will," Conan resolved aloud. "The rascal deserves a roasting for taking what belongs to me." He fell silent then, musing on the problematic question of the Star's ownership. A moment later he declared righteously to his horse, "After all, it was I, not he, who first snatched the jewel from the finger of a thieving prince!"

Sitting astride his jouncing steed, Conan watched with slitted eyes as the desert terrain around him gradually changed. Brick-hard soil gave way to a crazy patchwork of cracked sediment, with crevices deep enough in places to mire a horse's hoof. In other spots jagged crystal salt-towers jutted up weirdly out of the clay, like glistening, rotted fangs with necrotic blue shadows at their bases. Conan had to slow his steed to a walk.

"Steady, girl," he told her. "If your former owners are ever going to catch us, it will be here." But a careful survey of the desert behind him revealed no pursuers.

Far ahead the heat-waves glimmered and undulated more hypnotically than before, making the edge of the land wholly invisible. Yet the faint scuffs of his quarry's hoofprints continued forward into the eldritch landscape. Abruptly the mare balked, refusing to cross the broken ground even at a walk. With a sigh the caped man swung down from the saddle and led the beast by the reins, stepping gingerly over the deep cracks full of muddy salt crystals.

Then he blinked in amazement. Ahead was a round pool of water set in smooth clay, glimmering as clear as a burning glass under the sun. Passing near it, he knelt and took up water in his hand. It was warm, and the droplets sat thickly on his skin like glass beads. Widening the aperture of his cowl, he touched one of the drops to his tongue. Vehemently he spat; the taste of the water stung like scorpion venom. Spitting dryly, he led his horse on.

Finally, reluctantly, he took a swig from the half-empty waterskin slung behind his saddle and spewed it out in order to be rid of the vile taste.

More ponds and interconnecting mudslicks spread around him, even as the tallest of the salt-towers reared waist-high. Conan grew convinced that the glassy blue glare ahead was a larger body of water. Not a living sea, surely; yet once there had been life in it, as evidenced by the jagged fish bones and barnacle shells embedded in the clay at his feet. Some of the skulls were as large as a man's and many-spiked, like mace heads.

Conan looked up from examining these remains to catch sight of a dark speck ahead. It was low against the blue glimmer of water, broader and blacker than the pale ghosts of the salt-pillars. He fixed his gaze on it, staring through cupped fingers against the glare. As he drew nearer, it gradually took on a definite form: that of a stout man sitting against the belly of a dead horse.

Juvius had fled as far as his mount could carry him, it would seem, for he sat at the head of a shallow promontory of land lapped on three sides by the desultory ripples of the salt sea. The gleaming water stretched away behind him into a blinding mirage, patterned by only the mildest of waves, and probably no more than waist-deep at the limit of Conan's vision.

The unhorsed thief sat on a windrow of shell and bone at the dead sea's edge, facing the desert and his pursuer. He waited bareheaded, his stout body nested between the stiff, protruding legs of his expired steed. He was so still that Conan could not tell if he was dead or alive until a hand raised up in front of the man's red, balding skull, shading his eyes. That detail convinced the barbarian that the vision was real, not a mere trick of sun and desert-demons.

Conan stared at his enemy, lips pursed in wrath, and was struck by the bizarre aspect of the stranded thief. The fellow was pitiful, sitting there against his bloated steed like a king on his throne. The Cimmerian sighed and shook his head in resignation and mild disgust. It was hard even to be angry at the poor fool.

He stopped hauling on the reins of his horse, and the animal scuffed to a halt, its head drooping. With a sweep of his arms, Conan raised the caftan from his shoulders and flung it over the saddle; the motion exposed a sun-bronzed, muscular body clad in white silken shirt, brown leather kirtle, and sandals.

He untied the large, half-empty waterskin from his saddle-bags and slung it over his shoulder. Murmuring to his thirsty horse, he held his hand up to his animal's muzzle and trickled water from the bag into his palm. Then he turned and started toward the reclining thief.

When he felt the salt-crusted barnacles of the narrow strand crunching under his feet, he called out to the seated one, who was still a long bowshot away. "Ho, Juvius! Your trail has ended, I see." He paused, but there was no reply. "Are you ready, then, to deal with me for the Star of Khorala?"

"A deal, yes!" The voice came rough and faint from the distance, and the sun-reddened pate began to wag. "Juvius is always ready to deal! Even with a bloodthirsty barbarian!"

There was a wildness in the croaking shouts, and the Cimmerian decided that his quarry must be slightly crazed by the heat. He continued walking forward. "Aye, well," he shouted back, "I should carve you into strips, salt you down, and dry you in the sun for your treachery! But in truth I am too weary for the chore. So I propose a bargain."

"Yes, yes, a bargain!" Juvius's mouth flapped dark and hollow in the middle of his weathered beard. "Name your terms!"

"I want only that which you stole from me." Conan continued to close the distance while he spoke. "My ring— the Star of Khorala—in trade for a drink of water!" He held up his waterbag, sloshing it beside his ear.

"Water, yes! Gems for water! A fair trade! The ring . . . I

have it here somewhere . . . ." The rasping voice muttered on unintelligibly.

As Conan drew nearer, Juvius rummaged through a heap of saddle-gear at his side. His head and face were scorched and blistered cruelly red, and his lips looked whitish and parched.

Conan called to him, "You may guzzle as much water as you can hold—and then, if you have the strength, which I doubt, you can hang on to my horse's tail as I ride out of here. . . ."

He had no time to say more; at that instant, with a single, careless motion, Juvius raised a small arbalest from his luggage and discharged it at him. Conan felt a tearing impact at his waist as the bolt struck, and a warm wetness streamed down the outside of his thigh.

A wound in his side, but still he lived! There was no pain; perhaps the quarrel had struck sidewise. With barely a heartbeat's hesitation, Conan dashed forward across the loose seashore debris, clutching his pointed dagger, waterbag thudding against his side. The distance to his foe was a long sprint, but shorter than the dash out of crossbow range.

"Hiee, what a shot! I feathered him well! Now to finish him!" Juvius gloated aloud as he fumbled in his lap to recharge his weapon. "The barbarian wants his ring back! Wants to give me water! The fool!" Jerking the stock against his belly with both plump arms, he set the bowstring into the catch with a click. Careless of the attacker who rushed ever closer, he reached beside him for a new quarrel as he raved hoarsely on. "Can he not see that I've water aplenty? A whole lake of water, in easy reach! What do I need him for?" With a demented look he raised the crossbow.

Conan was still out of reach of the seated man. But, by an agile, desperate effort he stopped dead, putting all the energy of his dash into a throw of his heavy dagger. It flashed forward through the air and struck Juvius in the chest, thudding home to the hilt. With a gasp, the red-faced thief rocked backward against the carcass of his horse. His crossbow sagged and discharged its shaft into the beach, kicking up a spurt of barnacles.

So died Juvius, neither moving nor making a further sound.

Conan's side was still throbbing, his skin prickling with damp. Examining his wound, he saw that the bolt had left nothing more than an abrasion. The force of the treacherous shaft had been taken by the waterskin, now sliced open at the side. Only a few mouthfuls of water remained; the rest had drained out during his dash for life.

Cursing, Conan bound up the bag to secure what remained of the precious fluid. Then he turned to Juvius's body. He had dangerously underestimated the rogue, it was clear. The fellow had slowly been driven mad—first, no doubt, by the day-long hammering of the desert sun, and then, the gods knew how much further, by sucking up the dregs of this dying sea.

White encrustations discolored Juvius's beard; he had drunk deeply of the salt-thick water. When Conan bent over the corpse to retrieve his weapon, it pulled loose from the man's chest with a dry, eerie rasp. On the blade he found not blood but salt deposits, which had already begun to etch and blacken the gleaming steel.

But the cruelest surprise for Conan came when he ransacked the thief's belongings in search of the stolen ring, the Star of Khorala. It was nowhere to be found.

Conan searched again, turning out the dead man's every pouch and pocket. He examined each fold and cranny of his saddle-gear without success. Panting with the effort under the searing sun, he turned over the bodies both of man and horse to sift through the beach litter underneath them—in vain.

Baffled, he fingered the hilt of his dagger, eyeing the stout body of Juvius suspiciously. No, he decided, the ring with its huge gem was too large a morsel even for the gullet of this greedy thief. There was no point in slitting him open.

He turned his gaze to the terrain all around—the thin white beach, the jagged waste of salt-pillars and ponds behind it, and, on three sides, the rippling, gleaming, mirage-misted

sea. He could search the land in case Juvius had tossed away
the ring out of madness or slyness. The bauble was large
enough to show up to a careful scrutiny, even amid the
hellish maze of cracks and crystal towers.

But what of the water? Must he drag the bottom of the
poison sea, too? Glass-clear and shallow as it was, its bed
was light tan, feathery silt. He tasted the water and spat in
revulsion at the same foulness he had encountered in the
pond. Digging into his belt-pouch, he tossed a copper coin
into the liquid and watched it settle out of sight into the soft,
muddy bottom.

A short while longer he stood in the scorching heat, cursing bitterly to be stuck in this inferno with neither wealth nor
water to show for it. Then he glimpsed a sudden motion at
the corner of his vision; apparently the sea was not hostile to
all life. A wide, flapping thing with a yawning mouth and a
barbed tail, a wingfish or skate, splashed out of the water and
skimmed low across the surface like a spun stone. In a
moment it plunged back out of sight, spreading ripples afar in
oily circles.

With a last vain imprecation to Crom, Conan turned and
strode away.

Chapter 2

The Raiders of the Dead

The desert wind lashed the earth fitfully, like a drayman flogging his tired beast homeward. At the junction of two ravines cut into rising terrain, windborne sand had carved the exposed bedrock into a row of tall, minareted spires. Now they soughed deeply and thrillingly as stray gusts combed through them, making noises like sudden gasps of warning.

From between two of the spires a blunt, blinking reptilian head emerged. It was followed by a squat body, fat as a barnyard fowl and rainbow-hued under its coating of alkali dust. It slithered down the rock slope toward the bed of the gully, which was an expanse of sand dotted by the brown skeletons of shrubs.

Dry-lipped, dusty, and weak with thirst, Conan hauled himself up into the crevice the lizard had just scurried through. He was clad in the tattered remains of his caftan, torn off at the knees for easier walking. From his shoulder hung the shriveled husk of his waterbag. Having last quenched his thirst on the clotting blood of his dead horse, he eyed the rock-lizard greedily.

Throwing aside caution, he scrambled down the slope after the creature. Desperately he dove to grab it, rolling over bodily, then crashed to the sand with a grunt, scraping painfully against a spear-pointed bush. He fumbled beneath himself to clutch the struggling, scaly hide, dragged his catch up into view—and saw only the tapering, detached but still-twitching tail of the lizard. He looked up dazedly to glimpse the main part of the beast disappearing into a pile of rocks some distance away.

With thirst buzzing in his head, he examined the tail closely. It was dry and horny. To obtain what little moisture it had, he pressed the gory stump to his mouth.

"Is it human, I ask you?" The voice, deep and ironical, came from a man sitting astride the high hump of a camel; the beast had halted a few paces away, near the undercut stone wall of the canyon. "Or is it a sand-troglodyte, an imp of the barrens?" The rider was stocky under his traveling-cloak, blond and pale-skinned: a northerner, clearly, though he spoke in the mellifluous accents of Shem.

"Yea, Otsgar, if what I have heard is true." A second, smaller camel-rider jounced up from behind to join him. " 'Tis said the wild hill-apes sometimes filch the clothing of men and cavort in it, when their fur falls out from the scabby mange. . . ."

"Water," Conan croaked. The word was a short but imperative statement. He gathered his limbs under him and climbed to his feet. Unsteadily he moved toward the one called Otsgar, raising a hand to the dark-stained waterbag dangling from the northman's saddle.

"Wait, now!" Otsgar cried, catching at the reins so that his ungainly steed shuffled back from Conan. "Water is scarce in these parts, as you may have noticed." He frowned down at the Cimmerian with assumed severity. "We are traders by profession, and we do not give up our goods for nothing. What can you offer us in return?"

Other riders were coming up behind Otsgar, forming a party of a dozen and more; their mounts stood ruminating patiently, or nibbling at the stunted thornbushes. Most were curly-haired Shemites, younger than the blond man and the goat-bearded one who had spoken. Some of the newcomers sat smirking at Conan's abject appearance and at the chaffing he was receiving, while others stared at him grimly, striving in a youthful way to look hard and dangerous.

"You do not seem to be a man of wealth," their leader went on. "Perhaps you can pay for a generous drink in the coin of . . . information. Mere aid to honest traders who are lost and trying to find our way." Otsgar slapped the swollen waterbag at his side so that it sloshed audibly. "In your travels hereabouts, have you seen aught of ancient ruins or tumuli? Such monuments might be . . . useful landmarks to us!"

Conan took another step forward, and the northman reined back again, jostling among his comrades' snarling steeds. This time he scowled at Conan in earnest, laying a hand on the hilt of the crescent-bladed tulwar at his waist. Others of his band imitated him, rattling their weapons.

Conan fumbled under his ragged caftan for his own dagger-hilt. He failed to find it. Looking over his shoulder, he blurrily saw the knife lying in the sand beside the discarded lizard-tail.

"Hold! I know this man." One of the Shemites spoke—the bearded one who had first joined his chief and bantered with him at the starveling's expense. He slid down from his steed and came forward, unstoppering his own waterskin.

"Here, old friend! Drink, Conan of Cimmeria!" He held forth the sloshing bag as Conan eyed him dimly and suspiciously. " 'Tis fair payment to you for saving my life, or at least my good right hand, from the thief-catchers of Arenjun!"

He held the waterskin up to the thirsty man's mouth and squeezed water out in small portions. The barbarian fell to one knee, clutching at the Shemite's sheepskin coat and gulping greedily.

"Isaiab, what mean you by this?" Otsgar glared down angrily at his henchman. "I had further questions to put to him."

"It matters not. He would never have answered. These Cimmerians are stubborn unto death. Almost as stubborn as you Vanirmen," the Shemite added offhandedly as he pulled the waterskin out of Conan's eager grasp. " 'Tis enough, now! Let it soak in," he told him gently. "You can have more in a while."

"Just leave him the skin, and we'll be on our way." Otsgar shrugged impatiently. "We should quest farther to eastward now."

Isaiab regarded his chief. "That would be doing him no great favor, Otsgar, in this burning wilderness. This much water would only prolong his death. I say take him with us. Conan is a useful man to have on hand." He patted the barbarian's shoulder, which seemed already to have straightened somewhat from his few sips of water.

"Yes, take him with us, Otsgar." The new, sultrier voice came from a hooded rider seated close behind the northman. "From the bulk of him, methinks he would be good at . . . hauling and lifting." A slender hand flung back the dusty cowl to reveal the face of an olive-skinned, raven-haired woman.

The leader frowned a moment longer, then shrugged. Suddenly, disarmingly, he smiled down at the two men. A gold-filled tooth winked from his broad, lightly-bearded face. "Very well. We can always use more men. Conan, welcome to our band!"

"My thanks—to you, Isaiab," the Cimmerian rasped out. "I did not know you from afar." Half in friendship, half to steady himself, the barbarian placed a hand on the Shemite's shoulder. He looked up expressionlessly at Otsgar and the others. "In answer to your question, Vanirman, no, I have not seen any ruins hereabouts, nor any tombs." He released Isaiab and shuffled away to retrieve his dagger.

Meanwhile the party halted to rest, the beasts folding their legs tidily beneath them to let the riders step down. Isaiab offered Conan more to drink, with sugary dates to gnaw on as he came to feel better. The Shemite asked how he came to be afoot in the desert, and Conan told him in low, halting speech of the theft and pursuit of the Star of Khorala, keep-

ing the rueful tale from the ears of the others. Isaiab heard
him out gravely, commiserating deeply over his loss.

Later, after dozing for a brief time, Conan was given an
auburn-colored camel with a makeshift saddle. The now-
amiable Otsgar ordered the beast to be taken out of a train of
pack animals that followed the troop under the care of an
elderly, one-eyed Zuagir.

Weak as he was, Conan was relieved to get help from any
source. Nevertheless he wondered why such a party as this
would venture so deeply into the desert. They led some
unladen camels and some burdened only with water, food,
firewood, and clanking leathern sacks of what sounded like
weapons. They seemed an ill-assorted crew—mostly young
and untried men, with only Otsgar, Isaiab, and one or two
others having the look of experience and assurance. Not like
any merchant's caravan that Conan had ever seen.

And yet the woman, Stygian by her look, was somehow
too sleek. Seated daintily in the shade of her browsing camel,
preserving her ginger complexion from the sun while combing out her long black hair, she did not look nearly so rough-
and-ready as to throw her lot in among common cutthroats.

A suspicion formed in Conan's mind, but he kept his
thoughts to himself. Little more was said by anyone until
Otsgar ordered the band to remount.

Under the others' eyes, Conan managed to heave himself
up onto the hump of his kneeling camel unassisted; he was
quickly regaining his strength. He reined his sluggish steed
into line behind Isaiab and followed him down the widening
gully.

On reaching the open desert the riders fanned out wide
abreast, apparently by prearranged plan. The hooded woman
stayed with Otsgar, while the younger riders headed far out
to the flanks, each man keeping just near enough to be seen
by his neighbor. Isaiab gestured to Conan to stay with him,
and the two took a position near the center of the formation.

"A good way to search the desert," Conan said when the
others were out of earshot. He urged his camel up abreast of

his rescuer's, but not close enough to nip at the other steed's ears.

"Aye, but our vision will not carry far today. The wind is rising and hurling half the desert into the sky." Isaiab shrugged up his striped shawl against the breeze, which was indeed beginning to claw at them as it raised a grayish haze against the horizon. Conan knew that such a wind could suck the moisture from a man more quickly than the naked sun, wearing away at him all the while with the same force that it used to carve solid rock.

"Yes, it will be hard to search today." He kept his mount close up beside the Shemite's. "But for what? A wayward caravan? Just whom are you planning to rob, Isaiab?"

"None who will have any complaint about it," the other remarked with a sidelong, cryptic glance. "Only those greedy beyond greed itself, who seek to hoard their wealth past any earthly need of it."

"As I thought! You are tomb-looters." Despite himself Conan shivered beneath his bunched caftan.

"An unheroic term. Call us, instead, raiders. Raiders of the desert." The smiling Isaiab glanced once again at Conan, who was riding upwind of him and blocking some of the wind's force. "But why do you quail, O master-thief? Have you not faced greater risks plying your trade among living men, as I have?"

"I do not mind a fair risk, as you well know." Conan shook his head, frowning. "But tomb-robbing . . . 'tis the cravenness and the stench of it that I can't stand. Grubbing up graves and sifting amid rotting bones for trinkets! Fah! Besides, I like not spirits and spells, whereas old tombs reek with them!"

The Shemite looked pensive, stroking his curly beard. "I seem to recall a tale told to me once—doubtless in some disreputable tavern or brothel—a tale of a young Northron barbarian who violated the grave of an ancient king and stole a fine sword from the very skeletal arms that sought to snatch it back."

"Aye, true," Conan conceded. "But that was in desperation! I was naked in the snow and hounded by wolves! I had no choice but to enter that tomb."

"And is your situation so different now?" But Isaiab's observation went unnoticed as Conan spoke on.

"Anyway, your method savors of madness, combing this desolation for ancient tombs! How do you expect to find one?" He stretched an arm to indicate the stark landscape, changing under their camels' pads from barren, gullied clay to a sand waste with dust-rivulets blowing sinuously over the ground. "What makes you think that men have ever inhabited this wretched tract?"

"As to the past inhabitants . . . look there." Isaiab gestured to a flat circular stone embedded in a rock-hard expanse of clay before them. "Doubtless 'twas the base of a winepress or grain-mill, such as we still use on the plains of Shem. You can tell by the hole at its center." He waved expansively. "There was an age when this was fertile land, stretching from the slopes of yon mountains to the shores of a tranquil sea!"

Following the sweep of his friend's arm, Conan gazed about them. For a moment he could almost imagine green fields superimposed over sand and sun-glaring alkali, with fluffy white clouds sailing above blue waves in the distance. His imagination began to conjure a seaport of domes and towers . . . but then he blinked and shook his head to clear his mind of the enchantment. "Crom!" he muttered.

"As to how we find rich tombs," Isaiab went on, "I agree, 'twould be foolish to search at random. But Otsgar has keen ears." He grinned slyly, winking to Conan. "Back in Shem he owns an inn, a famed caravanserai. With friends among the desert-riders he is well-placed to learn of any new discovery they make. He also has connections among the merchants and aristocrats, so as to command the best price for what treasures we may find.

"He has used his knowledge to good profit in the past, and I with him, helping him to mine some rich lodes." The

Shemite shrugged. "So many, indeed, that undespoiled tombs and shrines have become nigh impossible to find of late—that is, the old pagan burials, which are not guarded by our religious authorities.

"But some days ago Otsgar began fitting out a new expedition more lavish than usual. It was because of the ramblings of an old gem-hunter, found on the brink of death by Zuagir herders. While he still lived, he whispered to them that he had seen a corner of an ancient monument newly bared by the drifting sand, a royal tomb where none was rumored to exist before! He told of seeing a carven stone cornice in the shape of a lizard-snouted demon.

"Word traveled to Shem, to Otsgar's ears. My master paid well to learn the exact location." Isaiab scanned the desert waste glumly. "But now I wonder whether there ever was any truth to it. If so, mayhap the sands have swallowed the tomb again."

Conan grunted. "And you call this crew a band of accomplished tomb-raiders?"

"Aye, of course. That is, Otsgar and myself, and Philo the Kothian, and the old camel-keeper Elohar. The rest of the party are young toughs from Abaddrah. 'Tis the kind of adventure that appeals to the idlers and bullies of Shemitish city squares. We can use them; the work requires plenty of . . . muscle."

"And what of the woman?" Conan narrowed his eyes against a sudden buffeting of the wind.

"Ah, Zafriti!" Isaiab laughed. "Otsgar would have left her at home, if he trusted her alone for so long an absence. Yet for some reason she was eager to come along. She is a Stygian with self-willed ways, a dancer at his hostelry." Isaiab leered at Conan. "She cleaves to Otsgar through no vows, and not overly closely."

Conan shook his head in bafflement. "And with this odd crew you plan to go delving into ancient tombs? Know you the hazards that lie ahead?"

Isaiab waved a hand to dismiss his question. "Conan, for

once and all, put aside your doubts! Over the years we've learned the tricks.'' He winked. ''Things have a way of working out, as you'll see.''

The rising wind was making it difficult to be heard, and so the riders lapsed into silence. Conan let his camel drop back behind his friend's as the desert passed away beneath them.

He was awakened from a nodding doze by Isaiab's cry. ''We must bear southward!'' The Shemite had reined his camel aside and was pointing. ''Philo has stopped. Look there, he waves his pennant at us! And here comes Otsgar racing down the dunes . . . They've spotted something!''

Chapter 3

The Mastaba

The camel-riders came together below the crest of a tall dune. Squinting against the stinging force of windblown sand, Conan could see a dark shape protruding from the side of the sloping drift. It was a squat, rectangular building of black basalt, an ancient mastaba of the type immemorially used to seal a tomb entry.

The stone hut brooded darkly angular and out-of-place in the windswept dunescape. Its blocks were aged and worn, but their elaborate carvings could still be traced by the eye. The three exposed corners were ornamented by leering, lizardlike demon-heads jutting out from it like horns. Serpentine patterns in deep relief squirmed along the sloping walls of the shrine. Its roof rose in a low, four-sided pyramid behind the guard-demons, whose long lizard-tails twisted together to form a broken spire at the peak.

As quickly as they arrived, the raiders found what shelter they could in the lee of the half-buried flank of the mastaba. The camels turned their scruffy shanks to the wind, restlessly shifting their splayfeet to keep from being mired in blowing sand. At Otsgar's order a few of the party rode along the ridge of the dune to wave their shawls as a signal to the approaching outriders.

"We found the place just in time," Isaiab called, leaning

19

back in his saddle to address Conan. ''The sand is beginning
to darken the sun.''

Indeed, looming dust-clouds now tinged the daylight a
sickly yellow-brown. A plume of sand streamed over the top
of the ridge like a steady, horizontal waterfall. Luckily the
angle of the gale seemed likely to expose the mastaba further
rather than bury it in the dune.

''Tether those camels! Step lively, there! Pile your gear in
one place or you'll lose it.'' Otsgar strode among the band,
roaring orders over the howl of the wind. Two men were
busy staking out a leather tent-floor, while others climbed
around the house-sized tomb, examining it.

As Conan dismounted, Isaiab shouted again to him. ''Pray
to El-Lil that this blows over by nightfall. No matter how bad
it gets, Otsgar will make us stay and ride it out.''

''The entry! I've found the entry!'' The shrill cry came
from one of the young recruits probing at the half-buried face
of the mastaba. ''Come and see!''

Conan joined others crowding forward after the youth. He
paused on the way, exchanging glances with one of the black
basalt crocodile-heads half-eaten away by wind. It seemed to
leer evilly at him from the corner of the roof. He moved past
it cautiously, trudging up the slope of the dune.

The woman, Zafriti, was behind the mastaba, and as he
passed her she half fell down the slope, her sandals catching
in the sand drift. Conan caught her by the waist and set her
aright. Her body was supple in his hand, and brown eyes
flashed up briefly at him from under her cowl. ''Steady,
there, lass!'' he told her. He turned away to see Otsgar
regarding him narrowly.

Along the back wall of the mastaba the stone carvings
stood out in bold, square relief, obviously framing a door.
The youth had dug shallowly near the top of this archway;
now he knelt, scooping up sand two-handed and flinging it
aside to expose a dark niche. ''See, it is not filled with sand!
The way is open!'' He shrugged back his robes and bent
forward, heedless of the wind, to grope deeply into the

aperture. Otsgar stood over the youth with silent attention while Zafriti clung to his side and watched in fascination. Conan opened his mouth to voice a warning.

"Aah! Aiee!" The young Shemite suddenly flung himself back from the hole, staring at his bare arm. From it dangled a half-dozen deadly red scorpions, affixed to his skin by their tail-stingers. He thrashed screaming in the sand, smiting madly at himself to shake off the creatures, while those around him stamped with their heels at the scurrying things or stabbed at them with knives.

"Bring up the shovels," Otsgar yelled authoritatively, shaking off the clutching hands of his horror-stricken mistress. "Smash the night-creepers! And clear away the rest of the sand from the door!" He stood over the victim, watching gravely as the lad's spasmodic thrashings turned first to a pale-faced rictus and then to the slackness of death.

The leader turned away to direct the shovel-wielders' efforts as they hunted out and destroyed the remaining scorpions. He spared hardly a glance for Zafriti, though she looked stricken as she watched the men dragging the youthful corpse aside.

Clearing the entryway of sand proved easy, for the diggers had merely to fling their shovelfuls high and let the wind carry them away. Conan and Isaiab joined those who were hammering slats into the sand to keep the wall of the dune from sliding into the digging. But as the wind grew fiercer it seemed to tear at the sand drifts near the tomb with an almost supernatural violence; soon a U-shaped notch had formed in the dune-crest above the mastaba.

The probing spades of the workers gradually revealed a new obstacle: a tall door of bronze, double-valved and brightly burnished by centuries of flowing sands. Unlike the stone wall and jamb around it, it was not sculptured or cast, but only studded with heavy diamond-shaped bosses. No hinges were visible, nor any handles. Otsgar ordered a hammer to be brought up and plied against the door; its low, bell-like resonance revealed the thickness and solidity of the metal.

"Hold! Hear that!" Isaiab exclaimed over the shriek of the wind. "The blows are echoing inside the tomb, deep into the earth!"

All those standing by nodded in apprehensive agreement as they listened to the gonglike, receding sounds.

Otsgar barked out more orders, and a leather bag of tools was brought up. Two burly youths with the look of accomplished sneak-thieves rummaged in it and knelt on the upward-sloping stone threshold. Expertly they went to work trying to part the door-valves by hammering pry-bars and chisels into the cracks.

In a few moments one of them looked back to Otsgar eagerly. "It comes free! I heard a bolt snap inside!"

The raiders crowded as one toward the door. Even wide-eyed Zafriti, who had recovered some of her interest in the treasure hunt, started forward—until Otsgar jerked her back with a firm grip on her arm. That motion caught Conan's eye, and he glanced to Isaiab, who stood stock-still beside him regarding the tomb.

Then Conan's attention was drawn back to the doorway by frightened wails and a mighty, crunching thud. The sand shook under his feet and his nostrils filled with an exhalation of foul air that the wind quickly snatched away as the bronze door toppled ponderously forward onto the two hapless lock-pickers and crushed them flat. Beyond it, darkness yawned.

The door was really a single broad piece of metal, Conan realized. Its central crevice was only a false groove etched into its face, containing some kind of trick release. It was a trap, and one more than massive enough to crush the life out of the unfortunate men caught beneath it.

But then came a rattle of bronze links and a massive grinding of stone, as of some great mechanism inside the tomb. Two chains affixed to the upper corners of the door-panel pulled tight and started to haul the portal shut again, exposing the gory remains of those caught underneath.

With a shout Isaiab ran forward, leaping atop the rising

door. He jammed a chisel into one of the links of the chain just where it disappeared into an aperture in the stone lintel of the doorway. Otsgar bellowed and promptly followed, running up beside the door and jamming the other chain with a pincer-handle.

Both men jumped clear. The grinding inside the tomb continued more slowly a moment, with a straining, creaking sound—then both chains snapped, and the great door-panel thudded back down atop its twice-crushed victims. From inside the mastaba came an uneven crash, as of massive counterweights falling free.

The other tomb-raiders stood watching for a moment, taken aback. But Otsgar stepped forward and grinned, his gold tooth gleaming. "The way is indeed open!"

He pointed in triumph to the stone steps leading down out of sight into the tomb, and his followers suddenly burst into cheers. Forgetting their companions who lay dead beneath the door, they rushed forward onto it, capering about and smiting their leader's shoulders with glee. Even Zafriti, throwing back her cowl, hugged her mate tightly and kissed him as the wild gusts howled and tore about them.

"Torches! Bring on the torches, and the ropes!" Otsgar cried. "We can soon be out of this cursed wind!"

One of the Shemitish recruits, a quiet youth who had been the friend of the scorpion-bitten lad, called worriedly in Otsgar's ear, yelling to be heard over the storm. "Sir, might it not be better if we finished making camp?" He glanced up at the darkness of the sand-choked sky. "We have labored long, and night is almost upon us."

Otsgar turned a withering glance on the fellow. He pointed to the gaping tomb. "Fool, what matters night or day down there?" He laughed harshly, bristling his blond beard. "In the underworld 'tis always night!" The others burst into laughter, and the young man's ears visibly reddened.

With quiet bustle the band took some refreshment and made ready to enter the tomb. Each raider armed himself under Isaiab's direction, not with swords, but with bars, hooks, and hammers. Conan took a pry-bar as long as his arm and slung a coil of rope over his shoulder; others kindled torches and thrust spare ones in their belts. The old Zuagir was designated to stay with the camels, driven now into the scant lee of the mastaba to huddle together for shelter.

"But what of the riches we shall find?" Zafriti, enthusiastic again, had shed her cloak to reveal a lush figure wrapped in silk blouse and pantaloons. She came running up with a pile of leather sacks. "Take these along to carry forth the tomb-treasure!"

She went around the group and passed them out, smiling at each man with moist lips and sparkling eyes. Now that her cowl was off, Conan could appreciate the slim, finely-drawn bridge of her nose and the delicate line of chin that marked a classic Stygian beauty.

Under Otsgar's stern gaze, the tomb-raiders fell into line. The recently-embarrassed youth held a guttering torch and, in an obvious effort to redeem himself, strode forward in the lead. Conan looked critically to Otsgar, but the Vanirman did not deter the lad. Another street-tough and the northerner called Philo took second and third position respectively, backed by Isaiab and Conan. Then came the rest of the Shemites, with Otsgar and Zafriti in their midst.

There was no spacious chamber inside the mastaba, which was made of nearly solid stone—only a narrow, descending stair. The corridor was tall but barely wide enough for one man to squeeze past another, and the stairs pitched steeply downward. Besides being choked with sand, the steps were treacherously worn and rounded beneath the slick sand grains.

"Priests or worshipers must have passed this way for centuries," Conan whispered to Isaiab. "Perhaps the stair leads down to a great underground temple."

The Shemite only grunted in reply without looking back.

Conan descended slowly, bracing an arm against either wall and striving to keep his gaze on the steps and shadows, rather than on the torches which bobbed just ahead of him at eye level.

As the band descended from the mouth of the crypt, the composition of the walls changed from cyclopean masonry to dusty-green bedrock, flawlessly hewn and smoothed. The ceiling of the corridor remained high, doubtless for ventilation, and the faint, foul odor of the place came to permeate Conan's nostrils. The shrieking of the desert wind gradually diminished to a whisper far above them. Ancient dust replaced the sand that had clogged the stair, though the footing remained steep and treacherous.

Then came an exclamation from the front of the group and a change in the shape of the shadows. "The stairs have ended," the voice of the lead youth called back excitedly "And there are pictures on the walls."

Indeed, Conan soon came to the spot where the stairs gave way to a smooth stone floor—which still, however, angled downward. Both walls of the corridor had been whitened with gesso and daubed with pigments showing brightly here and there through the dust and decay of centuries.

The paintings did not depict recognizable scenes. They were more a form of writing—not runic characters like those of the Hyborian lands, but a picture-writing similar to the texts used by the older civilizations of Stygia and Khitai. Marching in horizontal bands along the wall, the pictographs were artfully drawn and colored, containing some human, animal, and other recognizable figures. But their form was so rigid and stylized that Conan knew he could never interpret their meaning unaided.

One peculiarity he did notice, and it gave rise to an eerie feeling as he lingered in the unsteady light before sections of wall-painting that had not crumbled to the floor or been clouded over by the encrustations of time. The humanlike forms in the paintings—although they stood on two legs, wore garments, and carried tools and weapons—were invariably depicted as being green-skinned and as having long crocodile-snouts. The postures and props of the various figures were ordinary, recurring over and over, but he searched in vain for any truly human shapes.

Isaiab glanced back at Conan. "The men who dug this tomb must have come from a swampy land—their sacred totem animal was the crocodile, and thus they depicted themselves." He spoke casually but loudly enough to reach the others' ears. "Mayhap 'twas against their holy laws to render any human likeness."

From the back of the band came Otsgar's voice, rumbling powerfully down the tunnel. "Move along there! Quit dragging your feet! We come to make ourselves rich, not to look at pretty pictures!"

At the Vanirman's prodding the speed of their descent increased, and the pictographs rolled by unexamined on either hand. But Conan noticed a few places where the lines of text merged with larger frescoes that did, indeed, seem intended as illustrations. He glimpsed scenes of the symbolic crocodile-figures tilling the soil, rearing cities, launching ships, and excavating deep wells and tombs.

The strange, obsessive quality of these visions disturbed Conan, but he forced himself to go unflinchingly onward. Each fiber of his being dreaded anything mystical or arcane, yet he seemed fated ever to confront such things. Now, having thrown in his lot with this ragtag band of amateur ghouls, he thought it best to fight down his ancestral fears and see the enterprise through to its end.

Suddenly there was turmoil ahead and a diminution in the light. The frontmost torch had dropped abruptly out of sight even as its owner gavè a high, quavering cry. One of those in the lead—the scrawny, hook-nosed Kothian named Philo—pushed past Conan in fright and bolted for the back of the line.

Conan peered forward over Isaiab's shoulder to see the cause. The weight of the first man had apparently triggered a stone tilt-door, which now banged ponderously back up into place.

Meanwhile, from an unseen pit beneath the corridor, came a familiar mechanical sound of trundling, grating stones. This time it was accompanied by the fallen man's screams. They rose to a shrill, agonized crescendo, then ceased. Soon afterward the grinding sound halted.

After the initial shock the men in the rear of the band grew agitated. They demanded to know what had happened, while pressing backward to avoid further menaces. Otsgar's strident curses could be heard overriding their panic. Conan turned to see him railing at the cowardly Philo, dragging him back into line by his tunic.

At the front of the party the third man, a Shemite, had turned to Isaiab to speak.

"I saw the trapdoor that swallowed him. It was not very large." The youth shrugged his shoulders with attempted bravado, though his face was sweat-filmed in the torchlight. "I am a good jumper, and no coward! I could clear the pitfall safely."

Isaiab looked the fellow up and down a moment, then nodded curtly The younger thief promptly handed him his torch and squirmed out of his caftan, leaving only his long shirt and pantaloons. The rest of the company were herded back up the tunnel a dozen steps to make room for him.

The jumper clenched the end of a rope in his teeth, turned, and got off to a running start.

He leaped well beyond the floor-section that had engulfed his companion, landed with a thud, and turned around with a grin of triumph. In an instant the farther section of the floor began dropping away underneath him. He scrabbled and scampered against the stone, but not nimbly enough, and slipped screaming out of sight. The stone trap banged shut over him.

Again came grinding sounds and the frantic crescendo of shrieks. Conan and the others hauled desperately on the rope. When the cries finally ceased, the taut line jerked free, its end frayed and broken.

Otsgar shoved forward from the rear of the band, muttering darkly. Isaiab turned back to expostulate with him. "Others have passed here! There must be a way to lock the traps. . . ." The goat-bearded one stopped talking to turn and stare at Conan, who was throwing off his own cloak.

"Aye, that's my kind of northerner," Otsgar cried, "not discouraged by a little bad luck!" He shoved forward and clapped Conan on the shoulder. "I'll wager the Cimmerian can make the leap—what say you, Isaiab?"

"He'd be a fool—"

The Shemite shut up and watched as Conan knotted the rope around his waist and thrust his crowbar through it. Then he placed his back firmly against one side of the corridor and walked his feet forcibly up the other wall, his sandals grinding into the painted plaster.

Wedged firmly between the walls, he began to inch sideways over the treacherous segment of floor, first sidestepping with his feet, then sliding on his back and elbows. His progress was slow, but as long as he maintained a powerful stress along the arch of his knees, he could not slip downward. When he passed above the first trapdoor a murmur of encouragement sounded among the watchers. This was a tactic none of the flatlanders had seen before.

Conan's legs strained cruelly at the narrowness of the walls, and the footing was uncertain, with loose patches of the painted surface crumbling away now and again under his feet. As he passed the second telltale crevice in the stone floor he felt the reservoirs of his strength draining swiftly away. He realized how unwise it had been to try such a trick so soon after his ordeal in the desert.

He hurried his snaillike motions then, since moving was no more exhausting than staying wedged in one spot. Laboring till the tendons in his knees burned like hot wires and he felt his legs about to buckle, he allowed himself a glance downward and realized that he must have reached the far end of the double trapdoor. The stone surface felt firm to his prodding touch, so he eased himself down gratefully onto it. Panting and sore, he nodded in reply to his companions' shouts of congratulation.

Regaining the strength to stand, he hauled on his line and dragged over enough wooden wedges and props to anchor a tightrope. Under Isaiab's supervision the rope was slung and drawn tight. Then the rest of the party came across one at a time, walking on the raised line a short distance above the false floor while bracing themselves against the tunnel walls for balance. Otsgar urged Zafriti to stay behind and wait, but she refused, making the crossing more easily and gracefully than any of the men did.

With torches brought to the far side of the pit, it could now be seen that the corridor opened out a short distance ahead, widening into a gallery lined with carven pillars. One of the remaining Shemites, a short, robust youth whose ear glinted with one silver ring, crept forward with a lit taper to spy it out, but Otsgar called him back, warning him sternly of the traps that might lie in wait.

"Now he warns them!" Conan muttered to Isaiab. "Methinks he has more dread of our pilfering than he has of any traps." Isaiab responded only with a taciturn look, busying himself by kicking the rope-brace tighter.

Otsgar held the tomb-raiders in check until the last of them—the gangling Philo, who now wore an abashed, furtive look—had crossed over. Then the party continued forward.

This time they advanced more slowly, wary of new death-traps. Conan caught Isaiab pausing to stare at one of the last wall-frescoes, which showed the builders of the tomb dispatching war-captives in various gruesome ways. A disturbing aspect of the picture was that, while the captors were still portrayed as crocodile-faced figures in the same stylized fashion, the helpless victims whom they burned, beheaded, and impaled were clearly depicted as flat-faced humans.

"Doubtless their artistic taboo about showing the human form applied only to their own tribe," Isaiab mused to Conan as they moved quickly past. "They did not see their enemies as having sacred animal-souls."

The chamber they now invaded was of a majestic size; but it did not seem to boast the wealth they sought. The double row of stone columns loomed tall, round, and massive, their bases and capitals carved intricately in friezes of lotus roots and foliage, with birds and serpents twining among the branches. The high, arching walls were finished with color-fully painted trim and sconced with torch-brackets—but against them lay none of the rich sarcophagi and tomb-furniture that looters might expect to find. Except for dust and the shifting shadows of the pillars, the place stretched barren before them.

"Two men to each side aisle," Otsgar ordered, "and watch for concealed doorways!" He himself passed from side to side of the chamber, examining the stonework with a practiced eye.

Conan and Isaiab remained at the center, with Zafriti staying close between them and the ones who followed. She moved forward with a dancer's lightness, her eyes shining with mingled fear and fascination. They all watched and listened intently, hearing only the sizzle of their torches and the muffled echoes of their own footfalls as they breathed the cool, stale air of the tomb.

"I see something at the end of the chamber—'tis a door. And there beside it, two mummy-boxes!" The speaker was the earringed Shemite who carried the first torch. He did not rush forward, but paused warily to inspect the intervening part of the chamber.

Otsgar strode out from behind a pillar, holding his own light high and peering far ahead. Then he clapped the younger man on the shoulder. "Indeed, Asrafel! There we shall find our treasures! Come along; you can be the first to choose a prize!"

Coolly ignoring the raider-chief's urging, the young Asrafel led the way at his own unhurried pace.

As they drew near the end of the chamber they could see that it did frame another great door, this one flanked by two tall coffins propped upright against the wall at either side. Like the outer door, it was of bronze, but it differed markedly in that it was tarnished and scaled with verdigris. The edges especially, where they met the stone jamb, were swollen and green-crusted, frozen into place by the corrosion of centuries.

Isaiab nudged Conan. "There must be moisture on the other side of the door, to rot the metal like that!"

"Aye. And those mummy-cases . . . I like not the look of them."

The twin sarcophagi, pale with dust and mold, were smoothly sculptured and rounded, presumably to follow the contours of those ancients who had been laid to rest within them. Their shapes were no more human than the wall-paintings. The outlines of the heads were elongated, with long bulges that appeared to represent sharp, tapering snouts lying flat against the chests of the sleepers. Each mummy-form was depicted as holding both sword and club crossed before its midsection.

But the other tomb-raiders made no comment on the strange aspect of the bronze door and its two monstrous guardians. Hastily probing and pounding the stone floor before them and judging it free of traps, they swarmed forward around the coffins with enthusiastic cries. Philo, all his fear forgotten, pulled off his sheepskin coat and used it to wipe away the detritus from one of the cases; at the reddish gleam of gold leaf and the sparkle of gems thus revealed, a groan of pleasure went up from the watchers. An instant later the splintering of ancient, dry wood sounded; a crew likewise set to work with their crowbars on the other coffin.

"Push these cases clear of the doorway," Otsgar shouted. "Lay them flat and give us room to work!"

Even as some men dragged down the groaning, creaking boxes and pulled them across the floor, others were worrying away at them, peeling off the thin gold foil and prying out the turquoise and amethysts set into the wood. The raiders swarmed, like vultures over a fresh carcass, and in moments the linen-swathed corpses of the occupants had been exposed to view.

"No need for every man of us to work the coffins! Isaiab, take the Cimmerian and the youngster, Asrafel, and start on that door. That is where the real treasure lies!" As he spoke, Otsgar expertly slashed with his knife at the windings of the mummy in certain selected spots—the hands, the breast, and the forehead. With his free hand he fumbled busily in the incisions extracting rings, amulets, and other adornments, which he deftly tossed into the leather pouch at his waist. Zafriti stood close by his side, watching his efforts, pointing and speaking urgently in Stygian when she thought he had missed something.

"But look at that devilish thing," Conan exclaimed. "It's part man and part crocodile!" Staying well back from the ruptured coffin, he pointed to the huge, misshapen head that bulged recognizably beneath the mummy's bandages.

"Be not overly squeamish, Cimmerian." Otsgar emitted a gruff laugh. "Even to the present day, the priests in this part of the world are fond of stitching together human and animal parts. If you should wish it, they can furnish you at your death with the head of a dog, the talons of a hawk, and the loins of a bullock for your greater convenience in the next world!"

Otsgar's remark was greeted by raucous laughter from all sides. Conan, disgusted by the sight of the looters' hands rifling through charnel remains, turned away to inspect the corroding bronze door. Isaiab and Asrafel were already prodding at it in a gingerly way.

They decided that, even if this door was a fool's trap like the last one, its mechanisms would most likely have been ruined by corrosion. The best way to open it, Isaiab thought, was to clean the debris out of the edges of the jamb and pry at the door-panel, working from the sides so as to be ready when it fell flat.

"Answer me this, then," Conan asked. "What will happen to us if it springs open wide like a common double door, but with unnatural force lent to it by springs or weights?" After considering this, the others decided to guard against the eventuality by wedging the bottom of the door with metal chisels.

Soon their poundings and scrapings rang through the chamber, calling forth humming echoes from among the great pillars. As the others left off scavenging in the wreckage of the coffins, they gradually joined in the labor. Even Otsgar took his turn, wielding a pick with impressive strength. But most of the time he stayed well back, directing torchlight around the workplace with the announced intention of spying for traps and potential cave-ins. Zafriti flitted back and forth between him and the workers, enthusiastically following their progress. Of the others, Conan noticed that Philo the Kothian hovered farthest back, clutching his bag of peeled gold and ready to bolt at an instant's notice.

Even with most of the raiders working in shifts, it took time to gouge away at the edges of the door. Under the scabrous, green rust was a core of metal almost as tough as the greenish-black stone that framed it, and after hours of labor the floor was littered with chips of both.

"And what if the inner chamber is flooded?" Asrafel asked after a time. "That would account for the door's decay— might we not all be drowned like rats once we succeed in opening it?"

But Isaiab, working steadily, had bored deeply at one edge of the door, and he declared that he could feel a cold draft of air seeping through the hole. So the threat of drowning was dismissed, and the work resumed for more hours.

"Enough, there! That's plenty of nibbling and pecking! The portal should be loose enough for a couple of good men with crowbars to topple it." Otsgar scanned the exhausted crew. "You there, Cimmerian—you have the beef for the job. Here, take this bar! And how about . . ."

"How about you, Otsgar?" Conan caught the heavy bar that the leader had tossed him and defiantly met his gaze. "I'll put my best into it if you'll match me."

"Yes, uh, well . . . I suppose the two heftiest of us should be the first to try. . . ." He flashed his challenger a murderous look. "Very well, Conan. Both of us together!"

The others scurried back expectantly from the doorway. A moment later the two burly northerners braced themselves, digging their steel bars into the deepest crevices on either edge of the door. On Otsgar's count of three, they hove sideways against the steel rods.

Nothing happened.

Otsgar counted again, and again the two strained mightily, grunting and grimacing for long moments. There was no result but the fall of a few green flakes from the top of the door.

"Mannanan! Roast your Mitra-forsaken heart on a pyre of devil's bones! Move, blast you!" Conan's breathy curses startled the watchers as he threw his weight harder than ever against the steel, at the same moment that Otsgar gave his bar a mighty wrench.

With a slow screeching of metal, the two halves of the door began to yield at once. Ponderously they toppled outward, grinding and shuddering together, to clash down against the stone floor with an ear-numbing clangor. At first the watchers' shouts of elation were almost drowned out by the racket; then, as the ringing echoes died, their voices were likewise muted by wonder at what lay beyond.

The doorway opened on an eerie, misty realm lit with effulgent light. The subterranean source of the pale-greenish glow was not visible, yet it was strong enough to dim the watchers' torches and brightly illumine the fog beyond the archway. Stirred by air gusting from the fall of the doors, the mists swirled eerily above a balustraded stone terrace and a broad stair that led down and away out of sight.

The wisps of fog curled and drifted almost like living things, swirling at the limit of the watchers' vision. Then, to their amazement, moving figures did start to take shape in the pale nebulosity—a crowd of lurching, distorted shapes sweeping up the stairway and casting long green shadows ahead of themselves in the mist. They made a sound, too, as they came—a growing, full-throated roar. In an instant the raiders were matching it with their own cries of terror and alarm.

For across the stone terrace and through the doorway swarmed bellowing demons, crocodile-headed monsters who rushed up out of the glowing pit with eons-old hatred flaring in their eyes, as if summoned by the sound of the falling doors. They charged among the raiders, snarling with misshapen mouths and flailing with strange, antique-looking swords and clubs.

The humans were instantly embattled, for the monsters issued forth in hordes and moved with terrible quickness. They were undeniably the crocodile-creatures of the frescoes, Conan realized. He swung his bar before him to knock aside a slavering lizard-snout; the owner dropped his sword and clutched at a monstrous, broken-toothed face with leathery claws that were almost hands. Meanwhile the Cimmerian ducked back toward the line of his companions, who were scattering away rapidly.

The chamber thundered with roars and screams. One of the Shemite youths went down, his dagger-arm gripped in crazy-toothed jaws while a second enemy's green-corroded sword dug into his unguarded belly. Another of the monsters grasped the fallen Zafriti by one shapely ankle and dragged her toward his flapping maw.

Conan fell on the creature with savage clubs and kicks, battering its heavy body back against the base of a pillar. Dragging the hysterical Stygian upright, he hurled her along the chamber. At that moment Otsgar, swinging his bar with a Vanir war cry, burst through a ring of attackers and rejoined the band.

They could not hope to hold their ground, or even fall back in an orderly way. Some of the raiders were unarmed, and

the huge pillars of the hall broke up their ranks and made it
easy for the crocodile-faced ones to come at them from the
sides. In moments their retreat turned into a rout, and Conan
found himself racing full-tilt with the others away from the
bellowing of the monsters and the shrieks of their human
victims.

The pale glow from the subterranean gateway faded quickly
behind them. Luckily some of the humans had retained their
torches as weapons, and these, flaring and bobbing, lit the
fugitives' way through the dim subterranean gulfs. Their
flight was sped by terror, but those whom they had called
forth from the pit followed swiftly, and where the chamber
narrowed to a corridor, the crowding slowed the raiders'
pace.

Conan and Otsgar had to turn as the foremost of the
tomb-dwellers fell upon them, slavering and hooting in voices
like barge-trumpets. The creatures charged forward ferociously,
but soon learned at their cost to dodge back from the whizzing arcs of both men's crowbars and the short, savage jabs
of Conan's dagger. When the rear-guardsmen finally broke
away and fled up the passage, they left several of the ancient
reptilian race bellowing on the floor behind them. But count-
less more leaped across the writhing bodies in pursuit.

Immediately afterward came another bottleneck, at the
place where the tightrope was strung across the trapdoors.
Isaiab was just crossing by the light of Asrafel's torch while
Zafriti waited anxiously to mount the rope. Conan turned to
Otsgar with an unspoken question—who first?

For an instant the two men glared at each other; then, with
a grudging toss of his shoulder, the Vanirman urged Conan
forward. Growling, he turned back to swing his wrecking-bar
against the snout of his frontmost pursuer.

Conan bounded to the rope. Zafriti had started across it,
but this time her progress was slow and halting. Conan
realized that her ankle must have been wrenched earlier by
the grasp of her saurian attacker.

"You'll have to go faster than that!" Coming up from behind her along the rope, Conan clapped an arm around her middle and carried her swiftly across. As they reached the other side, however, he cursed and put her struggling form down untidily. "What in Set's flames . . . ?"

From his hand he untangled a costly piece of tomb-loot, an ornate silver wire necklace, age-blackened but glinting with gems. The Stygian, spitting with anger, snatched it away from him and shoved it back into her blouse where she had been concealing it. Grasping Asrafel's arm, she hurried onward.

Conan turned to see Otsgar making his way across the rope by the light of the disappearing torch. He finished with a leap and sped up the corridor close on the Cimmerian's heels. But the descendants of the tomb's makers must have remembered how to disable the trapdoors, for in a moment Conan glanced back to see them swarming unhindered in pursuit, ignoring the stretched rope.

Where the tomb-stairs began, the straggling fugitives bunched closer together; the footing here was treacherous, and the foremost of them did not have a light. Conan could see him beyond the wavering flame of Asrafel's torch—Philo the Kothian, scurrying up the sandy steps at the farthest probing limit of the torchlight, weighed down by his sack of gold.

Besides the Kothian only five raiders remained—Isaiab, with Asrafel and Zafriti pressing close behind him, Conan himself, and Otsgar, who could be heard in the rear, venting curses at his snarling pursuers and occasionally turning to beat them back. A pitiful remnant of the dozen and more adventurers who had come in search of tomb-wealth!

Then the thief Philo cried out excitedly, and Conan, peering ahead, could see why. A spot of pale blue light had appeared: daylight in the tunnel-mouth! They must have passed an entire night in the underworld; now, bright, unsullied dawn filled the doorway of the crypt. The sight of it was heart-seizing. It made the ungainly Kothian who was nearest

to it scamper even faster. All those behind him redoubled their
efforts too, drawing a few precious steps ahead of the hooting
tomb-dwellers.

As the doorway widened in his sight, Conan realized that it
would blind him at least temporarily. He caught up with
those in front, who in turn had gained on the encumbered
Philo. But the Kothian was still in the lead when he burst out
into daylight, gasping and shouting—then suddenly dropped
out of their pale, washed-out vision, his shouts twisting into a
shrill, fading scream.

"Hold, there! Don't follow him," Conan cried, grasping
Zafriti's shoulder while he blinked furiously and tried to
diffuse the morning light that was searing into his skull.
Beyond the Stygian wench, Asrafel and Isaiab had already
stopped short on the brink of what was now a sheer preci-
pice. Conan came up behind them, shading his eyes and
squinting down in disbelief.

During their sojourn in the crypt, the wind must have torn
away more sand from the tomb—vastly, incredibly more.
Now the structure could be seen in all its immensity. The low
mastaba they had found was only the tip, the uppermost
level, of a great step-pyramid that reared high above the
desert.

Below them Philo's broken body was still rolling down
first one, then the next of the titanic, sloping steps of the
tomb's wall, toward the desert's twisted sands. There, to one
side, the camel-train stood waiting, tended by the beckoning,
shouting Zuagir, Elohar.

The clash of weapons rang in the doorway behind them,
where Otsgar turned to face the first of a horde of flailing,
snapping crocodile-things.

"This way, girl." Conan seized Zafriti by the waist and
drew her sideways from the door along the narrow ledge of
the second-highest pyramid-step, to the rope which the old
camel-keeper had left dangling from one of the sculptured saurian heads at the corner of the tomb. Isaiab was

already starting down it, and Asrafel waited to follow. Once Zafriti was on the rope her handicap disappeared. Her supple dancer's limbs were able to bear her weight as the four let themselves down from one level to the next toward the highest rim of the sand dunes.

Moments later Otsgar hit the rope, fleeing his demonic pursuers. He jarred those below him with his weight, sliding down fast enough to crowd them.

But his haste was unnecessary. Above him the pyramid's entrance, which moments before had teemed with life, was now devoid of movement. The only sound was one which throbbed out over the desert like a solemn bell of warning: the clang of the pyramid's great bronze door, pulled shut behind the last of its ancient guardians.

Chapter 4

The Plain of Plenty

"And you said the builders of the place were humans who only worshiped the swamp-lizards!" Zafriti turned in her saddle to give Isaiab a petulant, angry look. "Conan guessed otherwise—didn't you, Conan?"

The Cimmerian's horse ambled some distance from hers, yet the glance of her artfully painted eyes brushed him so forcefully that he could almost feel its tingle.

Zafriti held up a ring poised in her fingertips for her companions' inspection. It was a large stone of pink carnelian with a greenish-silver setting in the form of two crocodiles biting one another's tails. "Knowing the truth, I could never bear to put this on my finger." She turned it glinting in the sunrays, affecting a shiver of her trim shoulders.

Conan made no answer, thinking of what she had not scrupled to hide inside her shirt. But Isaiab rode near her and reached out a hand. "If it offends, I will gladly relieve you of it."

"Nay." The Stygian promptly slipped the gem back into her belt-purse. "The profit from our expedition is slim enough already." This reproachful statement seemed to be directed at Otsgar, who rode at the head of the band.

But their chief went on in silence without looking back. He and the five other survivors, including Asrafel and the old Zuagir

41

at the rear, were now mounted on horses traded for along the way, because camels were less suited to travel the hills and meadows of western Shem. Fewer beasts were needed in any case since so little of their baggage had weathered the windstorm. The riders were winding through a magnificent cedar forest, going from the cool dark shadows of the trees and through patches of brilliant sunlight. Beside the trail meandered a sparkling, splashing stream.

The six had rejoiced at leaving the desert. In the first Shemitish hostelry they found among the western oases, they had gorged on wine, fruit, and fowl, then slept the sun nearly around its course. But their zest at mere survival quickly wore off. Now, as they thought of their future prospects, their mood was pensive and gloomy—all except Isaiab, who had been swigging at a wineskin along the day's hilly, winding trek, and whose exuberance showed it.

"Our profit may be slight," he declared, "but at least it is not divided many ways. As ever the hazards of the tombs have weeded out the unfit, thinning our numbers considerably in the process."

Otsgar swung back in his saddle and glared as if to silence the goat-bearded one. But it was too late; Asrafel already was aroused.

"Then it is as I suspected! You knew the dangers all along, yet goaded my companions onward in spite of them. Or rather, because of them!" The dark-eyed young Shemite spurred his horse forward, then reined it in angrily. He directed his rebuke first at Isaiab, then at Otsgar, his gold earring glinting in the forest rays. "Some of those fellows were my friends from boyhood—idlers, 'tis true, and not yet of manly parts—but they should never have died to serve your greed!"

Otsgar wheeled his horse to face the younger man. He made an imposing figure in the armor-plated coat and studded helm. "Speak not of my greed, stripling! Remember, I am the great loser in this adventure! My shares of the paltry treasure we found were scarcely enough to pay for the camel-fodder!'' Blocking the trail with his mount, the Vanirman swept his dour glance over the others as well as he spoke on.

"And yet I fulfilled my bargain with you and your overeager friends. If it had only been an honest tomb, you would now be happy enough with your wealth!''

The young Shemite seemed balked more by Otsgar's fierce appearance than by his words. He sat still in the saddle, sullenly eyeing the ground before his employer's horse.

Conan spoke up to break the deadlock. "Otsgar, the next time you choose a tomb to rob, try to be sure that the occupants are dead, and not just resting!''

Isaiab's tipsy guffaws dissolved the tension for the moment; with an irritated look at Conan, Otsgar wheeled his mount forward again. As the party moved on, the drunken Shemite drew his steed close beside the Cimmerian's. He spoke in a scarcely controlled whisper.

" 'Tis true, I would wager. Even with all the trinkets that he and the dancer managed to hoard in their clothing, Otsgar will scarce earn back his investment on this trip.'' He leaned even closer, to wink and to blow wine-breath in Conan's face. "It would not surprise me to find our captain casting about soon for a new venture. The debts of his business are pressing, and he has a northman's love of risk.''

"I shouldn't think it would be hard for him to line up something,'' Conan replied. "The Shemitish city-states have no shortage of tombs, I am told.''

"Oh, nay. There are tombs aplenty,'' Isaiab said. Then he blinked and hastened to amend his words. "Not like the land of Stygia across the river, of course! There the tombs outnumber the warrens of the living. The snake-worshipers dote on tombs; they build tombs on tombs and raze whole towns to try to make way for necropolises! In truth, 'tis disgusting.''

He pondered drunkenly a moment and sighed. "But then, we of Shem may go the same way, if the teachings of the prophet Horaspes continue to spread.'' The thief stroked his beard distractedly, as if trying to recapture his point. "But, ah, yes! the problem with most tombs in Shem is: they are very well-guarded, and the days when we dared loot them are long past. Enforcement is strict.''

''Do the people remember their past rulers so fondly, then?'' Conan asked.

''No. But the Priesthood is powerful, and they protect the graves vigilantly. Now, at Horaspes' instigation, we even have the tomb police to cut off the ears and noses of offenders and sit them down on sharpened stakes.''

''Who is this Horaspes, who looms so large in your difficulties?''

''Oh, he is a wandering prophet who has found eager ears among the royal courts of Shem. He preaches a facile doctrine of the glory of the Afterworld, as well as the latest innovations in tomb-crafting and embalming. For the last few years he has been entertained lavishly by King Ebnezub, the ruler of my own city, Abaddrah. He's talked the king into undertaking the grandest monumental tomb project in Shem. Now Ebnezub, as his health declines, rushes to finish it and gives Horaspes ever more sway in the city's affairs.''

''Tombs and monuments,'' Conan muttered. ''Rubbish! I'll never understand why men throw up hollow tributes to their own pomp! In my native land, a simple sword-post was enough.'' He shrugged. ''Adorned, perhaps, with the skulls of a few enemies. . . .''

''These giant tombs are a blight on the land of Shem!'' broke in Asrafel, who was riding nearby, still looking sullen from his clash with Otsgar. ''They are built on the blood and sweat of the farmers, and they take the place of more worthwhile public works. Meanwhile the small farms are all being taxed away from their owners.'' The young Shemite's earring flashed as he shook his head in indignation. '' 'Twas Ebnezub's folly that robbed me of my inheritance and turned me to this life of thievery!''

Isaiab shrugged. ''I would not be too quick to denounce the great tombs. They employ many idle hands, and they spread riches around that would otherwise lie idle in the king's coffers. Such wealth can filter into many pockets—

including ours." The Shemite grinned slyly to Conan and winked to Asrafel.

"Still, I agree, the notion is vain," Isaiab continued. "Going to one's grave with vast amounts of wealth, provisions, weapons—even with live servants and wives! I cannot say how the practice has gained such currency." The Shemite pondered further, twisting his beard more tightly. " 'Tis the Stygian influence, working through Horaspes. Stygia is a great land, and powerful, if not well-loved. With their vastness just across the river . . . here, look, you can see what I mean!"

Conan followed Isaiab's pointing finger. For some time the road had been trending downward through the trees, but now it emerged across the bald, rocky brow of a hill, opening a grand vista before the riders.

It was the great valley of the River Styx. The marshy plain stretched yellow-green toward the western horizon, where its bluish haze gathered upward in a jumble of clouds. To the left, under a layer of mist, lay the muddy-green, oceanlike expanse of the Last of Rivers; and beyond it, above the mist, pricked a half-dozen neat, symmetrical pyramid-tops of varying sizes. Conan knew that he was seeing, over a great distance, the tombs of Stygia—ancient symbols of the even more ancient land which commenced at the river's far bank and stretched southward to the haunted jungles of the Black Kingdoms.

"As you can see, the grandeur of the Stygian empire is ever before us." Isaiab sighed. "Yet I prefer our enlightened Shemitish ways. Yonder lies Abaddrah, our destination."

He swung his arm to the right, toward the rising ground marking the edge of the green bottomland. There a city of huddled white domes perched, surrounded by a thick, battlemented wall. The town itself was surprisingly upright and compact, a sturdy hub for the converging white spokes of road and sun-bright canal. But outside its walls, along the canal-banks, sprawled unplanned and undefended suburbs. And on the inland side, further weakening the city's defenses, were more buildings and avenues reaching back into the hills.

"There, behind the city, lie the tomb precincts," Isaiab explained. "Most of the slums on the farther side have been cleared for the king's new enterprise, which will dwarf the older monuments." He indicated a large excavation partly obscured by the city's heights.

"Glorious, is it not, Conan?" Zafriti, who had dismounted beside the trail ahead to take in the view, beamed at him as he rode up. " 'Tis more beautiful than my native side of the river. And the country does not suffer so under the heavy-handed rule of priests, with their piety and prudery!" She gave a lithe, expressive toss of her shoulders. "In Stygia, where public dancing is forbidden, I would have had to enter a governor's seraglio. But in Shem there is freedom to breathe. Yours is happy land, Isaiab."

"Not so happy for my dead father." The speaker was Asrafel, whose horse was ambling down the trail. "He was drowned in an irrigation canal for trying to hold back some of the extortionary tribute demanded by King Ebnezub's tax-gatherers!" The young man was sitting coolly in the saddle, though the sting of wrath was in his voice. "Nowadays Abaddrah is a happy place only for the well-born—and for the shrewd," he said with a pointed glance at Otsgar.

Isaiab spoke soothingly, "Now, lad, the hand of rulership rests heavy on the necks of lowly folk everywhere. Abaddrah is not the worst land in that regard—"

"I think it's a wonderful city!" Zafriti interrupted, adept at keeping herself the center of attention. "In my homeland, the audience for my arts would have been lost. But here, with Otsgar's backing, I am known throughout the land. You must see me dance tomorrow night, Conan! My ankle is mended!" Flashing her gaze up at him, she executed a brief, swaying step that ended with an earthy throb of her hips, causing a moment's silence among the men.

Otsgar, still seated in his saddle, had turned his gaze from the splendid landscape to his more splendid mistress. "Zafriti, you may be causing needless trouble for Conan. I did not think he meant to ride with us all the way to the Shemitish plain. Do you, Cimmerian?'' He looked meaningfully to his fellow northman.

"I would not mind seeing more of this part of Shem.'' Conan glanced to Zafriti. "It has pretty scenery.''

Otsgar scowled, ignoring Isaiab's braying laugh. "Tell me, Cimmerian, what business was it, anyway, that left you marooned days ago in the desert?''

Conan shrugged. "I was on my way to Ophir; I thought I would have dealings with the queen of that land. But it has come to nothing.''

"So you see, Otsgar, he can stay with us at the inn!'' Zafriti beamed as she swung herself up into the saddle of her dappled mare. "After all, he acquitted himself well in the crocodile-tomb. As well as any of us did.'' She flashed a demure look at her employer. "Perhaps he can join us in our next quest.''

"Indeed, I cannot decline.'' Conan looked to Otsgar earnestly. "I need to replenish my purse before I travel farther.'' He swung his horse back toward the trail. "Though I would just as soon avoid more tomb-grubbing, and the teasing up of ancient curses.''

"Well said, Conan!'' Isaiab said. "I, for one, have come round to your view. Let us reform and be honest thieves forevermore.'' He shook his wineskin and raised it to his lips. "Ali, I grow thirsty! I have talked myself near sober!''

Otsgar said nothing else, and the riders resumed the downward trail.

The road wound back into the forest, which eventually thinned to orchards of pomegranates and dates, and then to open fields, as the hills dwindled away beneath the horses' hooves. Here the trailside stream unbraided into a network of gleaming irrigation channels, whence field hands raised water by means of long, counterweighted dippers they swung back and forth on fulcrums of sunbaked mud. The slow, patient

swinging of the swapes and the gurgling of water into the
fields provided a rhythmic, monotonous background to their
ride. Conan felt the sweltering weight of the valley air on his
neck and saw the sprouts of barley and emmer it coaxed from
the lush soil.

"The lower fields have not yet been planted, for the Styx
has just begun its flood," Isaiab told him. "The city will be
crowded with farmers driven from their plots. The flooding is
worse this year—for, in his haste to finish his great tomb,
King Ebnezub has been letting the irrigation canals silt up
dangerously. But then, many of the homeless farmers have
been set to work on the project. This is the time of year when
tomb construction goes the fastest."

For the balance of the trip, Isaiab's garrulity flowed over
Conan like the waters of the eternal Styx. Zafriti was spared,
for as the road widened, Otsgar called her forward to ride
beside him. She immediately set about teasing him, as the
others could tell from the abruptness of his tones and gestures
and the laughter evident in hers.

As they passed onward the cultivation ended. The fields on
either hand turned into reedy mudflats, the dikes between
them frequently submerged or washed away. On stilts here
and there stood the vacant, reed-walled houses of the farmers, some of them sagging down into the water; the Styx,
swollen by rain-squalls in distant jungles and the melting
snows of southerly mountains, had swept into the plain with
devastating force. Soon the white-metalled high road was
nothing more than a low causeway through a waveless sea
that gleamed yellow in the rays of the western sun. Twice the
riders had to dismount to cross broad canals in reed boats
poled by breechclouted ferrymen, letting the horses swim
behind.

Then Abaddrah came into view, her spires and battlements
looming jagged against the western haze. The trumpets of the
priests could be heard braying from the ziggurats, and the
smokes of hearths and sacrifices colored the sun a deeper red.
Road and canal traffic grew heavy, even in the declining day,

consisting of ox-wains laden with fruits and furs, canopied, silver-chased chariots drawn by high-stepping horses, and barges hauling bundles of reeds and giant building-stones.

Soon the riders were passing among the habitations at the city's fringe: shanties of mud and sticks perched along the edge of the road or mere tents of ragged blankets strung up on the canal-banks. Naked, muddy children scampered out from under the horses' hooves with raucous cries. Their parents could be seen groveling in the shallows for eels and crayfish to eat, mere paces away from crocodiles that dozed or stirred sluggishly on the banks. At the sight of the reptiles Conan's gut clenched, his brain seeing dim, nightmarish flashes of his recent subterranean fight.

Then the raiders came up to the city's main gate, a massive, overarching fortification inlaid with colored tiles and lit extravagantly by torches in the fading day. To Conan's surprise, Otsgar led the party past the gateway; they had but a tantalizing glimpse of the trade goods being examined before the customshouse and the colorful rabble swarming just inside the portal.

Passing along the road outside the wall, they approached another junction. "Yon roads," Isaiab told Conan, "lead north to Eruk and the Hyborian lands, and west to Asgalun and the sea. Along them are clustered all the great city-states of Shem, like the jewels on a spangled golden pectoral. Down them passes the world's richest trade."

Just there, at the far corner of the crossroad, was a broad, low building of sunbaked brick, half a dwelling and half a fort. The gate to its walled courtyard stood open, and from inside came the flicker of firelight and the raucous voices of men and animals. As Otsgar led the way into the court he could be heard to bellow, "Awaken, servants! Attend, hostelers! Your master and host is returned!"

Chapter 5

Zafriti's Dance

Music and fragrance filled the air of the inn. The strum of strings and the clink of tymbals, the rich aroma of roasting mutton and the nectar of honeysuckle, mingled all together in a heady blend. And if the patron's senses of smell and hearing were not too wine-muddled, they could further feast on the murmur of voices in diverse tongues, the tinkle of feminine laughter, and a bewildering variety of perfumes, incense, and intoxicant herbs being dispensed in pipes and water-jars in the darker corners of the place.

The main chamber, though large, was divided into separate alcoves by low, curving arches perched on slender stone columns that supported the ceiling. Among these, at varying floor-levels, inn-guests sprawled on cushions before low tables laden with food and drink. Intricate mosaics gleamed from the ceilings of the alcoves—all except the largest and deepest-sunken one, whose only ceiling was the glinting starscape of Shem's sultry night. From the archways of this central courtyard hung flowering vines that stirred in gentle night-breezes, while at its center a tiled fountain plashed.

"I did not expect to find your bandit-chief so prosperous," Conan confided to Isaiab over his beaker of yellow palm wine. He sat cross-legged in a lamplit alcove, well-rested from his travel of the previous day. He sported borrowed silk pantaloons and vest, his black mane bound loosely in a striped turban. "The Vanirman sets a royal feast."

"Aye, he is accepted almost as a noble here in Abaddrah." The Shemite nodded toward the blond-bearded Otsgar where he stood robed in finery, greeting turbaned guests at the main doorway. "In his hostel you will find few of the dirty, brawling desert-riders of the eastern caravans. He prefers to lodge the richest merchants traveling with the most lavish goods and the trustiest retainers. Ofttimes they arrive from the caravan roads too late to enter the city gates." Isaiab winked. "More often, they wish to do some trading first, without the formality of tariffs."

"Well, at least Otsgar stays humble." Conan emptied his cup and reached for the pitcher on the table before him. "He has not forgotten how to poor-mouth it when he haggles over the division of spoils and their sale price back to him as art objects."

"Yes, he is astute." Isaiab swirled the dregs in his own beaker, examining them thoughtfully. "Abaddrah is like a deep pond left by the river-flood: bright and glittery at the top, dim and murky beneath. To swim smoothly between the different layers, it takes a special kind of fish. Like Otsgar." He looked up at Conan. "Sometimes that kind of cleverness is easier for a foreigner."

"Speaking of which, your town is an interesting place." Conan leaned close to Isaiab and spoke more confidentially. "Loitering today in the central market, I saw pigs of pure gold as big as a man's foot, tubs of gemstones, and chunks of jade I could scarcely have lifted. Great wealth changing hands, but all of it too well-guarded to touch. The place was abuzz with talk of the splendor of Ebnezub's tomb."

"Aye. The king pays top price for half the riches of the western world; hence Otsgar's greed for trinkets. The coffin-case is to be of alabaster and white gold, I have heard. All his gem-crusted personal belongings will be entombed with him, and the ceiling of his crypt-chamber will be speckled with twinkling gems in the patterns of yon stars." Isaiab pointed up to the heavens that shone above the fountain.

"Indeed." Conan thumbed his jaw thoughtfully. "And all extorted from the country's wretched poor. 'Tis enough to make a man ponder—a shame, truly, that so much wealth should be buried with a king, when his subjects wander hungry and homeless through the streets."

Isaiab looked up with surprise showing in his face. "Do my ears deceive me, Conan? Surely you have not taken up Asrafel's tireless grudge against the aristocrats . . . ?"

Conan smiled and ran a hand along the square edge of his chin. "Nay, not exactly. But as I wandered through the city yesterday, a thought did enter my head. What if—"

But then, suddenly, he left off speaking and turned to the back of the room. The throb of the lutes and the sting of the tymbals had grown louder, newly accompanied by a thin, twining melody from a pipe. All eyes turned toward the far side of the gallery where Zafriti emerged from a bead-curtained archway and began her performance.

She danced the courting-dance of the Zuagir women—though she went unencumbered by the many shawls and veils that a desert tribeswoman would wear. Those shreds and bangles which were draped about her athletic body strained at her every movement, mocking the very notion of modesty. She was also far more mobile than the Zuagir wenches, not being confined to a lamplit tent or a small carpet spread in the marketplace. Snapping out a brisk rhythm with her finger-chimes, she kept the bells at her waist constantly ajingle with movements both sinuous and sprightly.

Dancing she went among the alcoves of the inn. She was followed at a distance by musicians and by servant-boys shining reflecting-lamps to highlight her progress. She went nimbly, skipping over the pillows and legs of her audience and delighting each company in turn with some new trick or tease.

Otsgar hovered in the shadows behind her, clapping his hands in tempo and nodding to his guests with an air of smug proprietorship. He smiled approvingly as Zafriti shimmied before fat-faced merchants, letting them tuck silver coins into her girdle. Most of her time was spent with such patrons rather than the leaner, hardier travelers, Conan observed; in particular she seemed to ignore the part of the inn where he and Isaiab sat.

But then her dance suddenly changed direction. She bounded through the court, across the rim of the fountain, up to their very alcove and into it. Making Isaiab flinch, she leaped over him onto the stone table, her bare feet deftly scattering bowls, breadcrusts, and melon-rinds from the dark marble. There she paused, breathless and tense as an antelope stopped in midflight through the forest.

For an instant her blinding footwork ceased, and her finger-chimes strained against the melody, but the musicians soon understood, slowing their tempo. Zafriti then began a more slinking, sensuous phase of her dance, writhing unashamedly just before Conan's eyes. Occasionally she flashed a provocative smile over her shoulder at Isaiab, or serenely scanned the faces of the musicians, lamp-bearers, and eager patrons who crowded to the sides of the alcove. But her movements were plainly directed at the Cimmerian, who sat riveted before her.

She took great care tensing and rippling the golden flesh of her loins, commending each new wonder of her body to the watchers' eyes with slow, expressive passes of her bejeweled hands. She made shivers travel her full length from wrist to ankle, with sequins shimmering and bells rattling all along the way. She curved and twisted artfully, ever exposing new vistas of supple, sweat-glimmering skin to the silver lamp-light. Inching in perfect time to the throbbing rhythms, she went down on her knees and shins on the tabletop, pointing her scarlet-painted toenails back along the marble and arching her body away from Conan in a posture of abasement and invitation.

At this sight, the crowd of male onlookers sighed and murmured. Some of them commiserated in low voices at the plight of the northern barbarian seated so close to this living, shimmering flame—close enough to sweat from the heat, if not to be scorched by it.

Conan, his every nerve atingle, felt that he should take some action. He reached into his money-pouch and fumbled out the first thing that came to his grasp—a heavy, lozenge-shaped slug of golden Abaddran coinage. Zafriti was already shimmying upright again on arching legs and straining toes. As Conan reached forward to insert his coin into the dancer's silver-lined girdle, the tight-stretched shred of purple silk jumped back from his fingers, then spun entirely out of reach, as she bounded away from him with a flicker of dainty, dust-marked soles.

She whirled into the main corridor where a crowd of roaring, reaching inn-guests converged on her, thrusting forth coins or merely covetous fingers. But the dancer spun fast enough to keep them all at bay, throwing down a veil for them to toss their tributes upon.

Then Otsgar was crowding in front of her, slapping his dagger-sheath heavy-handedly and bellowing in loud acclaim—an applause which spread to the mouths of the audience in a widening tumult. Shielded by the innkeeper's bulky body, the dancer gathered up her wealth and disappeared through the archway, scarcely disturbing the strings of hanging beads.

In moments the hubbub dissolved. Patrons returned to their seats, calling for more food and drink, while youthful tavern-hostesses dispersed among them to attend to the yearnings that Zafriti's dance had aroused. To Isaiab's astonishment, Conan sullenly ignored the advances of several such flimsily-clad women.

He had put his gold-piece back into his purse, and now he sat dour and wordless. Isaiab deemed it wise to say nothing about Zafriti and tried instead to resume the topic of conversation that had been so tantalizingly interrupted by the dance. But as the festivity around them peaked, Conan became restless. He gulped down his drink and arose, declaring that he would venture forth alone by night. When Isaiab asked him on what business, he would not say.

Conan first headed through the bustling kitchen to fetch a cloak from the chamber that he shared with Otsgar's other rogues. As he was going down a rear passageway, he heard a door scrape open behind him.

He turned back to the portal made of stout, painted planks less sumptuous than the carved fittings in the public part of the inn. The half-open doorway was empty; nevertheless a hint of familiar perfume tinged the air.

He walked back and gazed into the room—to see Zafriti, still in her dancing-garb, but without her bells. She stood before a large mirror of polished metal, removing her remaining jewelry. The room was a bedchamber, but her bright, glittery costumes draped every piece of furniture in it.

"So, Conan, you did not see enough of me during my dance?" Zafriti spoke without looking at him, bending forward instead to loosen a stubborn ear-bangle. "I could scarcely have shown you any more! But come inside, close the door. Tell me what you thought of my performance!"

After a moment's hesitation Conan stepped inside and pulled the door shut behind him. " 'Twas as good as any I've seen," he admitted. "And in roving from Zingara to Khitai, I have watched more than a few tease-dances."

Zafriti flashed a glance at him, then looked down wryly at the coins heaped amid her pots of kohl and rouge on the mirror-table. "I wish you would tell as much to my other patrons. Their payments were far less heartfelt than their grunts and groans." She opened a drawer in the table and raked the coins into it.

Conan eyed her narrowly. "Are you sure you want me to know where your wealth is kept, girl? The rascals you run with do not steal only from the dead, you know."

Zafriti shrugged. "Tonight's take is small enough. I trust you at least that far, Conan."

"Yet you refused the gold I offered." Conan squinted at her appraisingly. "Most unlike you, it seems to me."

Zafriti turned to him, swinging her hips and shoulders independently of one another in a dancer's fashion. "Why should

I accept mere coins from you, Conan?'' She moved close up to him and placed her hands on his dagger-belted hips, gazing up insolently into his face. ''Why take your coins, when I could have it all?''

''All . . . ?'' He echoed her dully, his gaze fixed on her upturned face. Her eyes were sultry and green-shaded, her berry-stained mouth half-open. Below and very near were all the congenial curves of her body.

''Yes, I think I could possess it all—not only your money, but your body, your passion, and your northern savagery too, if only I ask.'' She stirred forward slightly but still did not touch him, except for the warm hands lingering on his waist.

''And what of the one who keeps you?'' Conan asked, striving to keep his guard up. ''What would he say to it?''

''Otsgar? Bah!'' Zafriti tossed her head to dismiss the thought. ''He is my employer, nothing more! He values me, 'tis true, as a costly possession or a good investment. But I have no bond to him!'' She shrugged impatiently, then smiled and slipped closer to Conan. Now, lightly, she brushed against him, letting one hand meander up his arm and chest toward his face.

''Nor would you have any bond to me, I think, once your fancy turns.'' Conan twisted his cheek away from her hand. ''I like it not, Zafriti. Never yet have I taken a woman from a faithful man—even such a loose, saucy wench as you from such a rogue as Otsgar. Though Crom knows, I might be doing him a favor. . . .''

''Barbarian prig!'' Zafriti's hand suddenly struck Conan's cheek a ringing slap. ''Rebuke me, would you? You are less than a man, in spite of all your bulky thews. . . .''

Conan had to seize Zafriti's wrist to keep her from smiting him again—and then her other one, to keep her hooked, scarlet-painted nails out of his eyes. Her dancer's muscles made the struggle an engaging one as she hurled herself repeatedly against him, spitting in rage.

He did not want to strike her; to immobilize her he clutched her close and drew her up off the floor. That brought her thrashing knees into play, and he had to twist sideways to protect his groin.

More violent moments followed—until suddenly, Conan knew not how, she was panting against him, clasping him hotly. Her small, hard teeth nipped at his ear and the side of his neck while he nuzzled hungrily into her fragrant hair. His hands roved free over her supple curves as she caressed him and clung to his shoulders, her compact body striving hard against his. She seemed to be seeking to climb him, as a monkey might frolic in a banyan tree.

From behind him Conan heard the scrape of the door opening.

He tried to turn, but Zafriti's strength and passion hampered him once again. He barely managed to shove her a handsbreadth away before a heavy fist struck the side of his head, knocking him free of her clutch and staggering him across the floor. An all-too-familiar voice bellowed in his ear.

"Confounded, thrice-blasted Cimmerian! Ever were your tribe women-stealers! Well, my kinsmen in snowbound Vanaheim do not stand for it—and neither will I!" As he shouted, Otsgar pressed forward against his stooping foe, raining blows on him with fists, knees, and elbows.

But as he drove Conan back against the wall he received a surprise. The Cimmerian rebounded from the mud bricks like an unleashed catapult, driving hammerlike fists into the Vanirman's chest and chin, drubbing him back into the center of the room.

Rallying quickly, Otsgar darted inside Conan's guard and tried to trap his extended arm in a wrestler's lock; Conan twisted free and kneed the innkeeper in the groin. But he did not expect the back of the blond, rocklike Vanir head to lash up into his chin, jarring him and piercing his vision with multicolored stars.

The two grappled in the center of the room, growling and gasping like dancing bears, until Conan's vision finally cleared. He got a leg behind Otsgar and seized him by the hair, throwing him over his hip. The toss sent the innkeeper lengthwise onto the corner of the bed, across a low heap of sequined costumes. The tortured wooden bedstead splintered beneath him, and he rolled onto the floor.

He came up cursing and brandishing the bedpost, from which long, jagged splinters protruded at right angles. Conan, ducking under its whizzing arc, bethought himself of the dagger at his belt—but Otsgar had not drawn his own. It would be a shame to end the brawl too suddenly and messily.

Instead he caught the innkeeper's whirling bludgeon in midswing, along with the wrist that held it. He received, as an unexpected bonus, a hard-soled foot in the belly.

The kick, followed through savagely, sent him staggering back into the cosmetics table. With a clang, the back of his head dented Zafriti's mirror. Bottles smashed to the floor, sending up a cloying fragrance.

Conan tried to regain his feet. He was resolved to end this fight soon, yet he could dimly sense a new and shrill distraction. It flitted in and out of his blurred vision, belaboring his shoulder fiercely like an enraged, shrieking bird. He realized that it was the dancer.

"Enough! Out of here, you two buffoons! These are my things, my livelihood!"

A moment later she turned from him to fly at Otsgar, flailing at the giant with small bare fists. "Get out, you potbellied ape! You've done enough damage! I don't want either of you with me now! Begone!"

Conan let himself be herded out of the chamber after his opponent, whom he found waiting in the corridor, his balled fist poised for another blow.

"Hold, Vanirman!" he said, raising an arm to ward off the innkeeper. "I have a business proposition for you." His speech felt thick because of a swollen, sore lip. "I don't want to cripple you—at least not until I've made you rich!"

Otsgar growled at him, his eyes large with anger. "What business might it be, Cimmerian? Do you want to don lace and sequins and join Zafriti in her dances?"

Conan shook his head impatiently. "Enough fighting over the Stygian." He scowled and prodded his sore lip ruefully. "Though she'll be one to keep your fighting arm well-exercised, if you indulge her. But let's stop this before it passes to blades." He eyed the Vanirman, whose arms were still held tense for grappling. "Come, what say you? What I have to propose is real and profitable."

Otsgar rolled the pinks of his eyes at him a moment more. Then his scowl broke into a grin, blond-bristling and gold-glinting, and he barked a laugh. "All right! We are friends again!" He advanced abruptly on the Cimmerian, reaching out an arm to clap his shoulder.

Conan fought down a combat urge that was almost involuntary and let the innkeeper near him. Then he cautiously grasped his hand in reconciliation.

"Ow," Otsgar said, rubbing abrasions on his knuckles. He reached up and waggled a loosened tooth gingerly. "I think I need another gold one." He looked at the Cimmerian and laughed again gruffly, then moved away to a businesslike distance. "But what is your proposal?"

Conan looked up and down the corridor, scanning Zafriti's closed door and the aproned kitchen help who had gathered in the corridor at the sound of the brawl. "It is for your ears only, and mayhap Isaiab's. And Asrafel, if he can be found."

"Very well." Otsgar turned and snapped his fingers at those standing near the kitchen-entry. "Fetch to my chamber the two men he names!" The servants departed hastily. With a wave of his hand, the innkeeper motioned Conan along the corridor.

Otsgar's room, though not luxurious, was appointed comfortably with furniture of dark wood and bronze. Its wide, silk-sheeted sleeping pedestal stood beside a dressing table cluttered with more of Zafriti's things. In lieu of windows, an overhead vent let in night breezes from the roof. Pouring out cups of palm wine from a lacquered decanter, Otsgar gave one to Conan, who settled down on a small bronze stool opposite him to wait.

Isaiab arrived, clutching his own wine-beaker and looking tipsy but interested. Then Asrafel came in wordlessly, and Conan spoke. "Welcome, friend. Close the door behind you." He arose from his stool and gazed at the others somberly.

"What I propose should be obvious to any professional thief: an easy means of gaining vast wealth, with no man the wiser." He shrugged to them. "But you three, living here and following the customs of the place, have probably never seen it. You ply the hostile desert and brave the ancient crypts for your loot, when a much greater treasure lies here under your very noses."

"You mean, robbing the hill-tombs of Abaddrah's kings and priests?" Isaiab interrupted. He glanced over his shoulder to make sure that the door was shut, then turned back to Conan. "Do not think of it! I told you they are too well guarded, both by men and spells. . . ."

"Nay, Isaiab. My plan is more daring than that." Conan spoke calmly and earnestly. "We can more easily rob the tomb of this city's King Ebnezub."

The Shemite's dark eyes widened. "But the tomb is not even built yet! The king still lives!"

Conan shrugged. "Not for long, if you and the market-place gossips speak truly. What is your understanding of Ebnezub's health?"

Isaiab stared at Conan a moment, then sighed and spread his hands. "I know only what the courtiers mumble into their cups when they come slumming here. The king's consort Nitokar is slowly poisoning him, as she did his queen before him. But in his infatuation with her he is too blind to see it."

"And may he stay blind until death!" Asrafel added. "The greedy snipe deserves no better!"

"Why, all this is madness!" Otsgar, bristling with outrage, broke his silence and arose from his chair. "Forget your idiotic whimsies, the lot of you! I am in too risky a position even to speak of such deviltry, with my holdings here in Abaddrah to safeguard! Even if it were successful, a theft like the one you suggest would cause such a hue and cry . . ."

"Not if the loss were never discovered," Conan put in quickly. "If, rather than breaking in, we spirit away the wealth by means of a hidden passage built for the purpose, why then it will never be missed!"

The Cimmerian's words stalled Otsgar's protest. He paused, brows knit, and settled back down into his seat.

Meanwhile Isaiab sat with his chin on his fist, alternately frowning and grinning as his mind ran over the implications. "You mean, we weaken the tomb during construction and make it easy to rob," he mused. "A risky business, that! But not likely to be foreseen or guarded against by the tomb police." The wiry Shemite slapped his knee in enthusiasm. "And easier than breaking in afterward, by Ishtar's girdle!" He paused to twist his beard. "But even now the site is guarded against pilferage, you know."

"Well, I'm for it!" Asrafel rose impulsively to his feet. "We should steal back the wealth old Ebnezub has taken from the honest folk, like my murdered father!"

Conan nodded patiently. "The best point of the plan is, it will circumvent all the traps and priestly spells. It's not really even tomb-grubbing, as I see it. Nor does it run the risk of embroiling us with haunts and long-dead things."

Isaiab raised his cup and spoke solemnly to Asrafel. "Conan here is a purist. He doesn't like the idea of robbing corpses, unless they are corpses that he has slain himself!"

Conan shook his head impatiently. "It's not that. Rather it's the foul, musty ancientness of it! In Cimmeria we have a proverb: 'Dead spirits are like drinking spirits; they grow stronger with age.' "

Otsgar's voice grated in over the others. "What makes you think you could sabotage the tomb so easily? Even if it only meant removing a single course of stones, it could be a task far beyond our strength. And it might be discovered by guards, and itself turned into a trap!''

"Aye. We dare not bring in many accomplices, lest some of them betray us.'' Isaiab spoke nervously, shifting his eyes toward the door. ''The tomb police are fiendish in their tricks and tortures.''

Conan shrugged. "It might not be hard to dig a tunnel inside. Ofttimes in a city wall, the large, well-fitted stones are set only in the face, while the core is filled with smaller stones and rubble. Mayhap Ebnezub's tomb is the same. I meant to go and make a reconnaissance of the place tonight, before I was . . . distracted.'' He paused, rubbing the back of his head where it had been softened in the recent fight. "But perhaps 'twould be better if I went along with you, Isaiab. Then you could guide me and tell me something of the tomb's nature and defenses.''

"Tonight, you mean . . . now?'' At Conan's nod, Isaiab looked uncertainly at Otsgar.

The innkeeper tilted his wine-cup in his burly, blond-bristled hands, eyeing its dregs. His blunt-nosed face wore an expression of taciturn thought. Then, suddenly, he looked up. "And why not? Why don't we all go?'' His gold-glinting grin flashed at Conan from between his battered lips. ''If we mean to beat old Ebnezub to his grave, we had better hurry.''

Chapter 6

The Night Excursion

Shemitish night lay sultry and heavy over the lanes at the city's edge. It was faintly reminiscent to Conan of the nights of Stygia, calling to mind certain black hours he had ventured abroad in the serpent-worshiping land to the south. Yet here was somehow less stillness, less isolation. Even, in spite of the hazardous venture they were embarked upon, less fear. Beneath the fragrant arches of the palms, date-pits rolled under his sandal-soles; the stars seemed to twinkle more softly on this side of the river, and the buzzing cicadas and chirping frogs played a more lulling harmony.

The neighborhood stirred with life in spite of the lateness of the hour. Gleams from oil lamps creased the doorways of rambling earthern villas at the roadside. From the canal-bank on the other hand came the murmur of voices and the flicker of campfires. Pedestrians, too, passed at intervals: flood-driven, homeless peasants, the women going quickly with their eyes kept to the ground, the men balancing on their shoulders the long wooden water-swapes, their only possessions. Conan also spied brightly-robed suitors serenading softly outside the shuttered windows of the villas.

"These are the homes of prosperous tomb-craftsmen," Isaiab was telling him.

"Shemitish girls are straightforward in their dealings with

65

men,'' Conan observed. He had seen a side door open to admit one harp-strumming dandy.

"Oh, aye!'' the Shemite nodded. "Some of these suburban lasses would make Zafriti seem straightlaced.'' He looked up slyly at Conan.

But the northerner grew pensive, turning his gaze ahead to where Otsgar and Asrafel were walking in a separate pair so as to avoid notice. "We must be nearing the tomb-district.''

Conan's remark was made as he regarded an ornate metal gate spanning the road some distance ahead. The wall into which the hinges of the grillwork were set was not more than man-high, but it seemed to mark the end of the realm of the living. Beyond it, tall white monumental stones gleamed in the light of the low eastern moon. Conan looked in vain for any sign of guards or a guardpost at the gate. He was surprised to see some of the homeless wanderers resting outside it, their swapes propped against the wall.

"Indeed, we are arrived. See, already they line up to beg for work on the great tomb—or for the honor of having their dead relatives, or themselves, embalmed and buried there.'' Isaiab slouched over to the roadside to avoid notice. "Watch where Otsgar goes,'' he muttered. "There! Now follow, but discreetly!''

Conan passed into dense reeds on the canal side of the lane, stepping high to avoid trampling the plants at the outer fringe. There were no squatters encamped here. Though the weeds loomed tall around him, the ground sloped sharply away; in a moment he found himself waist-deep in tepid water.

"Stop your splashing and follow me closely!'' Otsgar muttered irritably back to his companions. He led the way around the end of the wall, which stood out several paces from the shore of the weed-choked canal.

Conan advanced, placing his sandals carefully on the slimy bottom and reaching out to steady himself against the wet, slimy brick. He thought of the crocodiles he had seen in the local canals and scanned the moonlit, rippled surface of the water carefully.

Isaiab whispered at Conan's shoulder, "This waterway leads close up to Ebnezub's tomb. The king had it dug for the transport of large stones, but the river runs high enough to fill it only during the spring flood."

"If he is in such a heat to get the tomb done, why doesn't he have crews working night and day?"

Isaiab was slow to reply. "That would run the risk of offending the Sun-God, Ellael. By Shemitish belief the night is unclean, and outdoor work is proscribed."

Conan exhaled, keeping his voice in a hoarse whisper. " 'Tis evident you don't share that view—having been a night worker yourself for so many years."

The Shemite tossed his shoulders in a shrug that could have been half a shudder. "One should not dismiss a thing too lightly. Night harbors many dangers, especially in the tomb precincts."

Conan grunted and moved on in silence. The wall was behind them now, and the reeds were less dense. Otsgar slogged along the canal-bank in a crouch and motioned the others to do the same. He vanished into the gloom beneath a wooden bridge that arched high above the canal. Just as Conan followed him, a rattle of unguarded laughter sounded nearby. Conan drew Isaiab into the shadows after him as footsteps clumped on the planks overhead.

There were two sets of feet, treading with watchmen's stolid patience. They paused at the middle of the bridge to the sound of brief, bored conversation, then moved on.

"The tomb police," Isaiab hissed in Conan's ear. They waited motionless until the noises had passed well away, and then Otsgar muttered to them.

"The canal is blocked ahead. Our best approach now will be through the shrines."

Beyond the bridge a reed barge sat grounded in the oily-looking water, joined by a gangplank to the nearer bank. In its stern a brazier glowed, sending curls of smoke skyward.

To try to pass around it, either through shallows or deeps,
would be too risky.

A moment later, moving with the others, Conan dodged up
the muddy bank and over the dike beside the canal. They
crossed a low, weedy expanse and came to ground in the
shadow of a mausoleum.

The stone edifice was one of many—hundreds, Conan saw
as he propped himself up on a carved urn at one corner
and peered cautiously over the top. Avenues of sculptured
tombs stretched away up the hillside, forming a vast necropolis, an eerie vista devoid of motion and sound except for the
flitter and squeak of careening bats under the low-angled
beams of the moon.

Some of the structures were shaped from the unbroken
sandstone bedrock, while others rose overhead in towers and
ziggurats of jointed stones. Many of the tombs were decor-
ated with shallow, sculptured outlines of trellises and windows, like little mock houses; others were merely stone
portals set in the faces of hills, presumably forming the
entries to deep catacombs. There was no guessing the full
extent of the dead city, for the cramped processional ways
ran back to the base of the foothills, and some wound out of
sight into ravines.

"The pickings are too slim for you here, you say?" Conan
shook his head in wonder as he scanned the vast, funereal
vista. "There must be a hundred-dozen rich tombs!"

"Yes. But the place is too well protected," Otsgar muttered. "Here, keep down lest you be seen!" He tugged
Conan's arm to pull his head below the roofline. "One large
haul might pay off, as you have suggested. But to return here
night after night for petty spoils would be the purest madness. Now come along!"

Otsgar led the way, creeping among the huddled tenements
of the dead. The glare of moonlight on whited stones made
the thieves well-nigh invisible as they slunk through the
checkered underworld of shadow. Still, their leader moved
slowly and painstakingly, peering at least four ways at every

corner. The Vanirman's manner seemed to suggest that he was watching for more than mere human guards. And Conan soon came to share his watchfulness—for at times he thought he glimpsed furtive, noiseless movements along the stark-lit avenues of tombs.

Finally, after passing the canal's terminus, they came opposite a vast, shapeless pile in the midst of a level place. It loomed before them like a palace or a fort, buttressed by wooden scaffolds for men to climb on, and by earthen ramps for the transport of large stones. At the center of the ladders and mounds, near-vertical walls of pale stone rose to a jagged, unfinished crown. Conan knew without asking that it was Ebnezub's tomb.

Otsgar turned to face the other three. "Isaiab, you stay as lookout. From here you can see the whole excavation." He prodded a finger toward the others. "You two wait until I'm out of sight before you follow me."

Conan spoke up abruptly. "I want Isaiab along with us. If you must have a lookout, leave the youngster instead."

Otsgar turned a patient, matter-of-fact look on the Cimmerian. "If Isaiab sees guards coming, he will sound out the screech of an owl so that we can take cover. Asrafel, can you make such a cry convincingly?"

The young Shemite, who looked uncertain about the proposal, shook his head.

"So you see. Isaiab's the one. Now watch me." Otsgar turned to scan the work-yard without waiting for further protests. A moment later he darted from the covert, his own bulky shadow flowing first left, then right, to blend with deeper darknesses along the way. When he had vanished beneath a timber ramp, Asrafel launched himself forward, somewhat less expertly.

When his turn came, Conan hesitated. Yet he knew that if he wanted to use Otsgar's men and resources, he must acknowledge him as leader. All or nothing. Nodding a farewell to Isaiab, he followed.

Dodging forward through splashes of moonlight, he passed

rows of trapezoidal building-stones spaced evenly through the
yard. They were large, some taller than Conan himself, and
their height was their least dimension. Most were rough-
hewn and caked with soil; others near the tomb-site had been
dressed skillfully, almost to a gleaming finish. Passing these,
Conan had to skirt piles of stone chips that threatened to
rattle beneath his feet.

The finished stones had been raised onto cylindrical log
rollers. As the great blocks were rolled slowly toward the
tomb, crews would lay down more logs under the front edge
and pick up the ones that passed out from behind. Some of
the stones had long yokes of leather and rope already harnessed
to them, whose timber crossbars made places for twoscore
men to pull their weight. On the morrow, no doubt, they
would be dragged up the earthern ramps by work-gangs and
levered into place on the tomb. Conan had heard stories of
the gut-wrenching toil and mortal danger of manhandling
huge slabs of stone up the narrow ramps.

Such were his impressions as he stole catlike through the
work-yard; a moment later he was crouching with Asrafel at
the base of the tomb, under the shadow of a timber scaffold.
Otsgar had scrambled partway up the earthern slope by climbing along the props of the structure, and now he beckoned the
others to follow.

"They must not have enclosed the tomb-chamber yet, nor
started to lay in the rich decor," the raider-chief observed as
they joined him in climbing the rough-hewn timbers. "Else
there would be more guards."

"We chose a good time, then," Asrafel ventured.

"Aye. But there is little we can do to burrow between
these titanic stones." Otsgar spoke grimly without glancing
back. " 'Twould require a hundred of us to displace even
one."

Indeed, the massive geometry of the tomb looked well-
nigh impervious to sabotage. As the raiders reached the
uncompleted part of the edifice they saw that it was not
rubble-filled, but laid down in sloping, overlapping courses

of uniformly large blocks. These stones did not rely for their
fit on mortar or shims, which might be loosened; rather they
were held in place by friction and the sheer precision of their
shape.

The marauders had rapidly scaled the finished section of
masonry; atop it they had to cross one of the earthen ramps
that served the areas of new construction. At its jagged crest,
levers and scissors-cranes sprouted high against the stars;
nearby stood one of the great building-stones. It waited where
it had been left at dusk, resting on its log rollers which were
chocked with wooden wedges against the slope of the ramp.
The stone would not have to be drawn up much farther before
the cranes could be brought to bear on it.

Conan crept forward, trying to make sense of the jumble of
shadows. Beyond the tomb's rim he glimpsed the deeper
channels and shafts of its interior. He shaded his eyes against
the moon's glare . . . then suddenly heard a loud *"Hist!"*
from Otsgar.

He shrank back into the shadow of the great stone. A
moment later, from some distance away, there sounded again
the scuff of feet and the murmur of voices which had alerted
his companions.

Keeping low, Conan looked around. Otsgar and Asrafel
were not in sight; possibly they were lurking on the uphill
side of the same stone. No matter—even if the guards were
coming up one of the causeways to loiter here half the night, it
should be easy for the three raiders to steal over the edge of
the ramp and vanish down among the timber props.

Conan crept toward the corner of the stone block. As he
did so he heard a clatter, then another and another, and
looked around to see some chunks of wood go skittering
aside. He recognized them as the chocks that had been under
the stone's rollers.

Simultaneously there came a deep grinding and rumbling,
and the huge monolith at his side started to move. Conan was
directly before it; he felt it shudder, then felt its sharp,

squared lower edge catch at his ankle as it trundled forward on top of him with crushing force.

By a swift sidewise leap he managed to throw himself downslope, momentarily free of the accelerating stone mass. He rolled to his feet and at once had to stagger backward, a handsbreadth ahead of the juggernaut's gleaming face.

As the block gathered speed it began to turn askew, doubtless because some of the chocks were still in place. Desperately Conan dove toward the nearer side, his body clipping the steel-hard corner as he cleared it. Then, with the cold stone sliding swiftly past, he scrambled and danced desperately over the ends of the timbers rolling and grinding underfoot.

In a moment, running off its rollers, the stone was skidding to a halt in the earth of the ramp amid a blinding cloud of dust. Buffets and crashes still followed as the logs, set spinning by the stone's great weight, caromed free. Conan ducked beneath two; a third struck him in the chest, driving the breath from his lungs and making a red sun blossom in his stunned vision. He fell to his knees, rasping painfully for air; when finally it came into him, it was sulfurous with the smell of pulverized rock-dust.

Somewhere close at hand a brass trumpet shrieked. Rapid footfalls drew near.

Before Conan could regain his feet, long-robed men were seizing him by the hair and clutching his arms. He could only glimpse them through his smarting eyes, yet he kicked the legs out from under one and butted another in the belly with his head. More came to envelop him. In a tornado of hard-driving knees and sandals, he was beaten back down to earth.

When the blows ceased, Conan found himself gasping face-down on the earth with his wrists bound tightly behind him. An order was spoken, and several pairs of rough hands turned his body over. He blinked up at muffled shapes looming dark against the moon.

"A giant, this one! A northern lout!"

"Look at the damage the fool has done!"

"What is your purpose here?" This last voice, more authoritative than the others, spoke in cultured Shemitish accents. Its possessor was clad in a dark cape with nothing but a brass-belted girdle underneath, like the rest of the tomb police who crowded near; but his self-assurance, as well as the gold circlet on his brow, distinguished him as an officer.

The man leaned nearer to Conan, his face displaying wrinkles graven deep by a lifetime of fierce frowns. "Did you come here alone? Consider carefully before you answer!"

Conan stared in silence at the dour face. He listened for cries of pursuit elsewhere in the tomb-yard and heard none—until, faintly, his ears caught the sound of splashing in the distant canal. Likely it signaled the other raiders' escape.

For a moment he flirted with the notion of calling his captors' attention to it—or even telling them more, in repayment for his betrayal. But no, Isaiab was innocent of guile—possibly even Asrafel, who was still young and easily fooled. Otsgar, certainly, had set loose the stone to get Conan killed or captured; but that was a matter for him to settle later, on his own, if he lived long enough.

His tormentors had not noticed the sounds from afar; instead they resumed jostling and kicking him, in order to make him speak. "By Ishtar's girdle! Belikes the stinking savage does not even know Shemitish!"

"Aye. They come from ever farther away to toil on the great tomb!"

"What makes him think himself fit to labor with honest Shemites?"

"Quiet!" the officer bawled, casting a ferocious look around his gaggle of men. "Foreigner, hear me! You are in peril, both in body and soul. If you thought to creep into the work quarters and join the paid crew, you made a grave mistake. By committing this sacrilege you have placed yourself under divine justice!" He scowled and gestured to his men, who now kept silent as they grasped Conan's arms and raised him to his feet.

"Well, northman, what say you?" The officer reached up

and clutched Conan's chin. "Was that your motive in coming here? If so, why did you meddle and cause this costly accident? Speak now. What you say may save your life!"

In answer Conan silently resumed his struggles. Standing upright, he was head and shoulders above most of the guards, and they were barely able to keep him from dragging several of their number over the steep edge of the causeway. Only by jabbing at the prisoner with their long, curving daggers did they finally succeed in restraining him.

"Enough! He is addled, or else mute! Bring him to the gatehouse!"

At their commander's order the tomb police close-marched Conan away down the ramp. They took him under heavy guard through the moonlit work-yards to a gateway he had not seen before, on the side of the tomb-district nearest the city. This one had horse stables as well as a torchlit guardpost manned by two tomb police. The watchlights of the city wall loomed nearby across the roofs of canalside shanties.

While four men pinioned Conan's bound arms and two more held daggers to his gut, the gold-crested officer walked over to the gate. Conan heard one of the watchmen addressing his superior in a matter-of-fact tone. "Another trespasser! To be remanded for disfigurement and impalement, as usual?"

"Nay, though he deserves it better than most!" The officer sounded disgruntled as he rasped out the words. "This one is a northern brute, and something of a curiosity. His physique is . . . inordinate, as you can see." He tossed his head toward his prisoner, and the guard's eyes followed appraisingly. "The royal court will want him for their entertainments. We've done with him." After making a mark on a waxen tablet, the officer handed it back to the guard and spun away on his heel.

Squinting at Conan in the flickering yellow light, the gatekeeper asked the retreating officer, "Are we to hold him over till morning, then?"

"Nay. Send for a chariot at once." The dour-faced one

glanced back at Conan briefly. "I do not think you could keep him here safe, in any case."

Standing silent and expressionless, Conan listened. At his back one of the tomb police wrenched his bound wrists tighter and muttered, "Arrh, 'tis too easy a fate for one such as this! They let them go with a rap on the knuckles these days! Better to stake him out among the tombs and let the dead spirits do for him!"

Another guard somewhere behind the sullen captive replied, "Ah well, and what matters it after all? The court games will finish him soon enough!"

Chapter 7

Abaddran Evenings

Conan awoke to echoes of subterranean shouts and the scraping and banging of dungeon doors. The act of waking was merely that of raising his eyelids—for he was already sitting up, propped against the wall of his cramped cell. Sometime during the hot, weary morning hours he had braced himself there, his head cushioned against a curve in the stone, with a resolve to sleep and save his strength for whatever fate awaited him.

Gaining rest was not easy, for the cords which tied his arms behind his back had been augmented by a rawhide loop passing under his bound wrists, up his backbone, and around the front of his neck. In consequence he could scarcely relax the weight of his arms without throttling himself.

Yet his endurance, hardened by survival in war and wilderness, had allowed him a fitful kind of half sleep. Now the angle of the light filtering in through the tiny, single-barred window bespoke late afternoon. He blinked as wakening brought fresh awareness of his pain. The beatings administered by his various guards had weakened him, and the torment of keeping both arms wedged against the rough wall behind him made his upper body throb, where it was not numb.

As his own cell door skittered and creaked, he tried to roll forward to his feet in readiness. But his balance failed; he stayed on his knees, reeling and vulnerable.

Not that it would have mattered much—for the arching stone cell was not lofty enough to stand in. The door, which was only half his height, grated open, and an elderly warder entered in what looked like a habitual crouch.

"Your supper, slave!" He placed two trays beside the doorway. "By the king's generosity I bring you wine and a haunch from the royal table. I am to undo your lashings so that you may eat your fill. No tricks, mind you!" The wizened one crept toward Conan with a short, glinting blade extended in one hand. "After you have supped, you may bathe and clothe yourself for His Royal Splendor's service."

Conan would have tried to trounce the old one and make his escape, but the fellow only slashed his binding and scuttled quickly away. By the time the captive pulled loose from the thongs, the door had been dragged shut and bolted behind the warder. In any case, Conan soon found himself otherwise occupied—by the exhausting labor of straightening his limbs against the shuddering waves of agony that coursed through them. When he could clench his hands again, he crawled forward and gave attention to the food.

The much-acclaimed haunch of mutton had not left His Royal Splendor's table unscathed, Conan found. It was well-carved and whittled—after which it must have been gnawed by every set of teeth from the kitcheners' on down to the merest stableboy's. Conan spent a long time chewing off the paltry shreds of fat and gristle that remained, then sucking out the cold marrow. He hefted the bone with the thought of retaining it as a weapon, but it was too short and thin, yet not sharp enough for a dirk. He flung it aside, pausing then to massage his protesting shoulder.

Also on the food tray were an old, soiled scrap of bread and a clay cup of wine. The latter was the mixed dregs of several vintages, pulpy with sediment and sour to Conan's taste.

The second tray held a wooden bowl of primrose-scented

wash water, and clothing. Conan sniffed dubiously at the water; deciding that it was clean enough for washing but too tainted to drink, he laved and scrubbed himself with it as best he could in the cramped quarters. His garments had been torn in the fight and fouled by the muck of the cell, so he removed them and put on the fresh ones which had been brought—a tight-fitting, sleeveless jupon of green silk and a red cotton winding-cloth for his waist.

Conan thought the raiment odd for its gay color and athletic style. But he shrugged, resolving to go along with the game and see what was in store. No doubt perils lay ahead— somehow he could not work up as much concern about them as he could over the prospect of escaping, finding his way back to Otsgar's keep, and cracking the rascal's head open for the treachery he had shown. There was no doubt that the innkeeper had cunningly delivered him to the tomb police; at the thought, he clenched a fist and drove it into his palm, disregarding the pain of his strained hands.

Abruptly a new turmoil sounded outside the cell. As he turned toward the door it was kicked open, and the decrepit warder's voice crowed, "Ah, excellent! Our guest is well-fed and well-garbed, as prescribed by Shemitish law. He is ready to take his part in the court games. Come forth, you, by the king's order!"

Conan was quicker in issuing from the cell than the old man could have wished—but his speed was to no avail, for the fellow had already taken shelter behind a pair of silver-armored palace guards, whose bulk nearly filled the corridor. The two of them, one a black of Kesh, the other a brawny, curly-headed Shemite, extended their short spears and prodded Conan up the way, as one might drive a bull to a slaughter-gate.

The Cimmerian went barefoot and wordless, stooping in the passage, which was still not high enough for his northern frame. When he came to a spiral stair where two more guards waited, he climbed obediently, mindful of the razored bronze speartips hovering close before and behind him.

So it was that he passed through the corridors and anterooms of the palace of Abaddrah, an extensive building of stone and brick, beautifully tiled and nobly vaulted. Along its lavish passages the party encountered many richly liveried servants. These stepped aside to let Conan by, wearing expressions either of impatience or unconcern.

Then the Cimmerian found himself before a tall archway curtained with sequined velvet. His captors prodded him to pass between its folds, and upon doing so he gained his first view of the royal court of Abaddrah.

The place was splendid—a gallery lit by high, louvered windows, with the main doors set in the opposite wall. A dais rose at one side, clearly reserved for only the most royal. The vast room was vacant at its center, displaying an ornately tiled floor, while around its sides stood tables with long benches. Here sat several score Shemitish courtiers, with more arriving through the main portal each moment. The place was abuzz with conversation, and at the tables wine flowed freely from golden ewers tipped by servants.

With no time to gawk, Conan was herded to one side and into a small, sunken space enclosed by a stone railing which curved out from one wall and back to it. Another prisoner already squatted there—a swarthy eastern Shemite, clothed as gaudily and scantily as Conan. A pair of guards already stood outside the enclosure, their backs against the chamber wall. After ushering Conan through a gap in the railing, two more warders took places on either side of the narrow gate; the other two filed away to station themselves beside the curtained archway.

There were no seats or cushions in the railed pen, so Conan squatted near his fellow prisoner. The man did not acknowledge him, but stared off distractedly into space. Underneath his dark complexion he managed to look ashen-pale.

Conan tried muttering to him in Shemitish. "A rich gathering, eh?" He glanced up at the guards, but they did not seem to notice his talk. The other prisoner had not answered, so he used a Stygian dialect. "Do you know what they have in store for us tonight?" Still no response. He gave the Shemite's arm a cautious nudge; the man started violently and turned a wild-eyed look on him, but otherwise remained frozen. Slowly then he relaxed, and his gaze moved back to vacant air.

Conan grunted and edged away. The fellow's skin had felt moist and chill to the touch. Likely he was suffering from swamp fever—or else from an intense, paralyzing fear. The latter possibility was an unpleasant one to Conan, since presumably the man knew something more than he did, but he tried to dismiss it.

At least, he told himself, if they want me to fight him, there will be little challenge in it. He turned his attention back to the festivities about him.

The courtiers of Abaddrah were a talkative lot. They lined the tables on all sides, leaning one toward the other and earnestly gesticulating, their words lost in a babble of sound. A slack, effete look seemed to be fashionable among them, unlike the more robust and weathered appearance of the city's laborers and warriors.

Most of these nobles were paler than Conan had thought Shemites could be. Their clothing was rich, if scanty. And strangely to Conan's eye, the servants were garbed more chastely than the nobles. While the wine-pourers labored under linen smocks in the smoldering afternoon heat, their patrons lazed at the tables nearly unhampered by clothing. Many of the women were bare from hipbones to headdresses; others wore as upper garments mere jeweled straps crossed between their breasts. Except for a table of long-robed, bearded men at the front of the hall, which seemed to be a foreign legation, most of the males flaunted hollow chests and pot-bellies above their leather-belted kirtles.

Ebnezub, King of all Abaddrah, was no exception. He lounged on a gilded chair at the center of the dais and displayed his pale bulk to the company like a grounded sea cow. Conan recognized his face from the city's coins, and from a wall-plaque that was mounted over the very prisoners' dock where he sat—though in sculpture the king's visage was less fleshy and dissipated.

Conan glanced back to the ebony bas-relief, which showed
an upright, muscular Ebnezub standing before a broken city
wall; the king was poised brandishing his royal hatchet over
the stacked, headless bodies of his enemies. Conan had heard
of no recent martial triumphs of the Abaddran city-state, but
shifting his gaze with amusement from the carving to the
king, he judged that such an exploit must have been far in the
past, if ever.

Now Ebnezub sat dull and abstracted, rousing himself
from time to time only to make comments to a young servant
who knelt by his couch inditing a wax tablet with a stylus.
Looking for signs of the monarch's rumored illness, Conan
could see none, other than his general torpor and the gross
proof of his overindulgence.

Various privileged persons occupied the dais near the king.
One of them was surely Queen Nitokar; she drew Conan's
attention repeatedly by the force of her strongly-shaped features and her heavily painted eyes. Though not youthful, she
was among the least-clothed women in the gathering. Yet a
lavishly jeweled pectoral served her modesty somewhat by
dripping gaudy gemstones almost down to her navel.

The queen sat beside His Royal Splendor Ebnezub, hovering close over him and making up for his indolence by her
solicitude in calling servants and passing dainty-foods directly into his mouth. Her attentions were lavished to a lesser
degree on two younger members of the royal family, a
plump, dark-skinned, petulant-looking boy sprawled on a
couch at her side, and an older girl who sat apart, possibly a
princess or a consort. She was a slim, blossoming beauty,
barely of marriageable age, sheathed to the knees in a
shoulderless iridescent gown and wearing a high, feathered
headdress. She kept her eyes averted from the king and
queen, seeming bored or irritated by their antics.

On Ebnezub's other hand, in an upright chair, sat a figure
who comported himself in every way more regally and powerfully than the King of Abaddrah. He was gowned from neck
to ankles in a gold-bordered white robe and sandaled in

gilded clogs. Conan knew him as Horaspes, the prophet of whom Isaiab had said so much, for he had seen him and heard him named in the city the previous day; there he had been seated in a curtained sedar-chair in the marketplace, overseeing the purchase of tomb-stores in his role as chancellor.

Though not powerful of frame and in fact pudgy under his golden robe, Horaspes had an officious, energetic air. In one hand he fingered a short, gilded staff of office, never setting it aside but occasionally laying it in his lap. His pale, puffy face was stamped with a benign expression, and his balding head, fringed by short black curls at the back, stayed ever in motion, looking around the assembly or leaning over to deliver terse observations to the king and queen.

At other times he conferred with one seated just behind him, a tall, lean, leathery-faced man who stooped forward dutifully to listen but did not smile or make any reply. This one went armed, unlike any other person on the dais, wearing a short, cruelly-curved sword at the sash of his plain military-cut jerkin. Conan judged him a bodyguard, and not the king's own, for he recalled seeing his pinched, unemotional face looming behind that of the prophet in the shadows of the marketplace awnings. Now he sat and scanned the crowd just as coldly.

As Conan watched, Horaspes muttered brief words to Ebnezub, and the king nodded assent. With some effort His Royal Splendor heaved himself up onto one elbow, waved the other plump arm aloft, and began speaking. At first his voice could scarcely be heard over the hubbub, but Conan caught some snatches of his remarks: "This noble gathering . . . my subjects attend . . . the words of my honored chancellor Horaspes." Then the king fell back to his sofa, as if winded.

At His Splendor's gesture the courtiers had begun to harken to him, but their monarch's speech had ended almost before they could hear it. Now, with the room utterly silent, Horaspes arose. His face kept its look of bland goodwill as he scanned

the crowd, his white robe giving him an air of simple purity.
His voice rang out in rounded, resonant accents.

"O my queen, the radiant Nitokar; most royal Princess
Afrit; Prince Eblis, First Son and Heir to the Kingship!"
Horaspes spoke in cultivated Shemitish with many gracious
pauses. "Nobles and courtiers of the land, and loyal
minions of the Abbadran City and State—hear me." He
beamed to his listeners and raised both hands in practiced
acclaim.

"His Royal Splendor King Ebnezub of Abaddrah wel-
comes all of you to this reception given in honor of our
cherished allies, the noble emissaries of the city of Eruk!"
With a cordial wave he indicated the group of caftanned
foreigners seated among pliant, ribald courtesans at the table
close before the king's. "Wish them well, fellow Abaddrans!"

At once the room rang with cheers and the clanking of
goblets. Then Horaspes raised his hand, and the racket diminished. "His Royal Splendor the King has graciously allowed his humble servant Horaspes, exile and former priest
of Stygia"—the speaker briefly touched his own breast—"to
conduct the proceedings tonight. My eternal gratitude, O
Resplendent One!" He bowed deeply to the immobile king,
then turned back to the audience. "We shall, in a very few
moments, commence with our traditional entertainment. Then
a meal will be served, which I pray will meet your approval.

"And then—" Horaspes paused, his face losing a little of
its complacent look. "For the edification of our valued friends
from Eruk, I shall tell of a danger that threatens us all. Some
here have heard me discourse of it before, but I fear that
others of you may yet be ignorant of this menace that looms
so darkly over our lives, our property, and our very souls. So
I will deliver my prophecy once again."

Conan was surprised by this turn of Horaspes' words and
the sudden glower of his countenance. He scanned the faces
of the courtiers around the room, which was now darkening
with twilight. A few seemed unconcerned, but most watched

the prophet with serious looks, or nodded to one another solemnly.

"But first, gentlefolk of Abaddrah, our entertainment, and then our food!" Horaspes looked benign once again. "Noblemen and ladies, the traditional court games!"

At this, Conan's own sense of jeopardy drove all other thoughts from his mind. His earlier effort to subdue his fears had not been entirely successful, he realized, for they now mutinied and stabbed him under the heart with a steely chill. It was a foolish thing, he told himself. He had little fear in battle or other desperate straits; why quail here? But then, the scent of the unknown was ever enough to make his hackles rise.

He eyed the guards around him. All four were watching the prison-pen discreetly, waiting for any untoward move. His fellow captive still crouched where he had before, unchanged except that now he wrung his hands compulsively between his knees.

Servants were lighting oil lamps against the encroaching dusk, and by their light Horaspes pointed to a burly, outlandish figure who had swaggered through the curtained archway.

"Once again tonight the royal champion is Khada Khufi, the famed temple-fighter of Vendhya. Here he comes!" Horaspes' words brought a wave of applause from the company, who turned to greet the newcomer.

Naked except for a padded loincloth, he displayed a large expanse of cinnamon-colored skin that glistened with oil. His fat was muscle-slabbed in the fashion of a trained wrestler, and except for a short lock of hair at the back of his head his scalp was shaven clean. Under each arm he carried a large, square wicker basket. Reaching the far side of the open court, he bent to set them down. Then he dropped to one knee and bowed limberly toward the royal dais.

"To oppose Khada Khufi for the king's pleasure, we have two brave volunteers. First, Elam, a staunch goatherd of the eastern hills!"

Two of the guards had entered the railed enclosure; now

one of them circled behind the cowering prisoner and yanked
him to his feet. Conan stood up to protest, but the second
guard blocked his way with spear half-leveled. He could hear
the other two guards readying themselves at his back, so he
made no further move.

The Shemite's captor thwacked him across the small of the
back with his spear-butt to get him moving, then prodded
him unsteadily forward through the gate.

As the man entered the circle of tables, a cheer went up.
It seemed strangely disproportionate to the captive's pathetic
appearance, and Conan looked to the one called Khada Khufi
for the cause. The Vendhyan had opened one of his wicker
hampers and was bending low, reaching down into it. Then he
arose and turned to face his audience. The cheering became
more fervent.

Khada Khufi stood holding his arms spread forward from
his body; around each arm was twined a serpent. The wrestler's hands grasped the greenish-black, scaly bodies a little
behind the head.

The snakes were swamp pythons. Not venomous creatures
as far as Conan knew, but fair-sized for the breed, thick as
their handler's beefy forearms and longer than he was tall.
They writhed at ease in the Vendhyan's grasp, moving their
coils sinuously along his brown, gleaming skin and craning
their snouted heads at the audience while idly flicking their
black tongues. As Conan watched, the cinnamon-skinned
man brought the serpents close up to his face, crooning to
each one in turn and kissing it on the muzzle. Then he
extended his arms again, weaponlike.

The prisoner Elam was driven forward across the tiles by
his single guard. Someone had placed a short, knob-headed
bronze club in his hand, but it hung there limply and use-
lessly. The Shemite's dragging, debilitating fear was evident
in his walk. And yet Conan thought the captive went with a
certain resignation, as if drawn on by some fatal lure.

When he was close enough for the snakes' heads to turn and
fix their stares on him, his escorting guards stopped and

backed away. Still, by some dark miracle, the prisoner walked several steps onward before coming to an indecisive halt in the middle of the gallery.

Khada Khufi began to stalk, moving slowly and silently, with his legs bowed and his spine arched upright under the serpents' considerable weight. He crept forward, the heads of his twin pets swaying just above the eye level of his victim, until he was mere paces away.

Finally the one called Elam reacted. A low, quavering wail escaped his throat. He flung his club weakly at Khada Khufi's feet and turned to run.

His stalker leaped over the thrown club with unexpected agility, pursuing his quarry with two swift bounds. Then, abruptly, his whole body lashed forward and down. There was a blur in the air like a curling black lightning-bolt, and with an audible impact one of the snakes smote the Shemite's back, twining about his neck and shoulders.

The prisoner's scream ripped through the chamber as he sagged forward with the sudden weight. Yet he did not stop running. Indeed, he staggered all the faster while trying to tear the black coils from his neck.

Unavoidably his flight took him toward one of the tables. Two guards converged there to stand between him and the wide-eyed courtiers, but their precaution was unnecessary. Khada Khufi, dashing on quick-pattering bare soles, had almost overtaken his prey. Now his body arched forward once again.

This time the snake unwound from his arm like a lash, its tail remaining in his grasp, its forepart twisting around the Shemite's ankle. With a deft tug the Vendhyan jerked Elam's leg from under him. The hapless man crashed to the multicolored floor, thrashing now in the grip of two reptiles.

His struggles were piteous to behold. He rolled and twisted, emitting shrill, gasping cries, sounds that became less audible as the topmost python worked its hold tighter around his neck. Venomous or not, the snakes were vicious, using their long-toothed jaws to tear and worry at the victim's flesh even as they crushed his writhing body.

Standing aloof nearby with arms folded across his massive chest, Khada Khufi calmly scanned the open-mouthed courtiers, finally resting his gaze on the kingly dais. Then, at a discreet signal from His Royal Splendor, the wrestler unfolded his arms and knelt over his victim. Patiently he worked his hands between the snake's tightening coils and Elam's head. A moment later his shoulders bulged powerfully, and a popping crack sounded. The sheepherder gave one last kick and lay still. Ebnezub had decreed mercy.

The courtiers looked on for a moment, enthralled; then their applause began to sound. It built and built until the room was in an uproar. Khada Khufi bowed in all directions while Horaspes stood on the dais leading the acclaim.

Conan heard one thin, feather-caped woman at a nearby table addressing a male friend. She spoke loudly to be heard over the din. "Oh yes, I very much prefer wrestling to weaponsplay at these events. It's not nearly so . . . unappetizing. I hate bloodshed!"

Conan himself could not have said at that moment what he thought, only that he was lightheaded and experiencing a faint roaring in his ears. A numb, tingling sensation possessed his limbs, deadening the lingering pains as he flexed his hands.

"And so once again our king's champion proves his skill," Horaspes said, shouting to be heard over the steady tumult. "But the contest is not over; we have another challenger! A nameless northern barbar from the icy fringe of the world! I am told that he exceeds even our champion in size and ferocity. Khada Khufi, prepare for an even harsher test of your prowess! Challenger, come forward!"

At these words the two guards moved forward from the wall, touching their spear-blades lightly to Conan's back to urge him on. With a swift, impatient motion he wheeled, brushing aside their weapons at the cost of a scratch to one arm. His gaze crossed theirs, and on catching the look in his

eyes they halted, spears drawn back. Brusquely then the
Cimmerian turned, pushed past the third remaining guardsman, and stepped up out of the prison-dock.

As he emerged he felt all eyes upon him, in particular the
heavily painted ones of Queen Nitokar, who leaned across
her royal husband to make a smiling comment in Horaspes'
ear. The other courtiers regarded Conan with surprise or
audible mockery; as he strode into view, laughs and whispers
passed around the room.

Khada Khufi had just covered the snake-wrapped body of
the shepherd with a blanket and dragged it aside. Now,
gazing briefly at Conan and sizing him up, he raised the top
of the other wicker hamper and bent over it. When he
straightened and turned, an excited murmur sounded from the
onlookers.

The temple-fighter's arms were less burdened this time,
but the deadliness of their adornment was unmistakable. For
the Vendhyan held aloft two red asps—the legendary blood-
nooses of the Afghuli hills. Their bite, the hillmen said,
would bring gasping death to a man before he could even
recite the Last Prayer to Erlik and gain the safe passage of his
soul to paradise.

The serpents were scarcely as long as the arms that supported them, and they wound across the wrestler's oiled skin
like delicate coral bracelets. Yet even Khada Khufi seemed to
treat them with exaggerated respect; his hands held them
close behind their hissing, tongue-darting heads, and he did
not cherish them to his lips as he had their larger cousins.

Meanwhile Conan walked forward beyond the center of the
gallery to the slender bronze club that lay discarded from the
previous combat. Without taking his eyes off the wrestler, he
stooped to pick it up. The weapon had little use; it would not
allow him to strike effectively at his foe's head or body from
outside the serpents' reach; and if thrown, it could scarcely
knock down such a large man. Nevertheless he decided to test
it.

Melting into a catlike crouch, Conan advanced on Khada

Khufi. The audience murmured at his boldness, probably
unprecedented on the part of a "volunteer" in the court games.
The snake-fighter hastened to move clear of the baskets and
the slowly undulating cloth which draped the corpse of his
first adversary. He stood facing Conan, his arms spread wide
apart as if for a venomous embrace, his hawklike visage
set in a practiced sneer.

Abruptly Conan danced forward and began to strike back-
hand and forehand with his club—light, teasing strokes aimed
at the snake-heads and the massive fists that grasped them.
The Vendyan had no difficulty dodging, by twisting his agile
body and moving his hands up or aside, out of reach. But
then, swiftly, Conan dropped low and wheeled, speeding his
club in a flat arc against the wrestler's bare shin.

The blow was not a telling one, and its recipient only
blinked; yet the touch had angered him, as the insulted flare of
his nostrils showed. Conan brought himself swiftly upright
from his crouch, but the wrestler's agile arm was already
lashing out in a snake-cast—and a crimson projectile, lethally
envenomed, shot through the air toward the Cimmerian's breast.

Instinct alone, no matter how savage and swift, could not
have saved Conan from the fatal sting of that reptile; clever
planning must also have played a part. As the Cimmerian
twisted in midstride, his metal club was already swinging up
to ward off the flying asp. Its motion swept the scarlet blur
away from his throat, aside and around in a tight arc, to
redirect the peril back toward its source. At the final instant
Conan relinquished the club as well, jerking his hand clear of
a last, deadly stab of the serpent's fangs.

Seeing snake and club entwined and hurtling back at him,
Khada Khufi dove aside—proving in that moment both his
acrobatic prowess and his respect for the unloosed serpent. He
executed a smooth shoulder-roll, all the while managing to
hold his remaining asp clear of his body. Beyond him the
cudgel struck the floor and slid under one of the tables,
bearing the writhing creature along with it. Instantly there
were screams and scuffles at the table in question; courtiers

fell back wildly or leaped onto the tabletop, desperate to avoid the viper's fangs.

Meanwhile the nimble wrestler had come up on his feet, his remaining snake brandished high for attack or defense. But he did not allow for the astonishing quickness of the Cimmerian, who darted forward to intercept him. Conan clapped a hand on Khada Khufi's shoulder and worked himself around behind the Vendhyan's back. Driving close against his adversary to keep him off balance, he threw a forearm across the temple-fighter's neck whilst reaching with his other hand to grasp the wrist that held up the deadly serpent.

Conan groped in vain to catch the supple, oiled skin of the Vendhyan's forearm, and yet not snag his own skin on the viper's arching fangs. He clung grimly to the wrestler's bull neck, all the while shrinking and twisting to avoid the backward dashes of the snake-head, which was still clutched in the thick brown fist.

It was then, as the two men wrenched and pummeled to establish who in this mortal contest was the ravening wolf, and who the harried goat—then it was that the effect of Conan's recent captivity began to tell on him. He felt his straining limbs weighted down insidiously, not only by pain, which his harsh, uncoddled life had taught him to devalue, but by the debilitating legacy of his night and morning's struggle and torment.

At other times he might have borne all before him by the sheer force of his anger. Had he not snapped necks as thick as this one in past battles while barely able to see them through a red haze of barbarous fury? Yet now the strength was simply not to be found in his sore, racked arms and shoulders. With crimson death hissing in his ear each moment, darting ever closer to his throat, he could barely maintain his hold. He began to feel himself the beleaguered one, like an unlucky wolf tossed on the horns of an angered buffalo.

And the audience sensed it. Once the straying serpent was caught up on the blades of the guardsmen's spears, the uproar among the courtiers quickly died, giving way to restrained, earnest whispers. Now a hundred tense faces followed the wrestlers, awaiting the kill they knew was imminent. The royal entourage watched rapt—except for the girl Afrit, who kept her face rigidly averted: Even King Ebnezub raised up his inert bulk on one elbow so as not to miss the tiny flick of venomed fangs that would signal the end.

Under their hungry gaze Conan felt himself losing the advantage of position, as Khada Khufi's bulging, oiled shoulders and neck flexed and twisted beneath his desperate grip. Lucky it was that the Vendhyan could not let go the serpent. Clearly the keeper had no special defense against its venom, nor against its blind, retaliatory spite. With one arm kept low and out of action by Conan's choke-hold, the wrestler had to devote his other arm entirely to controlling the asp.

The reptile itself had grown frenzied under the punishment of the close combat; it worked its pale jaws open and closed in its handler's tight clutch, drooling forth droplets of clear venom that raised stinging welts where they struck Conan's skin. Its supple, red-scaled body had unwound from Khada Khufi's arm; now it lashed free, striking against the contenders' faces like a finely corded, blood-glistening whip.

Suddenly the Vendhyan drove forward, lunging like a bull and swelling his shoulders to break his attacker's grip. Conan's arms began to slip from the temple-fighter's sweaty, musk-reeking skin, but at that moment he saw a new chance, as the snake's tail happened to lash across the front of Khada Khufi's neck.

Conan's hands flew unbidden to grasp the writhing red strand where it brushed his enemy's shoulder. An instant later he shifted his grip so that his wrists were crossed at the nape of the Vendhyan's neck. His clutching hands drew the main length of the snake's body tight around his foeman's throat, like a vermilion strangle-cord.

The wrestler charged triumphantly a few steps forward, drawing the unresisting Conan behind him, before he fully comprehended the change. Then, still holding the snake's head immobile beside his own, he began to lunge and twist to break free—but in vain, for Conan's new position brought fresh muscles into play. It also gave him the leverage to tighten his garrote moment by moment.

Enraged, Khada Khufi resumed dashing the snake's head over his shoulder at his unseen tormentor. But he now had little of the snake's leathery length to strike with, whereas Conan had more freedom to avoid its sweep. And the tortured snake no longer bit wildly at air; knotted cruelly by the men's multiple grips, it was immobile and swollen, its eyes bulging with blood and its fangs folded half-in.

The Vendhyan's face, too, had begun to bulge and darken. His feet now shuffled and faltered on the tiles of the gallery as Conan drew him upward and backward in a strangler's close embrace. The grating sigh of air through his constricted throat ceased; his lips formed soundless blue curses, and his hands groped vainly behind him to rend his assailant.

At his shoulder Conan's face loomed just out of reach, nigh as dark with wrath as the other's was with strangulation. The Cimmerian fixed his whole concentration on the struggles of his victim, and on maintaining the tension in his aching hands and wrists—for he knew that here lay his last chance of victory.

Yet at the periphery of his vision, through a red-shot mist, he sensed movement—the palace guards inching forward, their spears raised, gazing up at the royal dais as if awaiting orders. Would they allow their costly imported wrestler to be killed by a foreign upstart, after all?

Conan wrenched Khada Khufi's flailing body around to face two of the advancing guardsmen and the dais as well. The entire royal party stared down on him, with even the young Afrit gazing open-mouthed, unable to maintain her studied disinterest. Horaspes' face looked grave, displeased by the turn the contest had taken. But Queen Nitokar's dark-stained lips curved in amusement as she whispered animatedly in her husband's ear. In response, King Ebnezub waved a brisk hand through the air; in a moment the guards were falling back to their places at the periphery of the hall.

Whether the Vendhyan could see their retreat, or recognize it as the ebbing of his hopes, was hard to tell. His eyes had begun to roll back in their sockets, and his struggles were even wilder than before. He released the lolling head of the asp to wrench and pluck with both hands at the taut, red-scaled cord of its body where it dug into the flab of his neck. His thick fingers were unable to insinuate themselves there; where they scrabbled at Conan's whitened knuckles, they had little more effect.

The serpent, once free of the wrestler's grasp near its head, seemed to recover some of its vitality. Its dull reptilian brain may only vaguely have sensed the constriction of its lower body; now its fangs protruded once again, and its gaping mouth arched and lashed through the air. The Cimmerian watched it with a thrill of horror. He was no longer able to protect his own fist as it clenched the beast's body, nor was he willing to release his strangle-grip on the Vendhyan.

An instant later the issue was decided—as the red asp's head darted sidewise and sank its fangs into Khada Khufi's ear.

At the viper's stroke the wrestler, whose purpling face seemed almost beyond earthly suffering, opened his jaws in a frothing, soundless scream. His body gave a mighty heave and broke free of Conan, who thrust him away at last in revulsion. The asp remained coiled around his neck and held fast to his ear, which swelled under the bite like a gray, venomous toadstool. Plucking vainly at it, Khada Khufi lurched two steps and flopped forward onto his face. There he died, making no further sound.

Chapter 8

Prophet of Peril

As the clamor of applause roared around the gallery, Conan stood weary and watchful at its center, wondering what the next menace might be. The guards had killed the red asp, pinning its body to Khada Khufi's with their spears. Now servants gingerly dragged the sheeted corpses and snake-baskets away. Whether the victor's prize would be freedom, or death, or some more complex fate, Conan could not tell.

Standing light-headed with fatigue and spent rage, he was approached from the direction of the royal dais by two smil-ing servant-girls. They were young, comely, and not over-dressed, swaying up to him barefoot in short linen togas. They took his arms and led him back toward the head of the hall.

As he went he felt himself intimately examined by the shining, kohl-dark eyes of Queen Nitokar—whose summons, he suspected, was the cause of his being brought forward. The other royalty glanced over him with only mild interest, except for Horaspes, whose beady eyes appraised him in evident annoyance.

But the servant-girls did not take Conan to the queen; instead they guided him around the low table before the dais and drew him down onto plush cushions next to the envoys from Eruk. The table was not close enough to the royal

95

divans for easy conversation, and once Conan was seated Nitokar regally ignored him.

To the delight of the courtly mob, food was served. Servants carried in fruit, bread, and cheese on huge golden platters, which were rapidly emptied as their bearers passed the length of the tables. Then came silver-chased bowls of sauces and puddings, to be fished in and scooped clean by dozens of eager hands.

Finally a great bronze chariot was wheeled forth, bearing the simmering carcass of a giant boar suspended on chains over a bed of glowing coals. It was carved and dispensed by a sweating, near-naked chef who could have been Khada Khufi's larger brother except for his Shemitish cast of features.

The envoys' table received the best of every dish. Conan, after sloughing away his worst memories of the recent fight with a beaker of wine, earnestly set about restoring his strength with ample helpings of fruit, meat, and bread. His servant-girls stayed with him, saying little and only nibbling a few morsels of food themselves. They devoted most of their time to caressing him and massaging the warps and knots out of his massive shoulders.

One of the goat-bearded northerners from Eruk sitting nearby seemed a down-to-earth type. Conan tried out a greeting in a Kothian dialect he guessed the locals would not understand.

"Hail, neighbor! A lush feast, is it not? Methinks yon worthy with the meat-ax, battling the wild boar, could head up a phalanx of Argossean heavy armor!"

The emissary, well along in his cups and holding up half the weight of a slatternly redhead as well, followed Conan's gaze and laughed. "Oh, aye. I think I have unhorsed him in battle once or twice myself." He turned to stare at Conan, squinting in the effort. "But you are no Kothian—a Nemedian, perhaps?"

"I hail from Cimmeria, north of there."

"Oh, aye, a hill-nomad. Well, I must credit you, Cimmerian." He sloshed his goblet upward in a splattering salute. "You dealt admirably with that eastern devil and his snakes! Too barbarous it was for this sort of occasion, to my thinking. A display like that would never be tolerated at a state dinner in Eruk!" He eyed the roistering courtiers all around, then looked narrowly back to Conan. "But I take it that you do not do this sort of thing by choice?"

Conan shook his head. "Nay. I was merely caught loitering in the wrong place at the wrong hour."

The envoy grunted. "Ah, yes, these southern customs. . . ." He glanced over his shoulder at the royalty on the dais, who were engaged in conversation with the leader of his contingent. "But as the saying goes, when in Abaddrah . . ." He shrugged. "And what will become of you now?"

Conan frowned and leaned closer, glancing at his wenches to make sure they were not following the conversation. "I have no idea," he confided. "I think I am called to this table by courtesy of the queen."

The man of Eruk raised his eyebrows and laughed. "I wish you good luck, then!"

Conan leaned so close that he was almost tickled by the northerner's beard-curls. "Why? What do you know of her?"

"That she is a famous voluptuary. That is no surprise—'tis evident just looking at her!" He flicked his eyes back toward the dais at Nitokar's undraped, pendulous figure. "One need not fear her husband, I am told. In his declining health and energy, he does not mind her dalliances." He turned a leering eye on Conan. "But I would be cautious nevertheless; I was warned that Her Queenliness's ways with younger men are rather rough . . . and that she does not keep them around long."

Conan took it in solemnly. "And what of the rumor that she is a poisoner, who killed Ebnezub's former queen and is doing the same to him?"

At this the envoy shifted abruptly backward from Conan. He showed no great surprise but eyed his goblet uneasily and set it down on the table before him. His wine-soaked amiability had suddenly chilled. "Indeed, stranger, how could an ambassador from a far-off country be privy to such details about the Abaddran royal family? If true, I would think it a well-kept secret"—he frowned sternly—"and a dangerous one to bandy about in public."

Conan nodded. "Even more dangerous to ignore."

The envoy blinked in acknowledgment, glancing at his food and drink again, but did not volunteer anything more. Conan decided that he had pressed the man far enough and slid back between his wenches.

The two gossiped in a low dialect of Shem as they kneaded and thumped his shoulders. He threw an arm around each and commenced a tickle-game, to their merriment. But it had not gone far when a new distraction arose.

Horaspes, the chancellor, dismounted from the dais and walked toward the center of the gallery. As he passed the envoys' table he saluted the foreigners with a courtly flourish that somehow managed to exclude the hulking Cimmerian. He moved with utter self-assurance, bearing in his hand the short scepter that Conan had seen him toying with earlier.

In the middle of the room he turned again to face the ambassadors and the royal family. Amid the spreading silence that heralded his arrival, the roasting-chariot with its tattered skeletal passenger was trundled away out of sight. Most of the servants departed, except for a few still tilting wine-ewers at the tables. Horaspes waited a long moment to let the stillness become complete before he spoke.

"My King and Queen, Abaddran and foreign nobles! We come to a time of reckoning that I promised you earlier. It is the least of my desires to trouble the ears of such an august company with religious preachments"—he smiled around the circle, palms spread—"and I shall not do so." He let his arms drop to his sides as if an unpleasant subject had been dismissed. "Nevertheless, we are persons of rank, mindful of the powers and responsibilities that are our birthright, and all of us are interested in preserving and extending those powers. Each of us cherishes our royal order and our Shemitish way of life. Myself not least, though I am a latecomer to this land so well-beloved of Ellael."

Here sounded a general murmur of assent from the listeners, combined, perhaps, with relief at the nonreligious turn of the rhetoric. Horaspes beamed at the audience and resumed.

"We of Shem are privileged to be in the forefront of human knowledge. Pagans far to the north and south of us may still squander their worship on petty, illusory gods with names as bizarre and uncouth as their practices—Erlik, Gwahlur, Orthyx, Crom . . ." The prophet spoke the foreign syllables roughly, with grimaces, and in so doing coaxed a gush of laughter from his listeners—all except Conan, who scowled.

"Still, in the cradle of knowledge that spreads majestically from either bank of the great River Styx, we have discovered and acknowledged the true ruling powers of the universe, the two mighty gods whose eternal conflict shapes men's destinies in this life and in the Afterworld.

"They are the beloved Sun-God, of whose many names Ellael is the one most cherished here in Abaddrah—and Set, the Undying Nemesis, whose fearsome incarnations are the jackal and the serpent. We worship the one and despise the other, yet we know it is their age-old struggle that orders the universe.

"Our sages, by dint of their clear-sighted reasoning, by tireless observation of the heavens and centuries of study in the priestly academies, have finally discerned the splendid order of divine and mortal life: from the great gods themselves and those gracious godlings who deign to rule us briefly here on earth"—the speaker made a low bow to King Ebnezub—"to the nobles, thence down to the lowly mortals who serve us, and the very beasts of the field.

"It is wonderfully simple, this serene natural law that has been revealed to our eyes. By the light of its reason we follow Ellael and promote his faith, so that all which is just and good may flourish on earth and hereafter." Horaspes paused reverently, his arms spread wide. But then the benign look on his face fell to a frown, and he lowered his hands to his sides. "Hard it is, then, to explain the great tragedy of our time: why those who dwell south of the river, in the vast Stygian empire, should offer their worship to the dark powers ruled by the hated Set!"

The prophet's words were met by a buzz of consternation from the crowd. But he did not stop speaking for long. "As a Stygian myself, a former temple-school acolyte and an exile from that nighted land, I am frequently asked why. What sinister twist of nature can cause a whole nation to worship at the shrine of evil? What unholy cincture holds Set's power so firm in the land of Stygia?"

Horaspes waved both hands aside, as if brushing away a noxious thing. "The answer to that question I cannot venture to guess, since my own belief differs so much from that of my countrymen. Perhaps 'tis their misguided failure to rear and homage a king, as we do. For when the firm hand of the priesthood wields the scourge of government, the combined power that results is strong indeed, strong enough to drive a great nation into peril!

"Deeper than that I cannot see into the dark pool of Stygia's iniquity. On fully glimpsing the enormity of their evil, I denounced their blasphemies and fled for my very soul to a more wholesome land.

"From experience, I can tell you this much: their will to evil is as strong and unflinching as ours is to good. Their knowledge and arts are as well advanced as our own, with further delvings and researches into areas that a just, enlightened nation like Shem would not allow. Their great wealth and military strength are known to all of us—and yet not greatly feared, it seems to me, by the rulers of Shem. Not feared nearly enough, perhaps." He cast a somber glance at the legates from Eruk. "It so happens that this is a time of peace between the two empires, which some may regard as a good thing." His scowl showed that his own opinion on the matter differed.

"In this day of peace, knowledge moves tirelessly for-

ward. Our crafts of metallurgy and stonemasonry are un-
matched among the Hyborian kingdoms. The medical arts
flourish as never before. Our priests of Ellael have developed
new techniques of embalming dead nobles and their favored
retainers, so that the souls' continuance into the Afterworld is
assured. By the boon of modern science, every highborn
person in this room can go forward into eternity with ample
possessions, livestock, and servants, with the hope of assum-
ing high rank in Ellael's bright domain and serving joyously
at his feet!

"But think you, fellow believers: as we take our place
among our honored ancestors, will we be able to uphold our
noble stations and prerogatives? We must be well prepared,
my friends, and fierce in our resolution to rule the Afterworld
as firmly as we do this one.

"This is a time of social upheaval and questioning of the
old ways. In these prosperous days every aging merchant
hews out a stone vault and lays into it a hefty tomb-dowry.
Even the lowliest pauper can scrimp together the coin to pay
for a cheap mummy-wrap and bundle up a few scraps of
food, in his pathetic hope of gaining the Afterworld. They all
have their eyes on eternity. How much grander, then, should
our own preparations be?

"Our engineering and administrative skills are greater than
ever before. It is in our power to build forts which will stand
against any army, and tombs which will weather the long
millennia. We must use all these skills, Shemites, to ensure
our place in the Afterworld, for Ellael loves the strong!

"Remember, this world is to eternity as a single drop of
water is to all the floods of the mighty River Styx! Our one
purpose in this life should be to prepare for the next! If by a
prudent expenditure we can secure or even enhance our rank
hereafter—why then, to do any less would be the most
pernicious folly!''

"Hold, Priest! A word, if you please!"

Here, though Horaspes scarcely paused in his speech, he
was interrupted by a voice from close beside Conan. "Are

you saying, Prophet, that these crass earthly problems will carry on into the Afterworld?'' It was the envoy from Eruk, whom Conan had spoken with over supper. He had overcome his doubts about the wine, consuming several more goblets of it, and now his gruff, martial voice rose in intemperate eloquence. ''Where in the holy tablets does it say so? I think of the Afterworld as a place of harmony and peace among men, under the serene grace of Ellael.''

''Honored emissary, let me answer you thus. . . .'' Horaspes began.

''Nay, Priest! I will say my piece!'' The envoy's drill-yard rasp was loud enough to override the speaker, and he shook off one of his companions who laid hands on his arm to try to hush him. ''If your intent is to make our kingdom of Eruk pour all its wealth into fancy tombs and trappings, and into the hands of your priestly cronies, then you waste your time! We have more pressing needs to attend to. . . .''

As the man of Eruk spoke, Horaspes strode forward to the opposite side of the table, so that he loomed close before Conan as well. Now, swiftly, the prophet leaned across the low marble board and laid a hand on the shoulder of the envoy, as if reassuringly. The Eruki started up angrily at first, but then settled back stiffly onto his cushion. Horaspes spoke directly into his face with an earnest intensity.

''My brother, I understand that you harbor doubts. But I beg you, hold your peace. All will soon be explained to your satisfaction.'' He waved his other hand, the one holding the short staff, to the audience at large. ''There is one proof I can give you, for after all, 'tis rightly that they call me Prophet.''

While speaking, Horaspes had not released his clasp on the Eruki emissary, who had grown strangely quiescent. Conan sensed something odd in his neighbor's silence and started to lean forward to his aid, but he found his own shoulders clutched tightly by the two serving-maids, who clung to him as if frightened, staring at Horaspes. By the time he shook them off, the chancellor had already straightened and released the envoy.

The Eruki was no longer belligerent. Dumb and uncomplaining, he stared up at Horaspes. And yet, where the prophet's hand had rested, just under the collar of the long traveling-cloak where shoulder met sun-darkened neck, Conan thought he glimpsed a livid white print as of a tremendously powerful grip. Then the Eruki's fellow envoys and his redheaded courtesan had laid hands on his shoulders, and he was nodding dully at their admonitions.

Meanwhile Horaspes turned back to the other courtiers. "To help you share the prophecies I bring, my helper Nephren and his slave will spread incense about the room." At his gesture, two persons entered the center of the gallery: the tall, lean, sword-bearing aide, and a young female servant, both of them carrying smoking censers. They turned left and right along the circle of tables and proceeded slowly, holding up the perforated golden cages with one hand and plying papyrus fans with the other to waft the curling fumes toward the seated watchers. Conan noticed that a separate incense-pot had been kindled on the royal dais behind him.

When the cadaverous Nephren passed near, Conan's dislike of his seamed, expressionless face increased, and he waved his hands to fan away the snaking fumes. But the scent, both acrid and spicy, wafted from all sides to penetrate the Cimmerian's nostrils. It brought with it an instant's dizziness and what seemed to him a faint flash of color in the lamplit room.

As the censer-bearers finished their round, Horaspes strode to a broad, blank wall at the back of the gallery. There he held high his staff. It was evidently a stylus of some sort, for he began to write on the wall with it. The markings were deep red, scrawled boldly across the stone in the wavy, looping characters of Shem.

When the prophet had finished, Conan studied the word in vain until he heard it mouthed faintly by one of his serving-wenches. "Jazarat," she whispered. Day of Doom, to Conan's understanding. The sound of the syllables spread among the

courtiers in an apprehensive murmur, like river reeds stirred
by the first breath of a storm.

"Fear not, my countrymen," Horaspes declared, "for I
will not reveal all that my inner eye has seen. I will spare you
the worst. For now, just gaze on these characters; study them
and ponder their meaning."

The leathery-skinned bodyguard Nephren moved along the
defaced wall, reaching up to his full, unnatural height to
snuff the lamps bracketed there. Methodically he squeezed
out the hot wicks barehanded, showing no sign of discomfort. Conan noted that as the light in the gallery diminished,
Horaspes' scrawl seemed paradoxically to become more visible, standing out in strange contrast to the colorless stone.

He found that in spite of himself he was staring intently at
the letters. At first they seemed to glow darkly before his
eyes. Then, with a prickling of his neck-hairs, he saw them
begin to shimmer and crawl, wriggling like the red snakes he
had wrestled earlier that evening.

An instant later the crimson characters blazed before him
and flew apart like burning leaves scattered by a sudden gust.
Their passing seemed to tear away the very stones of the
wall, but noiselessly; through it a jagged window opened on
bright, shifting realms. The gasps of surprise from all around
told Conan that the impression was shared by others in the
room; he looked wildly to the guards, whose figures were
half-lit by the lurid light—but they stood still and impassive
at this unnatural breach of the palace defenses. Apparently
they knew well that they were in the grip of sorcery.

"Here before you, nobles, is a monument such as it is in
our power to build—an enduring bastion shaped of stone and
flesh and blood, the triumphant expression of a ruler's ability
to unite his followers—a symbol of all we revere in omnipo-
tent kingship."

As Horaspes spoke, the floating dust that had obscured the
mystic gateway parted, and Conan saw before him, miraculously, a dazzling sunlit scene. He could not help but glance
up at the gallery's window-vents to confirm that they were

still gloomed with night, for before him shimmered the brightness of a desert day. He felt the hot, dusty breeze and heard the toneless rattle of men's voices in open air. A mere bowshot's distance from the royal dais, a gang of slaves were hauling a giant stone forward across the sand on wooden skids. The mutter of their work-chant and the crack of their overseer's whip came to Conan's ears, as did the faint smell of their sweat to his nostrils.

Yet, clearly, once the wonders of night-made-day and city-made-desert were accepted, the scene was a commonplace one of underlings' toil. The real marvel was the vaulting edifice in the background, toward which the stone was being dragged—a titanic, stair-step ziggurat whose white triangular face was split by the pylons of an archway as tall as twenty men, the arch just being joined at the top. The laborers swarmed on its distant slopes and scaffolds like ants, their movements directed by the faint blatting of trumpets. Conan recognized some of the contours of Ebnezub's tomb. Could it be the same structure, nearing completion? Its pattern put him more in mind of smaller monuments he had seen in Stygian Khemi, far to the east.

"So it goes daily, now and in the future. The humble and devout labor tirelessly in preparation for the next world. Their efforts are slow and painful, but well-spent." Horaspes, outlined in day-glare from the magic scene, waved his hand—and with a soughing noise, dust-clouds began to blow up and obscure the vista.

They billowed higher, till the noon sky became almost black, and sand began to drift into the palace court itself. Then the wind ceased and the dust settled swiftly out of the sky. The prophet proclaimed, "When death comes to such devout men, it is not tragedy but triumph. Thus the seed of afterlife is sown!"

This time the sky was darker, and the scene a funeral procession. The completed face of the pyramid was rosy with dawn's rays, its vast portals open wide, the parapets of its fore-corners flanking them like the paws of a sphinx. An endless train of mourners, chariots, and tribute-bearers labored toward the tomb. Outlined against the pink-gold horizon were ornate coffins on wheeled biers and crowds of richly dressed relatives and retainers. Slaves bore tomb-goods in bundles and copper vessels, and strings of oxen and kine were followed by platoons of armored guards. The air trembled with the hum of voices in a dirge, mournful yet resolute. A breath of the morning's chill touched Conan's face.

"Thus do a devoted people serve their ruler and their gods. No demand is too great; of every man's labor, three-fifth parts are given over to the Afterworld. We have the wealth and numbers to do this, if only we have the will. Our craftsmanship is equal to the task. And as I told you, brethren, by the improved art of embalming, each and every one of us in this room can take up at will the glittering garb of immortality." Horaspes paused and turned to regard his sorcerous vista—and as he did so the whispers of awe and admiration in the room gave way to a gasp of uneasiness.

For into the scene which the prophet had conjured moved a new group of mourners—black-skirted priestly acolytes, some moaning and scurrying forward in an odd, stooped posture while their fellows lashed their naked backs with the tails of living snakes. Their leader was a thin, shaven-headed man in a jackal-mask; he chanted in harsh accents and held high a carven standard depicting the crossed heads of fanged serpents.

"Priests of Set!" was the outraged whisper around Conan. "Stygians, curse them!" Indeed, Conan recognized them as such from his travels south of the river.

Horaspes turned back to the crowd, his face a bitter mask. "Alas, Shemites, you see truly. For the visions I show you are not of the future, but of the present—not north of the river, my friends, but south! Know you, the Stygians have long cherished the secret of immortality, as they share all our wondrous arts! While we prepare joyously to serve our god, they prepare, too. Grimly and resolutely they labor, on behalf of his Nemesis!"

The chancellor let his voice ring desolate a moment in the

silence of the chamber before speaking on. "But my friends, a prophet's skill is to show the future, and show it I will! Look ye here, brethren, to a momentous day yet to come, whose time I cannot fix exactly. But be assured that it is very near!"

At Horaspes' gesture, dust swirled up again abruptly, like a cyclone, obscuring the funeral scene and raising fantastic, shimmering clouds before the watchers' sight.

Then the clouds cleared away, but not totally, for the scene remained eerily dim. An overcast, brassy sky threw pale storm-light on a gray, mottled expanse of sands. It was almost the same vista as before, with the giant tomb rearing a good deal closer in front of the courtiers. But all was still except for the rolling clouds; there were no men or beasts in sight, and the towering edifice looked dusty and abandoned.

To the watchers' ears came a sound so soft at first as to be scarcely audible. It was a deep, groaning note that slowly swelled and intensified, until finally it rang deafeningly across the desert waste and into the chamber, like the note of some inconceivable, vast trumpet.

Abruptly Conan realized that the sound was made by the doors in the tomb's lofty archway, slowly parting outward, shuddering and resounding all the while with the friction of dry, protesting sockets. The great bronze valves yawned wider, propelled by no hand anyone could see, for the darkness beyond them was not pierced by the eerie desert light. Finally the metal doors struck the flanking arms of the tomb's stair-step facade, giving off a ringing clang that died slowly into stillness.

All eyes were focused on the black gulf of the archway—from which, in a moment, there issued a clattering formation of war-chariots. They were drawn by fiery-eyed horses and driven by stern, shaven-headed Stygian nobles and warrior-priests, waving high the tattered banners of their empire. The steeds' contours looked skeletal under their flying manes and armored hides, and there was the same taut, deathlike aspect in the drivers' sharp-boned faces. Nevertheless the chariots dashed forward with fierce vigor, their many-spoked, metal-shod wheels glinting with the spikes and whirling scythes fitted at their hubs.

Behind the trundling battle-cars came columns of Stygian foot soldiers holding hook-tipped pikes aloft and striding forward with a vigor that seemed truly superhuman. And the procession was far from ended, Conan could see, as on their heels new streams of horsemen and bowmen were disgorged from the pyramid.

Sweeping from the tomb, the demon warriors rode straight into battle against an unarmed throng; and amidst a growing murmur of surprise from those around him, Conan saw that the Stygians' hapless targets were clothed and coiffed in the Shemitish fashion. Some of them turned to flee the on-slaught, slowly, as in a dream, while others drew short swords in self-defense, but all were ridden down relentlessly by the thundering chariots, or surrounded and taken in charge by swarming cavalry and footmen. It was a shameful slaughter and enslavement of the sons of Shem. One square-bearded figure, more richly clothed and prouder of bearing than the others, raised the ceremonial ax of a rural governor and stood defiant—only to be cut down in a welter of bloody dust by the whirling scythes of a Stygian chariot, to the courtiers' wails of sorrow and outrage.

"Look well, nobles!" Horaspes turned his back on the gruesome scene, letting it play itself out before the court. "What you see, through my gift of prophecy, is a vision of the Great Day, a future which can be, and which most certainly will be, if Shemites do not mend their ways!" He made a swift gesture behind him with his stylus, and the violent images in the wall began to fog and fade, their unearthly light diminishing rapidly.

"I ask you, brethren—on that fateful day, when the sky reverberates like a vast copper gong, when all the petty works of man are swept away, when the tombs yawn and the River Styx turns to black sand—on that day, Shemites, will you be strong enough to stand against your enemies? For know you, to the victor in that final contest will go all eternity!''

Behind the prophet the radiance had all but died out, and the broad, sorcerous window was dwindling into disjointed patches and fragments. Before Conan's gaze these now congealed into the original scrawled letters, whose red pigment dripped and ran down the wall, staining the stones like molten wax or blood.

As the spell faded, the reaction of the crowd grew more intense, with cries and rantings of outrage and some nobles on their feet, pounding the tables. The lamps were relit, revealing tears in the eyes of some men and women, and harrowed looks on every face. Most gazed angrily or imploringly to Horaspes. He made as if to speak further, but then glanced toward the royal dais and extended his arm that way.

All eyes turned to King Ebnezub.

Chapter 9

The Royal Reward

The king, for the first time that evening, had arisen from his gilded seat. He stood none too steadily on the dais, clutching the head of his divan for support. His queen sat looking up at him and grasping his arm protectively while two guards stood close behind, ready to catch his wavering, near-naked bulk if it should start to topple. But Ebnezub, in regal defiance of mere gravity, detached one hand from the back of the sofa and raised it to the watchers in a declamatory gesture.

"Our loyal subjects be assured . . . what the prophet has shown you will not be the fate of our great city of Abaddrah. For we give our entire heed to his counsels. We have cast aside the petty concerns of this world, to fix our eyes solely on the next.

"Know you, with the help of mystic herbs, we too have had visions, shining glimpses of the wonders to come. Abaddrans, your king awaits them impatiently. You, too, should be eager to leave this life, and awaken beyond. Great Ellael knows, we prepare faithfully for the Day of Doom!"

The king's voice, not deep to begin with, became reedy with lack of breath; he lowered his arm to support himself a moment as his bare, flabby chest heaved. Then he raised it again, albeit less high. "When we are ready to betake ourself to the Afterworld, our place of refuge shall be the finest.

strongest monument this side of the Great River. No expense is being spared. This day we have ordered the acquisition of one hundred fine horses, with grooms and feed, to be preserved for the use of our officers in war and sport. Everything is being readied—kennels and rookeries, scribes and minstrels. No smallest need shall be unmet in the next life! Our providence is complete. Fear not for our welfare. . . ."

Although Ebnezub's enthusiasm was mounting, his strength was diminishing. His voice rapidly grew faint, and his bulky frame began to droop over the back of the teetering divan. Queen Nitokar arose and helped him down into his seat, assisted by the two guardsmen. The king went on speaking feverishly, if inaudibly, to those near him, and gesticulated urgently to his wife as she hovered over him. Meanwhile Horaspes' unctuous voice took up the speech.

"And so it is clear. The Abaddran state stands united behind a farseeing king. Ellael grant that we shall prevail." The prophet sank to one knee and bowed toward the dais. "My eternal obeisance to Your Royal Splendor. Subjects, thank your gracious gods for such a master!" He arose. "And foreign nobles, think deeply on what I have shown you tonight. Now farewell! I bid you good rest."

With a final sweep of his arm, Horaspes dismissed the company. There commenced a general cheering and acclaim, which seemed to Conan a good deal more heartfelt than the usual obligatory response to a king's speech. He stood up with the rest, but did no shouting or thigh-pounding—a fact which his two female attendants obviously noticed and strove to hide by their own bouncing exertions.

Of the others in the hall, aside from the stock-still guards, the only ones who seemed subdued were the emissaries from Eruk. These, as they bowed their respects to the royal family and filed away from the table, looked shaken but perhaps not wholly persuaded of the chancellor's message. Most pensive of them all was Conan's recent neighbor, the military envoy; his face had a blank, pale look above his goat-beard, and he held his shoulder cocked at an unnatural angle as his comrades led him away. He had not recovered from Horaspes' casual touch.

As the courtly audience dispersed toward the doors Conan also tried to take his leave. But he found himself detained by his wenches, who clung to his arms and urged him to wait. Alone they would not have been able to stop him, but a pair of guards also moved to head him off.

"Nay, Northron, do not hurry away!" Conan turned, surprised to see Horaspes himself addressing him. The chancellor had paused on his return to the head of the chamber, with a smile on his round-jowled face and a gleam in his beady eye. " 'Tis your night of glory! By your prowess you have won a place at the feet of the royal family; you may yet see wonders this night, and enjoy lush rewards! Do not forfeit them." His face creasing almost to a wink, he turned and proceeded to the dais, where Queen Nitokar greeted him from her place at the king's side.

The queen, for her part, glanced from the prophet's face to Conan's, and in her painted smile the Cimmerian saw covetousness and a shameless invitation. The look made a shiverish feeling travel across his shoulders—whether of lust or of unease, he could not quite tell. But on seeing that the guardsmen still hovered nearby, he let the two importuning servant-girls draw him back down onto the silken pillows, their hands lightly twining his arms.

The room was now almost clear of lesser courtiers, and curtains were being pulled across the entryways. Yet on the dais new drink was poured, and plates of sweetmeats passed. Amid the cluster of family and retainers King Ebnezub lay on his divan, muttering and gesturing feebly with his plump, pale hands. His queen leaned over him solicitously, her dangling ornaments brushing his chest and face. Then she turned to whisper to two male attendants, who nodded and hurried off on an errand.

In a moment they returned, bearing on a painted wooden cradle between them a strange contrivance. It was a low, potbellied vessel whose base was of beaten gold in the form

of the upspread petals of a pond lotus. At its heart, nested in
the golden petals, was a sphere of transparent crystal apparently filled with clear liquid. Its top was a cap of gold from
which sprouted flexible tubes and receptacles, like unearthly
flower stamens. The servants set their burden down on a low
table beside the king, and Nitokar busied herself with it. She
tapped colored powders into its openings from jeweled po-
manders that dangled at her waist, and by means of silver
tongs she transferred hot coals to it from the nearby brazier.

Before long the appliance was sending up wisps of yellow
smoke, the liquid inside bubbling intermittently. The queen
turned back to her reclining husband and held the ivory tip of
one of the tubes to his lips, which were still murmuring
inaudible royal decrees.

King Ebnezub did not seem to notice her at first. She held
the smoke-stained ivory nipple before him enticingly, fanning
the fumes into his face, until finally his head tilted up to meet
her gaze. She placed the pipe-tip gently in his mouth, spoke
softly in his ear, and turned back to the water pipe to make
some adjustments at its top. Then she took up a second
pipe-stem and blew into it vigorously, sending bubbles of
yellow smoke streaming up through the lotus's crystal belly.

The fumes must have been carried straight to the king, for
he gasped, and his body stiffened in a rictus, smoke seeping
from his nostrils. On seeing his reaction, Nitokar smiled
hungrily and clutched his trembling arm. She leaned close to
him, whispering long and intensely into his ear. Then she
blew again on the pipe, producing another spasm in her
husband. The fingers of his free hand twitched and scrabbled
aimlessly until Horaspes, who sat on the far side of the king,
clasped them discreetly in his own.

Nitokar observed the king's raptures with a gloating expression. Her hand idly stroked his sweating brow as she
laughed and joked with Horaspes across his racked body.

While the queen administered the fumes to Ebnezub, others on the dais busied themselves variously—the prophet
conversing with the queen, the gaunt bodyguard Nephren

listening attentively, the gangling boy looking arrogant and
pestering the servants who hovered about the royal family. At
one point he caused a disturbance, threatening one of the
servant-girls with a dagger drawn from his belt. The wench
spilled her drink-ewer in fright as she avoided the glinting
blade. For her clumsiness, an older male servant struck her
and sent her sobbing from the room; the royal youth was
given no rebuke.

The young princess sat apart all the while, marking a tablet
with a stylus and ignoring the spectacle going on a little
distance away from her. Once, however, she glanced at her
parents with what seemed horror or disgust, then quickly
averted her eyes.

In time the king fell into a stupor and let the pipe drop
from his lips, his face flushed and dreamy, his eyes rolling
back in his head to gaze on invisible realms. The queen
snapped her fingers, and four strong male servants gathered
round Ebnezub's divan. They bent to reach under his slack
body from either side, locked their wrists together, and hoisted
him up expertly in the cradle formed by their arms. At
Nitokar's nod they carried him off, presumably to the royal
bedchamber, with armed guards falling in before and behind
them. At this sign of the festivities' end, the others on the
dais arose from their seats as well.

Even Conan's wenches eased themselves out from under
his lazy caresses. As they strove to pull him to his feet, the
queen spoke to two more of the male attendants—her personal servants these, judging by the briefness of their costume. And eunuchs, if the insolence of their looks and the
sleekness of their oiled bodies meant anything. As she ad-
dressed them her gaze lingered on Conan; in a moment the
three stepped down from the dais toward him.

"Well, my valiant foreigner, you vanquished Khada Khufi
skillfully enough!" Nitokar's voice was of a deep, full timbre
and accompanied by a brazen arching of her painted lips and
eyebrows. " 'Twas a relief to me, I admit, since I was
growing bored of his snake-shows. But surely you are stiff

and sore from your trials." Stopping just before him with her
servants on either side, she extended a many-ringed, queenly
hand and squeezed his upper arm in a surprisingly firm grip.

Conan kept himself from flinching under her touch. "Indeed, nay," he replied, "for I have been kneaded and pummeled well enough by these two maidens . . ." Looking
around, he was surprised to see the wenches departing swiftly
toward a distant exit, their shapely tails twitching.

"Then you must come to my chamber and let me soothe
your stresses and strains," Nitokar declared. "For know you,
I am skilled in the healing arts and have numerous salves and
unguents that can restore your vigor." Her hand had clutched
his arm more firmly, its red-daggered nails nipping his skin.
Flanked closely by the two eunuchs, she drew him toward
her. "And while we dally there, perhaps you can tell me how
you gained such skill at grappling."

Conan let himself be led by the three toward a small door
at the head of the chamber. He had little choice at the
moment, although he felt distaste at the cruelty he had glimpsed
beneath the queen's sensuality. As they went they passed
under the eyes of the other royalty, and Conan felt their
looks—Horaspes' cold amusement, the thinly-veiled disgust
of the young princess as she turned to leave, and the others'
air of cynical knowing as Conan followed the queen's full-
bodied shape out through the door. Her men stayed close to
him, but he noticed that there were no palace guards following.

"Oh, yes, I enjoy the sport of wrestling," Nitokar continued, "although I never could endure the Vendhyan, with his
body-oil that always stank of rancid goat-butter. . . ." They
mounted a broad, tiled ramp beside a many-fountained indoor
garden, where pink and yellow birds flitted among orchard
branches by lamplit artificial day. "Khada Khufi was coarse
and barely able to speak Shemitish. And he was surly, like
so many of these costly, imported slaves. He could never
have appreciated my arts."

At the top of the ramp, a marble-columned porch opened
onto a broad corridor angling away out of sight; into it they

passed, with the queen bantering on. "There is an art, you know, of human sensation. Precious secrets have been handed down from ancient scholars, such as ointments that can heighten the sensibility of pain as well as pleasure." She arched her eyebrows and laughed with a purring tone in her voice.

"But then, of course, who can say where pleasure stops and pain begins? Is there really a difference between the two?" She leaned conspiratorially toward Conan, who felt her two escorts also drawing close.

"For example, I have in my possession a five-tailed whip, of which each barb is imbued with a different stimulant to create varying sensations against the flesh. A rich, varied feast of pain, with tangy pleasure for the sauce. After one has lain beneath my lash, I challenge him to distinguish surely between pain and pleasure ever again!"

Arriving at a tall, gilded door at the end of the passage, Nitokar turned to Conan. "I really think you would enjoy it." She raised her hand to caress his cheek. "Of course, when something is to be your fate regardless of your wishes, you might as well enjoy it."

One of the manservants threw open the heavy door, exposing a room that seemed less a bedchamber than an apothecary, with jugs and vials crowded on the tables and strange implements hanging from the walls. To Conan's eye, it was not a place any sane man would enter. As he was drawn into the doorway behind the queen he suddenly jerked free of her cajoling hand and drove an elbow into the midsection of the servant pressing close behind him.

He felt the baby-fat of the eunuch's belly give way to a layer of firmer muscle underneath, and heard a gasp of exhalation that sounded less than complete. As the man doubled over Conan spun and gave him a knee in the face as well, and a sledgelike fist to the back of the neck for good measure.

Still the fellow did not clear the doorway, but staggered forward in a crouch, groping blindly for Conan's waist. Perhaps the lout was under the spell of one of Nitokar's pain-killing narcotics; with a curse the Cimmerian bent down, clasped his arms about the man's waist, and hoisted him up with his legs kicking in the air. With a twist of his body he hurled the eunuch head downward against the doorpost.

"You unruly lout! You'll suffer if . . ." Nitokar cried out shrilly at Conan's assault, but did not intervene. "Guards, a mutinous slave! Come and seize him! Aah!"

Her screeching was finally silenced as her servant tumbled against her legs, bearing her back out of the doorway. This cleared the way for the other eunuch, who edged carefully around his mistress. He leaped over his fallen comrade and came pelting after Conan.

The Cimmerian had started down the corridor, but now he turned to face the manservant, who had seized up a weapon in the queen's chamber. It was a long, wavy dagger with sinuous curves that looked inefficient for battle. Perhaps it was intended to inspire esthetic appreciation or fear instead.

"Come on, then," Conan grated to his pursuer. "If you weren't already a eunuch, I'd . . ."

Snarling, the servant darted forward with the blade waist-high. Conan's arm struck his foe's to block it as he stabbed, driving his knife-hand up in a high arc over both their heads. But as their arms swept down on the far side of the curve it was Conan's fist that grasped the hilt. He drew the blade viciously across his opponent's belly, then slashed it back across the man's throat. The overstressed metal of the dagger-point caught in the tendon under the eunuch's chin and snapped off; the fellow clutched at it, gurgling, as he went down. Conan threw away the bloody hilt and fled.

"Surrender, barbarian! Guards, take him, I say! He defies his queen! Ooh!" Nitokar's railing ceased once again as she bent over the fallen, still-kicking slave. Conan, as he rounded the corner of the passage, glanced back to see her holding up a hand wetted with blood and staring at it in fascination.

In spite of her earlier clamor no guards had appeared. Yet Conan thought he heard a bustle in the corridor ahead; he cast about desperately for another escape route. One of the gilded doors in the passage was ajar, or just now gliding shut. Without hesitation he shouldered through it, his fist balled to quell any resistance within.

The thrust of the door sent a slim figure staggering back into the room, lit dimly by a single oil lamp. By its light Conan recognized the young woman from the royal dais, still wearing her dark green sheath. Her headdress was unpinned, and short brown curls brushed her cheekbones. There was no one else in the chamber.

The girl could have screamed, but she only gasped and stared at Conan, shocked to silence, perhaps, by his murderous appearance. Wary of losing his advantage, he pushed the door silently shut behind him and lowered the bolt.

"I warn you, make no outcry. If you do not oppose me, no harm will come to you."

She nodded, her eyes traveling down to his side. "Your hand is covered with blood." Her voice was faint but did not quaver.

He glanced at his gory fist. "Aye." He scanned the room, which was a sleeping-chamber with no other doors. Spying a gold washbasin on a table at one side, he went to it. He stayed half-turned toward the girl to make sure that she did not flee as he bent to cleanse himself. "You must have heard the outcry in the corridor."

She nodded, tossing her curls with a bold effort at unconcern. "Such sounds from Nitokar's quarters are nothing unusual."

Conan nodded, drying his hands on the edge of an arras near the basin. "You are the king's daughter?"

"Yes. I am Afrit."

With her hair unpinned she seemed almost a child, although the shape of her body was womanly under the sheer green cloth. She left her place in the middle of the room and moved forward past Conan with aristocratic assurance. She took up the basin of red-clouded water and emptied it into a tiled drain in the corner of the floor.

"Aren't you wondering whose blood it is?" Conan asked, a little bemused. "The queen still lives . . . ."

"More's the shame! I have no love for Nitokar." Afrit replaced the basin, flashing a defiant look into Conan's eyes. "If you have foiled her, I should help you as best I can."

"Aye, she is a perilous one. . . . ." he ventured.

"Perilous!" the princess flared and advanced on Conan. "The bitch poisoned my mother to get her place as queen, and now she is doing the same to my father! She corrupts the whole Abaddran court, and I am powerless to stop her!"

In spite of the girl's frail size, Conan found himself raising a hand to fend off her vehemence. But instead he ended up touching the side of her face, barely stroking her hair as she stood before him with tears of futile rage running from her eyes. "There, there, girl . . . ."

But Afrit shook off his hand and shook aside the tears. "Foolish, foolish! Why should you care aught about the sorrows of the mighty?" She turned from him abruptly. "Here I am, childish as ever, baring my soul to a commoner. A foreigner at that, who wants only to escape with his own meager life."

"True enough." Conan nodded earnestly. "In a few moments, if there's no hue and cry, I'll leave by that window and trouble you no more." He gestured toward a double-pillared opening in the opposite wall, shuttered by gilded wooden screens. "But tell me—the rumors I hear of Nitokar are all true, then?"

Afrit shrugged impatiently. "I suppose so. They could hardly slander her, monster that she is!" She flashed her tear-damp face back toward Conan. "She was my mother's personal physician, and by her wiles she pandered to the poor, sick woman, making her crave the very potions and fumes that finally destroyed her. My father did not seek vengeance. I fear he had long since tired of Mother." The princess shook her head sadly, a catch in her throat. "Nitokar was quick to seduce him and place him under the same evil power. Now his days are numbered, as all men know, though none dares lend voice to such a treasonous fact.''

Conan frowned perplexedly. ''And what if someone at court were to denounce the poisoning and stop it?''

''Father would die all the sooner, or go mad for lack of Nitokar's potions. When she is late with her treatments, his rage and anguish are dreadful to behold.''

''What does the queen stand to gain? Can she rule the city after he's gone?''

Afrit sighed. ''By Abaddran law, the king has the power to fix the succession. And I fear that Father will finally favor Nitokar and her treacherous brat, Eblis, over me. He says he loves me above all else in the world. He rambles on and on, when he is capable of speech, about how he hates the thought of ever being parted from me. But I am a woman, a mere child in his eyes. He will not take me seriously!''

''Hmm. A bold ploy indeed. Nitokar must have powerful friends at court.''

Afrit laughed bitterly. ''Aye, the most powerful. Horaspes, the only one whose means to evil are greater than her own. . . .''

At that moment the princess fell silent. She and her guest harkened to the faint sound of footsteps in the corridor outside.

''The queen may yet begin a search,'' Conan whispered, moving toward the window.

''Nay, wait! If they are watching for you, neither exit is safe.''

Afrit smothered the lamp and moved quickly across the room. In the sudden dimness of moonlight through the shutters, Conan strained to follow her form with his eyes, watchful for treachery. But she only unpinned her gown at armpit, hip, and knee, and threw it aside, showing him a sudden flash of brighter paleness; then, as swiftly, she covered herself by drawing a flimsy cotton shift over her head. She turned and beckoned, growing gradually more visible to Conan as his eyes learned the light.

''It would be folly for you to leave now. If they enter, I'll pretend to be asleep. You can hide here." She bent over her sleeping-pad, which rested on a high pedestal in the center of the room, and stripped aside the silken coverlet. It formed a sloping jumble that extended to the chamber's floor. "I often sleep thus when the heat is greatest."

Conan tried to fathom the expression on her face in the wan, slatted light of the window. The sounds from the hall had receded. "You would risk my being found here with you?"

She shrugged her bare, delicate shoulders. "Strange liaisons are the way of this palace, as you have seen. Why should it be gossiped that I am the only one to sleep alone?" She slid onto the mattress and sat upright on it in a chaste, girlish posture. "Besides, I enjoy talking to you. I have no friends at court. All here are so enmeshed in intrigue that I would never dare speak my mind to them."

"A shame, that." Conan sat on the edge of the bed, taking care not to trample the nightclothes. "A girl like you should have many friends, and faithful ones."

"Thank you—Conan, is it?" He thought he could detect a blush on her pale face as she gazed through the gloom to catch his nod. "But the court of Abaddrah is gravely ill, you know. Horaspes and the queen have bewitched it, and all the courtiers vie only for their favor."

"Ah yes, Horaspes! You do not believe his preachments, then?"

"No." Afrit shook her head bitterly. "But this is only the beginning. His teachings will spread far enough to ruin other cities than Abaddrah, by making the people pour all their sweat and blood into useless tomb building. Such ravings and sorcerous tricks have little to do with our ancient Shemitish belief. They are a hodgepodge, intended to dupe fools and commoners into following the prophet for his own ends."

Conan nodded. "That could be so. Crom knows, he lives grandly enough here, having gained the ear of the king."

"Yes, and his influence will increase if my stepmother takes the throne. She now helps him slap the courtiers into line." Afrit gazed pensively into the darkness. "And yet, I cannot help but think he may have even deeper motives. He seems so intense. I can't imagine him ever being satisfied just to prop up an all-powerful monarch, as most of the priests are." She turned a thoughtful look on Conan. "He is an ascetic, you know, with little care for the pleasures of the flesh. And that bodyguard of his, Nephren, is so cold and lifeless-looking . . . ugh!" She ended with a shiver, hugging herself in the sultry room.

"You hold an unlucky place in all this." Conan eased nearer to her on the bed and touched her arm. "And yet by rights you should have nothing to fear. A woman of your position, with your gifts, should be able to outdo Nitokar at courtly intrigue any day."

The princess clasped his hand against her shoulder. "I pray so, Conan. I am not yet a woman, and my youth is a burden to me. I am trying to learn, but can I possibly do it soon enough? Conan, you can help me!"

"I?" He caught her as she leaned against him, her soft hair brushing his shoulder. The pressure of her body was brisk and urgent. "How could I help . . . ?"

"Kill Nitokar for me! You can do it. You are strong and ruthless!" She turned her face up to his and gasped the words in warm, excited breaths. "After she's gone I'll find some way to heal my father! Go to her now, this very hour. I'll get you a knife."

"Nay, Princess, I'm no assassin. Nor a fool." Conan shook his head and started to push her firmly away. "I'm already embroiled deeper in your family affairs than I want to bè."

"Please, Conan! Not for me, but for the city!"

Again they fell silent because of a sound in the hall—this time the thump of nearby footfalls, followed by a rattle at the door and a voice.

"O Princess! Princess Afrit! Are you within?" The tone was a deep but subdued male one, and it was followed by the scrape of a key in the latch.

"Hide, quickly!" Afrit whispered to Conan. "They can open it from outside!"

Disengaging swiftly from her, he glided out of sight behind the bed. At that same moment the brass bolt flicked up, and lamplight invaded through the opening door.

"Princess! Pardon me for disturbing you! A dangerous prisoner has escaped." The voice paused a moment behind the half-open door, then the speaker proceeded inside carrying the light. It was a young guardsman in the feather-crested helm of a captain, with two more guards looming behind him. "I am ordered to search every room in this wing of the palace."

Afrit had taken a corner of the topmost, flimsiest sheet of bed linen to cover herself. "Captain Aramas, I was sleeping! There is no fugitive here, I assure you."

The officer paused just inside the door. He was flustered, no doubt attributing the princess's high color and breathy voice to her embarrassment at his intrusion. "I am sorry, Princess Afrit, but we must search. If he were hiding here without your knowledge, you would be in grave danger."

Aramas set his blazing lamp on the table as the two guards moved into the room and began their search, opening wardrobes, probing behind curtains, and peering out the window. Finally the elder and burlier of them turned back to Aramas. "Captain, there is no one here. No sign of anyone leaving by the window . . . aarh, what's this?"

In heading back toward the door, the soldier had trodden on the coverlet cascading from Afrit's bed and stumbled over something. As he bent to examine the fabric more closely, a large hand shot up from beneath it and grasped him by the throat. Then Conan's head and shoulders emerged, shaking off the coverlet. Struggling to kick free of the bedding and arise, he maintained his choking clutch on the guardsman while groping with his other hand for the man's sheathed sword.

"No, Conan! Stop it, please!" Afrit's entreaties, combined with the pressure of the other two guards' sword-points against his neck, caused Conan to relent. He shoved away the half-strangled guard, who staggered off red and gasping; then he knelt scowling before the others like a sullen, snared wolf.

"Stay down, you! One move and you're dead!" Captain Aramas looked reproachfully to Afrit. "My Princess, you told us there was no one here!"

Afrit had thrown off her coverlet when she crawled across the bed to implore Conan. Now she turned her face up to Aramas, all pretense of modesty forgotten. "Captain, look at him, and have pity! He is a poor slave struggling for his life!" She touched his sword-hand. "Captain Aramas, I have watched you from afar; I have seen your kindness and fairness. You know the cruelty of my stepmother's pleasures. Would you give him back to her as a plaything? Spare him, please!"

The captain, rather than looking to Conan as the princess urged him, seemed unable to tear his eyes away from Afrit. And indeed, the budding beauty of her face and body, scarcely masked by her shift, were distracting enough to make even Conan neglect the blades at his throat.

It was Captain Aramas's turn to blush. "Princess, how could I do anything . . . ? It is not in my power. . . ."

Afrit kept her eyes fixed on his face. "Captain, tonight, as a consequence of Queen Nitokar's perverse sport, a slave was killed. Turn over that body to the dead-wardens instead, and let this one go. Say that he died escaping."

Aramas finally glanced at Conan. "This man is dangerous, milady. A foreigner, and a skilled fighter. I would not release him."

"Then keep him under guard. Or set him to work on the tombs. He would be useful there."

"Aye, he would make a strong worker." The captain could not take his gaze from Afrit long. "But, Princess, you are asking me to place my own life in jeopardy."

Afrit waved to the other guards, who looked uncertain and only half-comprehending. "These men are faithful. They will not betray you. Do this thing for me, and I will . . . give you my protection, and aid you in every way I can."

If it was a bad bargain, the captain did not seem to realize it. He clasped his free hand over Afrit's as she withdrew it from his arm. "Very well, milady. I will spirit him out of here." He leveled his sword at Conan. "But you—you must go quietly or die. Come along, now."

As Conan walked around the bed and out of the room he was aware of the princess's parting look. Her gaze said *Remember me*.

Chapter 10

The Tomb-Workings

In the ensuing days, work on the Great Tomb of Ebnezub was hastened. Trumpets blatted shrilly from atop the vast stone-and-earth mound, and the whips of the overseers cracked sharp and fast, sending ever larger numbers of brown-skinned laborers swarming up its face like ant-soldiers to their gargantuan nest. Their ranks were swelled by the flood of peasants fleeing the countryside to escape the immemorially high waters of the River Styx.

The reason for speeding the project, according to the mutterings of the workers, was that the king's health was flagging faster in spite of the diligent efforts of his queen and chief physician, Nitokar. It would require a massive effort, it was said, to finish Ebnezub's tomb before the hour of his need for it.

But among the courtiers and city-sophisticates a different rumor held sway: that the powerful Chancellor Horaspes expected soon to be invited northward to the city-state of Eruk, and that he was anxious to see Ebnezub's tomb near completion before departing to sow the seed of his gospel in richer soil.

Amid the bustle and turmoil of the tomb-workings, Conan fit in well. Surprisingly, his foreign looks and speech and his special status as a remand from the palace guard made his lot easier by exempting him from the routine toil of the work-gangs. His size and strength were soon appreciated by the overseers, who liked to hold him in reserve for special tasks requiring exceptional force or leverage.

Often these jobs were in lofty or cramped places, where a number of weaker men could not bring their strength to bear. As mere shortcuts to speed the project along, they sometimes involved considerable risk. But the pace of the work suited Conan better than the plodding, monotonous labor of the crews, and it gave him the opportunity to visit all parts of the diggings and learn much about the tomb. On one occasion he had to swing a maul to break open the ill-fitting lid of a marble sarcophagus, inside which a howling stonecutter was trapped. Another time he was called into the Sacred College of Embalmers to help its frail acolytes lift the ponderous, mummy-wrapped corpse of an expired civil servant into its gilded coffin-liner.

Of course, escape was never far from his thoughts. By night, curled in his solitary, windowless pen, he soothed himself to sleep with the thought of making his way back to Otsgar's keep and giving his betrayer the throttling he deserved. This time, he fantasized, the little hussy Zafriti might find him quicker to respond to her coaxings, if she was still with the innkeeper and had not found some richer fool to tease into a jealous frenzy.

Another worry that prodded Conan toward flight was the ever-present danger from the palace. There was no telling when Queen Nitokar, with her drug-clouded brain roving between royal intrigues and sadistic diversions, might get word of his presence and send down the order for his death.

Worse it would be, to Conan's mind, if Princess Afrit should suddenly remember him and renew her importunings that he murder the queen. At their meeting the princess had seemed a frank and well-intentioned maiden; but the very air of the palace was poisonous with deceit. It might yet turn her into a more dangerous vixen than her stepmother. Since his transport here, he had had no word from Afrit except the pointed message left one night in his bed which he now kept wound in the back of his breechclout: a short, needle-sharp dagger wrapped in a familiar cloth of green silk. It might prove useful in his escape.

And yet, despite these goads and opportunities, Conan stayed on at the diggings. Why he did so was not entirely clear to him. Certainly it was not because of the small salary that was daily toted up to him and to each of the other workers by the scrawny-armed scribes—to be reduced to a pittance or a debit by the inflated cost of his milk and groats, his straw bedding, and the rent of his hippo-hide sandals.

In part he stayed because of the odor of wealth about the place, which was strong enough to hold an inveterate thief and pillager like himself in thrall. For not every laborer was so poorly paid as he, and overall their monthly payroll made a load of coin that would burden a train of ox-wagons. In carrying out his duties Conan had glimpsed gold and silver, lapis lazuli and amber, ruby and carbonyx enough to pay the purchase of any fair-sized northern city, all for use in the embellishment of the tomb. During construction these treasures were stored and worked in a well-guarded artisan's quarter of the camp, its fence liberally adorned with drying heads and limbs of pilferers and sneak-thieves. It was most dismaying to Conan to realize that even he, in a single night's haul, could have carried away only a small fraction of the loot.

Beyond the lure of any riches, Conan felt ensnared by a vexing uncertainty about the tomb itself, an air of mystery which hovered over the great work and ceaselessly pricked his curiosity. He felt it when his fellow workers spoke of the strange sounds and shadowy shapes they sometimes encountered at dusk around the tomb, or by day in its unlighted corridors. He felt it when they muttered low, or else kept strangely silent, about the unexplained accidents that beset workers in the lowest diggings, deep in the innards of the stone pile. He felt it most of all one dusk when he saw the prophet Horaspes passing through on an inspection trip, sur-

veying the project with an air of secret satisfaction, as if it
had a purpose and meaning which only he knew.

On that occasion Conan was careful to stay out of sight.
But Horaspes' man Nephren was harder to avoid, making
frequent visits to the site and questioning the architects closely
as they translated the rolled sheepskin building-plans into
solid earth and gargantuan stone.

Nephren's continual presence was odd in that, in spite of
his dark and weatherworn complexion, he obviously despised
the sun. He generally walked in the company of two slaves
who held a woven canopy up over his head to shade him.
And when he had to sit out-of-doors beneath his awning for
long periods, he was attended by a young female slave who
periodically sprinkled oil in his hair and applied pungent
salves to his skin, as if to protect him from the hot, chafing
delta breezes.

This maid always caught Conan's eye because, although
she showed all the restraint and humility required of a lowly
body-servant, an intense loathing of her master was apparent
in her every movement. At times when she touched him, her
face showed an involuntary look of horror and repugnance
that twinged at Conan's belly. Nephren, however, seemed to
regard her with sardonic amusement—insofar as his seamed,
immobile face could express any emotion. Her dread of him
was difficult to account for, since her minimal costume showed
her to be well-nourished and free of whip-marks.

Conan felt that Nephren's strangeness was somehow linked
to the undefined mystery of the tomb, and he rankled to
know more. Once, as the serving-wench drew water from the
communal urn, he went to join her and tried out his mastery
of a low Stygian dialect. "You fear your master," he said to
her, smiling. "And no wonder; I don't care for his looks
either."

She stared back at him in wide-eyed terror, her mouth
uttering a sound that could only have been made by the mute
or tongueless: "Ahr-ah!" Then she turned and hurried away,
water sloshing from her brass vessel. Nephren, seated below,

heard her frightened outcry; he turned in his seat to look up at Conan, his face wearing a narrowed gaze of recognition.

"Ready, there, you slackards. Now hoist, and hoist! Pull, you spawn of river-eels!"

At the overseer's command, fourscore sandals scuffed the stone, and forty brown bodies strained together like segments of a many-legged insect wriggling along the top edge of the unfinished tomb. Leather tackle squeaked in oiled blocks, and the huge, angular stone lifted up askew from its bed of mated stones, until its upper edge scuffed against one of the three stout timbers that supported it.

"Hold it there, now! Keep it aloft," the overseer said. Without making the rope fast, the laborers leaned against it, suspending the block a few handsbreadths above the stone bed.

"Now the levers! Pry it away evenly, lest you do more damage!" The stout, bare-chested overseer strutted officiously back and forth, but there was little more he could tell the three men who plied long wooden poles in the crack beside the stone, trying to force it away from its firmly bedded neighbor.

He walked to the edge of the wall and glared down at Conan, who hung from the end of a rope, probing into the crevice with a long wooden implement. "Work lively, there, barbarian! The whole crew is waiting."

"Quiet, whore's get!" the Cimmerian snarled. "You could do no better, even if you had the nerve to be down here! Tell them to pry harder."

Conan had been suspended down the near-vertical face of the wall with a hooked ashen stave, told to extract a shard of stone which had shivered away from the hoisted block and kept it from nesting evenly in its place on the tomb. The sliver was now wedged in the vertical part of the crevice by the weight of the dangling stone; Conan hung there with his feet braced wide against the wall, tugging and wrenching to work it free.

"It's coming," he called. "Pry more to this side. Aye, there!"

With a twist of his hook Conan swept the stone chunk out between his feet; it rattled down the stone face to end in a pile of broken timbers far below. The carved blocks thudded together, crushing the pry-bars and whipping them vertical before they were jerked out.

"Are there any smaller fragments? . . . No? Then lower away. Gently, now!"

In spite of the overseer's words, the strained muscles of the work crew let the stone drop with a screech of tackle.

"No, wait! Crom's devils!" Conan's shout was lost in the din as the great stone slid home. From beneath it hot air blasted into his face, laden with stone-dust, stinging fragments, and sparks. Blinded, he lost his footing and rolled away sideways along the wall, dangling loosely from his rope. Then, feeling something above him start to give, he twisted in air and slashed his hooked stave upward to catch on the edge of the stone above him.

Hand over hand he climbed the pole, finally hauling himself up to sit on the brink of the wall.

After knuckling both eyes vigorously, he examined his harness-rope—and found it frayed two-thirds through by its skittering journey along the sharp-hewn edge of stone. He muttered a stream of profanities and turned to the overseer. The lout was already far away, herding his work-crew down the broad wooden ladders to begin hauling up the next stone.

From behind him a voice called, "Is that the prisoner Conan? Here, you! I have a new assignment."

Conan looked around to see a guard in the cape and girdle of the tomb police beckoning him toward the ladder that led down to the inner pits. Standing nearby was a second man, a well-paid craftsman, judging by the trim and pleat of his cotton kilt. Conan shrugged and eased himself to his feet, grabbing up his sandals on the way.

"Well, he looks fit enough for the job," the higher-ranking one said. He was a young, clean-shaven man of slight build, less fit-looking than a physical laborer—and less deeply tanned, showing that his usual work was indoors or belowground. As Conan drew near he saw that the fellow wore a pair of calipers at his waist as another might wear a weapon or a baton of rank. A draftsman, then. Conan wondered what he was doing so far from his sheaves and inkpots.

"Barbarian, this is Mardak," the guard said. "He will be your overseer. Mind him well."

"I am heading a special project, Conan. It is a position of high trust, for which I want the very best workers. You are well spoken of." Mardak's manner had the openness and friendliness of youth, with none of the usual haughtiness of a skilled craftsman. "Most of the men under me will receive extra pay. I think that applies to you, too." He glanced to the guard, who gave a curt nod.

Conan regarded him skeptically a while, then shrugged. "It couldn't be any more thankless than the tasks I've had so far. Lead on." Mardak gave an impulsive smile and clasped Conan's hand. Then he started down the first of the wooden ladders. Conan followed, with the tomb policeman coming last.

Around them the diggings swarmed with activity, like a termite's nest torn open to the scorching midday sun. It was a bustling scene, and a strangely cheerful one; in spite of the arduousness of the work and its mystical, morbid purpose, the attitude of the tomb-workers was almost lighthearted. They were lean, sunbrowned river-children, life-loving and accustomed to harsh labor under stern masters. They took to the work stoically, viewing it best as a change from their toil in the fields and a chance, however illusory, to earn wealth rather than mere subsistence. Women labored alongside the men, some with small babes on their hips, and all of them tended to sing and chant, even during backbreaking exertions.

As Conan went from one ladder to the next, deeper into the tomb, the sound of the work-chants receded far above him with the dwindling rectangle of sky. The pit of the monument's interior soon broke into narrow descending shafts and galleries, for, tall and massive as the stone pile was, most of its rooms and passages were actually underground, hewn from the sandstone bedrock. While those deeper, darker regions also teemed with workers, the Shemites here seemed glum and quiet, as if brooding over the loss of the sunlight.

Long after the last crevice of blue sky disappeared, the three continued their descent by the light of oil lamps spiked to the walls—until the air swam with oil fumes and the stooping, sweating stone-carvers began to look like hunched troglodytes. Conan knew that he was deeper in the tomb than he had ever been.

Mardak, heedless of surroundings that were plainly familiar to him, began a one-sided conversation to pass the time. "I am a draftsman by training. But now I have the chance to try my hand at design and construction as well, from start to finish." He looked confidingly to Conan as they waited for the next ladder to be vacated by workers carrying out rubble in large baskets they bore on their backs. "Some parts of the project are limited to as few workers as possible. For reasons of secrecy, you understand. It leads to great opportunities, not only for me, but for a laborer like yourself as well."

Conan frowned as they started down the double ladder. "We'll be working on a secret part of the tomb, then?"

Mardak nodded. "The most secret of all. My design is for the closure of the Royal Chamber. Once sealed, it can only be opened from the inside, when the king and his escort awaken to immortality on the Day of Doom!" He smiled and spoke more volubly.

"My concept is brilliant, if I do say so! You'll see it soon enough. At Chancellor Horaspes' request I designed a unique mechanism, drew up all the plans, then supervised the stone-cutting. It was done in widely separated sheds by workers who could not have known what they were making. Now all that remains is to assemble the parts."

Conan could scarcely believe what he was hearing; he felt his heart begin skipping as his old schemes of raiding the great tomb rushed back upon him. But he took his time replying, anxious to conceal his interest.

"The chancellor must trust you a great deal."

"Aye, I have been promised . . . well, enough to say, it is a princely sum. All my laborers in the final phase will be paid extra—I'll see to it. But more important, it could be a step to greater things. . . . Ah, be careful here!"

They had been going in single file down a narrow passage, their progress lit only by a guttering lamp held high by the tomb-guard behind them. Now they came to a warning lamp which revealed that the way was blocked by timbers shoring up deep cracks spreading from one wall of the corridor across its ceiling and floor.

"This slippage must have occurred since yesterday. Likely the passage will have to be filled in! But I think we can make our way through." Mardak eased himself cautiously between the vertical timbers and the solid wall of the tunnel.

"I've heard of these cave-ins. They've cost a good many lives." Conan had to squeeze mightily to slip past the timbers; he thought he felt the cracked stone settling a bit further under his weight. "Is the tomb built on a rotten foundation, then?"

"No," Mardak replied. "It only happens in a few spots where older tomb-shafts have weakened the sandstone. Fear not, the Royal Chamber has been tested and is sound."

Beyond the shorings the passage joined a broader, sloping corridor lit by bracketed lamps at short intervals. "Here is the main corridor by which His Royal Splendor will be borne into the tomb," Mardak announced proudly. "To the right it leads up to the great entry doors. And here to the left is the vestibule of the Royal Chamber."

He led the way down to where the passage opened into an area with a vaulted ceiling. It was broad and tall, though not nearly so spacious as the pillared gallery in the ancient desert tomb, which now seemed only a dim memory to Conan. This open space was used to store angular building-stones packed in wooden frames, which some workers at the end of the room were busy uncrating. In the far wall could be seen a stately archway bordered with intricate carvings.

"Here, at the very heart of the tomb, is our workplace." Mardak turned to the guard and told him, "Many thanks. That completes my work party."

The tomb policeman responded with a curt nod; he had been sour-faced for some time, plainly offended by Mardak's intimacy with a mere foreign laborer. He turned and went to join two more tomb police who were guarding the approaching corridor.

Mardak escorted Conan over to the other workers. "These are some of the ablest hands in the diggings. But I needed one worker like you, of exceptional strength and reach. We are working in tight quarters." He raised his voice to address the others. "Men, this is Conan, the last of our crew."

The half-dozen looked up from their desultory labors. They were Shemites, a sturdy-looking lot, their skins smudged white with stone-dust in the wavering lamplight. There was something sullen in their gaze—whether because of Conan's foreignness or a resentment of their assigned work, it was hard to tell.

"I want every one of you to understand the nature of our task and its peculiar dangers. Here is where we shall work." Mardak conducted them under the ornamented arch into a short hallway of unusual shape, with odd channels and recesses in its walls. From beyond it, Conan was dazzled by the shine of turquoise and alabaster inlay in what must have been the Royal Chamber.

The inner room was dark and cavernously vacant, lit only by the glow of Mardak's lamp; he ceased talking and held the light high so that each man could gaze inside in turn. Although the light shimmered from the semiprecious adornment of the walls and floor, nothing of real value was installed there yet.

"You are not to defile this room or take anything from it,

on pain of death,'' Mardak said. "Our work will be out here in the entryway.''

He had more lamps brought in and pointed out the particulars of the hallway's design, explaining its workings and the construction methods to be followed. When the chamber door was closed, a set of fitted granite stones would fall to block the archway; these would be backed up in turn by other stones sliding down to wedge them firmly in place, in the manner of a Khitan puzzle-box. The extra stones would descend from narrow dead-ended shafts that angled up from the hallway, and would finally form a stone barrier many cubits thick.

The portal would be impenetrable to scavengers, ghouls, or even invading armies; yet when the king and his retainers awakened on the Day of Doom, they could make their exit easily by prying out the movable stones in a certain sequence from within, and finally throwing open the stone-socketed door.

Conan could not envision the exact mechanism, but he could understand that, as Mardak said, the work would have to be done from the outside inward, for the last stones they laid in place would clearly be the first to fall. The prime hazard, as the draftsman explained, was that the fall of the stones might be triggered early. If so, it would not only kill them all but cause untold difficulties for later crews.

Mardak finished his talk, and within the hour they commenced work. They knocked the protective boards away from the specially-shaped stones, most of which resembled chest-sized chunks of melon, and wrestled them into position. Conan's role was crucial, for as each new stone was raised up by a dozen hands, a single strong arm was required to wedge the previous one in place with a pry-bar.

Conan occasionally wormed his way up the stone shafts to clear away jams, and he sweated close beside the Shemites installing temporary wooden braces. Still his fellow workers remained sullen toward him. And to each other as well, he had to admit as he watched them toil together efficiently,

without needless talk. Mardak pressed everyone hard, keeping
them at it for hours—until finally one man's foot was crushed
in an accident caused by fatigue.

The overeager draftsman shed remorseful tears over the
casualty as the man was carried away moaning by two tomb
police. Then he ordered the others to rest. "We have labored
hard. Darkness has long since fallen in the upper world. But
we're not permitted to leave here until our task is done. We
spend the night in the tunnel."

Baskets of bread and dates had been brought, along with
wine in clay urns, which were later useful as chamber pots.
The men dined in silence, watching the guards change shifts
at the far end of the chamber. Then they plucked their
bedding from a bale of straw, scattered it on the floor, and
stretched their weary limbs out on it. The lamps were shaded,
and it was night.

Yet Conan could not quiet his mind so easily. He did not
slumber, but arose and ambled toward the head of the room.
There Mardak sat cross-legged beside a half-shaded lamp,
sipping wine and sketching on a waxen tablet. Conan stopped
beside the draftsman, who glanced up in surprise.

"Well, Mardak, your tomb-seal is quite an invention. I
look forward to seeing how it is triggered." He squatted
down next to him. "But I ask you—will it work when the
time comes? And if it does, how will any living soul ever be
sure that it did?"

Mardak looked tired and still woeful over the earlier accident, but he smiled at Conan. "I built a wooden model of it
and demonstrated it to Chancellor Horaspes himself. It worked
more than once, before we burnt it up in a fire for security's
sake. He trusts me, which is all I need to know."

Conan nodded, considering Mardak's words. "But will he
trust you afterward with the secret? Can he trust any of us
who know how the king's greatest treasures are to be
protected?"

Mardak raised an eyebrow. "Once the tomb is sealed,
there is nothing that we or anyone else can do from the

outside, no matter how much we may know." He smiled and shook his head. "Fear not, Conan. The chancellor gave me his solemn pledge that I am to be released after the project and paid the promised amount. And if I will, why not you?

"As to whether my device will work flawlessly or not" —the draftsman glanced aside and lowered his voice slightly— "can it possibly matter a thousand years from now to a flock of lifeless, shriveled mummies?"

Conan pondered the remark a moment. "So you don't believe in the reawakening of the dead in the Afterworld, as Horaspes teaches?"

Mardak shrugged. "There may be something to it, in some ethereal, mystical sense. But a man of my training would have to be gullible to accept such a notion without proof, on the word of priests."

Conan knit his brow. "Then why risk your life in building this tomb?"

"Why not? It works." The draftsman swigged impatiently from his wine-cup and set it down again. "The important thing is, the commoners believe in it and the king endorses it. It helps trade, and it creates great opportunities for the likes of you and me." Mardak looked up confidentially to Conan. "It's a question of other people's faith, like the value of money. After all, what good are gold and gems, really? You can't eat them, and you can't make decent clothes or houses out of them! Why not wall them up in tunnels like this, deep underground? What harm can it do?"

The draftsman glanced aside again to make sure no one was listening and spoke on in a low tone. "It's not as if I'm greedy, you understand. I take the risk because I have a large family, of whom I am the sole support. With this good fortune my younger brother will be able to enter priest school. My sisters will have dowries, and my old parents need never fear poverty." He smiled again shaking his head. "But here I am, rambling on about things that are of no interest to you, and you need your sleep." He reached out a hand to clasp his listener's shoulder. "Goodnight, Conan."

The Cimmerian went back through the shadows and lay down in his sleeping-place; still he could not rest. He propped himself on an elbow to face the man nearest him, who was also clearly awake—one of the eldest workers, a lean, bald man obviously respected by the other Shemites.

"I see only glum faces among your men, Esfahan, and I know there must be good reason," he whispered. "Is it your fear, then, that we will be silenced by the tomb police?"

The elder man could be heard to sniff in disgust, his beady eyes glinting in the faint light. "I know not whether they raise only fools in the northern countries, foreigner, but if you expect any of us to get out of here alive, you are just that. A fool!"

Conan cursed under his breath. "Well, whatever they have in store, we can try to plan against it. I, for one, will not hand over my life so easily!"

There was no answer; Esfahan had clearly finished with him, for he rolled over to face the other direction and lay hunched and still. In a while Conan settled down to a restless sleep.

Chapter 11

Beneath the Tombs

Morning was a new change of the guards, a rekindling of the lamps, and a groggy, sore-limbed awakening. After swallowing portions of cold gruel with goat's milk and figs, the men resumed their work under Mardak's fastidious eye.

They labored more deliberately this time, but also more efficiently; in several hours the last of the stone blocks was levered into place and the door was mounted. The timing mechanism, a sand-clock that would begin flowing once the portal closed, was fitted into its niche and primed. Mardak went to report the completion of the job, while Esfahan was left to supervise Conan and the others in dismantling the now-needless timber props.

By the time they were finished, the entry to the Royal Chamber had become a deceptively plain-looking hallway. The laborers turned to the task of cleaning up the vestibule and bundling the discarded packing-timbers.

But Conan noted a disconcerting change outside; there were now a half-dozen armed tomb police loitering at the foot of the central corridor, one for each of Mardak's crew. And looming among the rearmost of them was an eerily familiar figure—the chancellor's tall, unbending lieutenant Nephren, who was conferring with a guard-captain while eyeing the workers.

141

Conan elbowed his way over to Esfahan and muttered to
him, darting his eyes aside to direct the older man's gaze. "It
appears the time is here, Uncle. The guards are gathering.
We'd best make our move."

The other did not follow Conan's glance. "And what are
you proposing to do, northerner?"

Conan stifled his impatience and answered lowly, not wish-
ing to attract notice. "Why, fight, of course. Escape, or else
die like men! Look, I have a dagger." He eased the short
parcel out of his crotch-wrap and unwound the green silk,
screening the action from general view with his body. "Tell
your Shemites to arm themselves with clubs."

The senior man shook his head stubbornly, refusing to
meet Conan's eye. "There is no escape from here, foreigner!
The most you can do is prolong your death—if you are not a
spy. Better to use that knife on yourself!"

Conan snorted in disgust and turned away. He walked
among the scattered laborers toward the guarded passageway,
holding the dagger below waist level and flashing it in the air
to draw their attention. He hoped that none would raise an
outcry; as he went he scanned their faces, looking for companions. A couple of the younger ones trailed along behind
him, but with no great look of determination.

The guards maintained their pose of idleness, content to let
the doomed ones complete their labors. They had fanned out
inside the vestibule and were talking together in pairs or
lounging against the side walls. Conan strolled toward them,
his knife-hand now screened behind his body. One or two of
the guards looked up at him with annoyance. But they were
too lax; so smoothly did his pace accelerate to a run that he
was past them before they could react.

He headed for the side of the corridor, straight at Nephren,
since the two guards who conversed with the captain stood
with their backs to the vestibule. One of these, the captain,
heard Conan's approach and spun around, trying to draw his
sword. The motion interposed his body between Conan and
his target, so that the dagger-blow struck him instead. It was

a glancing stroke and the blade did little damage, though
Conan felt his fist break a rib or two. The captain staggered
against Nephren, bearing him back against the wall.

Then the Cimmerian was through the guards and hurling
himself up the corridor between the glinting lamp-flames.
Behind him he heard shouts and rapid footfalls as the tomb
police squared off against the laborers; a backward glance
told him that none of the others had made it, although they
may have slowed the guards, who were just starting after him
in pursuit. He redoubled his speed, the echoes of his footsteps ringing down the tunnel.

He knew the central passage would grow busy near the
surface and he resolved to take one of the narrow side
corridors to make his pursuers come at him single file. A
four-way junction appeared ahead, and he squinted at it in the
yellow light; were there really lamplit shadows moving there
in the dimness? Then an apparition emerged which made him
slow his pace to a halt.

It was his young overseer, Mardak, he realized, but with
dreadful changes: his eyes were glassy and his face deathly
pale except for the chin and neck, which were crusted with
bloodstains from his mouth. His arms ended in knots of
red-stained bandage at the wrists. He staggered forward weak
and dazed, guided by two priestly acolytes, one of whom
carried a small golden canopic chest.

Conan did not need to see inside the gilded box to know
that it contained the hands and tongue of Mardak the draftsman. Apparently Horaspes was keeping his promise to let
his trusted servant live.

Catching sight of the dagger-wielding northerner, the acolytes panicked and dragged their ward back into the tunnel;
meanwhile Conan gathered his wits about him once again.
He looked back toward his pursuers to find Nephren almost
upon him, borne well ahead of the others on his stiff, churning
legs. Swiftly Conan dodged into the narrow branching at the
nearer side of the passage.

It was the same corridor he had taken the previous day.

Some distance ahead of him a guttering lamp hung from the timbers shoring up the roof. He rushed onward, cursing the obstacle and the light; one or both might cost him his life. He scarcely slowed in squeezing around the first timber brace, and looked back to see Nephren in close pursuit. The Stygian's lean figure was well-fitted to the high, narrow corridor as he raised his sword to strike.

Instead of throwing himself backward, Conan ducked and hugged the shoring-timber close, stabbing a quick, vicious stroke at Nephren's midsection. His blade met hard resistance there, at the same instant that the other's sword struck the wood where he had been, hewing off a large splinter.

The sudden stresses must have been too much for the planks and the weakened stone. Conan heard a slow, cracking groan from overhead and felt the floor start to crumble beneath him. Then the world tilted up and the light was snatched from before his eyes.

In the brief time before consciousness was likewise snatched from him, Conan's mind retained a single, stubborn image: of Nephren's silk-shirted belly riven by his dagger, bleeding only a thin stream of pale sand and dry, flaking herbs.

Pain and darkness. Silence, constriction, pain. The world had new and unyielding limits; Conan felt as if he lay in the clenched jaws of a great stone beast.

He tried to lift his head, which throbbed even worse with the effort, and felt the coldness of sand trickling down from his cheek. Further movement was forbidden him by a rough, knifelike edge of stone that pressed the back of his neck. He eased his face back down onto jagged rubble.

The patter of gravelly sand continued a while on the rocks beneath him, falling from where it was strewn on his body. He stopped trying to move, wondering all at once who or what might be listening, hunting him. There was no other sound that he could detect—nor any light.

Or was there? Slowly the suspicion came to him that he might be blind. He blinked and twisted his head minutely, trying to catch some hint or crevice of light and seeing none. Yet the throbbing pain in his skull was not in his eyes; it was centered near one temple. So presumably he had sight, but was caught in pitch blackness.

After a further interval of fruitless listening, he tried out his bruised, abraded limbs. Though enmeshed in jagged stone, they were not buried deeply, and he could begin to free them. He used his less constricted arm to explore the area around his neck, aware that one clumsy move might turn the heavy overhanging stone shard into an executioner's blade.

He found a wider space at one side of his head; arching his back until pain racked it, he withdrew himself from the trap and lay panting in relief, cushioned on jagged rock. His next move was cautious; nevertheless it dislodged stones and sent him wallowing headfirst down what must have been the face of the rockslide.

The rubble did not shift far, and most of the sliding pieces were smaller than he was. He brought himself to a halt with both his palms pressed against a flat, cold surface.

He lay motionless once more, waiting for the clatter and trickle of debris to end. Still no sound of pursuit. He dared stretch himself and probe at his injured temple; it was tender but intact, crusted thinly with blood and gravel. Carefully he drew himself forward on hands and knees onto the solid stone.

It was level and tool-worked: no doubt the floor of yet another man-made tunnel. Or a monster-made one. Conan shivered, recalling what Mardak had said about the shafts of older tombs underlying Ebnezub's.

And yet the weakness of the king's tomb may have saved him, for the time at least. With any luck Nephren and his henchmen had been cut off from him or killed in the cave-in. If, that is, the Stygian had not been mortally wounded by his dagger-stroke. If a being with scented sand running in its veins could be killed at all.

Conan shuddered again. What would he not give to be free once and for all of these infernal sorceries and intrigues! He understood now that his assignment to Mardak's doomed work-crew must have been the result of Nephren's chance recognition of him the day before. It had been reported to Horaspes, most likely. And the priest, if not the queen herself, had ordered the transfer to effect his death.

Now, with luck, they would think him dead in the cave-in. And perhaps, after all, they were right. If he wanted to prove them wrong he had better do something. Conceal himself, at the very least.

His dagger was lost, so he groped and found a chisel-pointed stone for protection, clutching it in one bruised hand. Searchers might even now be clearing the passage somewhere above him; at any moment lights might pierce the subterranean dark.

He drew his legs under him and found that they would support his weight, if unequally. He reeled upright only long enough to grope above his head and determine that the ceiling was nowhere in reach, then dropped back to a crouch. There was no guessing the shape or extent of this room, and he dared not make a halloo to gauge it by echo. There was no movement of air, and the only odor was of dry, dusty age. He crept forward, probing for walls or chasms at the limit of his touch.

Beyond the radius of the rockfall the floor was covered only with dust and papery insect husks, the gritty, nameless spoor of centuries. Conan groped cautiously, reminding himself that snakes and scorpions usually lurked near the surface of the land and shunned the deepest caves and tunnels. He did not expect to encounter any living thing here. So he recoiled with shock when his hand brushed over the toes and thongs of a sandaled human foot.

It was made of stone, he knew a moment later, and was heaped with the same ancient dust as the floor. Following up the dusty curve of the ankle, he found that it was a part of a relief on the front of an upright sarcophagus. A gowned, full-length figure—a likeness, no doubt, of the occupant. He reached around the massive box and found the wall it stood against, made of smooth-hewn sandstone. Groping up the length of the carved coffin, Conan raised himself upright to touch the place where the statue's face should be. It was reassuringly human, its square beard rendered in intricately sculptured curls.

An old Shemitish tomb, intact for millennia, perhaps. Conan found no cracks or pry-marks on the coffin. No likelihood that it contained a weapon, though. Doubtless Otsgar would have smashed it open anyway and rifled it then and there.

The thought of his rival made Conan remember his purpose, and he edged along the wall in search of an exit—however unlikely that was in an ancient tomb covered over by the thousands of tons of rock that filled Ebnezub's great pile. He knew there was little chance.

What he found a short distance away was puzzling: a jagged corner to the smooth-carven stone, receding from it at right angles. He ascertained that it was a rough doorway cut into the wall at a level somewhat higher than the floor, and tall enough for a man of his height to walk through if he stooped. The stonework was cruder than that of the broad chamber, with a jagged surface of tool-gouges and protruding ridges; the tunnel was plainly newer.

So the tomb had been robbed after all. With that discovery, the hope of finding an exit freshened in Conan's breast. He stepped up into the rough-hewn burrow and began following it by touch.

Tracing the walls with his hands, he went a dozen careful paces. There were no curves or upward trendings that he could detect, and no branchings. Then his probing foot encountered glassy-smooth stone ahead. He stepped forward into the black vacancy of what his questing fingers soon told him was another tomb.

So the tunnel did not go to the surface, but only communicated between two lightless holes. What insanity was this? His hopes faltered, yet he had no choice but to go on searching.

After making a partial circumference of the room, he came to another rough-hewn tunnel. This one was dug partly into the floor, forming a shallow but treacherous hole at the base of the wall. Judging by its awkward angle and the feel of the toolmarks inside, it had been cut from the far end.

It began to dawn on Conan that whoever had made these tunnels had dug from one tomb to the next, and there was no telling the extent of the maze. But there was hope, for the angles and toolmarks of the shafts told him he was following them back toward their source. Even if the network had only one tiny, concealed entrance, he might find it by using his wits.

He traced the burrows through several more tombs—and then he reached a branching. It was not a chamber but a corridor, its walls surfaced to a rougher finish than the other tombs and coated with plaster which had mostly crumbled away to lie in heaps at the sides. Stamping his sandal on the floor, Conan heard echoes spanging away to left and right, confirming the tunnel-shape of the room.

Good, then, he told himself. A path that might lead somewhere! He started out in the direction that he imagined sloped upward.

Brushing thin trails of plaster from the walls with both hands, he soon had to stop in uncertainty, for there were archways on either side of the passage. But on probing within, he was relieved to find that they were only shallow alcoves, somewhat lower than his own height and shedding plaster the same as the broader corridor. They resembled the niches of a temple or crypt, made to hold statues or coffins, but they were empty.

Farther up the passage, however, he found that the alcoves occurred at regular intervals and were not all vacant; some held shriveled, desiccated mummies wrapped in lacquered bandages that flaked away like dry leaves under his questing fingertips. He did not examine these mortal relics closely, but he had the impression that they were poorly preserved even for ancient carcasses, some splitting open from improper embalming, others bent and twisted like winter twigs.

In spite of the alcoves' shuddersome occupancy, Conan was elated to have found what appeared to be a long-used tomb; that implied the existence of a reusable entrance, and one that might be reached by ramps or stairs rather than by a vertical shaft. Of course, the entry might also have been sealed at some date, or covered over by later constructions. Conan had no idea whether he was even out from under the vast bulk of Ebnezub's tomb yet, or of what direction he was heading. Those details were still imponderable, as was the question of what had happened to the occupants of the empty niches he now passed moment by moment.

He could not have said what made him freeze just then and stand breathless in the dark. It was certainly not a light, for no spark had showed itself other than the ghost-lights inside his skull. It must have been a clink or scrape of metal, or perhaps the scuff of a sandal on stone. His senses were tuned so finely to the silence that it required only the merest suspicion of a sound to alert them. For a long time he listened without hearing anything more. When another hint of noise finally did come—this time identifiable as the rustle of dry fabric somewhere ahead—his response was immediate. He slipped sideways into one of the alcoves, making no greater sound himself.

As luck would have it, it was one of the occupied niches. He crushed its frail, twisted inhabitant back against the wall and waited, afraid to move lest the mummy topple out and betray his presence. There was at least temporary concealment for him here, if only to gain the advantage of ambush over whoever or whatever was coming down the corridor toward him. He took the pointed stone from his waistband and held it ready.

The sounds were faint but definite, seeming to represent the steady progress of several walkers along the corridor. No voices, just measured, scuffing steps with occasional muted clanks, as of weapons or metal tools bundled together, or sacks of tomb-loot. The walkers definitely were drawing near, though it was hard to judge the distance by the soft sounds. Conan's keenest expectation was of finally glimpsing of their light, that most precious of all gems in this inky, mortuary maze.

When it came it would show them to him, and doubtless betray him to them as well. But he wanted it. Feverishly he schemed at how to fight them if need be, yet keep their lamp from going out. He held his sharp stone poised high for mayhem.

Then they were upon him, their scuffings and jinglings passing so near that the hairs on the outsides of his arms tingled. One, two, three . . . five walkers, by his count. Then they were past, their noises receding swiftly—and Conan awoke to the realization that they had carried no light.

The revelation froze him there as their feathery footsteps went on down the passage. What humans could move so surefootedly through darkness? No voices, no sounds of breath or exertion, either; did they even have bodies? Yet he was not blind, he told himself; the darkness must be total, for they had not seen him either. Whatever weird sense they navigated by had not revealed his presence, though he lurked close enough to feel the very breeze of their passing.

Sorcery it was, undeniably; else the walkers were night-beasts of some kind. Conan shifted in unease at the thought.

It was then that he noticed a strange constriction from behind him where he was pressed up so intimately against the withered mummy in the alcove. There was a tight prodding at his shoulders, a twinge he had overlooked in his earlier distraction. Since the passersby were well out of hearing, he stepped forward to shake off the bony relic.

And he found that he could not. It dragged forward with him, its attachment to him tightening perceptibly. Reaching behind, he swallowed an oath—for he found a half-bandaged skeletal hand clutching his shoulder, while that which pinched the skin at the side of his neck was undeniably a half-fleshed pair of jaws. The ancient lich was attacking him!

Conan groped frantically behind his head, unable to get a strong grip. His sharp stone was useless in the cramped quarters, unable to do more than prick his attacker, and so he dropped it. He lurched forward and tried to pull free of the clutching thing.

But it was tough, amazingly tough. Light as a straw husk it felt, its bandages crumbling away like old papyrus; yet underneath lurked hard bones and thonglike tendons that his grasping fingers could not pry back. And all the while Conan struggled, the thing slowly, inexorably tightened its grip, drawing closer against him as if it wanted to creep inside his skin and command his very flesh.

Staggering blindly into the opposite wall, Conan lurched sideways to scrape the clinging mummy off on the edge of the alcove. This forced the gaunt head and body around to where he could begin to shove against them. Again he battered the carcass against the wall and felt some of the ancient ribs shatter, jabbing him with their sharp points.

Yet his skeletal adversary did not seem to mind. He sensed a strange intensity and direction to its clutches as its bony fingers crept down his body. And now, as he pushed the skull-face away from his neck he felt sheaves of long, brittle hair fall from its head and cascade down his arms while his fingers closed over a metal diadem on the bony forehead, which could only have been worn by a female.

Driven by a new panic at the undead embrace, he shoved mightily—and felt the head break off in his hand. It clattered to the floor while he wrenched and twisted desperately at the still-clinging, still-groping body.

When his frenzy ended, the mummy was broken in several pieces at his feet. He stood panting, listening to the silence and vainly trying to brush the corpse-dust from his skin. Then he turned and blundered up the corridor.

More alcoves there were, more darkness, and more dead things that he now dreaded to touch. As he shuffled ahead he knew he was growing careless—knew, too, that his sanity was guttering dangerously low, like the frail flame of a candle lashed by black, sorcerous winds. It would be easy, he realized, to become a mindless, whimpering thing scrabbling with raw fingertips against the walls of these endless tunnels. He paused in a supreme effort to master his emotions.

Then sounds erupted all around him. Rough hands seized him, and a blinding light glared into his face.

Chapter 12

The Raiders' Ploy

The glow of sunrise was like the pink glare from the yawning door of a kiln, warning of the heat that would sear the land by midday. At this early hour the light shone brightest on the eastern walls of the city of Abaddrah and on the ramps and scaffolds of the nearly completed tomb that overshadowed them. But sunlight brushed likewise the distant pyramid-points of the great tombs of Stygia that waited out their vigil across the swollen waters of the Styx. Through the rising river haze the light tinted them red as the tips of heated needles.

By the time Ellael's shining orb rose high enough to throw the shadows of date palms onto the walls of Otsgar's inn, the hostel's gate had been flung wide, and hooves and wheels were clattering into the courtyard. The charioteer's bellows brought servants hurrying to attend his arrival.

"Ho, there, lackeys! See to the horses at once! They're foaming! And be careful carrying in these—ah, spice jars. I don't want the seals broken." Otsgar handed his reins to a stableboy and stepped down from the rear of the chariot as it tilted under his weight. "I've been driving steadily all night. Curse these flooded pig-troughs they call roads! Ah, well, it's a cool bath for me! And a soft, companionable bed!"

Slapping mud from his kilt, he strode through the main

door of the hostelry. He ignored the few early-rising lodgers who loitered in the commonroom.

"Where is my little dancer, Zafriti? I have something for her!" Scanning the mezzanine and the stairs, he brought his gaze to rest on a matronly female servant who stood nearby, looking slightly flustered.

"Sir, 'tis early. The mistress is not arisen yet; she sends word that she will greet you in a few minutes. . . ."

"Not arisen yet . . . a few minutes . . . so that's the way of it!" Otsgar's expression darkened abruptly as he pushed past the woman. "Dallying again, is she? And who is it with this time?" Moving swiftly for one of his size, he mounted the stairs by twos, cursing to no particular listener as he went.

"In my own chamber she cavorts! Who is it, I say? If it's that stripling Asrafel, I'll dangle him by the ears! I know all about him!" He reached the mezzanine and strode across the cedar planks toward a double door.

Without stopping, he thrust one sandaled foot into the midline of the doors. With the sharp crack of a snapping bolt they swung inward, and he continued straight through with a vengeful gait.

The room was plainly occupied, the bed in disarray, the floor strewn with gaudy clothing, but no one was in sight. At the back stood an ornate, four-paneled screen in dark wood and mother-of-pearl, depicting dragon-hunts in Khitai; from behind it Zafriti's voice sang out. "Otsgar, my love, is that you? You are impetuous! If you wait but a moment, I will join you. . . ." By that time the innkeeper had crossed the room and laid his hand on the nearest panel of the screen.

From a distance his recoil might have seemed instant and spontaneous—if one's eye was not quick enough to see the fist that dashed from behind the lacquered wood into his face. An instant later the screen toppled to the floor to reveal Conan, looking scrubbed and sleek, clad in nothing but a somewhat oversized kilt. Fists clenched and face tight with rage, he charged over the fallen partition after Otsgar, leaving Zafriti hurriedly dressing herself in the corner of the room.

Relentlessly the Cimmerian pressed his attack on the reeling innkeeper, darting after him with war-hammer blows whilst evading the bearlike man's attempts to grapple with him. In and out, forth and back his muscle-corded body danced, like that of a blacksmith working at an overheated forge. The impacts of his fists turned the Vanirman left, then right, staggering him time and again.

Then Conan drove forward even more vengefully, wading into his opponent with a rain of punches and kicks that forced the stouter man down to the floor and left him motionless— whether from senselessness or from prudent good sense, it was hard to tell.

"Conan! Don't kill him!" Zafriti had succeeded in partly covering her nudity. Now she ran forward and knelt over the prone man.

"Nay, how could I think of it?" Conan spoke bitterly, massaging his reddened, swollen knuckles. "I've gone easy on him. I know how much you need his wealth, and his skill at business and larceny."

"Every one of us would be roofless without Otsgar," a new voice said from the doorway. Conan wheeled to see Isaiab walk into the room; the Shemite nodded amiably to him. "But that doesn't mean a solid drubbing now and again won't do him good."

Behind Isaiab came Asrafel and two other ruffianly Shemites, new henchmen of Otsgar. Seeing their employer stretched motionless on the floor, they looked startled and uncertain. But they did not draw weapons. Asrafel waved away the servants who stood outside trying to peer into the room. He closed the broken double doors and took a place in front of them.

Otsgar's head, cradled on Zafriti's silk-fringed thigh, stirred feebly. His eyes opened, then his bloodstained lips. "My turtledove, how could you betray me . . . again, so soon . . . and you, Cimmerian!" His eyes rolled upward in his head to fix on Conan's, though his body did not do more than squirm. "They told me you were dead. Out of what pit have you crawled?"

"From the one you cast me into, pig! And I've thought long and lovingly of how to repay you for it."

"I know not what you mean. If you're thinking of our little tomb expedition—well, you were captured then through your own clumsiness."

"Blackguard!" Conan growled at him. "If you had your way I'd have been crushed alive."

"Nonsense." Otsgar's swollen lips blurred his speech. "But if you feel thus and want to settle things, why not do so right now?" Twisting his head weakly in Zafriti's lap, he pulled apart the lapels of his road-soiled leather vest so that a bush of curly blond chest-hair jutted out. "Just kill me and have an end to it—if you think you can!"

"Enough of this bluster!" Isaiab stepped forward and bent over the innkeeper. "It was at my entreaty, Otsgar, that Conan consented not to murder you! He has a business offer that might prove profitable, with your backing."

"Aye, he speaks true," Conan added, his anger subsiding. "If I had not met Isaiab, Asrafel, and these others prowling in the tomb-maze with a dark lantern, I might still be groping there. They've seen the same things I have, and they agree that our chances are good. . . ."

"You were delving in the local tombs in my absence?" At this Otsgar hauled himself up to a sitting position to face Isaiab, shaking Zafriti's lingering hands from his neck. "Are you mad? Do you want to lead the tomb police and holy torturers straight to my door?"

Isaiab shrugged. "You leave us precious little to do lately, with your urgent business affairs. Skilled hands like ours despise idleness, and this sudden boom in your smuggling trade hasn't put much coin in our pockets."

Asrafel interrupted from the doorway. "Otsgar, you should know what we found. There is a network of tunnels connecting the ancient tombs."

"Scavengers' burrows, you mean?" Otsgar waved the issue aside, stopping to rub a sore place under his ear. "Doubtless we are not the first men or beasts to despoil the place. . . ."

"Nay, these are man-sized tunnels cut through solid rock," Conan said. "Do you mean that you know nothing of the furlongs of corridors that travel under the tomb-district?"

Otsgar shook his head slowly and carefully, favoring his sore neck. "I am unaware of anything of the sort. Digging through stone is far too slow and noisy, as any good tomb-looter will tell you. In our prospecting, if we cannot prize open a tomb-entry, we leave it alone. Isaiab knows our methods." He gazed up at the latter man with grudging interest. "Has all the tomb-wealth been hauled away, then?"

Isaiab folded his arms, noncommittal. "Some of the crypts and sarcophagi look untouched and might still have treasures in them. We descended by our old entry through the Crypt of Cats near the north wall, and once we found the tunnels we had to be cautious about making sounds. We did not follow them far before we met Conan, so we carried away no loot. . . ."

"Aye, and if you found a royal dowry you would not tell me of it," Otsgar muttered suspiciously. "But go on."

"Well—a strange influence is at work there; we could sense it all around us. Conan was just escaping from a brush with something. He would not tell us what."

The Cimmerian returned their stares innocently. "It was black as pitch, so I couldn't be sure. I own that there is a certain . . . restlessness there among some of the dead." He stifled a shudder. "But nothing that a well-armed raiding party couldn't handle."

Otsgar nodded uneasily. "Aye. No doubt the result of Horaspes' warding spells. Just one more peril on top of all the rest." He climbed to his feet, using the shoulder of the still-kneeling Zafriti as a crutch. "The more reason for us to forget this petty thievery! If you knaves are restless, I can put you to work running caravans around tariff-posts." Otsgar

looked to Conan. "Even you. If you can learn to comport
yourself with respect in my household, I'll keep you on."

The Cimmerian shook his head. "Are you still dull-witted
from the beating I gave you? Don't you see, these tunnels
will let us carry out my former plan of robbing Ebnezub's
tomb!" Conan reached out a hand to clutch Otsgar, who
sidled back behind Zafriti to avoid him. "I myself went from
the great tomb to the labyrinth without even meaning to. It
shouldn't be hard to find our way back once the king dies."

Otsgar retreated to the bed and sat down, shaking his
head. " 'Tis foolishness even to talk of such things, the way
trade is flourishing just now. Do you have any idea how
much a set of steel chisels from Aquilonia is selling for? Or
jade from Turan, or good Argossean leather for slave-harnesses
and whips? All with steep tariffs, and with bonuses near as
steep for avoiding them! Why, I can make a bigger fortune
from the building of the tomb than from the looting of it!"

"Are you sure of that?" Conan slipped his fingers into the
waistband of his kilt, a gesture which made Otsgar flinch.
However, what the Cimmerian withdrew was not a weapon
but a medallion, molded of lustrous yellow electrum and
patterned with flashing gems. "Part of the treasure of the
great tomb," Conan explained. "I filched it from the outer
mummy-wrappings of one of Ebnezub's petty officials, who
was to be buried with the privileged.

"Thus are even the least of his servants adorned at burial,
as you well know. When he dies, treasures like this will be
squirreled away in his tomb by the thousand-weight."

Zafriti snatched the ornament. "Why, this is lovely! May I
have it, Conan?" At his nod, she placed it against her
half-bare bosom and flounced about, striking poses to model
it before the men's eyes. "Otsgar, Conan is right! We can't
afford to pass up this chance. We can be rich as kings
ourselves!"

Of them all, Otsgar had watched her capering only briefly.
Now he gazed down at the floor with a weary, aching air of
resignation. He rested his chin on his fist for a long while, as

if he saw his fate unfolding in the pattern of the carpet before him. Finally he spoke. "No doubt the retainers' tombs will have such trinkets aplenty. But you know, there will be heavier seals on the king's own hoard."

"Aye." Conan settled down opposite Otsgar on a carven stool, making it creak with his weight. "A bright draftsman named Mardak designed a barrier that we could never have penetrated—a fall of threescore fitted stones, triggered by a sand-clock. While we were working on it, I put a pebble in the reservoir to keep the sand from flowing. But there's no certainty in that. We'd best plan to be on hand the very hour the tomb is closed, so that I can jam the mechanism and make sure of holding open the Royal Chamber."

Otsgar had raised his eyes to Conan; now he watched him with pained amusement. "The knowledge you gained in the tombs makes you useful, Cimmerian. Even indispensable. Yet your scheme calls for extensive scouting and preparation; I can see why you need my backing." He probed thoughtfully at one of his battered cheekbones. "The irony is, you seem to have taken it into your head not to trust me. A difficult situation."

Otsgar stroked his chin in thought, gently touching the painful areas before he spoke again. "To remedy it, here is what I propose. I'll give you a free hand with my men; you need spare no expense in readying a path into the tomb. You lead the missions; I'll stay here and pursue my business. That way, you need not be watching me over your shoulder every moment."

Conan shook his head, smiling grimly. "Nay, Otsgar, none of your guile! I want you with me on every trip to the tombs. Zafriti, too. I know she still fancies such work." He glanced to the woman, whose moist-lipped, animated look confirmed his words. "That way I can be sure you're not selling us to the tomb police."

Otsgar rankled again. "A pox on your unending demands! I already stand to lose more by this folly than the lot of you will ever dream of possessing!" He scanned the faces of his hirelings, who were watching him patiently. "I have half a mind to forget tomb-loot and contraband both, and become an honest innkeeper!"

His gaze settled on Zafriti, who stood jaunty-hipped beside him. The electrum medallion had disappeared into a fold of her wrap; now she reached forward gently to massage his brow. "Very well," he sighed. "I'm in with you—for one-half the take. I only hope you have some inkling of the dangers we face."

That night and the ensuing ones served to cloak a good deal of furtive activity at Otsgar's inn, with many secretive comings and goings. Fortunately the servants were well-paid, and well-occupied with a press of lodgers caused by the continued flooding and the boom in local trade. Otherwise, even though inured to their master's smuggling, they might have guessed the nature of his current project and betrayed him to the tomb police out of sheer terror.

This risk was one the raiders sought to reduce by leaving their tools and dark-lamps away from the inn, hidden in the neglected animal crypt which they used as an entrance to the tombs. They readied an alternate exit through a nearby grave-shaft. And they observed strict caution, traveling between the hostelry and the tomb-district by separate routes and carefully noting the sentries' habits and deployment.

Yet once below ground in the mysterious tunnels, they faced guardians who could not be timed or observed. More than once they had to cower in dark corners while voiceless, rattling crews marched past them unseen. And often their ears caught the distant clink of hammers and chisels echoing down lightless corridors, as the nameless ones labored to extend their labyrinthine underworld.

The raiders, once out of the tombs and free of the need for silence, debated fiercely about the mysterious tunnelers. Whether, for instance, they would be as oblivious to the light of the lamps as they seemed to be to their warmth and their oily, smoky smell. While in the crypts, none dared to find out by unshuttering a light, for the strange creatures seemed to travel in sizable parties, clanking with tools and weapons.

As Conan learned the tunnels near Ebnezub's tomb and began to map them out, it became clear to him that these must be the least-trafficked areas of the maze, perhaps because they were already thoroughly worked out, with the tombs breached, the wealth removed, and most of the caskets emptied.

If, indeed, as Otsgar maintained, the tunnelers were Horaspes' expert looters, raiding the old graves either to furnish the new one or to enrich the chancellor, then it was obvious that their efforts had shifted to the vast and less opulent part of the necropolis lying farther back toward the base of the hills. That was where the noises seemed to originate and where the fresh work-parties were bound.

Regarding the tunnelers' ability to move unerringly without lights—"Horaspes has blinded the lot of them to inure them to the dark," was Asrafel's explanation. "I have heard that when vision is lost the other senses grow keen enough to take its place. And I would not put it past that fiend of a Stygian!"

As to the restlessness of the dead themselves, the raiders encountered no instance of it, and Conan never again spoke of his encounter in the tomb-niche. He did not want to frighten off his helpers or give them another unseen fear to tremble at. He had had brushes with the undead before, Crom knew. Likely the she-thing in the crypt had been some ancient succubus, or a vampiress making a last, desperate effort to imbibe life. Anyway, most of the tombs down here were empty, their crumbling occupants probably swept up and carted away with the rest of the rubble. He told himself that there was little risk of a recurrence.

Thus the raiders passed the time, skulking in tombs by night and sleeping or tossing during the sultry heat of noonday, amid the hubbub of the inn. Conan and Otsgar grew irritable, watching one another constantly and snarling over Zafriti. But the dancer did not seem to mind the attention.

She even provoked the men with sudden displays of affection
for one or the other. The third pawn in her game was Asrafel,
Conan came to see, although since his own return the young
Shemite's part was limited to yearning looks from afar.

All the while Zafriti continued her nightly dances, yet
ventured along boldly with the raiders on their nocturnal
trips. Isaiab plied the customers at the inn for news regarding
the king's health and the progress of the great tomb. Both
sounded promising from the raiders' viewpoint: Ebnezub continued his decline, and work on his resting place was speeded
up accordingly. Another reason for haste was Chancellor
Horaspes' expected summons northward. The emissaries from
Eruk had returned home with a favorable endorsement for the
prophet's teachings; that is, all but one of their party, the
military attache, who had died from a swift, wasting illness
en route. 'Twas divine punishment for blaspheming against
Horaspes' prophecies, the pious gossips said.

On asking after the prophet's knave Nephren, Conan was
disturbed to hear no word of any recent injury to him.
Apparently he was as full of his peculiar, rigid vitality as
ever. In fact, he was lately the focus of much acclaim,
having uncovered a treacherous plot to topple the great tomb
itself by weakening its foundation at certain crucial spots.

The city buzzed with the news. The saboteur, a foreigner
and probably a Stygian agent, had been confronted by Nephren
and had finally perished in one of his own abortive cave-ins
deep under the edifice. But there were continuing rumors
about the incident, including possible links to a captain of the
palace guard and other high persons at court. The chancellor
had promised the king a thorough investigation.

This twisted account gave Conan cause for bitter reflection. He did not doubt that he himself was the so-called
Stygian agent, and that his escape had been slyly used to
cover weaknesses in the tomb and to stir up warlike senti-
ments at court. By surviving, he had placed Princess Afrit in
jeopardy. No innocent child she, but a player with her own

motives; nevertheless he acknowledged his debt to her. Lately she was in his thoughts often.

The question of Nephren's wound was also disturbing. Surely he could not have misjudged the effect of his dagger-blow, not even in the wavering light of the tunnel, with the crushing imminence of the cave-in. Well, then, what if his enemy had worn a protective cumberbund filled with sand? Or a sachet of salts and herbs at his belt, to ward off illness?

No. Conan shook his head solemnly. He was sure his blade had bitten deep. The explanation was sorcery, a sorcery powerful enough to make Nephren, whether human or not, immune even to deftly-handled steel.

The news rankled Conan and strengthened his resolve to stay out of sight. Now, after all, there were any number of Abaddrans who thought him dead. They might view his sudden resurrection as unwelcome.

A pleasant chance occurred for him one evening, as Otsgar was called to the warehouse of a local merchant on pressing after-hours business. Irritated, the innkeeper insisted that Asrafel accompany him. Conan could not go along because of the public nature of the errand, and Zafriti was occupied in her nightly performance. So the harried-looking Vanirman departed, cursing bitterly. When Zafriti's dance ended, Conan was awaiting her in her dressing room to help her shed her bangles and her hot, constricting garments.

After a long, leisurely time of reacquaintance, he questioned the dancer regarding her youth in Stygia. "Did you know aught of Horaspes when you were there? If he is Stygian, why is he so pale?"

"They say he was a slave brought to Pteion in childhood from one of the northern lands. Corinthia, perhaps." Zafriti shifted on her cluttered couch, which had been splinted creak-ily upright since Conan and Otsgar's first fight. "Most of what I know of him is not from my Stygian days. I was young then, and my intrigues were not of the political sort." She gave Conan a sultry smile and reached out to stroke his hair. "Rather I have heard whispers from the southerners

who live here. Even Horaspes' fellow expatriates are leery of
him.

"The cause of his final exile is obscure. But then, so are
most affairs of the Stygian priesthood. 'Tis said he was
ambitious, and that his teachings were well calculated to
divide and weaken his opposition and to draw power firmly
into his grip. Then, as now, he preached resurrection and
afterlife in a daring, frightening way.

"Cunning he was, and adept at magic, but overbold in
challenging a faith that has held sway for thousands of years.
The elder priests renounced him and stripped him of office,
finally marching an army against his temple estates in the
eastern hills, across the river and upstream of here. Even then
he was not beaten." She shifted slightly, drawing up a veil to
protect her bare flank from night drafts. "There is rumor of a
battle, one in which the Stygian Army suffered even heavier
losses than Horaspes' supporters did." She shrugged as if
disclaiming the truth of the tale. "Finally he was forced to
board a boat and float down to Abaddrah. Though it now
appears that his ambitions are too grand for this small city."

"And what of his southern followers? Were they all killed?
The Stygian Army is not to be trifled with."

"A good question. The only retainers I know of who came
with him were Nephren and a few servants. But there were
stories told later." She shrugged the veil tighter around her
olive shoulders and huddled close against Conan. "Otsgar
was involved in river trade then, and he heard rumors of
barges being unloaded by night, east of the city. He went
prowling there with a group of his toughs to head off any
competition. But the only cargoes were human ones, he tells
me: hordes of starved-looking Stygians. Rumor had it that
they belonged to Horaspes. I suppose they became his tomb
builders and embalmers."

Conan grunted. "Or the skulkers we hide from nightly
down in the crypts. An interesting tale—I should ask Otsgar
about it. Though he will want to fight me again, if I mention
you."

"Why worry about Otsgar?" Zafriti purred, stretching herself sinuously beside Conan. "You are twice the man he is."

"You know I do not fear him. Nevertheless I'm leaving before he returns." Conan sat upright on the couch and began to fasten his garments. "In this enterprise our lives depend on smooth cooperation. It will be some time before I can come to a final reckoning with Otsgar."

The Vanirman must have felt the same way, for although Zafriti did not fail to tease him about her meeting with Conan, no violence flared. That night and the ensuing ones the raiders pressed their tomb-explorations further than ever; the spare hours in between were spent sifting their knowledge and elaborating their plan.

Tracing the tunnels close up under the great tomb, they found a half-dozen possible avenues of entry, including the rockfall by which Conan had escaped. This and other cave-ins had recently been buttressed and filled—unsoundly, using rough stones and mortar under a veneer of finished work. The repairs had been done hastily by laborers working from within the tomb, but it was clear that their inadequate efforts had been strengthened later by stronger shorings done from beneath.

"So the massiveness of Ebnezub's tomb is all for show!" was Asrafel's comment, made back in the safety of the inn. "It's a pathetic farce! Anyone who wants to gain entry can do so by scrabbling underneath."

"Likely Horaspes is relying on his spells to protect the underside of the tomb," Isaiab said, giving the others a significant look. "And who knows, they could be just as effective as stone walls. Even as long-lasting. We have not run up against the full force of them yet."

"Whoever these tunnel-diggers are, they're just as anxious to prevent cave-ins as the topsiders," Otsgar observed. "Apparently they want to keep their presence a secret."

And yet there were signs of commerce between the nether world and the upper one. In some places rubble ramps had been built leading up to thin areas in the patching of the tomb-chambers, where it seemed that the barrier might easily be breached. In one such spot the raiders found a rectangular, finished slab that had been set on a hinge-post to form a concealed door. It was stopped on the nearer side by a stone; when they rolled this away and pried open the door, their lamps shone in on one of the corridors of the great tomb. Here was their entry, ready-made.

They dared not explore further that night, but threaded their way out of the crypts with an elation that could barely brook the need for silence. On the way back to the inn, they risked attracting notice by walking together and carousing merrily like drunken revelers. And once there, as the first rays of dawn slanted through the tavern window-slats, they saluted one another with frothing mugs, cheering as Zafriti did a wanton victory-dance. Then, since none of them desired sleep, Otsgar called them into his chamber to finalize their plans.

"I know not what more we need to do, except wait for the fat tyrant to die," Asrafel proclaimed. "On the day of the funeral we hide ourselves in the crypts. Then, as soon as the treasure is laid in and the outer doors are sealed, we slip inside and grab all we can carry. Simple as that!"

"Nay, nay, 'twould be a waste!" Zafriti cried. "We should make many trips, over days or weeks if necessary! Hide the loot in one of the ancient crypts and then smuggle it out at our leisure!"

"But that way we're bound to run afoul of the tunnelers," Conan protested, shaking his black mane. "They have their own plans to rob the tomb, I'll wager. Probably at Horaspes' bidding. Our only chance is to beat them to it. I say we go the first time in force, and not count on going back again." He turned to Otsgar. "Can you find us a few more able thieves who would risk such a venture?"

"Perhaps." Otsgar shrugged away the question. "But be still, all of you. This is taking us nowhere. The heart of the matter is, we must know the layout of the place and not waste precious time blundering about in search of the treasure-rooms." He scowled at Conan. "I'm not going to rely solely on your memory of the tomb and your boasted ability to unseal the king's vault. We need to make one more trip, to enter the tomb itself and scout the place, so that we can plan ahead wisely." He drained his flagon and thumped it down. "Tonight will be as good a time as any."

Chapter 13

The Splendor Passes

"Confound these endless corridors! Why must they carve so many of them?" Conan's complaint was muttered furtively, even though there were no workers visible in the straight reach of passage they were traversing. He and Otsgar had agreed to pretend muteness in order to avoid recognition as foreigners and interlopers in the great tomb.

"Some of them are laid out in ritual designs," Otsgar whispered back. "Others are to carry in cool air and speed mummification." He walked in the midst of the group, grasping the rear handles of a large silver-plated box, while Conan bore up the front of the load. Both men wore stiff, formal waxen wigs to disguise their straight hair; the innkeeper had further sacrificed his blond moustache and chest-hair, and darkened his freckled skin with stain. Apart from this they were clad only in the kilts and sandals of ecclesiastic slaves.

The ark they carried was an ornate trunk from Otsgar's storehouse. Inside, under a layer of fine silk, it contained swords, hatchets, and pry-bars; the raiders had decided it was wiser to keep their tools and weapons out of sight within the great tomb.

"Quiet, you two, here's another turning." Isaiab led the party, walking in ceremonious single file with Zafriti and one of the new men who held a torch high; Asrafel and the other

torchbearer followed behind. They were disguised as a priestess and her acolytes, using chaplets and skirts from the
dancer's costume rack. They must have looked convincing,
for the few guards and workers they had met in their wander-
ings had not challenged them.

"Erlik blast me, now I know where we are," Conan
muttered as he turned the corner. "We climbed too far; ahead
is the central gallery. You're in for a sight."

Indeed, they soon emerged from the narrow passage onto a
railless ledge running around the walls of a vast subterranean
room. From a larger tunnel mouth ahead of them, at the
center of the gallery, a steep, massive stone ramp led down
to its floor, where more tunnels gaped. Smoky flames licked
up out of tall brass urns placed around the chamber, lighting
the scene dimly and infernally.

As they stepped forth onto the mezzanine, Conan glanced
upward toward what, mere days ago, would have been a vista
of sky or stars. Now it was a vast, shadowy stone ceiling,
vaulted solidly over as the tomb neared completion.

The place was well-conceived to create an effect of awe-
some vacancy. A sprinter would have become winded running across its floor, which stretched a dozen man-heights
below; and its ceiling soared twice as far overhead. During
this final stage of construction the place served as a work-
room, lined with tables and stacks of building material. Even
at this late hour, hundreds of laborers trod its long aisles by
special dispensation of Ellael's high priests.

Seeing that no listeners were near them on the ledge,
Conan risked speech again. "This gallery is the very heart of
the tomb. That centermost tunnel below leads to the Royal
Chamber; the one at the top of the ramp continues up to the
great entry doors."

"Look there! Gilded coffins!" Zafriti moved close to the
sheer ledge, attracted by the gleaming sarcophagi which were
lying on trestles close beneath them.

"Aye," Isaiab said, "but they're too big to carry away.
The gold would have to be stripped from them and melted

down." He gestured to a line of workers who bent over stone slabs with draped forms lying on them. "Yonder are embalming tables, where the innards of the deceased are plucked out and put into jewel-decked caskets. Sand and spices are poured into the mummy's paunch in their place, according to Horaspes' latest teachings." The Shemite resumed his affected, priestly gait as he walked forward along the ledge. "Then, on yon tables, the skin is lacquered over many times and wound with layer after layer of cloth, with gems and scarabs tucked between the layers like raisins in a sweetcake. . . . By the way, where are we going?"

Otsgar grunted from behind. "That ramp is the shortest way down, by my reckoning."

At this Isaiab grew silent, continuing forward with noticeable reluctance.

"At last, a real test of our disguises!" came Asrafel's nervous comment from the rear.

The Shemite spoke true, for there was continual traffic on the incline ahead. Accordingly they squared up their formation and walked with more dignity and purposefulness so that none would dare to stay them. Briskly, with eyes straight ahead, they passed between the two lamp-urns that blazed at the near side of the tunnel-mouth and turned down the great ramp.

"Back, you!" Suddenly gruff voices barked at them from the tunnel. "Clear the walk, there! Let no man obstruct the way!"

Startled, Conan looked around and saw the stern faces and crested helmets of six palace guards. Behind them came a larger descending group, but because of the tunnel's angle he could see only their feet.

Obediently he pressed aside, crowding back the weapon-box and Otsgar with it, while Zafriti and her escort scurried alongside him. In a moment they bunched on the terrace out of the way of the ramp, with a pair of guardsmen deploying stiffly in front of them. They peered over the guards' armored shoulders to watch the rest of the procession emerge from the tunnel.

The closely-grouped men following the troops were litter-bearers, who carried on their shoulders the long poles of a heavy sedan-chair. They walked barefoot, doubtless for the sake of their owner's smooth ride; in addition they stooped low in an uncomfortable crouch, so as to keep the head of their passenger from scraping the ceiling of the tunnel. Soon he came into view, lounging heavily against the backrest of the roofless conveyance, and the watchers gasped at the sight. For it was none other than His Royal Splendor, King Ebnezub of Abaddrah.

The monarch was even more unwell than when Conan had last seen him. His sparsely-clad bulk hung slacker now, with a dropsical look, and his skin had taken on the yellow pallor of jaundice. Yet a feverish glow of excitement lit his face, his small bright eyes drinking in the wonders all around as he lay propped in his padded litter.

As the king's high headdress cleared the rim of the tunnel his dozen bearers halted at a sharp command. The slaves, visibly taxed by the steep descent, used the interlude to stretch their cramped bodies and adjust the unwieldy weight of chair and king on their shoulders.

Conan, crouching among his fellows to avoid recognition, heard Asrafel muttering at his side. " 'Tis the tyrant himself. The greedy, murderous beast!'' The youth's treasonous mumblings were dangerously loud. Conan, still hampered by the burden of the chest, could only jostle him sharply and scowl in warning.

The officer of the guards turned back from the head of the ramp to address Ebnezub in a worried tone. Evidently he was concerned about the steepness of the road ahead.

"Nay, proceed!" the king croaked in reply; he even lifted one heavy hand and wagged it vaguely forward. "Let me see my own tomb this once with living eyes, before I am crated away in it!''

Dutifully the officer turned back to the incline, shouting

again to clear the last, hesitant walkers from the path. Then he barked an order and started down. The bearers followed him mincingly onto the ramp, which, although bordered only by ankle-high curbs, was grooved for traction and adequately broad for them. Those in the rear stooped low once again to compensate for the steepness of the slope, while the leaders raised the litter-poles high overhead in their hands; thus, on its descent, the king's platform canted only slightly forward.

When the chair was safely past, the last guards abandoned the mezzanine and fell into step behind it. Conan watched it go, exhaling in relief. Suddenly a booming clang dinned close at his side, and drops of scorching liquid stung his bare legs.

One of the great bronze lamps had overturned; now it rolled and wobbled across the stone, gushing forth a flood of smoking-hot oil. Luckily the torrent was not thick enough to overtop Conan's sandals and scald his feet. Its main flow was directed away from his party, toward the ramp where the royal party descended. The stone swiftly darkened with the spreading carpet of fuel, across whose surface blue ghost-flames raced.

Conan dropped the cumbersome chest and shoved his way clear of the other raiders, whose yelping, hotfooted rushes had been pushing him toward the brink of the mezzanine. He looked back toward the cataclysm just in time to see Asrafel dash forward and set a sandaled foot on the bulging belly of the second bronze urn. Yelling wildly, the Shemite kicked it over beside the first.

"This for you, drowner of my father!" he shrieked. "Death to the tyrant! May you drown and burn at the same time!"

A new gush of oil joined the first, turning it into a smoking flood whose rivulets now reached the guards at the rear of the king's party. They had gone less than halfway down the ramp, which was too lofty to jump from; all at once they began howling and leaping to avoid the torrent. They could neither stand still nor crowd downward. Some hopped onto the smooth curb with their oil-slicked soles, but they inevitably lost their footing and fell screaming over the side.

As the searing flood reached the unshod litter-bearers, some made a heroic effort to stand and hold up the sedan, but no human could bear such pain for long. The final stroke was the sight of the second, still-flaming bronze lamp belling and oscillating down the rampway toward them. Amid a chorus of yells the bearers bolted, and the litter slewed to one side, tipping the king's enormous body outward into vacant space. Twisting, it plummeted down the side of the ramp to strike with a thud atop a pile of building-slabs, sending workers scurrying back from the impact. Several bearers fell along with the king, accompanied by the chair, which splintered when it hit. The rest of those on the ramp went leaping or tumbling down its length to escape the bounding, clanging urn.

"Huzzah, huzzah, for the downfall of the mighty!" Asrafel shrieked in defiance as he capered gaily at the edge of the porch. "The great villain is dead! Now shovel him into his coffin!"

Isaiab tugged frantically at his arm. "Hush, fool, you'll betray us!" He gazed down at the upturned, outraged faces among the milling mob on the gallery floor. "Not that there's much chance we've escaped their notice so far."

"Arm yourselves and get moving!" Conan threw off the lid of the raiders' toolchest, hurriedly handing out swords to the others. Zafriti reached in and took out a puny dagger, which looked as if it might serve for suicide if little else.

Otsgar grabbed Asrafel by the scruff of the neck and dragged him away down the ledge. "Come along, you mad zealot!" he grated. "I don't want you taken! You'd be traced to me, even dead. Else I'd throttle you right here!"

"Why should you be so wroth?" Asrafel demanded. "The great buffoon is dead! Now you will not need to wait so long to rob his tomb!"

Isaiab wailed at him, "Aii, you fool, he would have died

within the week in any case! Why couldn't you just let him waste away?''

''If he is well and truly dead!'' Otsgar glanced backward at the shouting throng which now obscured the site of Ebnezub's fall. ''If so, and if by a miracle we manage to escape unrecognized, I would not dare venture back to rob him. All our plans are at an end!''

As they argued, they straggled hurriedly along the ledge. The few tomb-workers on the opposite flank of the mezzanine, driven away initially by the hot oil, continued to hang back in fear of the assassins, so there was no close pursuit. But in the gallery below, the officers of the guard were starting to brave the oil-slippery treads of the ramp with angry shouts, while other alarmed voices echoed from the upward tunnel; these things added fleetness to the raiders' steps.

Fresh trouble lay ahead, for a half-dozen priests and guards raced to intercept them along the ledge that followed the intersecting wall of the gallery. There was no chance of beating them to the tunnel-mouth. Hurling aside his waxen wig, Conan dashed forward to be first into the fray.

The attackers had to face him by ones or twos on the narrow ledge, and they hardly stood a chance, for he went among them like a wolf among lambs. He broke the sword of the first man, then gutted him; the second he gut-stabbed without bothering to meet his sword. The third, an armed priest, went down with a slashed leg and fell over the side, failing in his frantic effort to cling to the edge of the balcony, which was slippery with his own blood.

In all, those who threw themselves from the ledge fared better than those who stood before Conan's ravaging sword; by the time he gained the tunnel-mouth two more broken, bleeding human wrecks lay in the angle of the wall. With none left before him, he stood aside to let the other raiders enter the passageway.

''Well, you have hogged the fight so far,'' Otsgar panted

as he shoved Asrafel past the Cimmerian. "Are you going to handle the rear guard as well?"

"Aye, but I'll be close on your heels to guard against your treachery," Conan said. "Now go swiftly lest we reveal the secret way to our pursuers."

But after a breathless sprint down narrow passages, he and Isaiab closed the panel and quietly rolled the blocking stone before it, having seen no further sign of pursuit. Not waiting to learn whether their exit could be traced, they struck out into the blackness of the crypts.

Their flight was shadowy and treacherous, for one of the torches had been dropped, and Otsgar had not paused to kindle the dark-lamps. To Conan, something more seemed amiss. Some unidentifiable threat brooded in unseen corners, making the very air around them heavy with menace.

As he followed the single bobbing torch-flame far ahead, he smelled the tangy scent of his own fear for the first time that night. He heard scurryings and scrapings converging down lightless tunnels behind him, and whenever he paused, he sensed the brooding stillness of a black leopard about to pounce. He rushed the others along with urgent prods and whispers, refusing to say why, until, without apparent cause, they were all stumbling and panting through the jagged maze.

When finally they crept out into starlight, Conan wedged the crypt door shut tightly behind him. He felt as if he had just escaped a peril far greater than the sword of any foe.

Chapter 14

The Trumpets Wail

The days following the king's death were a time of strange, muted excitement in the city. Commoners walked the streets in mourning garb, with hair cropped close and faces daubed with blue antimony or black charcoal as the ancient laws required. Yet most of them went briskly or even enthusiastically, involved in urgent preparations for the grandiose funeral rites to come.

Over all sounded the chanting of the priests and the incessant shriek of brazen horns lamenting Abbadrah's loss, and celebrating the glory of His Royal Splendor's passage into eternity. The high priests declared a period of fasting, though a fast could scarcely diminish the sparse diet of the poor farm folk driven hither by floodwaters. The decree served instead to whet their appetites with thoughts of the lavish feasting the funeral would occasion.

The royal tomb, which in recent months had loomed ever vaster just beyond the city wall, now began to diminish as the workers attacked its sides, pulling away the earthworks and scaffolding from its finished gray stonework. The shape which emerged to the watchers' eyes was austere: a lofty, squarish vault with steeply sloping sides, curving shoulders, and a pyramid-point at its top. The tall, narrow, double doors of bronze—the massive jaws that were mystically to swallow

the departed sovereign in this world and spew him forth in
the next—faced eastward toward the city and were visible
from the whole length of the western wall. The folk of
Abaddrah took comfort in the knowledge that, on clear days,
this massive pile would be as prominent and intimidating to the
Stygians across the river as the southerners' huge monuments
were to them.

As the wooden shorings and cranes were pulled down from
the tomb, they were thrown into four great piles, one at each
corner of the edifice. These, by priestly decree, were set
alight each night, so that their towering flames gleamed redly
on the sweating backs of the crews who toiled there perpetu-
ally. During the long, sultry days the smoke remained, hanging over the city in a yellowish pall.

All the while Conan remained in hiding in a secret room at
Otsgar's, listening to the incessant blatting of the temple
horns. After one day of cautious waiting with no sign of
detection, the other raiders had been able to venture down-
stairs and into the streets without fear. Zafriti even continued
her nightly dances. Of them all, it was Conan who was
named by the priests' proclamation as a spy and saboteur,
and who was most likely to be recognized.

"If only we could dispose of you, Cimmerian," Otsgar
told him, "that is to say, spirit you quietly away from
Abaddrah," he hastily amended. "Why then there would be
no link between my people and the king's death." The
innkeeper shook his head regretfully. "But fear not; I will
provide for all your needs until we can smuggle you safely
out of here."

Conan made no reply he was well aware of his inconvenience to Otsgar. To avoid being stabbed or poisoned by his
protector, he had slept little and eaten less since his escape
from the tomb. Now, listless and dispirited, he slumped low
in his wicker seat at the back of the shadowy room.

" 'Tis you and not Asrafel they are blaming for Ebnezub's
death, you know," the Vanirman continued, seating himself
near an untouched tray of food on a low wooden table at the

center of the room. "Some of the tomb-workers recognized you as the notorious Stygian agent the authorities sought."

Conan shrugged, finally finding a voice for his gloom. "And what matters it, after all? 'Tis better that I be charged with the killing than hotheaded young Asrafel, who was only avenging his kinsman's death." He shifted desultorily in his seat, rustling the wicker. "Crom knows, they've already heaped me with enough false accusations. I may as well hang for the slaughter of a fat, lolling ox as for a nonexistent goat!"

He tipped his protesting chair back against the mud-brick wall with a speculative look in his eye. "In fact, with so little to lose, I may as well add to the stakes. I'm tempted to go forward with our theft plan. What think you of that?"

Otsgar smiled, shaking his head with incredulity at the shadowed figure. "By Ishtar's spangled teats, Cimmerian! You are surely mad! To be haunting the tomb-district now, with all the hue and cry that is afoot . . ." He paused and shrugged. "In a few months, perhaps a year, when things have cooled down . . ."

"Who are you fooling, Otsgar?" The Cimmerian's eyes glinted from the shadows. "We both know you'll be ransacking the place yourself the moment I'm dead or fled. But by then the richest treasure will be lost to you."

He stopped speaking at the sound of a sharp, coded knock on the chamber door. The innkeeper arose to unlatch it, admitting Zafriti and Isaiab through a portal that was a hinged section of finely carved paneling. As he closed it again, the dancer spoke enthusiastically.

"The news is good. The royal guards have no inkling how we escaped, nor where to seek us. Of course, they claim to be close on our trail, but that's just to appease the populace."

"Be not too sure." Conan spoke from his place in the shadows. "It would not surprise me if Horaspes can trace our path through the crypts or even beyond them, by supernatural means."

"If he knows that much, he's keeping it to himself,"

Isaiab said. "Who can tell, he may not even truly want to catch us. He has the court in enough of a frenzy now, denouncing our venture as a sorcerous Stygian plot."

"Aye, and the people are in a fervor over the tomb's completion and tomorrow's funeral." Zafriti sank gracefully to the floor beside Otsgar, resting an arm on his knee. "They mob the palace, petitioning the queen to have their newly buried relatives exhumed and laid in as Ebnezub's retainers. A dozen or more young soldiers have drowned themselves in the temple pool so that they can go to the grave with their king and serve him in the Afterworld." She shook her raven curls in amazement. "Even in Stygia we were never that bedazzled. The priests declared who would man the tombs, and none volunteered."

"You mentioned the queen," Conan put in. "Do you mean the old queen or the new?"

"The old and the new—they are one and the same!" Zafriti spread her hands. "The succession is well established, both by the king's own choice while he lived and by acclamation of the court. Nitokar rules Abaddrah, or shall, when the funeral and coronation are past. And I offer condolences to those who thought Ebnezub a callow leader!"

"What of the princess?" Conan asked from his distant seat.

Zafriti laughed lightly. "Another casualty of the royal skirmishing, I fear! Of course, she might have saved herself, had her name not been linked to treason."

"Treason? What do you mean?" The front legs of Conan's chair thumped to the floor as he sat upright.

"Why, the scheme of sabotage that Nephren uncovered, involving the guard-captain Aramas—and yourself, Conan, if I recall. Afrit was tied into it just before Ebnezub's death, on the evidence of a scrap of green cloth found in the depths of the tomb. Did you know that?"

"No, I had not heard." Conan gazed darkly at her.

"Well, the king exempted her from punishment on the grounds of his great fatherly affection. But the scandal has cost her any backing she might have mustered at court.'' The dancer glanced bright-eyed around the group, clearly relishing her account of misfortune in high places. ''Normally, you know, under Abaddran law, Nitokar would have been sent forward with Ebnezub to attend to his kingly comforts in paradise. But now, by his royal will, Afrit will have that privilege. And poor Nitokar will have to accept the dreary burden of queenship!''

''Confound it, woman, speak plainly!'' Conan was leaning forward out of his chair. ''You mean that Afrit is to be entombed with the king?''

''Indeed. By his command she is to be placed in the tomb alive, so that her fine young body will remain unmarked. She will be bound to his coffin with chains of gold.''

Isaiab chimed in, ''Aye, the queen has connived well. Now the crown will pass to her son, Eblis, who, though only of tender years, bodes to become an even more tyrannical leader than his mother!''

''It matters little.'' Otsgar threw down a fruit-core and belched. ''I can do business under any Abaddran monarch. The important thing is, the crime has not been traced to us. Not yet, at least. Now if we only lie low a while longer . . .''

''Lie just as low as you can cringe,'' Conan growled from the shadows, ''and curse you for a scheming Vanirman!'' Clutching his sword-hilt he sprang to his feet. ''But know you, I'm going to be at the tomb tomorrow as we planned! Afrit saved my life after the lot of you forfeited it, and I will not let her be tombed-up alive!'' He glared fiercely at the others' startled faces. ''I'll save her, or I'll kill her myself if need be!''

''Let go of that pig-slicer and sit back down.'' Surprisingly, Otsgar's reaction was steady and solemn, without a show of rage. ''I care nothing for your light-o'-loves, Conan. None of us here does. Understand me—we could never let you set forth on such a mad venture. You would be caught and tortured, or else your flight would draw the pursuit back

to us." He shook his head patiently, almost wearily. "It
would pose the gravest risk to all our lives, don't you see?"

"Are you so keen a judge of risk?" With a sudden rasp of
steel, Conan drew from its sheath the sword he had not let go
of for two days. "I'll give you risk! If you want to stop me,
do it now!" He gazed at them across the blade, with glints of
battle-lust in his eyes. "Or else wait, and betray me to the
tomb police, if you think I would not tell them fully of your
own crimes!" He leered at the three with a smile that danced
on the brink of madness. "Or come along with me, and make
yourselves rich! We know the way, and the preparations have
all been made. What is your choice?"

Otsgar sat with his hand on his dagger, glaring at Conan.
Zafriti looked up at her employer with what might have been
a veiled excitement in her dusky face. Isaiab twitched his
shoulders uncomfortably, saying nothing.

"In any event I'm going tonight, with or without you."
Conan faced them, unflinching. "Hinder me at your peril."

Chapter 15

Doors of Eternity

On funeral and coronation day, the folk of Abaddrah thronged the avenue that led from the palace through the west gate of the city. Nearly every soul of the kingdom was present, most of them tillers of the soil, many with their possessions wrapped in tattered bundles and their water-swapes propped over their shoulders. For although, as if by divine concession, the flooding of the Styx had begun to decline on the night of Ebnezub's death, nevertheless the waters were still high, and the peasants had delayed their homeward journeys until after the royal obsequies could be held. By midmorning their swarms were large enough to overflow even the broad, newly-cleared area before the great tomb, so that they trailed up onto the raised banks of the nearby canals.

Over the crowd hung an air of awed respect, for they knew they witnessed the passing of a being whose nature they could barely conceive, as remote and splendid to them as the sun. Soon, moreover, they would witness the ascendancy to the throne of another such mysterious demigod. The nobles, too, wore looks of devout contemplation and prayer as they filled out the funeral cortege in the palace courtyard or waited atop the city wall. For they knew that the transition of power from a mad king to a mad queen, orchestrated by a fanatic chancellor, gave rise to many opportunities for lavish gain, many chances of swift ruin, and much uncertainty in general.

When finally the procession issued from the courtyard and moved along the avenue, the throng pressed back without unseemly clamor or jostling. A phalanx of royal guards walked in the lead, stepping to the rattle of ivory drums, and the look of serene determination on their faces was enough to clear the street without any need for halberds or truncheons. These were elite volunteers on their way to a tomb-chamber specially blest by Horaspes. They would be sealed up alive there, to be set free by the king on the Day of Doom and lead his conquests in the Afterworld.

Behind them came more military equipage—encoffined nobles and officers, horses and grooms, rumbling chariots laden with the crated remains of their drivers, ranks and files of archers' and spearmen's coffins borne by foursomes of hurrying slaves, with the owner's weapons bracketed atop each mummy-case. All the carefully preserved martial dead of recent years were here, augmented by a good many newly-dead recruits. The spectacle caused an excited murmur in the crowd, whose pride was deeply stirred at the sight of their city's military might.

Stores and provisions followed—lowing flocks of scented, beribboned sheep and cattle, wainloads of camp furniture, slaves carrying baskets of food and urns of drink, slaves dragging the brightly-daubed coffins of slaves. On and on the parade unfolded, a show of more wealth than most of the watchers would otherwise have glimpsed in their entire lifetimes.

And that was but the merest prelude. Now came the king's own belongings. His golden, gem-glittering, little-used chariot, drawn by six matched silver-dappled horses. A scale model of the royal barge, big enough to have sailed across the Styx in its own right, carried high by twoscore slaves and laden with gold-encrusted furniture, exquisitely enameled and inlaid. Then came three resplendent coffins of favorite concubines, borne by transparently-gowned female slaves who sang dirges as they went. And finally, King Ebnezub himself.

It was as well, perhaps, that the king's litter had been demolished on the occasion of his death, for a larger one was needed to bear him in his massive coffin. This conveyance was more than twice as long, sustained on stout shafts which nevertheless curved visibly beneath their tremendous burden of sarcophagus and monarch, so that the centermost bearers, although the shortest, were forced to stoop low.

To make matters worse, the privilege of bearing the ruler to his grave was one traditionally allotted to favored nobles. These worthies were neither accustomed nor inclined to such heavy labor, and now, decked in their brief, humble pallbearer's kilts, they looked unequal to the task. Fortunately their ranks had been filled in with hardy slaves whose shoulders bore up most of the weight. This allowed the aristocrats to stumble along beneath the litter with a semblance of their habitual dignity.

Fortunately for them, it was the coffin itself that caught the eyes of the crowd. It was a true splendor, a gleaming carapace of platinum and gold, as astonishing for its craftsmanship as for its size and richness. So exquisite was the polish of its surface that, in the intense radiance of the morning sun, few could stand to gaze on it for long. Of those who did, some were fated to see its ghostly outline shimmering before their eyes for days and nights thereafter; a few, it was rumored, were struck totally blind. Anyone who so much as glimpsed it gasped in awe. As its mirrorlike rays washed over the crowd, a stir of excitement passed alongside and after it like the boiling wake of a many-oared galley.

Because of its stunning effect, little attention was paid to what came immediately after, a barefoot young woman clad from shoulders to knees in a paltry shift and laboring slightly under the weight of the golden fetters dangling from her wrists, ornaments which both matched and strangely belied the jeweled gold of the royal diadem resting on her brow.

She walked resolutely with head slightly bowed, keeping her eyes averted from the blazing glory of the royal casket.

By her side went one in even worse straits, wearing a soiled, tattered robe: a once-robust young man broken by torture, who could now barely shuffle his legs apace with the others, and whose weight was supported by slaves walking at either shoulder. From time to time the young woman moved close to him, clasping his hand or touching his dangling arm as if to comfort him. But he showed no awareness of her.

Any of the watchers could have explained that this was Afrit, the king's daughter, and that she was being punished for a treasonous conspiracy along with the former guard-captain, Aramas, who had aided her. Few of them cared about the matter one way or the other, in hate or compassion. On this day of wonders, this day of mighty destinies, she was simply too small and powerless to hold their interest.

In any event their attention was quickly diverted from the captives by what came next: Queen Nitokar, calling out greetings and strewing silver and copper coins from her own litter. The queen was arrayed to show off her earthy charms most favorably, with her mourning garb abbreviated to a low, stringy garment of sequined black and her customary eye-paint darkened in respect for the deceased. She did not look unduly stricken or mournful, but flung the coins wide with extravagant sweeps of her arm, leaning out over the crowd and eliciting their hails and cheers as they dove for her bounty. Her chair was low and light, built for speed and carried easily by six handsome, high-stepping male slaves.

And so the procession continued, with lesser nobles heading up trains of their tomb-gifts for the king. Additional ranks of guards brought up the rear, these walking more lightly than the foremost ones in the assurance that they would be coming back this way again after the ceremony.

Many noted the absence of Chancellor Horaspes and his servant Nephren from the funeral. The official explanation was that the prophet was working in solitude, finalizing important spells to safeguard the royal succession. Yet rumor held that he had already departed for the richer city-state to northward, having lost interest in Abaddrah now that his grand project here was complete.

In any case the people took in the procession avidly, thronging to follow it as it passed toward the city's west gate; this portal, though not as grand as the main one, opened toward the tomb-district and was used primarily for funerals. Soon the parade was threading into the great plaza at the edge of the tomb precincts, pressing back the crowds and sending them climbing the levees for a view.

From there, as from the city wall, marchers and crowd alike were dwarfed by the bulk of the great tomb. They swirled before it like a shallow tide eddying around a lofty sea-crag. Its near-vertical sides loomed gray and forbidding, broken only by the tall, vertical recess of the doorway at the front. Toward this Ebnezub's gleaming coffin was borne like a silver vessel afloat on a seething human surf.

As the procession neared the tomb, trumpets blared around its base. There came a deep groaning of metal and a grinding of winches from within. The great bronze doors, thick as a man's body and sculptured with friezes of the glories of Ebnezub's reign, began to swing open—the last time they would do so in this eternity, it was whispered by the onlookers.

The portals clanged wide just as the soldiers at the head of the procession reached the threshold. They passed into the black crevice with the accompaniment of a new fanfare. Cheers and lamentations alike rose from the watchers, echoing between tomb and city walls in a vast and growing murmur, until the royal sarcophagus itself reached the archway and was swallowed in shadow.

Once inside the tomb, the military contingents and stores were dispersed to their various chambers. The difficulty of carrying the huge coffin down the sloping tunnels had been foreseen; fresh slaves waited inside the tomb to relieve the panting nobles of their labor. Even so the great endeavor went arduously, blocking all traffic in the main passage and frequently halting the progress of the rear elements of the procession.

It had furthermore been resolved not to risk a repetition of Ebnezub's fatal mishap on the ramp. When the royal coffin arrived at the central gallery, it was made fast to ropes and lowered slowly down the incline on wooden skids.

More delays arose in the lower tunnel, and worse ones yet when the gleaming coffin reached the Royal Chamber, whose walls were now stacked high with treasure, and whose deep blue ceiling glinted in the lamplight like a star-jeweled dusk. Once borne into the sumptuous room, the coffin had to be lifted into the even more massive stone sheath of the outer casket and the locking stone lid lowered into place. Eventually, at the cost of crippling injury to a number of slaves, the task was complete, the fierce beauty of the sarcophagus quenched in cold stone. By that time Queen Nitokar was in a fury.

"Hurry, you wretched lackeys!" she railed at the gift-bearing servants. "Deposit your trinkets swiftly and go!"

Having sent her sedan and its bearers to wait in the central gallery, the queen stalked back and forth across the richly inlaid floor of the Royal Chamber. She was an imposing figure in her black halter and short, scalloped skirt, teetering on built-up sandals. She had kept the long, straight whip she used to speed her litter-boys; now as she prowled she flicked it left and right, dispensing cuts to the scurrying slaves as liberally as she had earlier dispensed coins.

"Much use this bric-a-brac is to me. Let it rot down here beside that fat lout!" She gave the foot of the stone coffin a swipe with her switch. "Fie, I am sick to death of loitering in these drafty tombs. I have a city to rule!"

"My queen, might I suggest . . . a degree of restraint in these sacred precincts, on this hallowed day?" Her one courtly companion in the chamber was a high priest of Ellael, a sequin-gowned man, tall and potbellied, who now hovered tentatively at her elbow.

"Restraint? Fool, what restrains a monarch?" Nitokar

whirled and raised her crop as if to slash it at his cheek. When he flinched away from her she laughed. "No, Priest, you need not fear. I am the very mistress of restraint. But if my nervous state disturbs you, then leave! Go survey the other chambers. I will send for you when this one is ready to be sealed."

"Your Splendor, my place is here with you and the king."

"Nay, run along." She took a further step toward him, and he retreated. "Don't let your priestlings skulk at the doorway, either. I wish to be left alone with my honored daughter, to bid her a last farewell." She watched the priest as he backed toward the entry, bowing and scraping his way out.

Then she turned to the head of the great coffin, where Princess Afrit knelt, desolate and silent. Her brown curls rested against her shackled wrists, which were suspended at shoulder height by heavy gold chains passed through an aperture of the stone casket. Her face was tearless, and pale as the fabric of her smock, showing a composure born of utter resignation.

"And so, my child, you will soon be rid of me for good. Rid of everyone, in fact, and of all the cares of the outer world, except your doting father." She patted the bulging belly of the stone casket at her side. "And excepting, of course, that wretch over there, your coconspirator in your treasons against me. You may talk and plot with him for as long as your breath lasts. He and I have already had long and interesting discourse." She pointed with her slave-crop to the crooked, slack-mouthed figure of Aramas, seated against the nearby wall and chained with iron anklets to a gilded stone block. He sat in a bandy-legged crouch, exposing discolorations and ill-healed gashes on his arms and shins that hinted at the suffering he had been through.

" 'Tis a harsh thing indeed for a young girl to connive against her parents," Nitokar went on, ignoring the slaves who still came and went bearing treasure. "What made you so hard, my child? I wish I'd had more time with you, to win your respect, if not your love, by my motherly care—and by a firm program of discipline.

"Discipline can do wonders, you know. As with that young fellow there—Aramas, is it? He was sullen and unco-operative at first, hardened by you in faithlessness to his rightful rulers. But before long he was whimpering to reveal his secrets. Pleading, even screaming out your name to me at the top of his voice! Oh, I have a winning way with young men!

"I could have done much for you as well, but your father would never give me a free hand. He wanted you kept inviolate. Even in death he has decreed that you go unpun-ished and unscathed. Much he can do to enforce it now!" Nitokar laughed and lashed out with her switch, stinging the girl across the arm; Afrit sucked in her breath sharply and clasped her hand over the burning welt.

"But, Princess, what is this? When the king's tribunal decided your fate, we said nothing of a garment for you to cower in! Off with it!" With a feral lunge Nitokar seized the hem of Afrit's shift and wrenched. Most of the thin fabric tore away in a long shred, while the girl screamed and writhed, straining at her wrist-chains. "There! Now try to hide your shame!" Nitokar darted in again with her lash, laying a flurry of strokes across the princess's naked legs and back. "This is what you should have had, when first you bore tales against me to your father—and this, and this, and this!" The princess dodged left and right, kicking out wildly once or twice at her tormentor, but was helpless against the lashing of whip and spiteful tongue alike. Finally the blows subsided, and Afrit sank down against the base of the coffin, sobbing.

"Well, what are you staring at?" Nitokar wheeled on a pair of slaves, male and female, who had lingered with startled expressions on seeing the princess's chastisement. She raised her switch to them, screaming at their backs as they hurried out. "When I am queen, you must learn to be blind as well as dumb!"

Nitokar would not let her frenzy subside. She now turned to the broken Aramas, who for the first time had raised his eyes as if in awareness of his surroundings. "And you—are you ready to woo me again? Well, here is my kiss!" She bent and slashed her whip across his face; wordlessly he averted his gaze, not even raising a hand to protect himself.

"You see, my child! There is devotion!" She turned to leer at Afrit. "No slinking hound could be better trained. Just give me time. . . . But who is this?" The queen turned once again to the door, where a man in the uniform of the tomb police had appeared. "I have no need of guards! I am in command here!"

"So you thought, haply for me." The intruder glanced back through the archway and gave a nod of assurance to someone outside. Then he turned to the queen, drawing his sword with a steely hiss. He was a large man, strongly muscled under his thin gray cloak, yet he moved with the grace of a mountain cat.

" 'Tis you, Conan! The meddling fugitive!" Nitokar's voice mounted shrill with fear and rage. "Guards! Guards! Come hither! Here is the assassin!"

Conan only gave a rumbling laugh, making no move to silence her. Behind him two heads in palace guard helmets peeked in at the door. But instead of rushing to the queen's aid, they moved to the chests and tables along the walls and began to rake treasures into sacks. "Aye, dogs," Conan called to them, "garner what you can. We must be out of here swiftly."

"What! You dare to defile the sepulcher of the king!" Nitokar drew herself up in indignation. "Would you take away the essentials of my dear husband's glory in the next world?" She turned an imperious gaze on the looters. "Leave at once, and I promise to wait a moment before summoning my followers!"

Conan laughed again. "If your followers know what's best for their city, they'll leave you here. I doubt not that some of them are even now thinking of discreet ways to be rid of

you.'' He watched the raiders depart with full sacks, while
two more entered with empty ones.

"Why, you black-hearted cur! You'll be cut apart with hot
knives in the city square for saying that!" The queen ruffled
her sequins self-righteously. "I have the devotion of the least
and the foremost of my subjects, including the national hero
Horaspes." She crossed her arms so that her whip protruded
to one side. "With his guidance I shall lead Abaddrah to
grander glories than ever before."

"Such as war with Stygia?" Conan narrowed his gaze at
her. "What plans does that priestly schemer have for your
reign, I wonder?" He turned briefly to watch Isaiab and
Asrafel departing with bulging sacks. "Anyway, it matters
not. You'll be out of the picture. With luck, a saner head will
wear the crown." He moved toward her.

"Conan, this is a great shame." Nitokar dropped her arms
to her sides, watching him. "Give up this insurrection and be
my consort! The first time I saw you, I could tell that you
were no ordinary man. Under my hand you can experience
new sensations. Don't you see, you could go further than the
others—beyond pain, beyond ecstasy!" Her hands lifted to
her breast and stretched forth to him, beckoning. "We could
learn together." She gazed intently into his face as he came
near.

"But no, you are set in your cruel purpose, I see. Now
I suppose you intend to butcher me, as you did my slave!"
She awaited him, open-mouthed, her lips moist.

"Do it, Conan, please! Don't be deceived by her!" Afrit,
standing just beyond the queen, strained at her bonds and
called out in anguish. "She made those same vile promises to
my father!"

Conan raised his sword above his head. "No." With a
whizzing slash that passed well over Nitokar's head, he
brought his blade down on the golden chains where they
joined the stone coffin. A dull clank sounded as the steel
edge sheared through the soft metal links, and the shackles

fell free. ''I told you, Afrit, I am no assassin. You'd best learn to do your own dirty chores.''

With a savage cry, the freed princess sprang on her step-mother, rending her skin with clawed fingernails and striking at her with the heavy cuffs of her shackles. The queen, for her part, did not use her whip; she screamed and struggled ineffectually, overwhelmed by the smaller woman's assault. In a moment one of her high sandals turned underneath her, and she fell to the floor. Afrit pressed the advantage, dragging the queen along the floor by the hair, kicking her.

''As much as I love a good catfight, Princess, we don't have time. Better end it quickly. Then you and your captain can come away with me.'' Conan reached to his belt and drew a straight, brass-hilted dagger, which he tossed pommel-first to Afrit. As it arched up between them it seemed to flash once, strangely.

The princess let go Nitokar's black tresses to snatch the weapon two-handed out of the air. But she gave a cry and dropped it, staring at her palms—which were reddened as if seared. The knife struck the floor, deforming oddly in their sight. Wide-eyed, Conan watched it melt slowly into a smoking, dagger-shaped puddle.

''My apologies to you.'' A familiar, resonant voice spoke from behind Conan in lightly-accented Shemitish. ''I hate to resort to low conjurer's tricks, but at times they can be helpful, if only to gain the attention of an audience.''

Conan wheeled, following the two women's stares, and froze. Into the room stepped white-robed Horaspes, flanked by his bodyguard Nephren.

Chapter 16

The Nightlings

The prophet smiled complacently at Conan, with his taller Stygian companion glaring down over his shoulder. Horaspes looked more bluff and capable than ever, while Nephren stood unchanged—his dark face woodenly immobile, his eyes fixed in an expression that almost suggested some strange, perpetual fear or astonishment.

Conan waited tense, already in a fighting stance, with sword drawn. Behind him Afrit and Nitokar ceased their struggles. In the space of a heartbeat their faces, each with the other, traded expressions, triumph for despair, despair for triumph. Only the broken Aramas, huddled in his corner, did not visibly react to the change of fortune.

"What, northerner, why so downcast? Are you worrying over the fate of your rapacious friends outside?" Horaspes' look was so benign that his round, pinkish face almost glowed. "They did not see us, for know you, I have ways of bypassing the most vigilant sentries, not to mention those." He spread his hands magnanimously. "And I, in turn, did not trouble them. They will find their fate soon, when they try to leave these catacombs.

"But, Queen Nitokar, my dear ally, it appears that I am arrived just in time to prevent another adjustment of the royal line!'' The prophet shook his head in mild disapproval. "As ever, you are too adventurous and reckless.''

The red-faced queen, her black hair snarled and hideous, climbed back to her feet. "Fah, Chancellor, what you see is only a mother's eternal trial in managing her ungrateful offspring. With your help I'll soon end it.'' She snatched at Afrit's wrist, and the girl retreated from her, spitting curses.

"Nay, nay, Queen, leave off your vengeance! I shall handle the matter henceforth.'' When Nitokar glared at him, Horaspes added patiently, "I support your reign because I need you to steer the affairs of Abaddrah as we agreed. But I expect you to maintain at least a facade of queenly dignity.'' A hint of firmness crept into the pleasantry of his manner. "Now go. Join your slaves and priests in the central gallery, where I told them to wait. You will find the main passage clear. And tend to your hair, if you please.''

The prophet ended with an unctuous smile. Amazingly, Nitokar moved uncomplaining to obey him—yielding, as Conan sensed, to a greater power and ruthlessness than her own. But as she passed the Cimmerian, he shot out an arm to block her.

"Why should we let her leave?'' he demanded of Horaspes. "Why not just cut down the three of you and go our way?''

The prophet watched Conan, shrugging with elaborate unconcern. "If you wish to see my little sleight of hand once again, it would be no great matter. You will achieve nothing of consequence whilst I oppose you.''

Conan fell silent, not wanting to see his sword turned into smoking slag as the dagger had been. When Nitokar edged past him he did nothing more to detain her. But she paused deferentially before Horaspes. "Shall I bring the guards back here?''

"No.'' The prophet shook his head. "I would rather keep them ignorant of this barbarous invasion. Lead the others out of the tomb, then commence the door-closing ritual. The stores and gifts have all been laid in by now. After dealing with this minor problem''—he waved a hand at Conan and the princess—"I shall seal the royal chamber for eternity. Then I will exit the tomb by magical means available to me."

His visage growing suddenly benign again, Horaspes clasped the queen's hand in his. "Now go; your subjects await your presence. Likely they are restless."

Nitokar gave a submissive nod and bent to press a kiss on the back of the prophet's hand. With a last, spiteful glance toward Conan and Afrit, she passed between the sage and his bodyguard and exited the Royal Chamber.

After watching her leave, Horaspes turned his beaming smile back on the room's occupants. "A dubious expedient, Nitokar is. But if all goes smoothly, the city will not be subjected to her inept rule for long."

Conan watched the two warily. "You have broader plans, wizard?" He spoke with no definite purpose other than delay, for he was not ready to rush his captors.

"Indeed, the broadest possible plans. Why should a man of real determination recognize any limits to his power on this earth. Or in other realms, for that matter?"

The princess had moved up close behind Conan, anxious to shield her nakedness from the gloating eyes of the prophet and his henchman. Now the Cimmerian, reaching one-handed, unhooked the guard-cape from his neck and passed it back for her to wear. "There are always limits," he told Horaspes, "as any true prophet should be able to see."

The chancellor smiled even more sweetly at Conan and Afrit, favoring them with the look a hungry cat might give a pair of nestling doves. "I foresee only a splendid victory, and one in which the two of you can prove helpful. That is why I lured you here." He stepped forward confidently into the chamber, disregarding the wealth and glitter all around, halting in front of a vacant side wall. "After all, northerner, I could scarcely let you and your tomb pillagers run free! And I knew of no surer bait for you than a hoard of royal treasure and a yearning princess." Behind the prophet, Nephren had remained in place, blocking the archway with his gaunt height.

"This is a time of unlimited opportunity, you know, if only a man is enterprising enough to recognize it and seize upon it." Horaspes spoke in a brisk, positive tone. "This part of the world, the lush valley of the Styx, is tremendously wealthy. Abaddrah in particular has vast resources—most of them underground, due to the age-old burial practices here.

"You perceived this fact and tried to exploit it by your endeavor to rob these tombs. For that I give you credit, Conan of Cimmeria." Horaspes nodded in ironic acknowledgment. "But in your shortsighted, primitive way you overlooked the real opportunity.

"In a land as old as Stygia, where I hail from, the dead far outnumber the living." He rested an unsmiling, contemplative glance on both of them. "The same is true here in Abaddrah, and in other districts where Stygian belief has taken root. In most places it would not matter, of course, for the dead are vanished and gone. Their flesh is the flesh of jackals, their bones are split and scattered to the four winds.

"But in these southern lands, as you have seen, they are carefully preserved, along with their entire households, for the future glory of the race." Horaspes smiled benignly on his listeners.

"It is truly amazing how well the dead can be preserved in these hot, dry climes. Why, I have seen centuries-old mummies exhumed with their contours still rounded, their flesh still firm, their skin supple. Such venerable relics can be softened and limbered even more, aye, and restored to an almost perfect semblance of life by applying the proper oils and balms. With adequate care this vivacious appearance can be maintained for many centuries.

"The great enemy, of course, is the sun, which parches and rots. The sun is the source of all decay. You may have noticed that I detest its light and avoid going abroad by day. Hence the healthy paleness of my skin." Horaspes held up his pinkish hands. "But of course, day is only a temporary thing, no more enduring or fleeting than the nighttime. And there was night, surely, before there was ever day!'' He shook his head in rhetorical puzzlement. ''Why, I wonder, should men arbitrarily choose the one over the other? There is no reason why all earthly pastimes could not be carried on by night. Then day, instead of night, would be shuttered out and shunned.

''Now you know the core of my plan: to resurrect the night, and restore its primacy over day. If you do not apprehend my means, well . . .'' Horaspes walked to the side wall of the chamber and struck it three times with the heel of his hand. ''Day represents life, does it not? And night is death!'' He stepped back from the frescoed wall to the corner of the room, as if to clear his audience's view. ''So, clearly, the Empire of Night is not to be carved out by the living!''

Conan watched the prophet in uncertain dread. He could not guess the exact thrust of Horaspes' ramblings, but their tendency was frightening. Afrit, shivering in spite of Conan's cloak, clung to his shoulder as if to gain strength from him.

The Cimmerian's gaze was drawn to the wall where Horaspes had pounded his fist. Something moved there. At first he thought the prophet had scrawled another rune that would grow into magical pictures—for a small, dark spot was twisting and enlarging in the midst of the pastel designs. But then chips of plaster rattled down, and cracks ran out from the black aperture, widening swiftly. Finally, with a crash, the whole central part of the wall crumbled to the floor, laying open a black, gaping void in the end of the chamber. Surely this was no illusion, as the scenes in Ebnezub's courtly gathering had been. Yet, there in the darkness, beyond the swirling wisps of plaster-dust, lurked eerie, spectral shapes.

Afrit's fingers dug fearfully into Conan's arm as both of them strained to distinguish what lay beyond the low mound of rubble. Then his stomach clenched in horror and dismay as he discerned the outlines of the waiting forms. They were monstrous, and scores of them crowded just beyond the rough threshold, peering back at him.

Conan stared into the gleaming eyes of a large hyena, whose half-rotted head rested incongruously atop a man's square shoulders. Just behind it glared a pair of smoldering sparks, deep in the eye sockets of a nearly fleshless, jewel-crowned human skull. Beyond that, out of the dusy folds of a priestly cowl, jutted the arched neck and scabrous, partly-feathered head of a holy ibis-bird, flicking sideways with brittle mobility so as to regard Conan first with one eye, then the other.

And so on, and on into the obscurity of the deep, unlit tunnel whence they issued. Some of the things stooped, others perched high on mounds of debris for a better view; some were clad in golden armor, some in decaying rags and bandages. All were humanlike in some way, most too monstrous to gaze on for long. They were, at least in part, the occupants of the riven tombs, Conan knew—the dead of Abaddrah's hoary centuries, thronging to life now at their prophet's summons, and poised to swarm forth into the world of the living.

"And so at last you meet my nightlings—the folk of the future!" Horaspes spoke over Afrit's sick gasps as she hid her face behind Conan's back. "Do not be distressed, I pray, at the semihuman nature of some of these poor clays. They are sadly out of step with fashion, I fear. They still wear the style of past centuries here in the valley of the Styx, when embalmers were fond of stitching together human and animal parts in imitation of their crude gods. Princess, I beg you, look kindly on them, for they, too, are your subjects! None could be more dutiful and obedient. But I warn you that they will always cherish a debt of gratitude to me, who magically rekindled the spark of life in their rotting chests!"

While the prophet gloated on, Conan forced himself to examine the nightlings more closely. Some were remarkably solid and robust-looking, with their leathery skin gleaming, doubtless from the preservative oils Horaspes had mentioned. So treated, the skins had far outlasted the crumbling garments which hung from them. Others were mere husks of sinew and bone, hunched and twisted by imperfect mummification, sometimes lacking a limb or a less essential body part.

In the course of his distasteful inspection, Conan saw ample evidence that the tomblings had not been idle. Most bore picks, chisels, and other tools for working the soft bedrock of the tomb-district—explaining the clanking that had signaled the comings and goings of the invisible tunnelers. The implements were dinted and worn by much use, and the wielders themselves had not escaped wear and tear. Many of the fingers that nervelessly grasped the steel tools were worn literally to the bone.

"And so you see, northerner, in all your thieving and plotting, you neglected the real treasure of the tombs—the dead themselves!" Horaspes preached at them with characteristic enthusiasm. "Starting with the few hundred dead souls whom I brought with me from Stygia—the survivors, though it sounds peculiar to use the term, of my clash with the army and the narrow-minded priesthood there—I have been able to undermine the entire tomb-district of Abaddrah.

"In so doing, I avail myself not only of the wealth, weapons, and materials buried here, but of the inhabitants themselves, rich and poor, man, woman, and child! No tomb is proof against their tireless delvings, not even this chamber made to be sealed so tightly against eternity! At this very moment my minions labor to free the last of their brethren trapped in the newest, remotest tombs. Doubtless the prisoners themselves twitch and scrabble in their coffins with anticipation, made restless by the spells I cast over this whole necropolis!

"I have the weight of numbers already on my side. With the further advantage of commanding troops who need no light, and who have already weathered the slight inconvenience of death, I could attack now and easily take this paltry city. But first I want to spread my teachings and my secret subterranean following through all the cities of Shem. When I strike, I'll command an empire large enough to threaten

Stygia and shake her stodgy, self-righteous priests to their sandal-soles!

"After all, why should I hurry, when each new tomb only enriches me and makes my ultimate triumph more total and inexorable. This one, for instance, whose plentiful troops and arms will strengthen my cause, and whose food-stores and live occupants will serve to nourish my hungry host. For know you, the dead do hunger, albeit more slowly and patiently than the living."

Here Horaspes paused in his harangue to gaze at the princess, who had long since clapped her hands over her ears and buried her faced against Conan's shoulder. "Alas, poor Afrit, I see that my words have upset you!

"But you misapprehend me. Do not think for a moment that I plan to give you to my minions as food! A princess of the royal line, no matter how self-willed and stubborn, is too valuable for that! Rather I propose to keep you intact to place on the throne of Abaddrah, once the people have sickened of Nitokar. Then I can seize the city as liberator rather than destroyer!

"Do not fear. If expertly done, the mummification treatment is swift and painless, and your death by smothering will cause no disfigurement. It will leave you looking much as you do now, but with considerably greater stamina. It should cure many of your girlish misgivings and help reconcile you to the simple, harsh facts of existence. Ask Nephren, here, who is my finest specimen so far. I expect Conan to be of considerable value to me as a bodyguard, too, after his conversion; surely, such a figure of a man is too splendid to be cut up as food . . . ."

At that moment Horaspes' voice faltered, and he staggered. In his maunderings about the princess's fate he had ambled near Aramas, the huddled, chained prisoner; now he was seized from beneath in a violent grip.

A grimace of rage contorted the prophet's face as he saw the impediment, and he clamped both hands down at the base of Aramas's neck. Yet for the moment his attention was diverted. The milling dead beyond him, though agitated by the sudden activity, did not swarm forward into the room.

Conan, seeing his long-awaited chance, had already moved. Yanking the princess with him, he rushed Nephren. The bodyguard still blocked the exit, sword raised, while gaping sidelong at his master's struggle. Conan's sword met hard resistance in the gaunt belly—this time he could hear the crunch of sand against steel—but it was his simultaneous kick that sent the Stygian reeling back against the broken remnant of the side wall.

The Cimmerian headed out into the short hallway, dragging Afrit after him; but her stubborn resistance slowed him, and her anguished plaints sounded in his ear. "Conan, what of Aramas? He was faithful to me!"

He paused, turning back in exasperation. "What am I supposed to do against Horaspes and all those zombies? Look there!"

Both of them stared back into the room to see Horaspes straighten over the captain's motionless form. Where the prophet's hands had clasped his attacker's chest were two black, smoking cavities.

Horaspes turned his face to them with a demonic look. Then their view of him was blocked by the giant form of Nephren, who strode into the hallway, sword raised, with sand streaming from the slash under his tunic. Conan shoved Afrit behind him and fell back slowly. Then, with a quick, sidewise leap, he swung his sword against the wall and smashed the earthen vessel embedded there.

Sand and pottery fragments poured onto the floor as Conan shoved Afrit farther back. Nephren paused, glancing overhead to find the source of the rumbling and grating which had commenced. Suddenly a pair of heavy, trapezoidal stones crashed down from the ceiling behind him. Then came two more, then four, blocking the passage entirely. The Stygian, with nearly human reflexes, leaped forward—only to meet a chest-high sweep of Conan's sword that crunched into his arm and drove him aside, spinning. Then the rest of the ceiling blocks rushed down with a shattering roar. The avalanche blasted sand against Conan as he leaped clear, crushing Nephren from sight under a massive, impenetrable wall of stone.

Afrit had been thrown down to her hands and knees by the shuddering shock. "The tomb-seal—?" she gasped.

"Aye," Conan said, overtaking her. "Designed by a clever fellow named Mardak, who is no more. But it will not keep Horaspes away from us for long. Up, girl, and run!"

Chapter 17

Day of Doom

Conan and Afrit sprinted up the sloping central passage of the tomb. It was deserted, its lamps guttering low in their wall-brackets. The princess, moving lightly in bare feet, proved a swift runner. At one place Conan stopped to pry the golden shackles from her wrists and dry her tears over Aramas. After that she pulled into the lead, her borrowed cape fluttering back to expose her flashing legs. But in time she slowed to ask him breathlessly, "What if the great doors are closed? Is there another way out?"

"No safe one, with all the dead afoot," he told her between heavy breaths. "Does the tomb-closing ritual take long?"

"I don't know." She fell back even with him, gasping with exertion. "It's so hard to judge the time in these tunnels!"

"Nonetheless, we stop at this junction," Conan told her. "Wait here. And give a cry if you see or hear any pursuit."

Afrit halted and rested against the wall while Conan jogged away down the side-passage. "Otsgar! Isaiab! Are you fled yet?" His shouts rang hollow in the high, narrow tunnel. "Beware the crypts. They are alive with sorcery!"

"Conan, where have you been dawdling?" Isaiab appeared around an angle of the corridor, grinning and shouldering a bulging sack. "The plunder here is splendid; we should make a dozen return visits." His smile dimmed slightly at Conan's aspect. "What, no loot? Did you find your princess?"

"Forget the loot." Conan brushed past him, rounding the corner to see the other five raiders busily at work along the corridor, sorting gleaming objects between chests and bags. He spoke peremptorily to them. "Drop those trinkets and come with me! We have to leave here by the main gates, and soon!"

Otsgar glanced up at him, looking only mildly skeptical. "What, fellow, another bout of madness? We would be torn apart by a ravening mob if we tried." He turned back to his labors, bending beside Zafriti over a pair of greasy sacks whose open mouths gleamed and caused gem-highlights to play up onto their faces.

"I mean it, Vanirman." Conan suddenly drew his sword, clashing it against the wall with a clangor that caused all six faces to stare at him. "I bring you your only chance to escape alive from this trap! Forget your treasure and come with me!"

Otsgar sprang upright, jerking out his own sword. "Curse you, Cimmerian, what trickery is this? And what trap? We were unnoticed by anyone down here, except for the queen you intended to slay! Now you rave at us to abandon all this wealth—"

His speech was cut short by a turmoil from behind him, farther down the corridor. Clinking tool-sounds, the crash of falling masonry, and then, a few heartbeats later, the shuffle of many feet through the rubble. "What in Nifelheim . . . ?" Otsgar seized a lamp and held it high, disclosing dim, distant forms that moved amidst the dust-swirls a few score paces down the corridor.

"Here they come! . . . Horaspes' rejuvenated corpses!" Conan shoved Isaiab up the passageway. "Keep clear of them and follow me!"

As he departed he could hear others dropping their loot and starting after him. He issued from the narrow corridor and bent his steps up the central passage, grabbing Afrit'sarm and pulling her along. "The nightlings have brokenthrough into the side-tunnel," he told her. "These are my companions. Not enough of us to work the doors, I fear, if they are already closed!"

Flying up the corridor past treasure-rooms sealed only with beeswax and priest-knots, they soon emerged into the central gallery. The tools and building materials had been removed, to be replaced by military stores; now the floor was lined with jars, bales, rolled tents, chariots, and horse-stalls complete with whinnying occupants. "A shame the place is infested," Conan told the princess as they started up the ramp. "We could live here for years, if not for the nightlings!"

Before they were halfway up the slope, the rest of the raiders were climbing at their heels, with Isaiab in the lead and Otsgar close behind him. Then, as they neared the top, the foremost of their pursuers burst into view—gaunt, martial-looking mummies armed with swords, axes, and picks, their legs working beneath them with the same relentless swiftness that Nephren's had. Although their appearance was heralded by the frightened screams of the horses, they ran on in ominous silence, neither shouting nor visibly panting.

On reaching the top, Conan looked for some way to block them. But the fire-urns were gone, and the ramp and tunnel-mouth were too wide for easy defense. He pressed on into the upper tunnel, pulling the exhausted princess along with him.

A moment later he heard anguished cries from behind. One of Otsgar's new men, who had tried to flee with a half-filled sack of booty, was overtaken and dragged down by nightlings. They swarmed around him at the top of the ramp, obscuring his final end as they struck and strove at his body. His death did not buy the raiders much time, for other fleet-footed mummies quickly arrived to press the pursuit.

"Pray that the gates are still open!" Conan yelled back to Otsgar, who labored up the slope alongside Zafriti. "If not we must hold them at the head of this passage."

Then he came up to a side door that looked stouter than the

others, carved of stone and barred with a thick metal bolt.
From beyond it, Conan swore that he could faintly hear
raised voices. With an oath he stopped to rip away the
priestly charms that dangled from the latch. As the other
raiders fled past him, he lifted the bolt and used it to lever the
door wide.

Huddled within were Ebnezub's elite tomb-guards, their
weapons stacked to one side. All were evidently drunk on
some narcotic the priests had dispensed; they were whiling
away their last hours in a quarrelsome dice game.

"If you must fight, dogs," roared Conan to their astonished stares, "then fight these Hell-demons that have invaded
your tomb!" As they tardily and confusedly began to react,
he was away, with the nightlings at his heels. In a moment
their pursuit was again slowed, as yells and the clash of
weapons sounded behind him.

Now he ran at his most desperate speed. He wanted to be
the first to face whatever peril awaited them at the top. He
passed most of the others—Otsgar and Asrafel both trying to
help Zafriti, who moved with unaccountable slowness, and
the princess who ran alone, near-exhausted. As the end of the
upward tunnel yawned ahead, Conan drew up behind Isaiab
and the last of Otsgar's new hirelings. Suddenly, to his inner
exultation, he saw the thieves' staggering forms outlined
against bright daylight.

Yet it was only a thin patch of light, and a narrowing one
at that. Topping the crest of the tunnel and bursting into the
vacant foyer, Conan found that the great bronze doors were
already half-closed; the lofty room resounded with the rattle
of the counterweighted machinery that would send the portals
clanging shut in a matter of moments, without any human
agency. Beyond the doors, in the vertical bar of daylight, his
dazzled eyes could make out a sliver of the densely-packed,
attentive crowd, with priests of Ellael kneeling in the fore-
ground waiting for the tomb-closing ceremony to be complete. If they saw the raiders laboring toward them in the
inner darkness, they gave no sign of it.

Conan did not understand the mechanism of the portals, and there was no time to puzzle it out, with the nightlings so close behind. Isaiab and the other man threw themselves panting against one of the metal panels; half-lit by the glare of day, they shoved against it with all their breathless might. But their sandals scuffed the floor in vain, not even slowing the relentless inward sweep of the brazen wall.

There were no loose objects nearby with which to jam the doors, Conan saw as he hurled himself forward. No way to wedge them against the polished stone floor, either. Yet there was still room between them for a man to pass, and Isaiab clearly debated the move. The scrawny thief's very silhouette wavered as he mentally weighed the threat of the approaching tomblings against that of the mob outside. The next man in line stood by, waiting to follow his lead.

Both were shouldered roughly aside as Conan charged into the narrowing breech. He did not pass through, but stopped directly between the closing valves. His upper arms bridged the gap, bulging, with forearms braced against the door-edges to resist their motion.

He sensed immediately that his shoulders alone could never exert enough force, even if he were not already panting with exertion. Shifting quickly sideways, he placed his back against one creeping door and braced his sandal-soles against the other, opposing their motion with the full strength of his legs. The pressure was soon redoubled by that of his arms as the gap narrowed enough for him to reach across and press with his palms.

Conan's appearance in the doorway elicited a startled exclamation from those outside, and so vast was the crowd that their spreading murmur echoed within the chamber. Yet none of the priests or onlookers moved forward; it was inevitable that, with the continuing sweep of the doors, the intruder would momentarily be squashed like an insect while they stood powerless to intervene.

So they watched and waited while Conan's bronze-hued body reddened with strain in the closing vice, and the mus-

cles of his thighs and shoulders bulged like knotted cables.
His tendons strained and cracked, his limbs bending beyond
the point of greatest leverage, past the time when he should
have thrown himself clear. He fought the machine to the
death as he would have fought a human assailant, probing
remorselessly for its weaknesses and striving to conquer it by
the sheer force of his savage will.

It was those inside the tomb who sensed the change first.
To them it was audible, as the grinding of the pulleys slowed
and the ratchet-pawls began to clack less and less frequently.
Then, miraculously, the inner gallery fell silent, the dusty ray
of daylight slashing undiminished down its center. The great
doors had stopped moving.

Even as a murmur of amazement spread outside, the last of
the raiders straggled up to the portal. Their continued pursuit
and the waning resistance of the tomb-guards were evidenced
by a rising clamor from the tunnel; now the fugitives halted,
panting and uncertain before the parted doors.

"Hurry and go, curse you!" was Conan's remark, muttered from between clenched teeth. "I'm being crushed alive!"

Hearing this, Isáiab was the first to shrug and step forward. He ducked low under the sinewy arch of Conan's legs
and went out to confront the watching crowd, followed closely
by the second man. Then the panting Otsgar stretched out a
burly hand to Zafriti. The dancer paused to straighten her hair
and clothing, and to pat ill-concealed tomb-loot out of sight
on her person. Then she followed her employer out with a
graceful dip. Asrafel ducked through the portal close behind
her.

Princess Afrit was last in line. She had been taking her
time, tearing away the trailing pieces of the shift that Nitokar
had shredded, and arranging the brief guard-cape to mask her
womanly charms and flatter them as well. Then she smoothed
her hair, setting the royal diadem straight on her head.

"For the love of Ishtar, girl, hurry!" Sweat beaded on
Conan's face, and his eyes darted to watch dim shapes

emerging from the inner tunnel-mouth. "If these doors don't kill us, the accursed mummies will!"

"Have patience, Conan," the princess said, stooping to pass underneath him. "The way I look when I leave here may be as important to our survival as your mighty thews!" Then she was out of the doorway, arising before her subjects and moving forward with a serene poise that belied her dress and situation. The crowd seemed to recognize her, their babble falling to a murmur as she appeared—except for a minor turmoil that erupted at one side of the throng.

Behind the princess, Conan braced himself in the door-crevice. Then he twisted and sprang free, dropping lightly to his feet, although his legs threatened to buckle under him. He followed her, trying not to stagger under the weight of cramp and weakness that surged through his strained limbs. As the faint sounds of the door-closing machinery resumed behind him, he pivoted carefully with the others to watch, hoping that the reeling of his brain did not show in his stance.

There was a motion inside the narrowing door-cranny—a human arm emerged holding a broken sword. A head and body in a gray tunic followed. It was an officer of the elite tomb-guards, fleeing the nightlings. He staggered out, dazzled by daylight. Behind him another guard squeezed through the impossibly thin crevice, his breastplate and scapular scraping the portals. He stood gasping and bloodstained, clutching an open wound in his shoulder. Conan glimpsed a few last, tentative flurries of motion within the tomb.

Then the doors met. They gave off a thunderous, deafening clang that shook the stones under the watchers' feet and resounded over the crowd, to echo from the city wall in the distance.

This great noise seemed to release the onlookers from their thralldom of silence. They did not rush forward, for only their frontmost ranks could see what was happening, and their assembled priests and leaders had made no move on the escapees. Instead, as the gonging echoes died, the vast multitude of voices rose up in a traditional Shemitish funeral

hymn. The mighty chorus swelled, washing across the plaza
like ocean surf across a shallow bay.

Yet at the same time, even amidst the echoing surge of
piety, the chief priests and their guards moved forward officiously to challenge the princess and her fellow refugees.

Conan's senses had finally recovered from the dimness of
the tomb and the intensity of his exertion; now he was able to
take in the scene fully. The grandeur of the monument's
towering facade and the vastness of the watching crowd
kindled in his belly an impression of wonder, which was
scarcely hampered by the awareness that he might soon have
to fight for his life against insuperable odds.

But what seemed most awe-inspiring was the unusual
weather. The sky, which had been so blinding when glimpsed
from the recesses of the tomb, was not really bright at all. It
was roofed over with a mottled layer of cloud that obscured
the sunlight and made the heavens seem to brood eerily, as if
in mourning for the dead king. The afternoon was darker than
any Conan had seen during his sojourn in Shem. Yet somehow it all seemed strangely familiar.

Conan flexed his shoulders uneasily to shake off the impression; then he moved up close behind the princess and the
others, trying to look wholly confident and quietly dangerous. Beneath the swelling strains of the Abaddran people's
hymn he could hear the ire in the voices of the elder priests
as they shot questions at Afrit, who stood before them with a
demure, regal air.

"What of your divine father's will?" a bald, weasel-faced
priest was demanding of her. "To quit His Splendor's tomb
with the aid of these . . . motley persons is a shocking
dereliction of royal duty."

"And that's not to mention the abrogation of afterlife,"
another punctilious voice put in. It was the tall, potbellied
priest who had been with Afrit and the queen in the depths of
the tomb; he stood at hand flanked by two guards with
gold-chased ceremonial halberds. "The question arises whether,

once properly inhumed and having subsequently fled the tomb, you can ever be elevated to immortal status again.''

"I have told you, sirs, that to belabor these points is to ignore a profanation of my father's tomb that is even now taking place.'' Afrit regarded her inquisitors with a lofty air. "There are hellish creatures loose under our very feet, summoned by magic to make a mockery of our devout purpose here.''

"You have no purpose here!'' an imperious female voice shrilled from behind the priests. Queen Nitokar strode up angrily in advance of her litter-bearers. She had left the portico of the tomb to go among her favorite courtiers in the front ranks of the crowd, but now she was back, making an intimidating figure in her jouncing black equipage. "Your flight from the holy tomb proves your faithlessness, and a profane attachment to the things of this world! For that, the fitting penalty is death.''

"But what of the monsters despoiling the tomb?'' Conan said loudly over her. He shoved forward briskly among his friends, whose little crowd was beginning to take on a defensive shape. "We came to warn you of the peril. 'Tis the work of the Stygian warlock Horaspes.''

The queen laughed harshly amid the shocked exclamations of her priests. "The only despoilers I see are yourselves! Punishing your crime should be but a matter of moments.'' She waved a hand to indicate the scores of guards holding back the crowd of courtiers and commoners. "As for your talk of monsters . . .''

"Monsters there are,'' said a voice behind Conan.

The raiders turned to gaze on the elite guard officer, who was helping his wounded subordinate approach. The recruit was dressed in a gray cloak like Princess Afrit's, except that it was slashed and bloodied—and as the officer led him forward he lifted up the fringe of the cape, from which something dangled. On looking closely, the watchers could see that it was a severed hand.

Shriveled, bloodless, and grayer even than the cloth itself, it ended in a shattered stub of wristbone where it must have been pinched off by the closing of the tomb doors. Yet it still clutched the folds of the fabric with a clawlike grip. Jerking the cloth of the tunic in the air, the guard officer shook it off; to the watchers' horror it fell on the smooth stone with fingers still squirming and grasping, like the legs of a giant beetle thrown over on its back.

"There, you see!" Conan exclaimed. "The dead of all the centuries have been raised up by sorcery. And not as shining immortals, but as creeping monsters! They've dug their way into Ebnezub's tomb!" The rest of the raiders nodded and muttered in agreement, but cautiously, none of them wanting to draw attention to himself.

"A clear case of necromancy!" one of the priests exclaimed. "Yet these interlopers blame it on Chancellor Horaspes, without offering any proof."

"Where is your prophet then, I ask you?" Conan confronted them fiercely. "I saw him down below not an hour ago, marshaling the ranks of the undead."

"Hold your treasonous tongue!" Nitokar was shrieking now in an unsuccessful effort to gain the ears of the priests, who were standing over the still-squirming hand and disputing among themselves. "Horaspes is the savior of our land!" she railed. "Any who slander him will pay dearly for it!"

"It cannot matter," the potbellied priest adamantly told a colleague. "If there is some kind of sorcerous invasion of the tomb, we can do nothing against it. Mortals are powerless to enter; the place is sealed until eternity."

His speech was audible largely because it lapped over into silence, as his interlocutor and most of the others turned to look up at the towering tomb doors. Their arguments stopped, and the crowd, which had ceased singing and begun to grow restive, now fell still.

In a moment the noise they had heard was repeated: a remote metallic clashing. It was followed by a grinding, as of some gear mechanism ponderously engaged. Then commenced

the creaking, grating moan of giant door-posts turning reluctantly in their sockets.

A stir of alarm passed through the great crowd as it stood
watching under the dark-mottled, lowering sky. It was very
much like the prophet's final vision, Conan realized: the
expectant silence, the dark, coppery heavens, the mournful
groaning of the portals. The awed folk of Abaddrah stood
frozen as the great doors swung slowly open. Then they
screamed in terror, trampling one another in their eagerness
to flee as the first ranks of the resurrected dead swept forth in
thundering attack.

Chapter 18

The Empire of Night

The Abaddrans' terror at the opening of the gates was mind-shattering. To them it signaled the end of the world, and the dread syllables of the word *jazarat* swept through the mob like the rustling wings of a locust swarm. The grim aspect of the heavens and the funeral trappings all around only intensified their fear.

They were a devout people, well-versed in their land's long and rich history; yet now they saw it all attacked and made a travesty by the horrors the great gates spewed forth. Visages and costumes from the city's past, traditions the townsfolk had learned to love through story and statuary, suddenly came shambling at them in the rotting guise of remorseless, undead attackers. Kings and heroes, grandsires and grandsons alike filled out the ranks of the tomb army. Instead of heralding a glorious afterlife, the honored ancestors stalked soullessly forth to hack their descendants down with rusted steel. The undead host emerged with dreadful swiftness, and before them the crowd quailed and fell back helplessly upon itself.

The tomb-raiders and Princess Afrit were spared the first crushing impact of the nightlings' assault, for while the attention of the mob was still fixed on the tomb doors, Conan quickly drew his companions aside. The battle-chariots clattered forth from the yawning portals, driven by skeletal warriors who lashed their frothing, terrified teams with long whips. They rode down priests and guardsmen alike, but they swept past the escapees without turning to engage them.

The footborne shock-troops which followed were quick to seize the main part of the terrace, making a hedge of their curiously-armored bodies and antique weapons to surround Queen Nitokar. Then they marched their formation forward with a rigid gait, clearing the porch and hewing down all who opposed them.

Yet a path of retreat was quickly opened for Conan and the others as the maddened crowd gave way. The chariots cut a widening swath before the tomb doors and circled there unchallenged, unimpeded by the mere human flesh which occasionally fell afoul of the glinting, whirling scythes at their wheel-hubs. Few of the funeral celebrants were armed, and all seemed smitten by a soul-chilling terror. In the angles and exits of the plaza, where the crowd surged back like sea-foam driving up a rocky beach, more Abaddrans died from crushing and trampling than from the blades of the nightlings.

Even the palace guards and armed priests were cowed almost into uselessness. Conan, acting on the theory that the bottle-neck of the tomb entry would be easier to defend than the open plaza, made a stand at the edge of the terrace. But only Isaiab, Asrafel, and a few survivors of the gate guards turned with him, the rest fleeing unashamedly.

Still, Conan told himself, it was enough of a force to cover his flanks. He raised his sword and tried it out on the shield-edge of a mailed, helmeted shambler from some remote era of the city's past, who marched forward amid a line of ragtag corpse-troopers. The green-rimmed metal of the ancient shield split easily, but the arm holding it did not sag with the shock and pain a living human limb would have felt. Instead it twisted aside craftily to entangle Conan's blade, while an ax wielded by a bony fist veered out from behind it toward his face. Conan ducked back, freeing his sword with a wrenching twist, then dodged farther to avoid the ax's backswing.

In his turn the Cimmerian struck with a swiftness born of rage and loathing, hacking at the base of the grill-faced helmet where it met the armored shoulder. The helm flew off and landed at his feet, the near-fleshless skull rattling inside it. But the headless body of the mummy fought on, caroming blindly against its neighboring warriors and striking them with the follow-through of its ax-strokes. Conan debated whether to whittle the thing down any farther, and decided not to; mayhap its wild blows would cripple a few of its fellows.

Beside him an armed priest had just used his spear to skewer a rag-clad, leather-faced Stygian mummy. But the thing refused to stop; with the bloodless steel point jutting from between its shoulder blades, it stalked forward relentlessly, forcing its body up the length of the spearshaft to jab its dagger into the throat of the astonished priest.

Conan, snarling curses, split the creature's brittle skull with one swordstroke and hacked through the bone of its thigh with another. Then he turned and fled with the rest of his outmanned force. As he departed, his last clear glimpse of the tomb entry showed the white-clad figure of Horaspes moving among the outrushing nightlings, directing his troops.

"Crom's hounds!" Conan swore as he joined the other raiders where they had gathered in the milling, shoving crowd beyond the radius of the chariots' sweep. "Have you ever seen the like of these fiends? Cutting them down will be harder work than felling and splitting an oaken forest."

"What does it matter, anyway? Why fight them?" Otsgar, who stood sheltering Zafriti under his burly arm, regarded him curiously. "We may have lost the treasure in this fiasco, but we still have our skins. We can make a clean escape."

Conan eyed him with contempt. "What, and let these stalking corpses murder all the living folk hereabouts? What would you do, flee northward?"

"You, Conan, would be well advised to take that course.

As for me"—Otsgar shrugged—"Abaddrah has seen changes of leadership before, and my inn and I have weathered them. This is a civil matter, the kind that an astute tradesman tries not to get involved in."

Conan's stare was incredulous. "You plan to stay and do your business as usual under Horaspes' reign?"

Otsgar waved a hand dismissively. "Whatever the nature of the prophet's rule, you can be sure that his kingdom will have trade, tariffs, envoys, and so forth. And that there will be a comfortable place in it for me. Unlike you, Cimmerian, I can make a better living in peace than in war."

Conan moved close to the innkeeper. "You fool," he rasped in his ear, "the sorcerer will slay every living man and beast! He plans to curfew the very daylight and ordain an Empire of Night!"

Otsgar frowned, careful to stay clear of Conan's grip. "Some of my best business is done at night. Except this tomb-robbing debacle of yours, which has come close to ruining me! Now go while you can, and leave us to our own livelihoods."

"FOLK OF ABADDRAH!"

Uncannily, as if in answer to the two men's words, a voice sounded from behind Conan, a voice loud enough to blot out the speech of every other tongue in the plaza. All eyes looked back in fear toward the tomb doors to see the white-clad prophet Horaspes held aloft on a platform over the heads of his milling nightlings.

"SUBJECTS, ATTEND ME."

The prophet was addressing the scattering crowd from his place in the recessed entry, and his voice echoed there and rang out over the plaza. Yet as Conan listened, he knew that no human lungs could achieve such force naturally; the wizard was using some devilish sorcery to increase the strength of his utterance as he cupped his hands to his mouth. Yet the loudness also lent the speech a gruff, inhuman quality, as if a great beast were mouthing mortal words.

"THERE IS NOTHING TO FEAR," the stentorian voice

boomed. "I COMMAND YOU NOW ON BEHALF OF YOUR QUEEN." He gestured to Nitokar, who waved to her subjects from a pedestal beside and beneath his own. "ALL WILL BE WELL IF YOU OBEY ME. THOSE WHO RESIST WILL BE SLAIN." He paused, lowering his hands to ask an inaudible question of Her Royal Splendor. Then he raised them back to his mouth, and his voice smote their ears again. "QUEEN NITOKAR WILL PROCEED TO THE PALACE TO TAKE UP HER THRONE. LEAVE THE CITY GATE OPEN FOR HER EASE."

The thundering voice ceased, and Horaspes stepped down out of sight. The effect of his speech was only to provoke a greater frenzy of fear in the crowd, which now swirled against the raiders and drove them apart. Multitudes found it impossible to leave the plaza; even those who had recovered from their initial panic were still driven in blind mobs before the marching nightlings. Conan was alone amid a sea of shouting, shoving brown bodies.

Luckily his height and size enabled him to breast the tide. He made his way toward a defensive square of palace guards that was formed up on a rise near the city gate; in their midst Princess Afrit held earnest counsel with surviving priests and officers. Also present, dwarfed by the adults and standing sullenly at one side, was Nitokar's son, Eblis. As Conan worked his way nearer, he saw each official bow a homage to the princess before turning away to issue commands.

When Conan finally came up against the line of leveled spearpoints, his tall stature easily caught Princess Afrit's eye; she clapped her hands and ordered the guards to pass him inside the formation. Approaching her where she stood between a pair of mailed warriors, he saw how well she maintained her poise in the face of the new threat. She greeted him warmly, reaching out both her hands to clasp his.

"Oh Conan, Horaspes has finally gone too far! The priests and officers have sworn to oppose him and Nitokar. They support me as the legitimate heir to the throne!"

"Wonderful, girl!" Conan reached out an arm to clasp her

shoulders, but drew it back on seeing the disapproving scowls of Afrit's newly-appointed bodyguards. "In any event, be cautious. Courtly factions have been known to shift their loyalties more than once." From the corner of his eye he caught the pale-faced look of young Eblis fixed narrowly on them. "And what is he doing here? That's Nitokar's whelp, is it not?"

"Aye, my half brother. He was swept away from the queen in the flight from the tomb. The nobles plan to use him as a hostage against her."

Conan spoke under his breath. "Well, beware him, whether he is hostage, fugitive or spy. Even at his tender age he's likely to have learned some nasty tricks from his mother. And be not overconfident. The nightlings will be hard to defeat in the field, especially with Horaspes' sorcerous skills behind them."

Afrit nodded, looking worried. "Our best hope is the city wall; loyal regiments have been sent to secure it. But we need the help of the people, too." The princess clasped Conan's hand again. "If you could help us by recruiting your friends to our side, or by rallying some of the commoners, it would make a great difference. But then, you have already saved my life once. I don't know how to repay you." She blushed and cast her eyes down, her hand lingering lightly in Conan's.

"I'll do what I can." Conan squeezed her hand and released it. "Crom knows I favor your cause, and Horaspes is too dangerous an enemy to run from. But I can't promise that any of my so-called friends will join us."

They bade one another farewell, and in a moment Afrit headed away to address her subjects from atop the city wall. She walked proudly among her new courtly allies, protected on all sides by the guard formation. And they departed none too soon, for Horaspes' minions soon regrouped and pressed forward in a new series of sweeps.

The square was chaos itself. The crowd had numbered in the tens of thousands, and exits from the place were few. The traffic-jammed west gate of the city was even now being closed by Afrit's forces in defiance of Horaspes' command. The wooden bridges over the still-swollen canals had quickly collapsed under the weight of fleeing throngs, and the high road running outside the city wall was preempted by military units.

In spite of Horaspes' conciliatory words, an ever larger area of the plaza was ruthlessly cleared by his war-chariots and infantry. The aspect of his troops was not one to allay fear, for they were only vaguely human. At best frigid-faced, at worst hideously decomposed, they efficiently slew all who came before them. Their victims, as all could see, were carried or dragged into the tomb—to be dressed out as mummies there, it was rumored, then revitalized and sent back into the fray on the side of the prophet.

In consequence most of the frightened men, women, and children could only climb onto the canal-banks, press up against the base of the city wall, or try to scale the high stone barrier to the tomb-district. Those lacking even such paltry refuge milled in the open, fleeing back and forth in response to wild rumors, and sometimes falling bloodily before the hooves and swords of the attackers. Many had been driven raving mad, or else into a dull stupor, by the conviction that doomsday really had come. All were unfed, since the carts of delicacies intended for the funeral-goers had been overturned in the initial rush and their contents trampled underfoot. Beneath the cloud-clotted sky that now darkened toward twilight, the scene was nightmarishly reminiscent of Horaspes' own grimmest prophecies.

Roaming at large, Conan fell in with some Shemites he knew from the tomb-workings. These men, wild with wrath and desperation, ran in a pack for their own protection. At his urging they obtained weapons by raiding a tool wagon. Then he led them against one of the nightlings' chariots.

It was a sturdy vehicle, trundled out new that very day and built to last an eternity; but its four costly horses were lathered and half-dead in their traces. On its first pass, the

skirmishers jammed one of its wheels to a dragging halt with
a pry-bar. Then they leaped on board and fought down its
Stygian charioteer and his dog-headed passenger, hacking
them into squirming pieces with shovels and hatchets, to the
cheers of the crowd on the canal-bank.

When a flying squad of tomblings was dispatched against
them, Conan rallied his men to stand fast. But by now the
worst of the mummies had crept forth from the tomb: ancient, decrepit, ill-preserved things, rotting where they stood
and patched with animal parts in a mad, monstrous array.
The Cimmerian felt shudders pass along his line as the
undead phalanx deployed toward them. To crown the horror, one of his companions screamed that he recognized the
freshest of the shambling creatures; it was his dead younger
brother, one of the elite tomb-guards, still dressed in his
immaculate funeral-garb. The fellow broke away, gibbering.

The other Shemites stood demoralized as two of their
number went down before the attackers' talons and their
flailing, rusted blades. Then Conan ordered a retreat. Merci-
fully, the older mummies were not as fleet of foot as the
living men, so the fugitives were able to regroup at the other
side of the plaza.

In spite of this defeat, the Shemites' skirmishing set an
example for all those before the city wall. Soon others began
to join them and form similar bands. Many, having heard an
impassioned speech by Princess Afrit from the gate, eagerly
spread the message of resistance to the prophet's army. There
were others, of course, who proclaimed their eternal fealty to
Queen Nitokar—but even the feuding between the two factions served to impede Horaspes' ends.

The prophet's next objective was evidently to be the west
gate; soon his force extended straight toward it from the
tomb, in a densely-defended cordon that cut the plaza in two.
Conan was mindful of his enemy's sorcerous skills and the
advantage the nightlings would have in the coming darkness.
He left the Shemites to carry out their depredations under

newly-appointed leaders. In trying to spy out the nightlings' attack plan, he happened upon Otsgar, Isaiab, and Zafriti.

Dusty and weary-looking, they had been unsuccessful in escaping the mobbed plaza, like so many others. Isaiab expressed a readiness to join Conan; even the haggard Otsgar acted less disdainful than he previously had.

"So you think Horaspes' reign will be the death of the city," he asked thoughtfully, watching the undead troopers march and wheel before the wailing crowds.

Conan nodded grim assent. "When his dead followers serve him so well, why should he put up with the inconvenience of living slaves?"

Zafriti clung to Otsgar, watching the sinister maneuvers going on before them, with a haunted expression. "This is horrid! It reminds me of my native Stygia, only worse, far worse!"

"Aye, 'tis bad." Otsgar nodded in his turn. "Horaspes' ascendancy may be hurtful to business after all."

Conan faced him earnestly. "Then help me fight him! The princess has promised us her friendship. This is your chance to gain a favored position with the new regime!"

"Indeed. Perhaps the time has come to switch sides."

Conan grinned wolfishly and reached around Zafriti to clap Otsgar on the shoulder. "Good, then! And what of Asrafel? Has he been slain?"

Zafriti shook her head. "Nay, he was swept up in the political fervor some time ago. He ran off jabbering some wild plan about how to defeat Horaspes' army."

"The fellow is a firebrand! I would call him harmless, had I not seen him deal with King Ebnezub!" Conan glanced around resignedly. "But it will take more than his zeal to save this day."

As they watched the steady deployments before the gate a Shemitish youth sought out Conan with breathless news. "Conan, my uncle Ezrah sends word: Horaspes himself moves forward! He is coming this way on foot amidst a phalanx of mummies."

Conan nodded thoughtfully. "He'll need to use his sorcerous power at close range to open the city gate. I thought he would wait until nightfall, when his troops will have the advantage. But it's better this way!" He turned to Otsgar and Isaiab. "I can throw a few hundred howling Shemites at him from the flank, but we'll need a strong spearhead to fight our way through. I want you two with me."

Otsgar considered a moment, then met Conan's look. "I'll go with you, fair enough. Mitra knows that the two of us are a match for any overfed sorcerer. But I want Isaiab to stay with Zafriti and protect her. None can tell what will befall tonight, now that hell is set loose on earth."

Conan glanced to Isaiab and the dancer, who did not demur; then he clasped Otsgar's hand. "The two of us, then. Death to Horaspes! And a second, more lasting death to those who serve him!"

Chapter 19

Long Live the Dead King!

At the rumor of a fight, scores of the rowdiest Shemites gathered near the city gate. Among them moved Conan, naming leaders, confirming the atttack signal, and doing his best to impart to each fighter in a single fierce glance what he or she lacked of a lifetime's military training. A poor expedient, he knew; he could only hope that a preponderance of the gods were on their side.

Otsgar also marshaled the troops, and of the two northerners the innkeeper was the better known. On finding him in their ranks, desperate men and women waved high their stolen swords and makeshift weapons, flashing brave smiles.

Yet the knot of enemy troops where Horaspes was said to walk drew nearer, moving up the corridor of armed nightlings, and Conan soon passed the word for silence. From his place at the center of the mob he stepped up onto the side of an overturned cart to reconnoiter the scene.

The enemy cordon stretched four hundred paces from tomb to gate, with a broad margin on either side where the living feared to tread. Inside a triple square of heavily armed undead marchers strode the white-clad figure of Horaspes. Queen Nitokar was not in sight; an informant told Conan that she remained in command before the tomb, which reared ever darker against the murky sky.

On the city wall opposite, torches paraded in readiness for night. Defenders lined the battlements, clustering thickest above the shut and barred city gate. Conan could make out the tower-top where Afrit and others of the highest rank stood watching. Far below them, the nightling pickets stood heedlessly close to the gate, within easy spear-cast; obviously, having already suffered the discomfort of death, they were unafraid of the mortals' barbs.

The situation worried Conan. If Horaspes could approach so near the gate, there was little doubt that he could pry it open by some sorcerous trick, or else a political one. When that happened, it would likely cause another rout of the defenders and the ultimate fall of the city. Only a swift, unexpected attack might prevent it. Like the one he intended to unleash momentarily.

Meanwhile, powerless to escape, the undiminished crowds huddled at the perimeter of the killing-ground. Sobs and wails sounded on all sides as the stricken peasants awaited the night and the outcome of the siege. Conan spied some purposeful activity along the canals: lines of workers, their plodding forms etched darkly against the red-weltering clouds of the western sky, were displacing the refugees and moving up onto the banks carrying tools or weapons of some sort. A few among them shouted faintly and waved their arms, as if directing the others; perhaps they were planning to bridge the treacherous water with ropes, or float a makeshift ferry.

In any event, their efforts were far from the focus of Conan's interest. Horaspes' party was almost opposite him now, and he braced himself to give the attack signal. Shemitish faces, variously sullen or wild-eyed, glanced to him expectantly; it was clear that they were ready to throw every hope they had into this effort. Otsgar looked around with a somewhat more doubtful expression on his beefy face; but he was hemmed in too closely by ruffians to back out now. Conan placed a hand on his sword-hilt in readiness.

Suddenly the marching square of nightlings halted just short of the spot Conan had intended for the attack. As he

watched, the guards at the fringe of the marching column
stepped outward to form a broader perimeter. At its center a
group of them grasped the edges of a large, leveled shield,
and the white-clad figure stepped up onto it, his gold-hemmed
robe flapping at his sandaled ankles. The bearers then raised
it shooulder-high into the air, elevating Horaspes well above
the throng on the makeshift platform. He bowed shallowly
toward the city gates and cupped his hands to his mouth.
Once again his shattering stentor-voice roared out, this time
near enough to rattle Conan's teeth.

"PEOPLE OF ABADDRAH! YOUR LIBERATION IS
AT HAND!"

The earthshaking announcement was greeted with wails and
shrieks from those cowering nearby, and with shocked silence from the city wall. Conan's segment of the crowd
stayed tense and quiet; their eyes shifted from Stygian prophet
to Cimmerian warrior as they nervously awaited the signal
amid the hammering peals of the voice.

"SHEMITES, NEVER DOUBT THAT ELLAEL FAVORS
YOU! A GLORIOUS DAY IS COME! I GIVE YOU—WHAT
BROUGHT YOU HERE, AND WHAT YOU CHERISH
ABOVE ALL ELSE." As he spoke, Horaspes waved his arm
grandiloquently toward the tomb; then he returned both hands
to his mouth to trumpet the next words. "ABADDRANS, I
GIVE YOU BACK YOUR KING!"

As the last syllables blared out and the prophet waved
toward the tomb again, Conan's eyes followed his gesture to
see a flurry of activity before the great mausoleum. There,
indeed, a new body of troops was forming up, and in their
midst was a great platform or litter on which something large
and pale reclined, stirring listlessly. In spite of the failing
light there could be no doubt what it was.

"CITIZENS, HIS ROYAL SPLENDOR EBNEZUB RE-
TURNS! OPEN THE CITY GATE TO WELCOME HIM!"

The reaction of the nearby crowd was vehement but confused. From atop the wall rang astonished outcries; apparently some guards rushed to obey while others opposed them.

A wave of violent reaction swirled along battlement while
through the mob below passed stirrings of mingled horror and
hope.

The prophet's voice trumpeted again. "FORM A DELE-
GATION, NOBLES, TO HONOR YOUR KING! SEND
FORTH HIS CHILDREN TO GREET HIM!"

Conan shuddered at that; now the prophet wanted hos-
tages, including Afrit. He could not guess how the Shemites
would finally react to Horaspes' demands and the rebirth of
their king, but he knew that he himself dared not wait any
longer. He drew his sword and flourished it on high.

"Forward, dogs, for Shem! Death to the wizard!"

His own shouts sounded pathetically weak after the prophet's; yet in a moment they were rebounding from a score of
throats, as those who had long been primed for action threw
aside their doubts and started to move. Sweeping across the
open space, they fell on the nightlings in a yelling horde.

It was a savage fight from the start, for the ancient mummies knew not the notion of retreat. They hacked and flailed
stubbornly where they stood, letting themselves be cut or
dragged down without any thought of falling back to re-form
their ranks. Standing in a rigid line, they were set upon by
dense mobs of Shemites who jabbed or clubbed with makeshift weapons and knocked their feet out from under them;
some were lifted overhead and literally torn apart by scores
of eager hands. Soon the battle line consisted of swirling
knots of humans who beat and rent at the isolated undead
things in their midst, venting their wrath and disgust on the
cold, dry, mummified flesh. At their success, more of the
watching crowd swarmed in to join them.

Yet that was only the first rank of Horaspes' defenders;
beyond them stood the second line of fresher and better-
armed tomblings surrounding the prophet himself. These were
mostly deceased officers and aristocrats of the city's recent,
prosperous past. Attired as they had been entombed, in
costly ceremonial armor or good, functional plate, they were
distinguishable from living men only by the wizened pallor of

their features and the gaudiness of their embalming-paint. A few were immaculate, youthful-seeming warriors who had relinquished life fairly recently, including some of the elite guards slain inside the tomb earlier that day and hastily embalmed. They strode into the melee in a tight line, swinging their blades against the mortals with devastating skill and halting the momentum of their charge.

Against these warriors Conan and Otsgar hurled themselves to good effect. All along their front the nightlings were engaged by the mob, but no single defender or pair of them could stand against the two giant northerners. The first to try was a stout, bush-bearded noble of some past century, his face pale as a shark's belly; Otsgar's stroke split his rubied headband and the bloodless skull beneath it while Conan's blade struck aside the swing of the gem-crusted sword and ran its owner through the middle. His thrust must have severed the aristocrat's spine, for as Conan wrenched his blade free the mummy bent impossibly backward. Shedding dry sand from its riven belly, it folded grotesquely beneath the shuffling feet of its fellows.

The next to oppose them was a trim, youthful officer of the tomb police, whose handsome aspect was marred only by a mouth that hung open with the bloated look of the freshly drowned. Likely this was one of those who had slain himself in his eagerness to accompany his king to the Afterworld. The thing raised its curved sword already beaded with human blood and swung it down at Otsgar. Both the northmen's weapons struck it at once, breaking the blade in two places. Their subsequent strokes hacked away the arms that still tried to hammer vainly at them with the hilt. Wide-eyed, the thing turned and tottered away, its hideous mouth working with soundless screams.

"SUBJECTS, YOUR KING COMES." Horaspes stood on high ignoring the turmoil at his feet. "OPEN THE GATES SWIFTLY AND MAKE READY!"

Conan thought it unlikely the nobles would open the gates; yet haste was called for. He chopped a gaunt, ax-wielding

priestly warrior in twain while Otsgar fought off a burly
tomb-guard.

Then the two northerners were through the line and in
among the nightlings, with no new defenders rushing to fill
the gap they made. For a few moments they struck out
savagely left and right, hacking the necks and hamstrings of
the embattled mummies they had outflanked. Conan cut a
knee from under one fat-bellied, richly cloaked, courtly corpse;
it fell to earth with a muddy splash. He glanced down,
astonished to find himself suddenly ankle-deep in water.

It washed all around, flowing in a scummy tide which
stirred the bodies and the detached parts of nightlings more
buoyantly than it did the fresher human remains. Excited
shouts rose amid the battle cries. "They've broken the levees," the voices yelled. "Father Styx comes to save us!"

With new understanding, Conan dared to glance back over
his shoulder toward the canal-bank. Large crowds labored
there in earnest unison against the background of darkening
vermilion sky. Water-swapes swung high, and shovels rose
and fell feverishly; even at that distance and over the battle-
din, their faint, exultant cries could be heard. The river-
children were fighting back against the nightlings with the
weapons they knew best.

A bold plan! Conan wished he'd thought of it himself—
though it might end by drowning them all. He was uncomfortably aware of the water rising around his shins as he
sloshed up to Otsgar, who was hewing off the flailing sword-
arm of a fallen mummy. "The peasants are opening the
canals," he gasped in the Vanirman's ear. "The river will
flood the tomb-district and wipe out the undead reserves!"

"By Mitra, that was Asrafel's mad notion!" Otsgar looked
around him in evident surprise. "The lad must have found
other fools to help him!"

Conan grinned to himself. It stood to reason, farm child
that Asrafel was, and his father drowned by Ebnezub's men.
Yet there remained more urgent matters.

"Now we face Horaspes," he muttered to Otsgar. "Stay

wide apart, and beware him! He can melt projectiles in air, and his touch brings death.''

Ahead of them, among swarming fighters whose struggles were barely visible in the fading light, the only real opposition was the last circle of nightlings standing close under Horaspes. These picked guards were all richly robed, becrowned personages—late kings of Abaddrah, their white hair and fingernails grown long and tangled over centuries in the grave. Two of their number now supported Horaspes at waist level on the raised shield while the rest stood staunchly, hacking at the wild Shemites as they flew past.

The prophet himself, from his lowered vantage, finally took in the peril of the mob's attack and the flood. He rapped out orders in a harsh dialect to the nightlings standing nearby and turned an anxious glance toward the tomb. Thence, judging by the shouts and screams of battle, the new force of mummies flanking dead Ebnezub's litter were swiftly approaching to aid him.

The moment was ripe, then. With a savage bellow the Cimmerian hurled himself at one of Horaspes' bodyguards. His blade clanged to block the sweep of the dead king's broadsword, while his foot swung up high to strike the creature's chest.

The kick splashed his foe with muddy water, which was now knee-deep; whether it broke the gaunt old neck he could not tell, since the shriveled monarch staggered back with its shaggy head only slightly askew. But the stroke bought Conan time to chop off the ax-hand of an even hoarier mummy-king that menaced him from the side. He turned back to hack the belly stuffing out of the first before its great sword could descend again, then kicked it aside to flounder helplessly in the water.

Otsgar dealt similarly with the guards on Horaspes' other flank, driving them down into the swirling muck with savage sword-blows, to the prophet's audible rage. But his angry exhortations to his troops ceased as he and his attackers both

turned to stare at the city wall. There the clanking of heavy
chains signaled that the gate of Abaddrah was opening.

The broad, heavy cullis door was already raised nearly
halfway, and through it filed a torchlit procession of armed
guards and courtiers. At their center Conan glimpsed the
crowned tresses of Princess Afrit, the errant, rebellious daughter sent forth to greet her royal parents whether she wished
to or no.

Horaspes' victory was almost complete, then. The courtly
fools feared the monsters and the mob at the gate less than
they feared the wrath of their dead king. Neither did the flood
deter them, for city and wall were on raised ground, and the
water had not yet risen to the gate.

Now, with the prophet's undead reinforcements clamoring
close on one hand and the city welcoming its own destruction
on the other, Conan felt rage blossom in his heart. Instead of
despairing he became a living blur of havoc. His sword
spewed water left and right like a sea-tornado as, with savage
blows, he cut the legs from under the last of the kingly
guards. The flailing mummy toppled back against one of his
undead brethren supporting the shield, who in turn slipped to
his knees in the flood. The platform tilted, and the cursing
Horaspes was forced to leap down into the rising water
directly between his would-be assassins.

For Conan it was a cherished chance. Ignoring all the other
perils around him he drew back his sword for a mighty
thrust. At the same instant Otsgar raised his weapon high in
the air to cleave the prophet's unprotected head.

The Stygian's response was quick and astonishing. As the
blades swept toward him, his bare hands shot out to grasp
each one in air, showing no concern for their force and
keenness. The power of his grip took his attackers by surprise,
and not only because he arrested their strokes in midflight.

As soon as Horaspes' hand touched his sword, Conan felt
its hilt grow warm in his grasp; the metal burned with a
mystical, smoldering energy that coursed through it more
intensely each second. Was it just his imagination, or could

he already see the steel blade incandescing pink before him, giving back the great heat that had forged it—and perhaps that which had first welded its metal into earth's ancient stone as well? Paralyzed for the instant, he watched it glow. The nerves of his arm shrieked with pain; his nostrils filled with the smell of the burning shagreen hilt-winding, and of his own scorching skin.

It was feral stubbornness that caused him, rather than letting go. to bend his knees low and force his end of the sword down beneath the swirling surface of the flood. The water had risen nearly waist-deep and its dark coolth closed swiftly over his agonized hand, soothing it a little. The sword-metal glowed red even underwater, and bubbling. gouts of steam exploded upward, scalding his skin where they jetted against it.

Meanwhile, Otsgar, unable to stand the searing heat and likewise unable to stanch it, released his sword—as did Horaspes an instant later. Where the weapon plunged into the water between them an even denser steam-cloud rose, obscuring the Vanirman almost entirely from view. Strangely, the steam-billows did not die out swiftly as they would have in a smithy's trough, but kept gouting violently upward. And into the midst of that living cloud Horaspes' arm plunged with a quick, feral gesture that boded no good for its target.

The sight spurred Conan to further effort. The agony in his hand remained just bearable to his rage-dulled nerves; and the wizard's attention was distracted, though his impervious grip still held the Cimmerian's sword low and out of action. Clenching his blistered fingers tighter on the hilt, Conan twisted it underwater and, with all the strength of his pain and desperation, drove the blade upward and forward.

He felt it slide through the prophet's momentarily relaxed grip; an instant later it went home, its glowing point searing through Horaspes' wet gown with a hiss, stabbing into his belly. The glaring, superheated blade cut slack wizardly flesh like cold butter. When the force of the thrust was exhausted, the sword's point tented out the prophet's robe in back and scorched through the damp fabric to glow there like a hot brand in the twilit dark. Swiftly Conan let go the sword, evading the prophet's claw-curved hand as it snatched at his wrist.

Horaspes' face swung toward him, bulging-eyed. His mouth contorted in an agonized snarl, exhaling a small, round puff of steam. The sword transfixing him glowed brighter than ever. As his pudgy, uninjured hand plucked at it, his whole body writhed and twisted in pain, resembling not so much a mortally wounded man as a cutlet of meat broiling and curling on a spit. With a dying gasp the prophet slipped backward into the water.

Conan did not turn away; he sensed no other imminent threat. Carefully he watched the wizardly corpse floating and scalding at the base of its spreading pillar of steam, as he would have watched a severed viper to make sure it was dead. Guardedly then he circled the abomination to get near Otsgar. He dragged his fellow raider's bulky body up from the unnaturally heated water where it had settled motionless.

His friend was dead; in the middle of his chest was a charred cavity, sickeningly familiar to one who had seen the end of the guard-captain Aramas. Letting the limp body settle back into the water, Conan looked to the dead prophet's protruding hand, in which was clutched a coal-black lump: the Vanirman's heart.

With a shudder Conan finally dared to touch the wizard's warm, parboiled flesh. His own hands, he noted with surprise, scarcely felt burned. Gingerly he prized the charred lump free of Horaspes' clawed fingers and dropped it into the water near its rightful owner.

Around him the battle seemed to have dispersed in the night, with the surviving humans crowding into the shallows near the city wall. A few undead fighters still roved the plaza aimlessly, chest-deep in water. They had trouble making their way, their desiccated bodies less solid and stable in the swirling flood than live human torsos. Conan watched as several of them were swept away, thrashing helplessly. Of the resurrected king and his queen, and of the chariots, wagons, and the rest of the undead army, there was no sign. Between Conan and the great tomb, the surface of the water was lit by red-gold reflections of the torches that still flared high in brackets around the monument's base.

And as Conan gazed across the dimpled, littered Stygian tide, he suddenly realized that its motion had direction and purpose. For the scum, the bodies, all the nameless debris that littered the surface of the water, were moving together. All flowed toward Ebnezub's vast edifice, and into its yawning gates; the noise of their descent to the underworld echoed forth over the plaza like the roar of a cataract falling deep in a cave.

An irony it was, truly. All those who had died that day, as well as those who never should have arisen from death, were being laid together into the tomb by the tireless, efficient hand of Father Styx.

Another sound came to Conan's ears from nearby—the clangor of steel. There, on the high apron of ground before the open city gate, enough leaderless nightlings still remained to engage the delegation from the city in a brisk fight. All around the combat, flood refugees thronged through the shallows to shove their way into the city. A perilous situation, with Afrit likely caught in the middle of it. Weaponless, half-striding and half-swimming, Conan made his way toward the gate.

Chapter 20

Life to the Queen!

Morning found the city dazed and unrestful, its folk harrowed by their glimpse of apocalypse. As in time of war, the broad boulevards and narrow lanes were cluttered with displaced rural folk from outside the walls, who either stretched themselves out on the hard paves for a comfortless sleep or wandered listlessly in search of food and shelter. In the streets where they prowled, some of the houses and shops were tightly shuttered, while others, their owners absent or dead, stood rifled open by the mob. The city-dwelling Shemites waited passive but watchful; as always in the absence of any acknowledged rule, doubt and instability reigned.

Every inhabitant sensed the vacuum of royal power, and none could say what dark contender would march forward to fill it. Yet there was also a sense of relief, a dawning wonder shared by all those who had doubted that they would ever again see the sun rise to paint the walls of their city pinkish gold.

The light first touched the lofty battlements, where loitering watchmen debated what officer or faction they should report to that morning. They had been unrelieved all night and were weary; nevertheless, they lingered to admire the vast, mirrorlike pond that stretched from the escarpment before them to the broad base of Ebnezub's tomb. Sometime before dawn the echoing roar of water rushing down the throat of the tomb had stopped; now the estuary's limpid bays and channels extended far back into the ancient necropolis, reflecting the shapes of its monuments up to the sky.

As the sun began to probe into the urban lanes, the scene remained tranquil. More of the fitful sleepers arose and roamed the streets, passing sooner or later into the market square. Acquaintances met and talked there, and families reunited joyously. They told one another of the funeral and the fight, and of all the terrors and wonders of the previous day.

Those who had been near, but not too near, the great tomb just at nightfall described how flood waters had surged across its low threshold, sweeping the raving Queen Nitokar and her guards and servants into the dark depths—and how, buoyed up by his great litter, King Ebnezub, if such the corpulent figure really was, had likewise been drunk down the tomb's greedy gullet shortly thereafter. None dared to say whether this was a good thing or an ill one, but the story was repeated a thousand times that day, and furtively relished with each telling.

On a lane just off the city's main street stood a draper's shop which had been looted during the turbulent night. As morning brightened, a stout door at the back of the establishment's jumbled interior was unlatched and opened. From the gloomy inner room a broad face, blue-eyed and vigilant, peered out into the vacant shop.

Then the door swung wide, revealing the bare-chested figure of a muscular, black-maned northman, who had to stoop low under the lintel to pass through. Following him closely was a lithe female, also dark-haired and crowned with a jeweled diadem that glimmered in the slanting, dusty rays. With girlish craft she had pinned a length of pale-blue draper's cloth across her shoulders to fashion a fetching shift, yet beneath the scanty garment she was every bit a woman. The intimacy with which she clung to the northerner's arm told much about their night's adventure.

"Conan, I wish . . . I truly wish we never had to go back

to the palace! Royalty is boring!'' She flushed in remembrance. ''Not lately, I mean, with all the troubles at court. But most of the time it's just decrees and taxes, and courtiers endlessly promoting their own welfare!'' She twined her arms around his torso. ''I would rather stay here with you forever!''

''I too, girl.'' The Cimmerian turned to place an arm around her waist. Drawing her close against him, he brought her face up to his and kissed her long and deliberately; then he gently set her down. ''But now is the time for us to move. Bringing this city under your thumb will be enough of a challenge to hold your interest, I'll wager.'' He resumed picking his way over tumbled spools and racks, toward the door.

''You really think I have a chance?'' she asked, clinging to him.

''Aye. Even last night would not have been too soon to make your bid. But the fickle fools had almost sent you to your death, and in all the turmoil none of them could be trusted.'' He hitched up the stolen sword at his belt. ''Better to let the various parties sort themselves out overnight, so they can vie and plead for your favor this morning!'' He paused and glanced aside at her. ''Know you, there will be ill-wishers, too. I pledge my life to keep you alive long enough to make contact with your allies. The rest is up to you.''

''And afterward''—Afrit brushed her cheek against his massive shoulder—''there will be a place for you in my royal court.''

''Perhaps.'' Conan peered out through the splintered doorframe, then drew the princess outside with him into the lane. ''Such plans have failed in the past. But for now, all we need is to get you safely before the nobles.''

As they moved through the streets the princess's bearing and her royal adornment drew exclamations and stares; but rather than causing the menaces and delays Conan had feared, her aspect made the citizens open the way respectfully. Afrit now accompanied him with more restraint, walking serenely beside him and letting her hand rest lightly in the crook of his arm. Not his sword-arm, he made sure. He was aware of others following along behind them. On entering the market square and glancing back, he was surprised to see that the crowd of friendly-seeming subjects who had fallen in with them extended out of sight along the winding lane.

In the pillared square there was even more of a flurry at the sight of Afrit, and Conan tried to conduct her swiftly through the mob. But then, hearing eager hails, he turned. Jubilation flooded his chest as Isaiab and Asrafel approached him through the crowd.

"Welcome, rogues! Never have I needed you more!" Keeping the princess close by his side, he clasped his fellow raiders' hands and smote their shoulders heartily. Then, abruptly, solemnity fell over him. "Otsgar is . . ."

"We know, Conan." Isaiab nodded. "I saw it, and I told Asrafel."

The younger Shemite nodded. "Aye, a cruel death. But a worthier one than I foresaw for such a knave as Otsgar."

"Aye, indeed!" Conan grinned again. "Near as worthy as your own part in the fight, Asrafel! This town should be grateful to you!" He turned to Isaiab. "And what of Zafriti?"

"She is safe at the inn, getting bathed and rested." Isaiab shrugged. "I think she will bear up, Conan."

"Good. But do not call me by name again." Conan glanced suspiciously over the crowd that was forming around them. "I need you to help me escort the princess to the palace. And that may be just the beginning of the danger. Are you game?"

Afrit stepped forward and said earnestly, "Any help you render us now will only increase the debt I owe you."

The two raiders assented in a show of bravado, with courtly bows to the princess. They pressed on through the market, making better time once they struck the colonnaded central boulevard. Before long the broad portico of the palace loomed ahead.

There was no lack of activity there, in spite of the early

hour. Chariots were pulled up at the base of the wide marble stairs, and at least three different kinds of troops shared the porch—palace guards, tomb police, and armed priests, each group eyeing the others uncertainly. Piles of burnt-out torches suggested that their vigil had been an all-night one.

Leaving the trailing crowd behind them at the base of the steps, the four climbed toward the doors. As they approached, the princess gazed boldly at the guards. Either because of her regal assurance or because of the uncertain division of authority, none of them blocked her way or issued a challenge. But as the four approached the half-open portals, a priestly figure hurried forth to greet them.

"Ah, Princess, at last!" It was the tall, potbellied priest whom Conan had grown to recognize and mistrust. "We knew not what had become of you! We feared . . . But come with me, my Princess, into the presence of the high counselors! I see that your subjects have come forth to welcome you, too." He glanced at the sizable crowd below. "Ellael be praised, this is a signal day for our land! Your escort can stay here." The unctuous fellow extended his welcoming arms to Afrit while simultaneously managing to convey his disapproval of her friends.

"Your Sanctity, these men have protected me thus far, and I want them to remain at my side." She clasped the priest's hand in hers, deftly avoiding his hug, and swept him along with her into the palace. In its shadowy interior more soldiers lounged in ready disarray, looking up suspiciously; the princess did not pause there but moved toward another archway with open doors.

On passing through it, Conan found that they were in the huge chamber where he had first seen the royal family and fought the snake-wrestler Khada Khufi. Here at the raised end of the cavernous room were not guards but nobles and priests, most of them haggard and disheveled, still clad in soiled ceremonial garb from the previous day's obsequies and fight. They stood or sat in a loose group centered around a padded sofa, where the gangling boy Eblis reclined in a pose that would have suited his royal father.

On the entry of his half sister, the young prince looked up with surprise and distinct displeasure. The reaction of the courtiers was more enthusiastic. They arose and moved toward Afrit, bowing cordially and greeting her with expressions ranging from intense relief to cautious evaluation, with occasional wary looks at her bodyguards.

In a moment she was engaged in a half-dozen conversations about the fate of the kingdom. The talk quickly took on immediate political significance; Conan gathered that she was being nominated by the priestly faction as a regent who could quickly pull the city administration together and avert civil strife, at least until the male heir came of age.

Afrit's response was impressive. She talked easily of large concerns, all her poise and naturalness coming to the fore, her cheeks showing a little of the same happy flush that Conan had been privileged to see earlier that morning. The courtiers, too, found her engaging, and those who tried to lead her into damaging statements and premature commitments failed in every attempt. Conan saw little need for his own violent talents and did his best to fade into the background.

Of all those present only Eblis, sitting where he had been abandoned by the royal retainers, looked displeased. At length he slouched to the periphery of the discoursing nobles, his arms folded tightly under his foppishly spangled cape.

Asrafel, likewise watching the courtly negotiations unfold, spoke quietly aside to Conan. "It looks as if the princess will be enthroned before the sun is high, and with our help! Strange, I never saw myself as having a favored place with this royal house."

"Aye, Conan," Isaiab put in gaily. "This little errand was not as hard as you expected."

"Conan!" The young prince Eblis's voice rose, cracking with excitement, to interrupt the various conversations. "So this is the foreign spy, the slayer of my father! How dare you come here!"

Seeing all eyes turn his way, Conan stood startled, momentarily at a loss to answer. He was further astonished when the lad darted at him, jerking a long, curving dagger from beneath his cape.

It was no great difficulty for the Cimmerian to sidestep the youth's impetuous rush. But Isaiab was less swift and received a slash on his arm as he reached for his sword-hilt. The prince turned back to Conan, dagging wildly at him again.

Without drawing a weapon, Conan balled his fist and struck at the hand that held the knife. His blow moved faster than any eye could follow, and the prince's blade was knocked back against the side of his head and out of his grasp, skittering away across the floor.

Eblis felt his ear, which had been cut. Holding his bloodied hand before his face, he gave vent to anguished screams. The courtiers hurried forward to restrain the youth and comfort him, but only Afrit dared to approach Conan and his two cursing swordmates. She clutched his hand, then swiftly relinquished it. "Conan, listen to me! You must go!"

He nodded sullenly. "Aye, I'll go away for now. Luckily no great harm is done. The lad bellows lustily, but 'twas only a small cut."

The princess shook her head and spoke urgently, her face pale. "No, Conan, you don't understand. That was a poisoned blade, given to the prince by his mother! Eblis almost certainly will die. Your friend too, I fear!" Her stricken gaze flashed briefly to Isaiab, who stood pale-faced, pressing with his palm against the deepest part of his gash. "And the nobles will surely have your life for the boy's murder!"

Conan's brain reeled, even as his ears coldly measured the footfalls of soldiers converging outside the doorway. "And what of you, Afrit?"

"I will be well. Fear not, I'm the last royal heir they have! But you—" She grasped his shoulder in her frail hands and tried to turn him bodily toward the door. "You must flee while you can!" She glanced anxiously over her shoulder, then continued in a lower voice. "Once I rule, I'll try to protect your friends. But for you, Conan, there is no safety in Abaddrah! Now go—my love!"

Conan heard the sob in her words and cast a final look her way; then he turned toward the archway, hauling Isaiab and Asrafel along with him. Soldiers had straggled across the exit, but some of them now gave back before his gathering speed. The less swift ones were bowled bodily out of the way by the three, who burst into the antechamber to the ringing hiss of drawn swords.

Still the troopers were under no single commander, and Conan confused them by aiming his charge between two groups of guards with differing uniforms. He brandished his sword high, but used it only to block the thrusts of those opposing him. With a few swift, clangorous bouts of fencing, they made their way outside onto the palace steps, into full view of the townsfolk who stood watching. A high, flying kick from Conan's sandal sent the last two armed priests clattering down the steps out of their way. Then Conan was dragging the faltering Isaiab down the stairway, with Asrafel defending their backs.

Conan headed for the chariots standing idle at the base of the stairs. Reaching the nearest one, he leaped aboard, seized the startled charioteer by the collar, and hurled him headlong over the side. While his friends dragged themselves aboard he snatched up whip and reins and roused the team of four black geldings. With a flurry of whip-cracks and cries he wheeled the frightened beasts around and away, straight through the crowd, who scattered wildly to left and right before him. Gathering speed, he headed down the broad central avenue which led to Abaddrah's southern gate and the high road.

Some time later, throwing up clots and spatters of mud, the chariot slewed through the main crossroads outside the city. The giant charioteer, his black mane flying, craned his neck for signs of pursuit and saw none. With a whistle and a tug at the reins, he drove the team into the open gate of Otsgar's inn.

"Hey, stablers, shut and bar these doors! Zafriti, are you here? Bring help, we have a wounded man with us!" Driving the team around in a half turn inside the hostel yard, Conan halted the panting animals, made fast the reins, and jumped down from the platform to kneel beside Isaiab.

The wiry Shemite lay limp in the chariot, his head cradled in Asrafel's lap. His olive skin had taken on a grayish hue, and his arm, though it only seeped blood, was swollen and discolored purplish green up to the shoulder. When Conan prodded gingerly near the wound, a moan rattled from Isaiab's chest; his head rolled from side to side, and his eyes bulged with pain.

"Come, Isaiab, you'll weather this! In a while we'll have you indoors in a bed, with soothing compresses on that cut. You've survived worse wounds. . . ."

"Nay, Conan. I can feel the poison creeping through me, like fiery snakes gnawing to my heart." Isaiab's voice was breathy and pathetically weak. "I'll soon be as dead as old Ebnezub. But please, no mummy-wrap for me!" The dying man gave a feeble cough that trailed off into a wheeze. "Just throw me into the Styx. Keep me safe from such as Horaspes."

"Aye, old friend." Conan nodded solemnly. At Zafriti's summons a matronly servant arrived carrying poultices and ointment-jars, but she only stood helpless, her dismay at Isaiab's condition showing in her face, until the Cimmerian waved her back.

"Conan, I have something for you." The dying man rallied slightly and fumbled with his good arm at the front of his shirt. "I might never have dared to tell you . . . but now it doesn't matter any more. It's yours."

"Don't trouble yourself, Isaiab," Conan told him. "Just rest."

But the Shemite bestirred himself, drawing from his shirt a plum-sized leather pouch attached to his neck by a thong; he

plucked eagerly at it one-handed, craning his head to see
the parcel as it lay on his heaving chest.

"Here, I'll help." Conan reached forward and tugged at
the binding, which came loose with a glint of blue. The
pouch turned outward, revealing a golden ring set with a
giant blue sapphire—the Star of Khorala.

"When first we found you in the desert," Isaiab gasped,
"I had already stolen it. I snuck up on that fool you hunted,
while he napped under a bush at midday. I filched this from
the lining of his saddle-bag and left a lump of quartz in its
place. Belike he never even missed it."

Isaiab held the blazing blue stone up in his unsteady hand,
and Asrafel's mouth fell open at the sight. Zafriti peered
greedily, moving closer; even Conan's eyes were large with
astonishment. "And you carried it with you all this while?
Why, man, you could have bought and sold the lot of us with
it!"

Isaiab exhaled a croak that might have been a laugh.
"When you said it was worth a roomful of gold, I knew not
what to do with it. Normally I sell my prizes to Otsgar for a
pittance. Such a gem is too great for a common thief. Too
dangerous to possess."

Wheezing, Isaiab tried to draw in a new breath and shuddered with the effort. His hand slipped back down to his side,
and Conan plucked the ring from his slack fingers to hold it
up before the dying man's eyes again. "Besides," Isaiab
whispered, "getting wealth is only a small part of it. One
steals through habit . . . for the fun, and the fellowship . . ."

His wheezing ceased as, with the reflection of the Star still
bright in his eyes, he died.

Conan, after laying an ear to his friend's chest, closed his
slack eyelids. He helped Asrafel shift the body out of his lap,
laying it lengthwise in the chariot, and arose. The gem had
disappeared from his hand into some thieves'-stash on his
person. He looked around at the last of his fellow raiders,
who now numbered only two.

"Well, that ends my business here. I should warn you, this

place may soon be swarming with guardsmen in search of me. A while ago I lopped another limb off the royal family tree." He rumbled out a laugh still heavy with emotion. "But there should be no real danger to those at the inn. I'll take this chariot and lead the chase away from here. On the way I'll throw our old friend into a fast-flowing canal."

"Splendid, Conan! I'll come with you!" Zafriti, clad in a pale violet wrap that swept across one of her dark shoulders, gestured abruptly to the female servant. "Hama, pack a few of my best things." As the wench departed, the Stygian swept close against Conan with her sultry dancer's grace and with cupidity lighting her eyes. "Once you ransom your legendary gem in Ophir, the two of us can live like royalty! We'll make a bold show in the Hyborian lands . . ."

"Nay, wait!" Asrafel's voice, harsh and tremulous, challenged both of them. "Zafriti, I love you! Conan, if you mean to take her away, you must deal with me first. I have watched and suffered long enough!" The Shemite, though trim and cleanly muscled, was a mere stripling compared to Conan. That he knew it was evidenced by the paleness of his face and the trembling of his hand; this he stilled by clutching the sword-hilt at his belt.

"Here, both of you. . . ." Conan disengaged his arm from the dancer's twining hands and stepped clear of her. "Zafriti, I did not mean for you to come with me. Asrafel"—he palmed his own sword-hilt as he faced the youth—"if you want to fight me for the gem, then have at me! But do not trouble over the girl. . . ."

"But Conan!" Zafriti threw herself yearningly against him. "Surely you don't intend to leave me, after all that's passed between us!" She managed to get her slender hands about his sword-arm, and clung there. "Why, consider, Otsgar is dead. I'm free at last! And there's nothing left for me here."

"If you are free, Zafriti," Conan said, a cold note entering his voice, "then be free of me as well. For I think you would be no more faithful to me than you were to Otsgar." He shook her off again, keeping a watchful eye on Asrafel, who stood by without drawing his sword. "Crom, woman! The Vanirman may have been a knave, but he loved you, and he provided for you to the last! I am no lovesick hound like him, to be whistled up or spurned away at your whim. The roads I travel are too perilous for such games."

"Conan, you are cruel!" The Stygian pressed her hands to her face, her shoulders suddenly heaving with sobs. "You were keen enough to steal me away from Otsgar when he was alive!"

"No, Zafriti, I am not cruel, but kind. Here stands one who craves you more than life itself, judging by his willingness to fight me over you. He may be more tolerant than I am of your little dramas—but not as tolerant as Otsgar, I hope, for his own sake." Conan grasped one of the dancer's wrists. Slowly he drew her hand away from her face, which looked remarkably dry underneath. He gave her a nudge toward the trim young Shemite, who waited with one hand outstretched, his gold earring glinting in the sun.

"Asrafel is an able man, and he stands in good favor with the city's ruler. Together the two of you can hold onto what Otsgar built and carry it forward"—Conan stepped up onto the back of the chariot—"or not, as you please. In any event I leave it to you." He waved a hand. "Farewell, Asrafel, and good luck to you!"

Then he took up whip and reins, shouting to the servants. "Stablers, open the gates and stand aside! I will pass through at a gallop! It's the high road for me!"

Conan
the
Indestructible

by L. Sprague de Camp

The greatest hero of the magic-rife Hyborian Age was a northern barbarian, Conan the Cimmerian, about whose deeds a cycle of legend revolves. While these legends are largely based on the attested facts of Conan's life, some tales are inconsistent with others. So we must reconcile the contradictions in the saga as best we can.

In Conan's veins flowed the blood of the people of Atlantis, the brilliant city-state swallowed by the sea 8,000 years before his time. He was born into a clan that claimed a homeland in the northwest corner of Cimmeria, along the shadowy borders of Vanaheim and the Pictish wilderness. His grandfather had fled his own people because of a blood feud and sought refuge with the people of the North. Conan himself first saw daylight on a battlefield during a raid by the Vanir.

Before he had weathered fifteen snows, the young Cimmerian's fighting skills were acclaimed around the council fires. In that year the Cimmerians, usually at one another's throats, joined forces to repel the warlike Gundermen who, intent on colonizing southern Cimmeria, had pushed across the Aquilonian border and established the frontier post of

Venarium. Conan joined the howling, blood-mad horde that swept out of the northern hills, stormed over the stockade walls, and drove the Aquilonians back across their frontier.

At the sack of Venarium, Conan, still short of his full growth, stood six feet tall and weighed 180 pounds. He had the vigilance and stealth of the born woodsman, the iron-hardness of the mountain man, and the Herculean physique of his blacksmith father. After the plunder of the Aquilonian outpost, Conan returned for a time to his tribe.

Restless under the conflicting passions of his adolescence, Conan spent several months with a band of Æsir as they raided the Vanir and the Hyperboreans. He soon learned that some Hyperborean citadels were ruled by a caste of widely-feared magicians, called Witchmen. Undaunted, he took part in a foray against Haloga Castle, when he found that Hyperborean slavers had captured Rann, the daughter of Njal, chief of the Æsir band.

Conan gained entrance to the castle and spirited out Rann Njalsdatter; but on the flight out of Hyperborea, Njal's band was overtaken by an army of living dead. Conan and the other Æsir survivors were led away to slavery ("Legions of the Dead").

Conan did not long remain a captive. Working at night, he ground away at one link of his chain until it was weak enough to break. Then one stormy night, whirling a four-foot length of heavy chain, he fought his way out of the slave pen and vanished into the downpour.

Another account of Conan's early years tells a different tale. This narrative, on a badly broken clay prism from Nippur, states that Conan was enslaved as a boy of ten or twelve by Vanir raiders and set to work turning a grist mill. When he reached his full growth, he was bought by a Hyrkanian pitmaster who traveled with a band of professional fighters staging contests for the amusement of the Vanir and Æsir. At this time Conan received his training with weapons. Later he escaped and made his way south to Zamora (*Conan the Barbarian*).

Of the two versions, the records of Conan's enslavement by the Hyrkanians at sixteen, found in a papyrus in the British Museum, appear much more legible and self-consistent. But this question may never be settled.

Although free, the youth found himself half a hostile kingdom away from home. Instinctively he fled into the mountains at the southern extremity of Hyperborea. Pursued by a pack of wolves, he took refuge in a cave. Here he discovered the seated mummy of a gigantic chieftain of ancient times, with a heavy bronze sword across its knees. When Conan seized the sword, the corpse arose and attacked him ("The Thing in the Crypt").

Continuing southward into Zamora, Conan came to Arenjun, the notorious "City of Thieves." Green to civilization and, save for some rudimentary barbaric ideas of honor and chivalry, wholly lawless by nature, he carved a niche for himself as a professional thief.

Being young and more daring than adroit, Conan's progress in his new profession was slow until he joined forces with Taurus of Nemedia in a quest for the fabulous jewel called the "Heart of the Elephant." The gem lay in the almost impregnable tower of the infamous mage Yara, captor of the extraterrestrial being Yag-Kosha ("The Tower of the Elephant").

Seeking greater opportunities to ply his trade, Conan wandered westward to the capital of Zamora, Shadizar the Wicked. For a time his thievery prospered, although the whores of Shadizar soon relieved him of his gains. During one larceny, he was captured by the men of Queen Taramis of Shadizar, who sent him on a mission to recover a magical horn wherewith to resurrect an ancient, evil god. Taramis's plot led to her own destruction (*Conan the Destroyer*).

The barbarian's next exploit involved a fellow thief, a girl named Tamira. The Lady Jondra, an arrogant aristocrat of Shadizar, owned a pair of priceless rubies. Baskaran Imalla, a religious fanatic raising a cult among the Kezankian hillmen, coveted the jewels to gain control over a fire-breathing dragon he had raised from an egg. Conan and Tamira both yearned for the rubies; Tamira took a post as lady's maid to Jondra for a chance to steal them.

An ardent huntress, Jondra set forth with her maid and her men-at-arms to slay Baskaran's dragon. Baskaran captured the two women and was about to offer them to his pet as a snack when Conan intervened (*Conan the Magnificent*).

Soon Conan was embroiled in another adventure. A stranger hired the youth to steal a casket of gems sent by the King of Zamora to the King of Turan. The stranger, a priest of the serpent-god Set, wanted the jewels for magic against his enemy, the renegade priest Amanar.

Amanar's emissaries, who were hominoid reptiles, had stolen the gems. Although wary of magic, Conan set out to recover the loot. He became involved with a bandette, Karela, called the Red Hawk, who proved the ultimate bitch; when Conan saved her from rape, she tried to kill him. Amanar's party had also carried off to the renegade's stronghold a dancing girl whom Conan had promised to help (*Conan the Invincible*).

Soon rumors of treasure sent Conan to the nearby ruins of ancient Larsha, just ahead of the soldiers dispatched to arrest him. After all but their leader, Captain Nestor, had perished in an accident arranged by Conan, Nestor and Conan joined forces to plunder the treasure; but ill luck deprived them of their gains ("The Hall of the Dead").

Conan's recent adventures had left him with an aversion to warlocks and Eastern sorceries. He fled northwestward through Corinthia into Nemedia, the second most powerful Hyborian kingdom. In Nemedia he resumed his profession successfully enough to bring his larcenies to the notice of Aztrias Pentanius, ne'er-do-well nephew of the governor. Oppressed by gambling debts, this young gentleman hired the outlander to purloin a Zamorian goblet, carved from a single diamond, that stood in the temple-museum of a wealthy collector.

Conan's appearance in the temple-museum coincided with its master's sudden demise and brought the young thief to the unwelcome attention of Demetrio, of the city's Inquisitorial Council. This caper also gave Conan his second experience with the dark magic of the serpent-brood of Set, conjured up by the Stygian sorcerer Thoth-Amon ("The God in the Bowl").

Having made Nemedia too hot to hold him, Conan drifted south into Corinthia, where he continued to occupy himself with the acquisition of other person's property. By diligent application, the Cimmerian earned the repute of one of the boldest thieves in Corinthia. Poor judgment of women, however, cast him into chains until a turn in local politics brought freedom and a new career. An ambitious nobleman, Murilo, turned him loose to slit the throat of the Red Priest, Nabonidus, the scheming power behind the local throne. This venture gathered a prize collection of rogues in Nabonidus's mansion and ended in a mire of blood and treachery ("Rogues in the House").

Conan wandered back to Arenjun and began to earn a semi-honest living by stealing back for their owners valuable objects that others had filched from them. He undertook to recover a magical gem, the Eye of Erlik, from the wizard Hissar Zul and return it to its owner, the Kahn of Zamboula.

There is some question about the chronology of Conan's life at this point. A recently-translated tablet from Asshurbanipal's library states that Conan was about seventeen at the time. This would place the episode right after that of "The Tower of the Elephant," which indeed is mentioned in the cuneiform. But from internal evidence, this event seems to have taken place several years later. For one thing, Conan appears too clever, mature and sophisticated; for another, the fragmentary medieval Arabic manuscript *Kitab al-Qunn* implies that Conan was well into his twenties by then.

The first translator of the Asshurbanipal tablet, Prof. Dr. Andreas von Fuss of the Münchner Staatsmuseum, read Conan's age as "17." In Babylonian cuneiform, "17" is expressed by two circles followed by three vertical wedges, with a horizontal wedge above the three for "minus"—hence "twenty minus three." But Academician Leonid Skram of the Moscow Archaeological Institute asserts that the depression over the vertical wedges is merely a dent made by the pick of a careless escavator, and the numeral properly reads "23."

Anyhow, Conan learned of the Eye of Erlik when he heard a discussion between an adventuress, Isparana, and her confederate. He invaded the wizard's mansion, but the wizard caught Conan and deprived him of his soul. Conan's soul was imprisoned in a mirror, there to remain until a crowned ruler broke the glass. Hissar Zul thus compelled Conan to follow Isparana and recover the talisman; but when the Cimmerian returned the Eye to Hissar Zul, the ungrateful mage tried to slay him (*Conan and the Sorcerer*).

Conan, his soul still englassed, accepted legitimate employment as bodyguard to a Khaurani noblewoman, Khashtris. This lady set out for Khauran with Conan, another guard, Shubal, and several retainers. When the other servants plotted to rob and murder their employer, Conan and Shubal saved her and escorted her to Khauran. There Conan found the widowed Queen Ialamis being courted by a young nobleman who was not at all what he seemed (*Conan the Mercenary*).

With his soul restored, Conan learned from an Iranistani, Khassek, that the Khan of Zamboula still wanted the Eye of Erlik. In Zamboula, the Turanian governor, Akter Khan, had hired the wizard Zafra, who ensorcelled swords, so that they would slay on command. En route, Conan encountered Isparana, with whom he developed a lust-hate relationship. Unaware of the magical swords, Conan continued to Zamboula and delivered the amulet. But the nefarious Zafra convinced the Khan that Conan was dangerous and should be killed on general principles (*Conan: the Sword of Skelos*).

Conan had enjoyed his taste of Hyborian-Age intrigue. It became clear that there was no basic difference between the opportunities in the palace and those in the Rats' Den, whereas the pickings were far better in high places. Besides, he wearied of the furtive, squalid life of a thief.

He was not, however, yet committed to a strictly law-abiding life. When unemployed, he took time out for a venture in smuggling. An attempt to poison him sent him to Vendhya, a land of wealth and squalor, philosophy and fanatacism, idealism and treachery (*Conan the Victorious*).

Soon after, Conan turned up in the Turanian seaport of Aghrapur. A new cult had established headquarters there under the warlock Jhandar, who needed victims to be drained of blood and reanimated as servants. Conan refused the offer of a former fellow thief, Emilio, to take part in a raid on Jhandar's stronghold to steal a fabulous ruby necklace. A Turanian sergeant, Akeba, did however persuade Conan to go with him to rescue Akeba's daughter, who had vanished into the cult (*Conan the Unconquered*).

After Jhandar's fall, Akeba urged Conan to take service in the Turanian army. The Cimmerian did not at first find military life congenial, being too self-willed and hot-tempered to easily submit to discipline. Moreover, as he was at this time an indifferent horseman and archer, Conan was relegated to a low-paid irregular unit.

Still, a chance soon arose to show his mettle. King Yildiz launched an expedition against a rebellious satrap. By sorcery, the satrap wiped out the force sent against him. Young

Conan alone survived to enter the magic-maddened satrap's city of Yaralet ("The Hand of Nergal").

Returning in triumph to the glittering capital of Aghrapur, Conan gained a place in King Yildiz's guard of honor. At first he endured the gibes of fellow troopers at his clumsy horsemanship and inaccurate archery. But the gibes died away as the other guardsmen discovered Conan's sledge-hammer fists and as his skills improved.

Conan was chosen, along with a Kushite mercenary named Juma, to escort King Yildiz's daughter Zosara to her wedding with Khan Kujula, chief of the Kuigar nomads. In the foothills of the Talakma Mountains, the party was attacked by a strange force of squat, brown, lacquer-armored horsemen. Only Conan, Juma, and the princess survived. They were taken to the subtropical valley of Meru and to the capital, Shamballah, where Conan and Juma were chained to an oar of the Meruvian state galley, about to set forth on a cruise.

On the galley's return to Shamballah, Conan and Juma escaped and made their way into the city. They reached the temple of Yama as the deformed little god-king of Meru was celebrating his marriage to Zosara ("The City of Skulls").

Back at Aghrapur, Conan was promoted to captain. His growing repute as a good man in a tight spot, however, led King Yildiz's generals to pick the barbarian for especially hazardous missions. Once they sent Conan to escort an emissary to the predatory tribesmen of the Khozgari Hills, hoping to dissuade them by bribes and threats from plundering the Turanians of the lowlands. The Khozgarians, respecting only immediate, overwhelming force, attacked the detachment, killing the emissary and all but two of the soldiers, Conan and Jamal.

To assure their safe passage back to civilization, Conan and Jamal captured Shanya, the daughter of the Khozgari chief. Their route led them to a misty highland. Jamal and the horses were slain, and Conan had to battle a horde of hairless apes and invade the stronghold of an ancient, dying race ("The People of the Summit").

Another time, Conan was dispatched thousands of miles eastward, to fabled Khitai, to convey to King Shu of Kusan a letter from King Yildiz proposing a treaty of friendship and trade. The wise old Khitan king sent his visitors back with a letter of acceptance. As a guide, however, the king appointed a foppish little nobleman, Duke Feng, who had entirely different objectives ("The Curse of the Monolith," first published as "Conan and the Cenotaph").

Conan continued in his service in Turan for about two years, traveling widely and learning the elements of organized, civilized warfare. As usual, trouble was his bedfellow. After one of his more unruly adventures, involving the mistress of his superior officer, Conan deserted and headed for Zamora. In Shadizar he heard that the Temple of Zath, the spider god, in the Zamorian city of Yezud, was recruiting soldiers. Hastening to Yezud, Conan found that a Brythunian free company had taken all the available mercenary posts. He became the town's blacksmith because as a boy he had been apprenticed in this trade.

Conan learned from an emissary of King Yildiz, Lord Parvez, that High Priest Feridun was holding Yildiz's favorite wife, Jamilah, in captivity. Parvez hired Conan to abduct Jamilah. Meanwhile Conan had set his heart on the eight huge gems that formed the eyes of an enormous statue of the spider god. As he was loosening the jewels, the approach of priests forced him to flee to a crypt below the naos. The temple dancing girl Rudabeh, with whom Conan was truly in love for the first time in his life, descended into the crypt to warn him of the doom awaiting him there (*Conan and the Spider God*).

Conan next rode off to Shadizar to track down a rumor of treasure. He obtained a map showing the location of a ruby-

studded golden idol in the Kezankian Mountains; but thieves
stole his map. Conan, pursuing them, had a brush with
Kezankian hillmen and had to join forces with the very
rogues he was tracking. He found the treasure, only to lose it
under strange circumstances ("The Bloodstained God").

Fed up with magic, Conan headed for the Cimmerian
hills. After a time in the simple, routine life of his native
village, however, he grew restless enough to join his old
friends, the Æsir, in a raid into Vanaheim. In a bitter struggle
on the snow-covered plain, both forces were wiped out—all
but Conan, who wandered off to a strange encounter with the
legendary Atali, daughter of the frost giant Ymir ("The Frost
Giant's Daughter").

Haunted by Atali's icy beauty, Conan headed back toward
the South, where, despite his often-voiced scorn of civilization, the golden spires of teeming cities beckoned. In the
Eiglophian Mountains, Conan rescued a young woman from
cannibals, but through overconfidence lost her to the dreaded
monster that haunted glaciers ("The Lair of the Ice Worm").

Conan then returned to the Hyborian lands, which include
Aquilonia, Argos, Brythunia, Corinthia, Koth, Nemedia, Ophir,
and Zingara. These countries were named for the Hyborian
peoples who, as barbarians, had 3,000 years earlier con-
quered the empire of Acheron and built civilized realms on
its ruins.

In Belverus, the capital of Nemedia, the ambitious Lord
Albañus dabbled in sorcery to usurp the throne of King
Garian. To Belverus came Conan, seeking a patron with
money to enable him to hire his own free company. Albanus
gave a magical sword to a confederate, Lord Melius, who
went mad and attacked people in the street until killed. As he
picked up the ensorcelled sword. Conan was accosted by
Hordo, a one-eyed thief and smuggler whom he had known
as Karela's lieutenant.

Conan sold the magical sword, hired his own free company, and taught his men mounted archery. Then he persuaded King Garian to hire him. But Albanus had made a man of clay and by his sorcery given it the exact appearance of the king. Then he imprisoned the king, substituted his golem, and framed Conan for murder (*Conan the Defender*).

Conan next brought his free company to Ianthe, capital of Ophir. There the Lady Synelle, a platinum-blond sorceress, wished to bring to life the demon-god Al'Kirr. Conan bought a statuette of this demon-god and soon found that various parties were trying to steal it from him. He and his company took service under Synelle, not knowing her plans.

Then the bandette Karela reappeared and, as usual, tried to murder Conan. Synelle hired her to steal the statuette, which the witch needed for her sorcery. She also planned to sacrifice Karela (*Conan the Triumphant*).

Conan went on to Argos; but since that kingdom was at peace, there were no jobs for mercenaries. A misunderstanding with the law compelled Conan to leap to the deck of a ship as it left the pier. This was the merchant galley *Argus*, bound for the coasts of Kush.

A major epoch in Conan's life was about to begin. The *Argus* was taken by Bêlit, the Shemite captain of the pirate ship *Tigress*, whose ruthless black corsairs had made her mistress of the Kushite littoral. Conan won both Bêlit and a partnership in her bloody trade ("Queen of the Black Coast," Chapter 1).

Years before, Bêlit, daughter of a Shemite trader, had been abducted with her brother Jehanan by Stygian slavers. Now she asked her lover Conan to try to rescue the youth. The barbarian slipped into Khemi, the Stygian seaport, was captured, but escaped to the eastern end of Stygia, the province of Taia, where a revolt against Stygian oppression was brewing (*Conan the Rebel*).

Conan and Bêlit resumed their piratical careers, preying mainly on Stygian vessels. Then an ill fate took them up the black Zarkheba River to the lost city of an ancient winged race ("Queen of the Black Coast," Chapters 2–5).

As Bêlit's burning funeral ship wafted out to sea, a down-hearted Conan turned his back on the sea, which he would not follow again for years. He plunged inland and joined the warlike Bamulas, a black tribe whose power swiftly grew under his leadership.

The chief of a neighboring tribe, the Bakalahs, planned a treacherous attack on another neighbor and invited Conan and his Bamulas to take part in the sack and massacre. Conan accepted but, learning that an Ophirean girl, Livia, was held captive in Bakalah, he out-betrayed the Bakalahs. Livia ran off during the slaughter and wandered into a mysterious valley, where only Conan's timely arrival saved her from being sacrificed to an extraterrestrial being ("The Vale of Lost Women").

Before Conan could build his own black empire, he was thwarted by a succession of natural catastrophes as well as by the intrigues of hostile Bamulas. Forced to flee, he headed north. After a narrow escape from pursuing lions on the veldt, Conan took shelter in a mysterious ruined castle of prehuman origin. He had a brush with Stygian slavers and a malign supernatural entity ("The Castle of Terror").

Continuing on, Conan reached the semicivilized kingdom of Kush. This was the land to which the name "Kush" properly applied; although Conan, like other northerners, tended to use the term loosely to mean any of the black countries south of Stygia. In Meroê, the capital, Conan rescued from a hostile mob the young Queen of Kush, the arrogant, impulsive, fierce, cruel, and voluptuous Tananda.

Conan became embroiled in a labyrinthine intrigue between Tananda and an ambitious nobleman who commanded a piglike demon. The problem was aggravated by the presence of Diana, a Nemedian slave girl to whom Conan, despite the jealous fury of Tananda, took a fancy. Events culminated in a night of insurrection and slaughter ("The Snout in the Dark").

Dissatisfied with his achievements in the black countries, Conan wandered to the meadowlands of Shem and became a soldier of Akkharia, a Shemite city-state. He joined a band of volunteers to liberate a neighboring city-state; but through the treachery of Othbaal, cousin of the mad King Akhîrom of Pelishtia, the volunteers were destroyed—all but Conan, who survived to track the plotter to Asgalun, the Pelishti capital. There Conan became involved in a polygonal power war among the mad Akhîrom, the treacherous Othbaal, a Stygian witch, and a company of black mercenaries. In the final hurly-burly of sorcery, steel, and blood, Conan grabbed Othbaal's red-haired mistress, Rufia, and galloped north ("Hawks Over Shem").

Conan's movements at this time are uncertain. One tale, sometimes assigned to this period, tells of Conan's service as a mercenary in Zingara. A Ptolemaic papyrus in the British Museum alleges that in Kordava, the capital, a captain in the regular army forced a quarrel on Conan. When Conan killed his assailant, he was condemned to hang. A fellow condemnee, Santiddio, belonged to an underground conspiracy, the White Rose, that hoped to topple King Rimanendo. As other conspirators created a disturbance in the crowd that gathered for the hanging, Conan and Santiddio escaped.

Mordermi, head of an outlaw band allied with the White Rose, enlisted Conan in his movement. The conspiracy was carried on in the Pit, a warren of tunnels beneath the city. When the King sent an army to clean out the Pit, the insurrectionists were saved by Callidos, a Stygian sorcerer. King Rimanendo was slain and Mordermi became king. When he proved as tyrannical as his predecessor, Conan raised another revolt; then, refusing the crown for himself, he departed (*Conan: The Road of Kings*).

This tale involves many questions. If authentic, it may belong in Conan's earlier mercenary period, around the time of *Conan the Defender*. But there is no corroboration in other narratives of the idea that Conan ever visited Zingara before his late thirties, the time of *Conan the Buccaneer*. Moreover, none of the rulers of Zingara mentioned in the papyrus appear on the list of kings of Zingara in the Byzantine manuscript *Hoi Anaktes tês Tzingêras*. Hence some students deem the papyrus either spurious or a case of confusion between Conan and some other hero. Everything else known about Conan indicates that, if he had indeed been offered the Zingaran crown, he would have grabbed it with both hands.

We next hear of Conan after he took service under Amalric of Nemedia, the general of Queen-Regent Yasmela of the little border kingdom of Khoraja. While Yasmela's brother, King Khossus, was a prisoner in Ophir, Yasmela's borders were assailed by the forces of the veiled sorcerer Natohk— actually the 3,000-years-dead Thugra Khotan of the ruined city of Kuthchemes.

Obeying an oracle of Mitra, the supreme Hyborian god, Yasmela made Conan captain-general of Khoraja's army. In this rôle he gave battle to Natohk's hosts and rescued the Queen-Regent from the malignant magic of the undead warlock. Conan won the day—and the Queen ("Black Colossus").

Conan, now in his late twenties, settled down as Khorajan commander-in-chief. But the queen, whose lover he had expected to be, was too preoccupied with affairs of state to have time for frolics. He even proposed marriage, but she explained that such a union would not be sanctioned by Khorajan law and custom. Yet, if Conan could somehow rescue her brother from imprisonment, she might persuade Khossus to change the law.

Conan set forth with Rhazes, an astrologer, and Fronto, a

thief who knew a secret passage into the dungeon where Khossus languished. They rescued the King but found themselves trapped by Kothian troops, since Strabonus of Koth had his own reasons for wanting Khossus.

Having surmounted these perils, Conan found that Khossus, a pompous young ass, would not hear of a foreign barbarian's marrying his sister. Instead, he would marry Yasmela off to a nobleman and find a middle-class bride for Conan. Conan said nothing; but in Argos, as their ship cast off, Conan sprang ashore with most of the gold that Khossus had raised and waved the King an ironic farewell ("Shadows in the Dark").

Now nearly thirty, Conan slipped away to revisit his Cimmerian homeland and avenge himself on the Hyperboreans. His blood brothers among the Cimmerians and the Æsir had won wives and sired sons, some as old and almost as big as Conan had been at the sack of Venarium. But his years of blood and battle had stirred his predatory spirit too strongly for him to follow their example. When traders brought word of new wars, Conan galloped off to the Hyborian lands.

A rebel prince of Koth was fighting to overthrow Strabonus, the penurious ruler of that far-stretched nation; and Conan found himself among old companions in the princeling's array, until the rebel made peace with his king. Unemployed again, Conan formed an outlaw band, the Free Companions (*Conan the Renegade*). This troop gravitated to the steppes west of the Sea of Vilayet, where they joined the ruffianly horde known as the *kozaki*.

Conan soon became the leader of this lawless crew and ravaged the western borders of the Turanian Empire until his old employer, King Yildiz, sent a force under Shah Amurath, who lured the *kozaki* deep into Turan and cut them down.

Slaying Amurath and acquiring the Turanian's captive, Princess Olivia of Ophir, Conan rowed out into the Vilayet Sea in a small boat. He and Olivia took refuge on an island,

where they found a ruined greenstone city, in which stood
strange iron statues. The shadows cast by the moonlight
proved as dangerous as the giant carnivorous ape that ranged
the isle, or the pirate crew that landed for rest and recreation
(''Shadows in the Moonlight'').

Conan seized command of the pirates that ravaged the Sea
of Vilayet. As chieftain of this mongrel Red Brotherhood,
Conan was more than ever a thorn in King Yildiz's flesh.
That mild monarch, instead of strangling his brother Teyaspa
in the normal Turanian manner, had cooped him up in a
castle in the Colchian Mountains. Yildiz now sent his General Artaban to destroy the pirate stronghold at the mouth of
the Zaporoska River; but the general became the harried
instead of the harrier. Retreating inland, Artaban stumbled
upon Teyaspa's whereabouts; and the final conflict involved
Conan's outlaws, Artaban's Turanians, and a brood of vam-
pires (''The Road of the Eagles'').

Deserted by his sea rovers, Conan appropriated a stallion
and headed back to the steppes. Yezdigerd, now on the
throne of Turan, proved a far more astute and energetic ruler
than his sire. He embarked on a program of imperial conquest.

Conan went to the small border kingdom of Khauran,
where he won command of the royal guard of Queen Taramis.
This queen had a twin sister, Salome, born a witch and
reared by the yellow sorcerers of Khitai. She allied herself
with the adventurer Constantius of Koth and planned by
imprisoning the Queen to rule in her stead. Conan, who
perceived the deception, was trapped and crucified. Cut down
by the chieftain Olgerd Vladislav, the Cimmerian was carried
off to a Zuagir camp in the desert. Conan waited for his
wounds to heal, then applied his daring and ruthlessness to
win his place as Olgerd's lieutenant.

When Salome and Constantius began a reign of terror in
Khauran, Conan led his Zuagirs against the Khauranian capital. Soon Constantius hung from the cross to which he had

nailed Conan, and Conan rode off smiling, to lead his Zuagirs on raids against the Turanians (''A Witch Shall Be Born'').

Conan, about thirty and at the height of his physical powers, spent nearly two years with the desert Shemites, first as Olgerd's lieutenant and then, having ousted Olgerd, as sole chief. The circumstances of his leaving the Zuagirs were recently disclosed by a silken scroll in Old Tibetan, spirited out of Tibet by a refugee. This document is now with the Oriental Institute in Chicago.

The energetic King Yezdigerd sent soldiers to trap Conan and his troop. Because of a Zamorian traitor in Conan's ranks, the ambush nearly succeeded. To avenge the betrayal, Conan led his band in pursuit of the Zamorian. When his men deserted, Conan pressed on alone until, near death, he was rescued by Enosh, a chieftain of the isolated desert town of Akhlat.

Akhlat suffered under the rule of a demon in the form of a woman, who fed on the life force of living things. Conan, Enosh informed him, was their prophesied liberator. After it was over, Conan was invited to settle in Akhlat; but, knowing himself ill-suited to a life of humdrum respectability, he instead headed southwest to Zamboula with the horse and money of Vardanes the Zamorian (''Black Tears'').

In one colossal debauch, Conan dissipated the fortune he had brought to Zamboula, a Turanian outpost. There lurked the sinister priest of Hanuman, Totrasmek, who sought a famous jewel, the Star of Khorala, for which the Queen of Ophir was said to have offered a roomful of gold. In the ensuing imbroglio, Conan acquired the Star of Khorala and rode westward (''Shadows of Zamboula'').

The medieval monkish manuscript *De sidere choralae*, rescued from the bombed ruins of Monte Cassino, continues the tale. Conan reached the capital of Ophir to find that the effeminate Moranthes II, himself under the thumb of the sinister Count Rigello, kept his queen, Marala, under lock and key. Conan scaled the wall of Moranthes's castle and fetched Marala out. Rigello pursued the fugitives nearly to the Aquilonian border, where the Star of Khorala showed its power in an unexpected way ("The Star of Khorala").

Hearing that the *kozaki* had regained their vigor, Conan returned with horse and sword to the harrying of Turan. Although the now-famous northlander arrived all but empty-handed, contingents of the *kozaki* and the Vilayet pirates soon began operating under his command.

Yezdigerd sent Jehungir Agha to entrap the barbarian on the island of Xapur. Coming early to the ambush, Conan found the island's ancient fortress-palace of Dagon restored by magic, and in it the city's malevolent god, in the form of a giant of living iron ("The Devil in Iron").

After escaping from Xapur, Conan built his *kozaki* and pirate raiders into such a formidable threat that King Yezdigerd devoted all his forces to their destruction. After a devastating defeat, the *kozaki* scattered, and Conan retreated southward to take service in the light cavalry of Kobad Shah, King of Iranistan.

Conan got himself into Kobad Shah's bad graces and had to ride for the hills. He found a conspiracy brewing in Yanaidar, the fortress-city of the Hidden Ones. The Sons of Yezm were trying to revive an ancient cult and unite the surviving devotees of the old gods in order to rule the world. The adventure ended with the rout of the contending forces by the gray ghouls of Yanaidar, and Conan rode eastward ("The Flame Knife").

Conan reappeared in the Himelian Mountains, on the northwest frontier of Vendhya, as a war chief of the savage Afghuli tribesmen. Now in his early thirties, the warlike barbarian was known and feared throughout the world of the Hyborian Age.

No man to be bothered with niceties, Yezdigerd employed the magic of the wizard Khemsa, an adept of the dreaded

Black Circle, to remove the Vendhyan king from his path. The dead king's sister, the Devi Yasmina, set out to avenge him but was captured by Conan. Conan and his captive pursued the sorcerous Khemsa, only to see him slain by the magic of the Seers of Yimsha, who also abducted Yasmina ("The People of the Black Circle").

When Conan's plans for welding the hill tribes into a single power failed, Conan, hearing of wars in the West, rode thither. Almuric, a prince of Koth, had rebelled against the hated Strabonus. While Conan joined Almuric's bristling host, Strabonus's fellow kings came to that monarch's aid. Almuric's motley horde was driven south, to be annihilated at last by combined Stygian and Kushite forces.

Escaping into the desert, Conan and the camp follower Natala came to age-old Xuthal, a phantom city of living dead men and their creeping shadow-god, Thog. The Stygian woman Thalis, the effective ruler of Xuthal, double-crossed Conan once too often ("The Slithering Shadow").

Conan beat his way back to the Hyborian lands. Seeking further employment, he joined the mercenary army that a Zingaran, Prince Zapayo da Kova, was raising for Argos. It was planned that Koth should invade Stygia from the north, while the Argosseans approached the realm from the south by sea. Koth, however, made a separate peace with Stygia, leaving Conan's army of mercenaries trapped in the Stygian deserts.

Conan fled with Amalric, a young Aquilonian soldier. Soon Conan was captured by nomads, while Amalric escaped. When Amalric caught up again with Conan, Amalric had with him the girl Lissa, whom he had saved from the cannibal god of her native city. Conan had meanwhile become commander of the cavalry of the city of Tombalku. Two kings ruled Tombalku: the Negro Sakumbe and the mixed-blood Zehbeh. When Zehbeh and his faction were driven out, Sakumbe made Conan his co-king. But then the

wizard Askia slew Sakumbe by magic. Conan, having avenged
his black friend, escaped with Amalric and Lissa ("Drums of
Tombalku").

Conan beat his way to the coast, where he joined the
Barachan pirates. He was now about thirty-five. As second
mate of the *Hawk*, he landed on the island of the Stygian
sorcerer Siptah, said to have a magical jewel of fabulous
properties.

Siptah dwelt in a cylindrical tower without doors or windows, attended by a winged demon. Conan smoked the
unearthly being out but was carried off in its talons to the top
of the tower. Inside the tower Conan found the wizard long
dead; but the magical gem proved of unexpected help in
coping with the demon ("The Gem in the Tower").

Conan remained about two years with the Barachans, according to a set of clay tablets in pre-Sumerian cuneiform.
Used to the tightly organized armies of the Hyborian kingdoms, Conan found the organization of the Barachan bands
too loose and anarchic to afford an opportunity to rise to
leadership. Slipping out of a tight spot at the pirate rendez-
vous at Tortage, he found that the only alternative to a cut
throat was braving the Western Ocean in a leaky skiff. When
the *Wastrel*, the ship of the buccaneer Zaporavo, came in
sight, Conan climbed aboard.

The Cimmerian soon won the respect of the crew and the
enmity of its captain, whose Kordavan mistress, the sleek
Sancha, cast too friendly an eye on the black-maned giant.
Zaporavo drove his ship westward to an uncharted island,
where Conan forced a duel on the captain and killed him,
while Sancha was carried off by strange black beings to a
living pool worshipped by these entities ("The Pool of the
Black Ones").

Conan persuaded the officals at Kordava to transfer
Zaporavo's privateering license to him, whereupon he spent
about two years in this authorized piracy. As usual, plots were

brewing against the Zingaran monarchy. King Ferdrugo was old and apparently failing, with no successor but his nubile daughter Chabela. Duke Villagro enlisted the Stygian super-sorcerer Thoth-Amon, the High Priest of Set, in a plot to obtain Chabela as his bride. Suspicious, the princess took the royal yacht down the coast to consult her uncle. A privateer in league with Villagro captured the yacht and abducted the girl. Chabela escaped and met Conan, who obtained the magical Cobra Crown, also sought by Thoth-Amon.

A storm drove Conan's ship to the coast of Kush, where Conan was confronted by black warriors headed by his old comrade-in-arms, Juma. While the chief welcomed the priva-teers, a tribesman stole the Cobra Crown. Conan set off in pursuit, with Princess Chabela following him. Both were captured by slavers and sold to the black Queen of the Amazons. The Queen made Chabela her slave and Conan her fancy man. Then, jealous of Chabela, she flogged the girl, imprisoned Conan, and condemned both to be devoured by a man-eating tree (*Conan the Buccaneer*).

Having rescued the Zingaran princess, Conan shrugged off hints of marriage and returned to privateering. But other Zingarans, jealous, brought him down off the coast of Shem. Escaping inland, Conan joined the Free Companions, a mer-cenary company. Instead of rich plunder, however, he found himself in dull guard duty on the black frontier of Stygia, where the wine was sour and the pickings poor.

Conan's boredom ended with the appearance of the pirette, Valeria of the Red Brotherhood. When she left the camp, he followed her south. The pair took refuge in a city occupied by the feuding clans of Xotalanc and Tecuhltli. Siding with the latter, the two northerners soon found themselves in trouble with that clan's leader, the ageless witch Tascela ("Red Nails").

Conan's amour with Valeria, however hot at the start, did not last long. Valeria returned to the sea; Conan tried his luck once more in the black kingdoms. Hearing of the "Teeth of Gwahlur," a cache of priceless jewels hidden in Keshan, he sold his services to its irascible king to train the Keshani army.

Thutmekri, the Stygian emissary of the twin kings of Zembabwei, also had designs on the jewels. The Cimmerian, outmatched in intrigue, made tracks for the valley where the ruins of Alkmeenon and its treasure lay hidden. In a wild adventure with the undead goddess Yelaya, the Corinthian girl Muriela, the black priests headed by Gorulga, and the grim gray servants of the long-dead Bît-Yakin, Conan kept his head but lost his loot ("Jewels of Gwahlur").

Heading for Punt with Muriela, Conan embarked on a scheme to relieve the worshipers of an ivory goddess of their abundant gold. Learning that Thutmekri had preceded him and had already poisoned King Lalibeha's mind against him, Conan and his companion took refuge in the temple of the goddess Nebethet.

When the king, Thutmekri, and High Priest Zaramba arrived at the temple, Conan staged a charade wherein Muriela spoke with the voice of the goddess. The results surprised all, including Conan ("The Ivory Goddess").

In Zembabwei, the city of the twin kings, Conan joined a trading caravan which he squired northward along the desert borders, bringing it safely into Shem. Now in his late thirties, the restless adventurer heard that the Aquilonians were spreading westward into the Pictish wilderness. So thither, seeking work for his sword, went Conan. He enrolled as a scout at Fort Tuscelan, where a fierce war raged with the Picts.

In the forests across the river, the wizard Zogar Sag was gathering his swamp demons to aid the Picts. While Conan failed to prevent the destruction of Fort Tuscelan, he managed to warn settlers around Velitrium and to cause the death of Zogar Sag ("Beyond the Black River").

Conan rose rapidly in the Aquilonian service. As captain,

his company was once defeated by the machinations of a traitorous superior. Learning that this officer, Viscount Lucian, was about to betray the province to the Picts, Conan exposed the traitor and routed the Picts ("Moon of Blood").

Promoted to general, Conan defeated the Picts in a great battle at Velitrium and was called back to the capital, Tarantia, to receive the nation's accolades. Then, having roused the suspicions of the depraved and foolish King Numedides, he was drugged and chained in the Iron Tower under sentence of death.

The barbarian, however, had friends as well as foes. Soon he was spirited out of prison and turned loose with horse and sword. He struck out across the dank forests of Pictland toward the distant sea. In the forest, the Cimmerian came upon a cavern in which lay the corpse and the demon-guarded treasure of the pirate Tranicos. From the west, others—a Zingaran count and two bands of pirates—were hunting the same fortune, while the Stygian sorcerer Thoth-Amon took a hand in the game ("The Treasure of Tranicos").

Rescued by an Aquilonian galley, Conan was chosen to lead a revolt against Numedides. While the revolution stormed along, civil war raged on the Pictish frontier. Lord Valerian, a partisan of Numedides, schemed to bring the Picts down on the town of Schohira. A scout, Gault Hagar's sons, undertook to upset this scheme by killing the Pictish wizard ("Wolves Beyond the Border").

Storming the capital city and slaying Numedides on the steps of his throne—which he promptly took for his own—Conan, now in his early forties, found himself ruler of the greatest Hyborian nation (*Conan the Liberator*).

A king's life, however, proved no bed of houris. Within a year, an exiled count had gathered a group of plotters to oust the barbarian from the throne. Conan might have lost crown and head but for the timely intervention of the long-dead sage Epimitreus ("The Phoenix of the Sword").

No sooner had the mutterings of revolt died down than Conan was treacherously captured by the kings of Ophir and Koth. He was imprisoned in the tower of the wizard Tsotha-lanti in the Kothian capital. Conan escaped with the help of a fellow prisoner, who was Tsotha-lanti's wizardly rival Pelias. By Pelias's magic, Conan was whisked to Tarantia in time to slay a pretender and to lead an army against his treacherous fellow kings ("The Scarlet Citadel").

For nearly two years, Aquilonia thrived under Conan's firm but tolerant rule. The lawless, hard-bitten adventurer of former years had, through force of circumstance, matured into an able and responsible statesman. But a plot was brewing in neighboring Nemedia to destroy the King of Aquilonia by sorcery from an elder day.

Conan, about forty-five, showed few signs of age save a network of scars on his mighty frame and a more cautious approach to wine, women and bloodshed. Although he kept a harem of luscious concubines, he had never taken an official queen; hence he had no legitimate son to inherit the throne, a fact whereof his enemies sought to take advantage.

The plotters resurrected Xaltotun, the greatest sorcerer of the ancient empire of Acheron, which fell before the Hyborian savages 3,000 years earlier. By Xaltotun's magic, the King of Nemedia was slain and replaced by his brother Tarascus. Black sorcery defeated Conan's army; Conan was imprisoned, and the exile Valerius took his throne.

Escaping from a dungeon with the aid of the harem girl Zenobia, Conan returned to Aquilonia to rally his loyal forces against Valerius. From the priests of Asura, he learned that Xaltotun's power could be broken only by means of a strange jewel, the "Heart of Ahriman." The trail of the jewel led to a pyramid in the Stygian desert outside black-walled Khemi. Winning the Heart of Ahriman, Conan returned to face his foes (*Conan the Conqueror*, originally published as *The Hour of the Dragon*).

After regaining his kingdom, Conan made Zenobia his queen. But, at the ball celebrating her elevation, the queen was borne off by a demon sent by the Khitan sorcerer Yah Chieng. Conan's quest for his bride carried him across the known world, meeting old friends and foes. In purple-towered Paikang, with the help of a magical ring, he freed Zenobia and slew the wizard (*Conan the Avenger*, originally published as *The Return of Conan*).

Home again, the way grew smoother. Zenobi gave him heirs: a son named Conan but commonly called Conn, another son called Taurus, and a daughter. When Conn was twelve, his father took him on a hunting trip to Gunderland. Conan was now in his late fifties. His sword arm was a little slower than in his youth, and his black mane and the fierce mustache of his later years were traced with gray; but his strength still surpassed that of two ordinary men.

When Conan was lured away by the Witchmen of Hyperborea, who demanded that Conan come to their stronghold alone, Conan went. He found Louhi, the High Priestess of the Witchmen, in conference with three others of the world's leading sorcerers: Thoth-Amon of Stygia; the god-king of Kambuja; and the black lord of Zembabwei. In the ensuing holocaust, Louhi and the Kambujan perished, while Thoth-Amon and the other sorcerer vanished by magic ("The Witch of the Mists").

Old King Ferdrugo of Zingara had died, and his throne remained vacant as the nobles intrigued over the succession. Duke Pantho of Guarralid invaded Poitain, in southern Aquilonia. Conan, suspecting sorcery, crushed the invaders. Learning that Thoth-Amon was behind Pantho's madness, Conan set out with his army to settle matters with the Stygian. He pursued his foe to Thoth-Amon's stronghold in Stygia ("Black Sphinx of Nebthu"), to Zembabwei ("Red Moon of Zembabwei"), and to the last realm of the serpent folk in the far south ("Shadows in the Skull").

For several years, Conan's rule was peaceful. But time did that which no combination of foes had been able to do. The Cimmerian's skin became wrinkled and his hair gray; old wounds ached in damp weather. Conan's beloved consort Zenobia died giving birth to their second daughter.

Then catastrophe shattered King Conan's mood of half-resigned discontent. Supernatural entities, the Red Shadows, began seizing and carrying off his subjects. Conan was baffled until in a dream he again visited the sage Epimitreus. He was told to abdicate in favor of Prince Conn and set out across the Western Ocean.

Conan discovered that the Red Shadows had been sent by the priest-wizards of Antillia, a chain of islands in the western part of the ocean, whither the survivors of Atlantis had fled 8,000 years before. These priests offered human sacrifices to their devil-god Xotli on such a scale that their own population faced extermination.

In Antillia, Conan's ship was taken, but he escaped into the city Ptahuacan. After conflicts with giant rats and dragons, he emerged atop the sacrificial pyramid just as his crewmen were about to be sacrificed. Supernatural conflict, revolution, and seismic catastrophe ensued. In the end, Conan sailed off to explore the continents to the west (*Conan of the Isles*).

Whether he died there, or whether there is truth in the tale that he strode out of the West to stand at his son's side in a final battle against Aquilonia's foes, will be revealed only to him who looks, as Kull of Valusia once did, into the mystic mirrors of Tuzun Thune.

L. Sprague de Camp
Villanova, Pennsylvania
May 1984

CONAN

☐	54238-X	CONAN THE DESTROYER	$2.95
	54239-8	Canada	$3.50
☐	54228-2	CONAN THE DEFENDER	$2.95
	54229-0	Canada	$3.50
☐	54225-8	CONAN THE INVINCIBLE	$2.95
	54226-6	Canada	$3.50
☐	54236-3	CONAN THE MAGNIFICENT	$2.95
	54237-1	Canada	$3.50
☐	54231-2	CONAN THE UNCONQUERED	$2.95
	54232-0	Canada	$3.50
☐	54246-0	CONAN THE VICTORIOUS	$2.95
	54247-9	Canada	$3.50
☐	54258-4	CONAN THE FEARLESS	$2.95
	54259-2	Canada	$3.95
☐	54256-8	CONAN THE RAIDER (trade)	$6.95
	54257-6	Canada	$8.95
☐	54250-9	CONAN THE RENEGADE	$2.95
	54251-7	Canada	$3.50
☐	54242-8	CONAN THE TRIUMPHANT	$2.95
	54243-6	Canada	$3.50
☐	54252-5	CONAN THE VALOROUS	$2.95
	54253-3	Canada	$3.95

Buy them at your local bookstore or use this handy coupon:
Clip and mail this page with your order

TOR BOOKS—Reader Service Dept.
49 W. 24 Street, 9th Floor, New York, NY 10010

Please send me the book(s) I have checked above. I am enclosing
$ _____ (please add $1.00 to cover postage and handling).
Send check or money order only—no cash or C.O.D.'s.

Mr./Mrs./Miss _____
Address _____
City _____ State/Zip _____
Please allow six weeks for delivery. Prices subject to change without notice.

For the millions of people who have read the books, enjoyed the comics and the magazines, and thrilled to the movies, there is now -

THE CONAN
FAN CLUB

S.Q. Productions Inc., a long time publisher of science fiction and fantasy related items and books is announcing the formation of an official Conan Fan Club. When you join, you'll receive the following: 6 full color photos from the Conan films, a finely detailed sew-on embroidered patch featuring the Conan logo, a full color membership card and bookmark, and a set of official Conan Fan Club stationary. Also included in the fan kit will be the first of 4 quarterly newsletters. **"The Hyborian Report"** will focus on many subjects of interest to the Conan fan, including interviews with Conan writers and film stars. And there'll be behind-the-scenes information about the latest Conan movies and related projects, as well as reports on other R.E. Howard characters like Solomon Kane, Red Sonja and King Kull. Fans will also be able to show off their talents on our annual costume and art contests. **"The Hyborian Report"** will be the one-stop information source for the very latest about Conan. Another aspect of the club that fans will find invaluable is the **Conan Merchandise Guide,** which will detail the hundreds of items that have been produced, both in America **and** Europe. And as a member of the club, you'll receive notices of **new** Conan products, many created just for the club! Portfolios, posters, art books, weapon replicas (cast from the **same** molds as those used for the movie weapons) and much, much more! And with your kit, you'll get coupons worth $9.00 towards the purchase of items offered for sale.

Above all, The Conan Fan Club is going to be listening to the fans, the people who have made this barbarian the most famous in the world. Their suggestions, ideas, and feedback is what will make the club really work. The annual membership is only **$10.00.** Make all checks and money orders payable to:**CONAN FAN CLUB**
PO Box 4569
Toms River, NJ 08754

Response to this offer will be tremendous, so please allow 10-12 weeks for delivery.